TACHYON TUNNEL 3

Michael Gorton

Cover Graphic Design: Shefa Rumby
Text and Flow Edits: Shelley Laine
Grammar, Text, Flow, Content Edits:
Makenzie Ozycz, MA, MFA
Contributing Editors: Derek DelCarpio, Rick Childs

**For more information, or to book an event, contact
Michael Gorton mg@mgalcor.com
https://MichaelGorton.us/**

Much of this story takes place in our home, the Milky Way Galaxy. Unlike most other galaxies, we do not have a photo of our home galaxy, so this is a rendition. It contains more than 200 billion stars and is approximately 100,000 light years across. We are located about 30,000 light years from the center.

Special Thanks to the Launch Team

No journey to success is ever walked alone. One of the greatest gifts in any endeavor is the support of those who believe in the mission and lend their time, talent, and inspiration. My launch team of editors, plot shapers, cheerleaders, and reviewers on this adventure have brough insight, elevating every page. **Thanks to every one of you.**

Aaron Handwerker	**John Wingate**
Anthony Williams	**Laurel Gorton**
Bob Blount	**Laurie Choquette**
Brett Sandstrom	**Leanna Pezzini**
Brian Stieglitz	**Lynn McGinnis**
Cheryl Quillian	**Makenzie Ozycz**
Chuck May	**Mary Begia**
Dan Bedell	**Megan Widner**
Dan LaBroad	**Neeraj Chitra**
David Waldon	**Noel Geren**
David Zakariaie	**Quentin Faust**
Derek DelCarpio	**Rick Childs**
Genevieve Castelline	**Shelley Laine**
Greg Echt	**Sandi Santino**
Harvey Castro	**Terry Phillips**
Jay Maymi	**Ty Gabriel**
Jeannie Lewis	**Yuriy Vasylenko**

Recap

Storyline recap from Tachyon Tunnel
Brilliant engineer Alex Durant secretly develops a ship capable of traveling through tachyon tunnels, using the strange faster-than-light particles to cut pathways through space and even time. His only companion at first is Emily, his AI, whose evolving intelligence soon feels more human than machine.

When Alex learns that his closest friend, Paula Campbell, has been killed in a horrific car accident, he decides to save her. Risking paradox and meltdown of his reactor, Alex pulls Paula from the fatal moment of impact,

Together, Alex and Paula take the ship, Tranquility, across interstellar distances, visiting Alpha Cassiopeia and confronting the dangers of imprecise time exits. Their bond deepens, rekindling old sparks from their Princeton days, while Emily's hybrid silicon-organic mind grows in ways Alex himself cannot fully predict. The first book closes with Alex, realizing he has stumbled into forces far greater than himself.

Recap from Tachyon Tunnel 2
After Alex Durant and Paula Campbell are pulled back from near-certain doom in the timeline-shifted events of Tachyon Tunnel 1, they, along with Alexander Bell and Lyra, safely return to Earth. But Earth is not the same. The galaxy's shadow is lengthening, and the Daklin Empire has turned its gaze toward humanity.

Alex, Paula, Zander and Emily, now a cybernetic AI, and a growing band of allies including the fiery hacker Megan Hoglund and nerdy scientist Mark, are forced to balance discovery with survival.

Alex and Paula encounter Atroz, a Caretaker from the distant star Bint, who reveals a shocking truth: Alex's tunnelling experiments have created new corridors in the galactic network, something thought impossible for millions of years. This breakthrough could alter the balance of power across the galaxy while it also paints Earth as a target.

Meanwhile, the Daklin Empire prepares annihilation. A giant planet killing ship named Sector 437B charges a planet-killing weapon, intending to destroy all life on Earth. Onboard Tranquillity, Alex and Emily push tachyon physics to the limit, collapsing tunnels and timing hyperspace hops with surgical precision. Their desperate gamble destroys one Daklin ship in deep space, a first in fifty million years. But another ship remains in Earth orbit, its destructive wave primed to extinguish nine billion lives.

Maria, grounded on Earth, works frantically on plasma-based defences, suspecting plasma itself may hold answers to faster-than-light communication, or even sentience.

The novel closes on a knife's edge: Earth spared only by the narrowest of margins, the Daklin threat looming, and the secrets of plasma and tunnel creation hinting at humanity's chance not only to survive, but to change the course of galactic history.

1

The Death of Sector 437B

For fifty million years, the Daklin Empire have ruled the spiral arms and central hub of the Milky Way with an iron grip, their power enforced through a vast network of tachyon tunnels. These conduits, relics of an ancient and forgotten civilization, enabled instantaneous travel across the stars and became the arteries of commerce, culture, and conquest. Entire fleets could travel hundreds of light years in just days.

Yet no Daklin engineer ever learned how to create new tunnels. Instead, the Empire seized existing ones by force, expanding its dominion along their routes and crushing any world that dared resist. For those civilizations on the grid, the Empire promised order and demanded absolute compliance. Any civilization that so much as whispered defiance was summarily extinguished.

That unbroken order began to unravel on a backwater planet called Earth. Primitive by galactic standards, its people had only just begun to explore the edges of spaceflight. And yet, one of them, an engineer-scientist named Alex Durant, had achieved what no Daklin had in the entire history of their empire: he had discovered how to create new tachyon tunnels. With his invention, Durant opened pathways where none had existed before. In his early explorations, he encountered warnings about the Daklin and the terrible grip they held on the galaxy.

Suspecting that Earth had developed this technology, the Daklin sent a delegation to demand compliance. When their demands were refused, they responded with force, dispatching a scientist to acquire the technology and two ships to destroy the planet. One of those ships had disappeared. The other now loomed over the third planet in the Sol system, preparing to carry out Earth's destruction.

ooooo ∞ ooooo

Daklin science officer Fortak checked the power interface on his latest acquisition: the Earth-built T-Portal. The tablet interface switched on easily, cycling through its diagnostics. Earth engineering was crude by Daklin standards but somehow, they had achieved what the greatest Daklin minds had failed to do. They had built a functioning portal.

Fortak had spent months on Earth studying its customs, economy, and technology. In time, he found a way to connect with T-Portal's CEO, Maillew Pascal. From there, it was only a matter of price. Fortak had been prepared to take the technology by force, but on Earth he discovered a truth as old as the Empire itself: money could be more powerful, and far more efficient, than weapons.

Now the device sat in his laboratory aboard *Sector 437B*, and while Pascal and every living thing on Earth faced imminent destruction, Fortak's interests were consumed by his new T-Portal toy.

Sector 437B was no ordinary warship. At 45 kilometers long and taller than most mountains on Earth, it was a mobile fortress, larger than New York City. It housed nearly a million inhabitants: Daklins and human subjects bound to the empire. Its hull, forged from an obsidian-black alloy, was etched with crimson energy veins that pulsed like a living heart. From a distance, it resembled a predator lurking among the stars, mercilessly stalking its prey.

But inside, Sector 437B breathed with life.

There were schools and academies for families, auditoriums where children performed, and holotheaters showcasing art and history. Restaurants served the finest cuisine, curated from a hundred conquered worlds. Parks and plazas offered stretches of greenery beneath simulated sunlit skies, where the scent of alien flowers mingled with the faint ozone of the ship's ventilation systems. In the lower districts, neon-lit bars and music clubs pulsed through the night cycle with the heartbeat of a restless population that chose the freedom of interstellar life over the pull of planetary gravity.

For Fortak, 437B had been home for nearly three decades. He had learned its rhythms, the morning bustle of officers on duty, the glow of shopfronts along the promenade, the quiet comfort of a ship that was both fortress and sanctuary. Fortak was a soldier, but in reality, he was much more of a scientist.

Even with all the signs of humanity aboard, the ship's true purpose was never out of sight. Sector 437B was one of over a million death-ships built to enforce the Empire's will. Though its residents enjoyed restaurants, family life, and parks within its protective shell, the vessel had been designed for one purpose: the ruthless annihilation of entire planets. It was both city and weapon. And its people lived beneath the constant shadow of that primary purpose which was destruction. It was a mission they all understood and had accepted.

If a planet was slated for destruction, it was assumed to be for good reason. Every resident of 437B accepted that the moral debate had already been settled at the heart of the Empire. Today, the target was Earth. No one questioned or cared why. That decision belonged to the Empire. It always had.

Fortak knew Earth better than anyone on 437B, and he didn't think twice about its destruction. He had been back on board for less than two hours when the ship-wide announcement echoed through the corridors: the command had been given. The energy pulse was charging. In a matter of hours, it would fire. Soon, Earth would be nothing more than a scorched, lifeless satellite orbiting a G2-class star.

He might have gone to watch the spectacle from one of the upper decks, but his mind was elsewhere. What interested him now was the T-Portal. He wanted to see whether it would respond to Daklin interfaces, to test if this primitive human design could truly be understood. Earth's fate no longer concerned or interested him.

As Fortak connected the power grid to the T-Portal, alarms suddenly howled. Red light spilled into his quiet lab, pulsing through the corridor like blood in water.

On the bridge, Captain Borzat slammed a fist against his console. The holomap flickered, then stabilized before displaying something impossible. The energy wave hadn't consumed Earth. Instead, it was bending, reversing course… and accelerating directly back toward them.

"How?" Borzat roared. "How can a primitive world deflect this?" His voice cracked into comms. "Fortak! Options?"

In his lab, Fortak's hands flew across the control pads, data streams cascading past his eyes in a blur. The energy pulse, engineered to annihilate all life on a planet, had been deflected and was now racing straight toward his ship. He ran the numbers.

They had less than a minute.

"The energy required to generate the pulse has drained the ship's reserves. There is no escape, Captain," Fortak said flatly. "You could deploy the pods, but they'll be overtaken. The tachyon tunnel has collapsed, so it will be years before another Daklin ship can reach us. I'm sorry, Captain. Our ship, Sector 437B will not survive."

"Shields?" Borzat barked.

"Energy is spent. We burned it all in the pulse. There is nothing left."

Borzat's voice cracked with rage. "Then die doing something, Fortak!"

But Fortak was already moving. The T-Portal hummed on its platform, its screen glowing with an improbable destination: *Dallas, Texas*. The energy signature was low, but stable. A primitive human city, yet familiar at least to him. Dallas was where he had spent most of his time on Earth. He didn't even know if the device would function in space. Nineteen million miles separated him from Earth. Could it work over such a vast distance?

For half a second, he considered the situation. Even if the T-Portal *did* work, he would be tunneling directly into the heart of the enemy world. Would anyone on Earth know the intent the Daklin had on this day? It was unlikely, but still, he hoped they did not.

Before he could fully evaluate the situation, the ship screamed as its own destructive energy wave tore through the hull. The air trembled as bulkheads crumpled like paper. The destruction had begun.

"No," Fortak whispered to himself. "I will not remain here to face certain death. I will take a chance on this Earth technology and tunnel into life."

He pressed the activation pad and stepped through the glowing portal.

The lab dissolved into white fire as the pulse ripped through Sector 437B. Captain Borzat, and a million other souls, were reduced to interstellar dust and plasma. Fortak felt the wrenching pull of the T-Portal, weightlessness swallowing him, darkness flooding his vision. His mind told him it was the end. But his heart pounded with the possibility that it wasn't.

And then, he fell through.

Approximately two seconds passed between stepping into the T-Portal and tripping onto the ground in the Dallas port.

"Are you okay, sir?" A tall man in a business suit reached out to help him up.

Fortak opened his eyes and focused on the T-Portal structure he had just fallen though.

He was in a large building with 40-foot ceilings made of glass. This was the central hub for the T-Portal company built on Earth.

Fortak took the man's hand, "Thank you. I am fine."

"First time through?" the man asked.

"Yes," He looked back and saw only the T-Portal, and thousands of people walking to portals to their next city.

"You get used to it, sir," the man smiled. "There's a food court over there where you can sit and get your bearings," he pointed. "I've been coming through every day, and now it's just like walking from the kitchen to the living room."

"Thank you, I appreciate it." Fortak turned and began walking to the food court.

Just under two minutes after he stepped through the portal, everyone was pointing through the glass roof at a sudden flash in the sky. For a brief moment, it blazed brighter than the sun, then faded to a glowing red ember before it finally vanished.

When he realized that flash marked the destruction of his ship, Sector 437B, his home, he did the math in his head. 437B had been stationed in L5, roughly 19 million miles from Earth. His own transport vessel, capable of traveling 1,200 miles per second, took over four hours to reach the ship. Yet the T-Portal had delivered him almost instantly. It had beaten the speed of light by more than two minutes.

His Daklin suspicion was now confirmed: Maillew Pascal had cracked a secret that had eluded Daklin engineers for millions of years.

And then he laughed; a deep, ragged sound that echoed through the quiet. He had survived the destruction of his ship, the fall of Borzat's command, and now found himself stranded on a primitive planet marked for annihilation.

But his focus was clear: survive. And find a way to deliver technology back to the Empire.

○○○○ ∞ ○○○○

Maillew Pascal's Dallas office was tucked into the upper floor of a modern research complex, funded by the T-Portal company. Since its inception, T-Portal had become the fastest growing and most valuable company in the world, and Pascal, the world's richest man.

Fortak stood in front of the glass door for a full minute before entering. He adjusted his jacket. It was civilian style, soft navy cotton, secondhand. He glanced at his reflection once more. He closely resembled an Earth human, and that was the point. The Daklin were human in biology and form. Culturally divergent, yes, but on the streets of Dallas, and the hallways of this building, he passed without suspicion. He had been in Pascal's office many times and was instantly recognized by the executive assistant.

"He will see you now, Fortak," she smiled.

He pushed the door open.

Pascal was hunched over his computer, immersed in a glowing 3D molecular rendering. He didn't look up as Fortak entered.

"If you're here to sell me another AI data scrubber, save your breath," Pascal said, voice gruff.

"I'm here to ask questions," Fortak replied evenly.

Pascal turned, startled, then squinted his eyes in the direction of his visitor. "Oh, Fortak?" Pascal was one of the few people on Earth who knew that Fortak was Daklin. "Was that your ship? That flash in space earlier?"

"Yes, my home and ride back to my sector of the galaxy."

"Holy shit! What the hell happened, Fortak?" Pascal stood, curious, but feigning concern.

"I'm not sure," Fortak started. "I had just docked when the alarms started going off. The whole thing happened too fast for me to have done an assessment." He tried to keep a straight face in the lie.

"From here, it looks like it blew up. The news is buzzing, trying to figure out what happened. Some amateur astronomers are even saying the ship was as big as a small moon?"

"There were nearly a million humans onboard that ship, Pascal."

"I am so sorry," Pascal said, rubbing his chin thoughtfully. Nothing in human history had ever claimed a million lives in an instant, like what happened with the Daklin ship. "It's a monumental tragedy."

"Yes… it is indeed," Fortak replied, studying Pascal's face carefully, searching for any hint of what he might know. In his short time on Earth, Fortak had seen nothing to suggest that Earthlings possessed the technology or capability to destroy a Daklin destroyer. While they had developed tachyon tunneling technology, nothing else on this planet came close to the wonders of the Daklin Empire.

"I cannot even begin to perceive how you must feel."

"I suspect human connections and interactions on Earth are different from those in the Empire, Pascal. Though I am saddened, I accept their fate."

"Saddened?" Pascal was shocked by the response. He couldn't imagine how he would feel if a million people from his planet suddenly died.

Fortak simply shrugged.

"How many of you managed to escape?"

"I am the only one." Fortak answered. "I used your T-Portal to escape right as my ship was being destroyed."

"Wait, *being destroyed*, Fortak?" Pascal was startled by his phrasing. "What do you mean by that?"

Fortak took a slow breath. "This morning," he said, "a high-intensity energy burst was aimed at my ship. Massive power, enough to destroy a planet. Maybe even yours."

"What?" Pascal frowned, shocked. "Destroy Earth? Why would anyone do that?"

"I don't know," Fortak lied. "Earth wasn't destroyed because the energy wave was redirected toward my ship. From what I saw, it looks like Earth had some aggressive intent toward the Daklin Empire."

Pascal leaned back, the blood draining from his face. "I'm not a decision-maker at the UN or in DC, but from what I've seen, humanity has been celebrating our new friends in the galaxy. As for Earth creating an energy beam powerful enough to destroy a planet…that's just not possible. Our government has plenty of secrets, but the ability to generate or redirect an energy field capable of wiping out Earth is far beyond the scope of our technology. Hell, we can't even produce enough power to meet the needs of the people on this planet."

"You say that, and yet, your T-Portal is beyond our capabilities, so I wonder, could Earth have done it?"

Pascal shook his head. "We don't even have the capability to detect something like that in real time, much less deflect or reverse it. Are you saying we, *Earth*, bounced or created a planet killing energy wave? Like a mirror?" Pascal started to laugh at how absurd the proposition was.

"Or absorbed it. Or redirected it with a counter-frequency. Something. Right now, this is a dangerously grave issue. Physics and engineering aren't the problem. The intent, or perception, is."

Pascal narrowed his eyes. "Whose intent?"

Fortak met his gaze evenly. "Hypothetically… let's say an alien power sent the energy burst. And Earth responded in defense. What kind of technology would be required?"

Pascal stood and walked over to the window. "You've got to be kidding me, Fortak. Look at us! We barely have the technology to put a base on our Moon. Outside of movies like *Star Wars*, we don't have a clue how to create or stop planet-destroying death rays."

Fortak met his gaze. "Humor me. Speculate."

"I don't know what you're fishing for, Fortak, but my company builds T-Portal gateway systems, not planetary shields and death rays. No one here even talks about that level of weaponry. We don't have it, and if we did, the Pentagon would've kicked my door down a *long* time ago."

"So," Fortak said carefully, "you're telling me you don't know of any civilization that might have targeted Earth for destruction?"

Pascal turned back to him, his expression now dead serious. "No. As far as I know, your people are the only alien race humanity has ever encountered. And I sincerely doubt anyone on Earth has the intent, or the knowledge, to build something like your death ray. But I'll tell you this: if the Daklin want the T-Portal technology, we can sell it to you. All day long."

Fortak leaned back, calculating.

Either Pascal was a masterful liar… or genuinely ignorant. Fortak leaned toward the latter. The man seemed to care only about money and molecules, not war.

That made him useful.

Fortak stood. "Thank you, Maillew. You've been more helpful than you know."

Pascal raised an eyebrow. "That's it? You show up in an alien tinfoil hat, drop a few bombs, and then disappear again?"

"Tinfoil hat?"

"It's a saying we use for conspiracy theories that are mostly outlandish and bizarre, Fortak."

"I see. Anyway, it looks like I'm stuck here, so I need to understand this place. I'm going to need a friend; someone who can help me navigate the people, the tech, and everything I don't know."

Pascal raised an eyebrow, wondering how he could possibly profit from this connection.

"And?"

Fortak knew where he was going, "I think you could be… a valuable friend."

Pascal scoffed. "You're a weird bastard, Fortak. But if you keep paying like last time, I'll listen to just about anything."

Fortak extended his hand. "Then let's start with a drink. You can explain how this planet keeps evolving in spite of its chaos."

Pascal shook his hand. "You buying?"

Fortak smiled faintly. "I just suffered the loss of a million Daklin souls. I think, at least for today, you are buying."

Pascal nodded with a grim look. "I am really sorry about that, Fortak. Yes, I will absolutely buy."

A few minutes later, they stepped out of the building and onto the hot, sunbaked streets of Dallas.

"There's a quiet club at the top of that building," Pascal pointed at a building located about two blocks away with a keyhole near the top. "It's a short walk."

"That works," Fortak followed Pascal's lead. "Can you explain the physics and engineering of the T-Portal?"

"Well," Pascal started, "I am not an engineer or physicist, but as I understand it, we are doing some kind of mass to energy conversion."

Fortak was shocked by the response, which showed virtually zero knowledge of engineering. "Pascal, my ship was 19 million miles from Earth, and T-Portal transported me in about two seconds."

"Oh no, Fortak. You must be mistaken. I'm not a physicist, but what you just described is faster than light travel. If light travels 186 thousand miles each second, it should take over 100 seconds to go that far."

"Correct, and that is exactly what happened, 19 million miles in less than two seconds."

"No, that can't be…"

"Listen to me, Pascal, I am an engineer and physicist. I understand the difference between energy moving at the speed of light, time dilation, and Lorentz transforms. The fact is that just under two minutes after I used T-Portal to travel from my ship to Dallas, people were looking up in the sky to see the destruction of 437B."

"What's 437B?"

"That was the name of my ship," Fortak watched a car drive by. How could a society using internal combustion engines have developed tachyon tunnelling? It made no sense. "Look, Pascal, Your T-Portal is using something we call tunneling. Tachyon tunneling, to be precise."

"I'm sorry, I don't even know what that is, Fortak. Is it like warping space or something?"

"Unbelievable," Fortak replied, studying Pascal. "Nobody warps space. Gravity does that, and creating gravity on that scale is too expensive for travel." He paused as he looked across the street at the building, then back to Pascal.

"You must know that we've only been putting humans in space for about 70 years." Pascal replied.

Fortak nodded. "Interstellar travel is done with far more efficient means using tachyon tunneling. It's how we traveled to Earth from my sector of the galaxy. Any other means would take too long, and too much energy."

"I just," Pascal stopped. He was rarely confused, but he had never made an attempt to understand the inner workings of the T-Portal technology.

"Who developed the tech, Pascal?"

"Well, my co-founder Zander. Zander Bell."

"Then I suggest we invite this co-founder Zander to our meeting today."

"Unfortunately, he died in a car crash."

The two men had reached the building with the bar and Fortak stopped out front. "You are telling me that the man who invented T-Portal tech *died* in a car crash," he asked incredulously. "In a *car crash?*"

"Yes. It was a head-on collision." Pascal paused, thinking it over, then the realization hit him. *Could that really have happened?* Why would the inventor of the T-Portal be traveling in a car?

Fortak watched the realization hit Pascal, then grinned at him. "Let's find your Zander Bell, and while we are looking, maybe I can get a couple of your engineers to help me understand how this T-Portal thing works."

After a drink and a bit more conversation, Fortak left the meeting and stepped back onto the street, where the Dallas heat engulfed him once more. The late afternoon sun pressed down, baking the pavement as the city pulsed with chaotic noise unlike anything on 437B. Horns blared, traffic lights flickered, engines growled, and voices rose around him, thick Texas accents mingling with foreign tongues. He kept walking, letting it all wash over him until the sounds blurred together, fading into a steady, indifferent white noise.

At that point, the realization hit him. He froze as he looked around. He was isolated and stranded on a primitive world.

In some ways, this was harder than the destruction of his ship. When the Daklin returned, their response would be swift, merciless, and Earth would be obliterated. Fortak had no comm-link, no long-range beacon. He was trapped in the planet's gravity well, with no way to escape or to tell the Empire he was still alive.

Even if he found a way to use a primitive Earth rocket, he would never be able to locate the tachyon tunnel portal, or travel in it.

He was cut off from the Empire in every possible way. For a Daklin science officer, isolation was worse than exile.

He stopped in the shade of a glass-walled café, watching people pass. Their lives moved on as if the galaxy didn't exist beyond their skies. The simplicity of it was almost infuriating.

He resolved to set a goal to thrive and eventually return. To do that, he would have to rebuild a line of communication back to the Empire. That meant securing resources, gaining access to high-energy transmission arrays, and creating a tunnel endpoint that could bridge the void between this planet and the tunnel network.

The fastest path forward was obvious: unlock the full mechanics of the T-Portal.

Pascal believed that Zander Bell, its inventor, was dead, or otherwise removed from the equation. If indeed true, that left Fortak with only one option: work with Earth engineers, exploit their strengths, and dissect the device from the inside out.

The thought brought a slow, deliberate smile to his face. Earthlings were primitive in many ways, yet one engineer here had mastered tachyon tunneling without the centuries of layered science the Daklin had accumulated. Somewhere within that system lay the key, not only to his return, but to something far greater. If he could unlock its secret, he could win favor with the Emperor, and that favor would land him in the middle of a new life far from the battles and the suburbs where he now lived.

He stepped back into the sun, weaving through the crowd with renewed purpose.

2

Human Innovation

Maillew Pascal delivered on his promise the next morning. Fortak found himself standing in a cavernous engineering lab three floors underground, surrounded by humming servers, diagnostic stations, and the unmistakable sterile smell of freshly unpacked electronics. Several variations of the T-Portal in stages of testing were connected to screens and power.

"This is Ronald Clyper," Pascal said, nodding toward a good looking, muscular man in his mid-thirties with an untucked shirt, a smirk, and a cup of coffee that looked too big for human hands. "Everyone just calls him Clyper." Pascal walked over to the other man and placed a hand on his shoulder, "And this is Art Adamez, a Marine veteran, engineer, and the reason projects stay on track in the facility."

Art, shorter than Clyper, with dark eyes and a squared jaw, gave Fortak a polite nod but no smile. His posture said military. His toolbox was open on the bench before Pascal had even finished talking.

"Gentlemen," Fortak said evenly, scanning the two men. "We will be reverse engineering the T-Portal interface. I require your full cooperation and no delays."

Clyper raised his coffee. "Well, you're in luck, Fortak. You have me fully cooperative until five p.m., and then I have very important business with a margarita machine."

Fortak frowned. "Five p.m.?"

Pascal stepped in, "Gents, you are lucky to be working with a Daklin engineer…"

"Holy shit," Clyper's eyes grew to full circles as he reassessed Fortak. "I guess that explains the unusual name?"

Fortak looked at Adamez, "Are you okay working with an alien engineer, Marine?"

"Yes, sir. I look forward to the opportunity to collaborate, Fortak."

Fortak turned back to Ronald, "What's the 5 p.m. thing, Clyper?"

"It's a human tradition," Ronald said. "Work-life balance."

Art walked back to his toolkit. "Some of us keep working after five. It's all a function of motivation, though I have known Clyper long enough to attest to the fact that he's only a great engineer until about 5:00, then he turns his focus to other stuff."

Fortak shook his head. The reality is that Daklin work ethic is perhaps a notch below even that expressed by Clyper. Daklin longevity was such that no one was ever in a hurry. "Fine, let's get started."

They gathered around the open T-Portal core, its lattice of energy channels pulsing with a faint blue glow that cast shifting shadows across their faces. Fortak moved quickly, directing them through a series of tests with precise, clipped instructions. He was focused on one goal: understanding the function of every component within the portal.

Clyper handled the calibration rig but kept tossing out questions that seemed half-serious. "Hey, what happens if we swap the polarity on the harmonic regulator? Would it implode, or just make the room smell funny?"

"My guess is that it would destabilize the field," Fortak replied without looking up. "In Daklin science, we do not…" He stopped mid-sentence, catching himself. "Why would you suggest such a thing?"

"Sometimes you learn more from breaking something than from following the manual," Clyper said. "Besides, manuals are just… suggestions."

Art glanced over. "That's why your laptop dies every three months."

Fortak didn't understand the fact that it was just a joke. He was still turning over the comment in his mind. Daklin engineers didn't break things on *purpose*. They built. They maintained. Everything was done by the book, with precision and caution. Daklins did not invite chaos in the name of insight.

Later in the day, Art proposed altering the diagnostics harness to simulate a portal burst without powering the full system.

"It's not how we usually run tests," he admitted, "but it could save us three days of wasted work if we want to understand the impact of phase alignment."

"Three days?" Fortak asked. "You would alter a proven test process to save three days?"

Art met his gaze. "Of course I would. Heck, I'd alter it to save three minutes if I thought I would get a positive result."

Fortak filed the moment away. Two humans, different in discipline, opposite in methodology, and both were willing to challenge the existing-working process if it meant progress.

Daklin engineers had no such reflex.

By late afternoon, Clyper was packing up his bag. "Shift's over. Bar time," he announced. "You coming, Art?"

Art kept working. "Not tonight."

Clyper shrugged. "Suit yourself. Fortak, you should come with me sometime. Might loosen you up."

"Am I not loose?" Fortak asked.

"Not even close," Clyper grinned and walked out.

When the door shut, the lab seemed quieter. Art tightened a coupling and glanced at Fortak. "Did you want to go with him?"

Fortak studied the human for a long moment before answering. "Life is… short. Even for a Daklin. Perhaps that is something we share."

"How long do you live?" Art asked.

"I am 346. In Earth years, that is."

"That can't be right!" Art asked, his mouth hanging open in disbelief. "346?"

"Aging is a disease, Art," Fortak responded in a matter-of-fact tone. "Daklin technology has cured that disease."

Art nodded once and went back to work.

Fortak turned to the T-Portal core, its energy threads weaving and shifting like liquid light. *They know less than we do,* he thought. *But they see more possibilities.* And for the first time in centuries, Fortak felt a strange new hunger, not for conquest, but for discovery.

The following morning, he studied Clyper and Art. Both were good in their own way, but Art had the military discipline that came along with a strong sense of ethics. He needed a project done, and didn't want questions about why it needed to be done. Clyper seemed to be the best choice for that task.

"Hey Clyper, can I borrow you for a few minutes?"

Clyper walked over to Fortak's desk. "What can I do for you, bud?"

"I need to find a way to communicate back to one of the nearby Daklin bases."

"Communicate? Like radio?" Clyper was rubbing his chin. "That's gotta be a slow way to say hello. Don't you guys have any faster technology than that?"

"We do, but nothing using Earth tech. Anyway, we have a relay outpost at Rigel Kentaurus, which is only 1,597 days away at the speed of light."

"Wait, that's like, 4.5 light years. You mean Alpha Centauri, Fortak?"

"Yes," Fortak smiled. "And I am going to need something where I can transmit a fair amount of data. At least megabits per second, but anything higher would be great."

"I can't build it, but I can source that for you, Fortak. Should have it in a day or two."

"Thanks, Clyper." Fortak fist pumped him and watched him walk away. Clyper didn't ask a single question regarding the purpose, and that was the perfect scenario.

○○○○ ∞ ○○○○

Two weeks later, Fortak had been broadcasting to Kentaurus for ten days, transmitting daily updates and files detailing everything he was learning about the T-Portal.

The two Earth engineers and Fortak were functioning as a solid team. Art was used to, but still apologetic about, Clyper's constant jokes, frequent coffee breaks, and loud music during lunch. Despite their shared creativity, Clyper was, in many ways, more like a Daklin engineer than Art. When faced with an important problem, Art would keep working relentlessly, pushing past exhaustion. Like creativity, that kind of stubborn persistence was a trait Fortak had never seen in Daklin engineers. Hard work was a foreign concept to the average Daklin.

Fortak came to appreciate that Clyper's strange mental leaps occasionally hit on something important. Art on the other hand was steady, methodical, and the kind of engineer who triple-checked a connection before calling it finished. Both methods seemed to work, and both styles were completely unfamiliar to Fortak.

That morning, Art had stripped down a subassembly from the T-Portal's inner core. Inside, he discovered a set of copper-wound modules bolted to the emitter housing. He was methodically tracing the lines with a continuity tester when he suddenly stopped.

"These lines don't go anywhere," Art concluded.

Fortak looked up from his console. "Explain."

Art handed him the schematic he had been sketching. "Power leads run in, then stop. No return path, no load. They're not connected to the emitter or the phase controls."

Clyper rolled his chair over to Art. "Let me guess… are they decorations?"

"They're wired like they matter," Art said. "But electrically, they're dead weight. As far as I can tell, they do nothing."

Fortak pulled one of the modules free. The casing was high-grade composite, the kind used to shield against tachyon leakage, yet inside was nothing but an empty core and a loop of inert fiber.

"Did either of you know or work with Zander?" Fortak asked.

"I came after he left," Clyper answered.

Fortak looked at Art, "How about you?"

"I was here. Zander was the best damned engineer I have ever worked with. The man was in his own league. I cannot understand why he would build in circuits that do nothing."

Fortak took a breath and exhaled slowly. "Do you keep up with him?" He asked, attempting to catch Art unexpectedly.

"What?" Art's face turned to one of pain. "Zander's dead, Fortak."

"I see. Sorry," Fortak feigned. "Why would a brilliant engineer add useless components to a system this critical?" Fortak asked, half to himself.

"To mess with anyone trying to copy it," Clyper replied, with sudden certainty. "Classic misdirection. You publish schematics with a bunch of fake parts and the competition copycats waste years chasing ghosts."

Art nodded thoughtfully. "That's one possibility. Or maybe he wanted to hide something else, shield a signal, or mask a signature. Zander was always deliberate."

Fortak turned the module over in his hands. Daklin engineers did not waste material. Every component had a function. Yet here was Zander Bell, building decoys into one of the most advanced machines Fortak had ever seen.

"Could also be hiding from someone," Clyper added, spinning lazily in his chair. "If your enemy can't figure out what's real, they can't shut you down."

Fortak set the module down with deliberate care. "Let's start testing components and systems in this device. We'll map every nonfunctional component. And then, perhaps we can determine what Zander Bell was hiding from."

○○○○ ∞ ○○○○

That evening, Fortak entered Pascal's office without knocking. Pascal stood at the bar cart in the corner, pouring something amber and slow into a glass.

"You've been quiet lately," Pascal said, handing Fortak a drink without asking. "Are you and my engineers making progress?"

Fortak took the glass but didn't drink. "We have found multiple assemblies inside the T-Portal that serve no functional purpose. They consume power, generate no output, and are sealed with materials difficult to penetrate without destroying them."

Pascal shrugged. "Zander was an odd guy. Maybe he just liked symmetry."

Fortak leaned forward. "I believe he was hiding something."

Pascal sipped. "Here we go again, your obsession with finding Zander."

"Have you searched for him?"

"Everywhere," Pascal said. "We checked property records, travel manifests, old contacts. The guy's dead, Fortak. Car crash. I saw the wreck."

"Stuff like that can be faked," Fortak scoffed.

Pascal set his glass down on his desk hard enough for the ice to clink. "And sometimes, people just die. If you want to chase ghosts, fine, but I'm telling you, you're wasting your time searching for Bell. The man is gone."

Fortak studied him for a long moment. "You do not believe your own words."

Pascal gave a tired smile. "No, I believe them. What I don't believe is that you're going to let this go, so, knock yourself out and continue the search. But if Zander Bell is alive, he's not coming back here."

"How about the possibility that he's not on Earth?"

"What?" Pascal asked incredulously.

"I stepped through the portal 19 million miles away from Earth. That's half the distance to Mars, Pascal." Fortak thought for a second. "At opposition, Mars is about 34 million miles. Isn't it possible he could build a T-Portal to Mars?"

"Wait, you're suggesting he went to Mars? There's no atmosphere, no food."

"I would not rule it out," Fortak paused and walked over to the window overlooking the Dallas skyline. A regular flow of airliners passed in the field of view, heading to Dallas Love Field. As was often the case, Fortak was reminded of just how primitive this Earth society was compared to Daklin technology.

"The T-Portal technology requires a portal or gateway on both sides. I heard Zander say on more than one occasion he needed both sides to make it work." Pascal explained. "There's no way he could have gotten one to Mars."

"Pascal, you should know that what Zander did with T-Portal is special. It's unique on a *galactic* scale." He emphasized. "In fifty million years of Daklin technology, no one has ever figured out how to do what Zander did. I think he could have figured out a way to do it without both sides."

"You are putting on that tinfoil hat again. This discussion makes no sense, Fortak. Didn't you say you came to Earth using tachyon tunnels, or some such?"

"We fly our ships in a network of interstellar tunnels, but we did not build those tunnels, and we do not know who did, or when."

A chill ran down Pascal's spine, the hair on his arms standing up. "You're telling me the Daklin travel the galaxy through tunnels, and you don't know who built them, or *how* to make more?"

"Correct. It is a problem that has perplexed our engineers for millions of years. We use the tunnels, but we don't know how to create new ones."

"Do the tunnels go to every star in the galaxy?"

"No," Fortak responded.

"How do you travel to places that have no tunnels?" Pascal continued the query.

"We can do it, but it takes a lot of energy and a very long time. Interstellar travel without the tunnels is subject to the laws of relativity. It would be like walking to the southernmost tip of South America as opposed to flying there."

"I had no idea."

"All those stars that are not on the tunnel network remain isolated. They don't get to enjoy the benefits of our culture, trade, and of course, protection."

Pascal wanted to ask *protection from what* but ultimately decided against it.

"So, you see, Pascal," Fortak quipped, "Zander Bell is special. Whatever it takes to find him is energy worth taking."

"And if he's dead?"

"He's not dead." He answered with confidence, finished his drink in one slow swallow, and set the glass on Pascal's desk.

"If you say so…" Pascal responded with skepticism.

"Look, Pascal, I keep thinking about the fact that I stepped into the portal from L-5, which is 19 million miles from Earth. Maybe it's time to take T-Portal into space."

"Into space?" Pascal leaned forward with renewed interest.

3

The City in the Stars

Alex glanced at Maria and then Emily as the Tranquility ship shut down primary systems.

"Thoughts?"

"I have run thousands of simulations based on the small data I have collected," Emily started. "I see no reason why we should be concerned."

Maria nodded, "Agreed."

Alex grabbed young Steven's hand and opened the portal.

He quickly looked around the room. A tall, thin, and distinguished-looking man stood waiting in the docking bay just outside Tranquility. When Alex looked behind his ship, he froze. The massive opening they had flown through was still wide open to the vacuum of space.

The tall man looked at Alex, then at the opening. He raised his hand and smiled. "It's okay, Alex Durant," he spoke in perfect English. "There is an electromagnetic field that keeps the atmosphere in and the radiation out. This bay is safe." He smiled in a friendly way.

Alex's caution immediately turned to fascination, but he stopped himself from pelting this man with engineering questions. "And you are?"

"My name is Polonius. I am captain and governor of *Andromeda Prime,* the name of this ship." He stepped forward with the easy confidence of a statesman who had welcomed visitors from across the spiral arms.

"Alex Durant," Polonius said warmly, before Alex could introduce himself, clasping onto Alex's forearm in greeting. "I have done my research. Many believe you are the greatest living mind in the Local Group of Galaxies today."

Alex tilted his head. "That sounds like a compliment that I have no hope of living up to, but thanks."

Polonius turned to the others. "Welcome, cybernetic Emily, Maria, young Steven. For a while, I hope that this ship can be a sanctuary, so welcome aboard Andromeda Prime. You arrived at a good hour. The city is awake and at its best."

"City?" Steven tilted his head. "I thought we were on a spaceship."

"I know you must have a million questions, but please allow me to give you a brief tour." Polonius smiled knowingly. "You'll see."

The moment the inner hatch opened, warm light spilled in, along with the scent of flowering trees. The air was soft, carrying the sound of distant laughter and the faint rush of water.

"This is… a ship?" Maria's voice carried a rare edge of wonder.

"It is far more than a ship," Polonius chuckled. "It is a self-sustaining home to three million inhabitants. Allow me to show you around."

They stepped onto a promenade that curved gently under a transparent canopy. Overhead, the Earth was visible, filtered through atmospheric shielding. Below, lush parks sprawled like green ribbons, broken by crystal-blue lakes. The air was alive with birdsong, and somewhere nearby, a street musician coaxed a melody from an instrument that resembled an acoustic guitar with shifting metallic strings.

Maria slowed as they crossed a footbridge. Children splashed at the edge of a pond while students painted at easels under the shade of broad-leafed trees. The smell of baked bread and roasted spices curled from an open-air café, mingling with the fragrance of wildflowers planted along the walkway.

"This reminds me of Pronimos. Everyone is happy and carefree," she murmured to Alex. The parks, the open water, the blending of science and nature. It was the closest thing she had seen to her adopted home world. For a moment, her eyes softened, the weight of all the challenges slipping away. "On Pronimos, our cities were built into the natural environment, not over it. This... what you have here feels like coming home."

"Maria," Polonius began, "this entire ship was designed as a natural habitat to support human comfort. There's no real natural environment here, just architecture and engineering. While your home of Pronimos was a living breathing planet, Andromeda Prime began as an engineering project. We created the nature, if you will."

Maria took a deep breath and surveyed her surroundings. "Of course," she said with a smile, somewhat embarrassed by her oversight. "The sky, the scenery...it feels like we're actually on a planet."

Alex jumped lightly, "How are you simulating gravity?"

"Oh, we are not simulating gravity. We create it, but we do it without all the mass you would expect in your traditional equations."

"How?" Alex asked.

"No science yet, Alex. Besides, I'm a politician, not a scientist. You'll have plenty of opportunities to learn what you need to know."

Steven tugged on Emily's hand. He pointed toward a green park where kids were playing.

"Steven is what, three Earth years old?" Polonius asked, observing the child's curiosity.

Emily looked at Steven, "Tell Polonius how old you are."

Steven held up three fingers, backed by a proud smile.

"A smart young man, like his father and mother," Polonius affirmed.

"Oh, I am not his mother," Maria corrected.

"We know. Paula Campbell was his mother," Polonius winked at Maria.

"Wait, how do you know all this?" Alex asked. "It's concerning that you seem to know so much about us."

"Yes, Alex, I understand your concerns. But like with the science, let's finish our tour first, then we can start answering the million questions you have." Polonius looked to the other adults for their agreement. "I promise, there will be no secrets."

"Okay, let's finish the tour," Alex hesitantly agreed.

"When this city was built, just under a million people lived here. But with immigration and," Polonius motioned to the playing children, "families joining, we're now closer to three million. Hundreds of civilizations are represented, and each culture brings its own recipes, music, and art. That's what keeps the city alive."

"How old is the city?" Alex asked.

"One thousand, two hundred thirteen years," Polonius replied, glancing up as a tram whispered past, gliding silently on thin air. Residential towers rose on either side, wrapped in cascading vertical gardens.

As they walked, Polonius stopped every few blocks to point out something notable: the academy for engineering and sciences, a public holotheater that allowed residents to immerse themselves in historical or entertaining environments. At one stop, he gestured toward a clinic where medics used bio-resonance fields to accelerate healing and handle any accidents.

One side street opened into a school courtyard where children were practicing with instruments of strange geometry, their music accompanied by holographic waves that danced in the air. Another led past a zero-gravity gymnasium where young acrobats tumbled and laughed, learning balance in three dimensions.

Steven's curiosity got the better of him when he spotted a group of boys chasing a floating, glowing sphere across the grass. Without waiting for permission, he darted toward them.

"Steven!" Alex called after him, but Polonius held up a hand.

"Let him go. It is good for visitors to join the games of the city's children. All of those children will immediately know who he is and how to play around him."

They watched as Steven joined the chase, darting and leaping, his laughter blending with the others. The sphere shifted colors as it moved, forcing the group to adapt their strategy in real time.

Emily, her senses attuned to patterns of behavior, observed quietly. "They've integrated play with cognitive development. The game forces cooperative problem-solving, reflex training, and emotional bonding. The design is intentional."

"Precisely, Emily," Polonius answered. "And Alex, he is perfectly safe. There is no crime on Andromeda Prime."

"How is it that the name of this ship is Andromeda Prime?" Alex smiled as Steven came running back over to the group and took his father's hand.

"That's simply the English translation, Alex. We don't call our galaxy Andromeda, nor do we call yours the Milky Way," Polonius explained, leading the group up a spiral staircase.

They ended the tour at an observation deck high above the central hub. From there, they could take in the ship's full scale: hills, buildings, waterways, and parks, all seamlessly integrated into an environment indistinguishable from Earth.

Maria leaned against the rail; eyes fixed on the glowing heart of the ship. "If you had shown me this years ago," she said quietly, "I would have believed humanity had already reached its pinnacle."

Polonius inclined his head. "Perhaps we have. Or perhaps this is just the beginning."

Steven tugged on his father's arm. "I scored twice," he announced proudly. "And I made a new friend."

Alex smiled. "I think, perhaps, we all have."

"Ahead is the childhood learning center Alex." Polonius pointed at a small building next to a park. "You can choose to keep Steven with you or immerse himself with educators and other kids during your stay."

Alex looked to Maria, then Emily. Both nodded approval.

Steven clung to Maria's hand as they stepped into the early center. Bright murals shimmered along the curved walls, alive with animated animals and neon-colored starships. Holographic storybooks floated in midair, and the other children, all of whom were human, were busy building intricate towers from blocks that rearranged themselves when tapped on.

A gentle caretaker with iridescent skin knelt to Steven's level. "Welcome, young traveler. My name is Dimitria, and I am a cybernetic, like Emily. I will be your teacher and guide. Today we'll explore the worlds of color and sound."

Steven's eyes went wide at the promise of adventure. After a reassuring nod from Alex, he released Maria's hand and followed the cybernetic teacher inside.

Polonius motioned to Alex, Emily, and Maria. "Come. I have some friends who have been anxiously waiting to meet you."

They entered a conference room with a panoramic window overlooking the ship's inner cityscape. Three figures awaited them. The first was a tall, lean African man dressed in a dark blue tunic. His smile was warm, but his eyes held the weight of someone who had seen too much.

"This is Jabari Minja," Polonius said. "AI systems specialist, and a refugee from Earth. Minja was selected same as you were, Alex."

"Selected?" Alex asked.

"It is complicated, but a traveler from our Galaxy came to Earth several hundred years ago. Jabari is the great grandson of that traveler."

Jabari inclined his head. "I've followed your work, Alex. I know that I will be assigned to Emily, but I hope we can accomplish the impossible together."

Beside him stood an Andromedean woman whose eyes seemed lit from within, their deep sapphire glow hinting at millennia of thought. Her skin, hair, attire, and figure were absolute perfection, and her presence a combination of both calming and electric energy.

"This is Hypatia." Polonius said. "She is a plasma physicist and scholar of reincarnation. She's one thousand one hundred twenty-one years old, and she'll be working with you, Maria."

Maria smiled politely but couldn't help feeling a thrill. On Pronimos, many lived beyond a thousand years, but Hypatia had likely witnessed civilizations rise and fall in an entirely different galaxy.

The final figure was shorter and broad-shouldered, with pale skin, a receding hairline, and a tool harness slung across his chest. His gaze took in Alex as though he was measuring every molecule.

"And this," Polonius concluded, "is Torvek, the finest engineer aboard Andromeda Prime. He is yours to collaborate with, Alex. My research on Earth scientists and engineers suggests that Torvek is likely very similar to many engineers you have known and worked with."

Torvek frowned and tugged on his earlobe. "Are you complimenting or insulting me, Polonius?"

"You are the finest engineer on Andromeda Prime, Torvek. Need I say more?" Without waiting for a response, Polonius turned to the others and motioned for them to take a seat. "We have much to cover, so please, let us get started."

Polonius stood at the head of the conference table, the ship's cityscape glowing through the wide viewport behind him. Alex, Emily, Maria, Jabari, Hypatia, and Torvek took seats and focused on Polonius.

"You've all wondered why Andromeda Prime has assembled this group," Polonius began, his voice calm but weighted. "Our Andromeda Republic has enjoyed 60 million years of peace and prosperity. We are a democratic republic, collaborative and peaceful. Our people have no military, nor have we needed one for tens of megaanum."

Jabari raised an eyebrow as he glanced at his handheld computer, which translated "megaanum" to millions of years. "60 million years without war? That's… hard for me to imagine. Dinosaurs, not humans, walked the Earth that long ago."

Hypatia folded her hands. "That is because our society was shaped by the recognition that every life is a cycle, and that every individual has a purpose. Destroying even one life diminishes the whole."

Polonius gave a small nod, but his expression darkened. "For that same reason, we have avoided contact with the Daklin Empire. We have observed them for hundreds of millennia, never interfering, hopeful that their empire would fall, but alas that has not happened, and is not likely to happen."

Alex leaned back in his chair. "Before we dive into all this, I have a question. If the Daklin Empire is so oppressive, why wouldn't its subjects want to see an end to their rule? Wouldn't they rise up the moment they had the chance? I think we could inspire and give them that chance."

Polonius' eyes softened. "It is a natural question, and one your own history can answer. The people who became the first citizens of the United States left monarchies and kingdoms behind. They knew what freedom was and had tasted enough of it to be willing to fight and die to keep it. But they were an exception. Almost every other attempt to liberate nations from dictatorship has failed."

Jabari tilted his head. "You're saying the will to fight depends on knowing what you're fighting for?"

"Exactly," Polonius said. "Take the recent fall of your Soviet Union. Its subjects had lived so long under central control that they had no living memory of genuine liberty. When the system collapsed, most were unprepared to build something better. They drifted toward familiar patterns with strongmen, centralized authority, and control disguised as stability."

Hypatia's voice was quiet but firm. "The Daklin subjects will be no different. They have never known freedom. To them, the Empire is not oppression, its stability, and the only structure they have ever seen. They will not rise willingly against it. They will, in fact, stand against *you* if you try to liberate them."

Polonius clasped his hands. "We have an advanced think tank called the Andromeda Mathematical and Historical Institute, aka the AMHI, that runs simulations and evaluates trends using a form of what you would call calculus. The AMHI does not merely project troop movements or economics, it models the deep inertia of cultures. The way human and non-human societies resist change. It accounts for psychology, resource distribution, cultural myths, and a trillion other constants. And in this calculus, the Daklin populace will not be a force for liberation against their ruling class. They will be, at best, neutral… and at worst, a willing tool to serve their rulers."

Polonius took a slow breath, his voice gaining weight. "Now, you must understand the larger reason for your presence here. As I mentioned, our Republic has endured for 60 million years, but the AMHI has completed a new projection, and it shows the Daklin are approaching a dangerous threshold."

Alex leaned forward. "Let me guess, this has something to do with tachyon tunnels?"

"Exactly," Polonius said. "The AMHI models behavior the way your mathematicians on Earth model bacterial or viral growth. In our case, AMHI studies cultures, civilizations, and empires. Only they have mastered the mathematics and can produce results with vastly greater precision than your molecular biologists."

"I think I see where this is going," Emily broke in solemnly.

"Yes, I would guess that you do," Polonius frowned. "The AMHI incorporate trillions of variables: resource availability, cultural momentum, technological leaps, even the probability distributions of leadership traits. Our simulations predict the Daklin will soon recreate your work, Alex."

Torvek's gravelly voice broke in. "I assume they won't just recreate the tech, they'll weaponize it."

"That is correct, Torvek," Polonius affirmed.

Maria frowned. "What's their first move?"

Polonius tapped a control and a holo-map appeared over the table, star clusters pulsing in slow rotation. "They have captured a rendition of the technology called T-Portal. Fortunately, it is not capable of accomplishing what your Tranquility Ship can do, but our intel tells us a Daklin scientist has realized that Daklin engineering is devoid of creativity."

"Engineering without creativity?" Alex challenged. "How is that possible?"

"I could answer sarcastically and say laziness, but we have learned that much of engineering, even in Andromeda, is simply learning how to work with what we already have. There is little room for innovation and creativity when the base of knowledge gets as voluminous as it is in a 50-million-year-old civilization."

Alex took a deep breath and shook his head slowly. "Can I assume that the Daklin scientist is using Earth engineers?"

"Yes, Alex, but your technology is way beyond their grasp. It is going to be a long time before they catch up and fully understand what you have done. Once they do, they will use the tunnels to crush the Pronimos insurgency. We expect that to happen in 27.8 years."

"Wait," Alex broke in, "27.8 years? Are you being sarcastic, or is that a real calculation?"

"It is real math, and quite accurate, Alex." He stopped and studied the group. "Emboldened by that rapid victory, and armed with the new tunneling technology, they will expand beyond their galaxy. The AMHI's long-term projections show them conquering neighboring star clusters, then whole galaxies."

Emily's tone was sharp. "How certain is this?"

Polonius looked at her without blinking. "We ran 3.48 trillion simulations. In all but two, the Daklin succeed."

Jabari shifted in his seat. "Two out of nearly three and a half trillion? I understand how big a trillion is and that's not a margin. That's not even a miracle. Statistically, it's zero, no matter how you look at it."

"It is why you are here," Polonius said. "In one of those scenarios where the Daklin are stopped, there is one constant, and that is Alex Durant. The first human from the Milky Way in 50 million years to build engineering capable of tachyon tunneling."

Alex glanced at Torvek, then to Polonius. "What is the other scenario?"

"The other scenario is one that I do not think anyone in this room would agree to."

Emily stood, "I know what it is."

Everyone turned and focused on Emily.

"If we destroy Earth today, or very soon, we change everything." Emily spoke in a calculated response.

"Please sit, Emily," Polonius commanded. "Her assessment is correct, but we are not here to even consider the destruction of Earth."

"Wait," Torvak asserted himself. "Computer, approximately how many humans will be killed in a Daklin scenario where they have tachyon tunneling?"

"Just under one quintillion," Emily responded before the computer had a chance.

"Emily is correct," the computer answered. "The worst-case scenario is nine hundred twenty-two quadrillions, which is just under a quintillion."

Torvek's mouth curled into something that might have been a smile, but more likely was a calculated frown. "Eight billion Earthlings die today to save 922,000,000,000,000,000? It seems like obvious math to an obvious answer."

"Absolutely not!" Alex blurted, horrified by the possibility.

"Alex is right," Polonius added. "We will not employ a statistical analysis that results in killing anyone. What we need is a lever, and AMHI has concluded that Alex *is* that lever."

Emily spoke softly. "And levers require fulcrums. That is why each of us has been chosen. Jabari for artificial intelligence strategies and his legacy to our own galaxy, Maria for deep scientific inquiry into plasma and the cycles of existence, Hypatia to integrate ancient knowledge with modern physics, and Torvek for engineering education for Alex."

"Emily, you have been a half step ahead of me this entire meeting." Polonius replied as he studied her with a furrowed brow.

"No military, and no firewalls on your central computer. It was easy for me to hack in and access everything I needed," Emily said, smiling despite the gravity of the situation. "I agree, Alex is in a category of his own. Without him, I wouldn't exist."

Polonius clasped his hands behind his back. "We knew you would be extraordinary, Emily. I don't think we understood just *how* extraordinary. In any case, we do not have a military, but we do have knowledge, science, and this team. The AMHI cannot fight this war for us, but it has given us the best framework to successfully execute that 1 in 3.48 trillion scenario. For a period, we will be at your disposal and will do whatever you need to improve your probability."

4

Collapsing Tunnels

"Why were you insistent on naming the ship, *Vega*?"

Zander stared at his wife Lyra, smiled, and took her hands. "Vega is the brightest star in the constellation, Lyra."

Lyra kissed him on the nose, "I didn't know that, but I promise to thank you later, my love," she winked and returned to her console.

Zander stood at the command table, the glowing lattice of the Daklin Empire's tunnel network hovering above the glass surface like a web of light. The threads shifted as Lyra manipulated the display, collapsing tangents until only one pulsed crimson.

"That's the one," Lyra said, her voice calm but resolute. "Primary, high-density traffic. Collapse it here, and three outlying systems are effectively isolated."

Zander exhaled, steadying himself. "Seventh one in five weeks," he murmured. "Feels like we've been at this for years already."

Lyra glanced up at him. "We always knew the math was going to be brutal. Thirty thousand primaries, more than a hundred thousand feeders in the tunnel network…and only *three* ships to cut them. But every collapse matters."

He nodded. His fingers danced across the control matrix, aligning the ship's tachyon emitters. Outside, the Vega adjusted position, engines humming at a resonance frequency very similar to her sister ship, Tranquility, as the targeting grid locked into place.

"Tunnel resonance matched," Lyra reported. "T-Fields holding stable."

"Can you detect any ship in the tunnel?" Zander and leaders on Pronimos had made the decision to isolate the empire with a minimum cost in lives.

Lyra checked for energy emissions in the tachyon spectrum. "All clear."

"Execute," Zander ordered.

The deck shuddered as energy surged through the emitter array. The crimson thread on the display flickered, wavered, and then snapped. Vega ripped through the fiber of the tunnel wall, which collapsed the entrance and exit. Their ship created its own mini tunnel, hopping a few million miles away so they could observe the collapse. On the main screen, they watched as it unraveled in a cascade of fractured tachyon flux, a brilliant flash fading into nothingness.

Lyra leaned closer to the display, her eyes reflecting the fading light. "Confirmed. Collapse successful."

Zander allowed himself a rare smile. "Seven down. Twenty-nine thousand, nine hundred ninety-three to go."

She smirked. "I'll take progress where I can get it."

He leaned back in his chair, but his mind was already calculating. Six months earlier, he and Lyra in Vega, along with Megan and Mark aboard their ship, *Singularity*, had set out to isolate the Daklin

Empire by collapsing critical tachyon tunnels leading to the hub of their empire.

The plan had worked. When the Daklin attempted to destroy Earth, they suffered their first failure in what was likely fifty million years, thanks to his father, Alex Durant, and Emily, their cybernetic AI, who had discovered how to collapse the tunnels.

It was even more effective when the tunnels were collapsed *with* Daklin planet-killers inside them. But the true mission had never been about destruction. It was about isolation. The Daklin used and controlled the tachyon tunnels, but they didn't know how to create them.

Fortified by a military of tens of billions of weaponized ships, the Daklin's true strength lay in their control and use of the tachyon tunnels. But the ability to *build* those tunnels was a piece of engineering lost to history, forgotten for fifty million years.

…Until Alex Durant.

Zander re-focused and looked at Lyra, "If she's kept pace, Megan's probably close to ten collapses herself. And the third member of the tunnel collapse group, Calit Engress…" He trailed off, shaking his head. "That one's harder to read. He doesn't share his numbers, and he sucks at communication."

Lyra gave him a look. "Well, Calit is Tilka. They look at science in a very different way but he's brilliant and a talented pilot. In any case, does it matter? We each play our part. The Daklin won't know what hit them until the lattice starts falling apart from the outside in."

Zander's expression darkened. "Unless they figure it out sooner. And if they do, they'll come looking for us."

Silence hung for a moment, broken only by the faint thrum of the ship's engines. Lyra reached across the console and touched his hand. "Let's get some dinner, and then, I believe I have a promise to fulfill." She winked and followed with a seductive smile.

"Here's to seven down," Lyra said finally, holding her glass in the air. "I think that calls for at least a moment of celebration. We're still alive. We're still moving."

Zander managed a half-smile. "If the Daklin haven't noticed yet, maybe we…"

The alarms cut him off with a shrill, insistent, vibrating through the hull like the cry of some mechanical beast. Both Lyra and Zander were on their feet instantly, food and drinks forgotten, sprinting toward the control deck.

The main screen lit with the unmistakable silhouette of a Daklin warship. It was a vast, angular monster, dwarfing the Vega. Its hull bristled with weapon arrays, glowing with the telltale charge of imminent fire.

"Contact." the ship's AI announced, its calm tone a stark contrast to the blaring klaxons. "No communication received. Hostile action detected."

Lyra gripped the railing, her knuckles pale. "They've found us."

Before Zander could respond, a lance of energy erupted from the Daklin vessel, a searing beam that tore through space toward them. The Vega shuddered violently as the AI slipped the ship into tachyon space just seconds before the beam reached them.

The tunnel outside twisted, stretched, and a second later, dissolved as the Vega leapt a million miles in a heartbeat.

The alarms ceased. The void was calm.

Zander let out the breath he'd been holding. "We lost them."

The words had barely left his mouth when the screen flickered, anomalous readings spiking. Space rippled ahead. And then, impossibly, another Daklin warship burst into view, tearing through the void as if Vega's escape had been nothing more than a delayed invitation.

"They followed," Lyra whispered, horror in her voice.

"Impossible," Zander shouted as he watched the AI process the next jump.

They fired again.

"Jumping." the AI announced coolly.

The Vega buckled under another surge as the universe stretched once more in a second hop.

They emerged in dark, empty space. For a fleeting moment, the stillness was absolute. Zander's heart pounded as he checked the scans. "Maybe this time..."

The Daklin ship appeared again, ripping into existence less than a minute later, energy banks already flaring for another strike.

"They're locked onto us," Lyra said, her voice steady despite the fear in her eyes. "No matter where we go, the find us."

The Vega lurched again as Zander gritted his teeth, voice cutting through the roar of alarms. "Longer jump. 10 million miles. Now!"

The AI acknowledged in its calm, even tone: "Trajectory aligned. Tachyon field stable."

The universe twisted violently, and the Vega vanished into the shimmering blur of tachyon space. Five seconds later, Lyra clutched the rail as the stars reformed around them.

For three heartbeats, there was only silence. Then the warning lights flared crimson.

"They're back," the AI reported. "Daklin vessel emergence detected. Range: closing rapidly."

On the forward display, the monstrous warship burst into view, firing before its form had even stabilized on the screen. A brilliant energy wave sliced across space.

The AI managed to dodge the burst.

"Jump again!" Zander shouted. "Push it farther. Let's do 200 million miles this time."

The Vega tore away, plunging deep into the pale currents and hum of tachyon space. The crew could almost feel the Daklin breathing down their necks. Emerging once more into normal space, Zander barely had time to shout a curse before the enemy vessel clawed through after them, faster, closer. They were learning and improving with each jump, while the Vega was fleeing like a scared rabbit.

"I calculate they will hit us in the next jump," the AI announced. "Margin for error: unacceptable."

Lyra's voice was tight. "They're adapting. Every time we run, they follow faster, react faster."

"They'll gut us on the next one," Zander muttered.

The AI interjected, "Initiating extended tachyon transit. Fifteen minutes."

The ship opened a new tunnel and entered the calming hum of tachyon space. For once, they had a stretch of time to breathe, though every second felt stolen.

"They're not just predicting us," the AI said after a pause. "They are following. The Daklin ship is entering the tunnels we create. The are learning how close they can get, and exiting the tunnel with guns charged."

Lyra's brow furrowed. "So, every jump is just a trail we lay for them to walk?"

Zander clenched a fist. "Then we have to cut the trail."

Lyra's eyes lit. "Brilliant, Zander. We collapse it behind us just like we are doing with their network."

"Exactly, they are expecting us to just run, but this time we will rip out of the tunnel and collapse it behind us."

The AI hesitated for a fraction of a second. "This is different, Zander. Our tunnels are small compared to the galactic network. We'll need to run a new set of equations to avoid the risk of Vega entanglement."

"Run those calculations," Zander commanded.

"Done." The AI responded less than two seconds after.

"Do it," Zander said firmly. "On my mark."

The ship ripped itself from tachyon space collapsing the tunnel as it exited.

"Mark!" Zander barked.

The Vega leapt forward, vanishing into tachyon space, then popping out a million miles away. Five seconds later, the sky lit with the fire of a tunnel collapsing around the Daklin ship.

Then, silence.

They were drifting in a quiet starfield. Nothing behind them. No alarms. No pursuit.

Zander stared at the scans, chest heaving. "Is it...?"

"Confirmed," the AI replied. "Daklin vessel destroyed. Tunnel collapse successful."

The control deck of the Vega was strangely quiet now after the chaos of the chase. The hum of the engines felt almost comforting, a reminder that they were still alive.

Zander could feel his heart pounding in his temples.

Lyra leaned back in her chair, rubbing her own temples. "That was too close. One more cycle and that thing would have turned us into stardust."

Zander stared at the scan results still hovering over the console. The violent fluctuations where the tunnel had collapsed were already dissipating into the void. Nothing remained of the Daklin ship.

"They weren't just chasing us," he said finally. "They were learning, evolving in real time. Every jump, they were faster. Smarter."

The ship's AI chimed in, voice steady and analytical. "Observation consistent. Daklin adaptive algorithms appear to have modeled our escape patterns in real time. Had the pursuit continued, the probability of Vega's destruction would have exceeded ninety nine percent in the next encounter."

Lyra glanced at the AI's interface panel; her voice edged with awe. "Then collapsing our own tunnel wasn't just a trick. It was survival."

Zander nodded slowly. "But it's a trick we only get to use once. The Daklin were adapting and figuring it out in real time, so we can only assume they were relaying their chase to the Empire as it progressed."

For a long moment, they sat in silence. Finally, Lyra whispered, "So many tunnels left, and now we know the enemy can run us down. This…. well, this changes everything."

Zander's jaw tightened. "Then we change first." He leaned forward over the comms console, fingers flying across the interface. "Open secure channel. Link the *Singularity* and *Tilka 934*."

"Channel open," the AI confirmed.

A moment later, two holos shimmered into being, Megan Hoglund's face sharp and intent, her wild curls pulled back, and beside her the stern, angular features of Calit Engress, captain of Tilka 934.

"Zander," Megan said, her tone brusque. "We were in the middle of a run. This had better be important."

"It is," Zander replied. His voice carried the gravity of the encounter. "We've just destroyed a Daklin warship, but it nearly destroyed us first. They're using our tunnels against us. Every jump we make is a path they can follow. They're getting better at it."

Megan's expression hardened. "So that's how they tracked me last week. I thought it was coincidence."

"How did you escape, Megan?" Zander asked.

"I exited the tunnel, did a two-hour time hop, then jumped into a second tunnel."

"I am not sure time jumps are wise, Megan," the Vega AI responded.

"Well, it's a hell of a lot smarter than getting destroyed by a Daklin ship," Megan quipped.

Calit narrowed his eyes and focused on Zander. "And you destroyed one?"

Zander nodded. "Collapsed our own tunnel as they came through. It took them with it. But if they are learning, it's only a matter of time before they turn the trick on us. This is gonna turn into a game of Russian Roulette."

Lyra leaned forward. "The lesson is clear: we can't assume a jump makes us safe. We are going to have to develop a new set of tactics."

Megan, realizing she had the tactical skill set exhaled, muttered a curse under her breath. "Understood. Thanks for the warning. I'll adjust our strategy."

Calit's hologram tilted its head. "What you've called Russian Roulette is an excellent way to respond to the Daklin chasing us in our own tunnels. Thank you."

The channel flickered, static rippling as the encryption cycled. Zander's eyes lingered on the fading images of the other captains. "Stay alive," he said quietly, though the link had already closed.

The deck lights dimmed slightly as the ship settled into a quieter power state. Zander sat back, the weight of the galaxy pressing down on him.

"Eight down," Lyra said softly. "And thirty thousand more to go."

Zander's gaze drifted to the stars. "And now, the Daklin are hunting us too. This war just became real." He turned and looked at Lyra who was studying him intently. She had been beautiful and intriguing from the first moment they had met.

"You made a promise to me, gorgeous wife."

"Really? You are thinking about *that*, after a day like this?"

"Especially after a day like this, Lyra."

∘∘∘∘ ∞ ∘∘∘∘

The tunnel behind Vega folded in on itself with a thunderous ripple. Another tunnel eliminated, this time with a Daklin warship in it.

To his surprise, Megan Hoglund's ship, Singularity, popped out of a second tunnel, just a hundred meters from Vega.

Megan leaned forward over the console. "Vega, do you read?"

"Aye, Megan," Lyra answered. "We didn't expect you."

"What you should be asking is how did I find you," Megan corrected.

Zander thought about her comment for a second. All three ships had purposely been operating in stealth mode. They had sectors and preplanned tunnels to collapse, but with over thirty thousand each, and no preplanned order, they shouldn't have been able to find each other. This was intentional, protecting the others if one was captured.

"Can we dock and meet in person?" Zander asked.

"Yes, but first, a few jumps," Megan hammered away on a screen. "Can I have access to Vega?"

Zander looked at his cybernetic AI and nodded. A fraction of a second later, Vega began a series of tunnel jumps. Five minutes later, Singularity and Vega docked.

"Okay, Megan, how did you find us?"

"Two things you are doing wrong, Zander. First, you are being methodical in your tunnel collapses. It wasn't difficult to write a routine that predicts your next collapse and track you. I guarantee, if I can do it, the Daklin are doing the same."

Zander looked at Lyra, then at his AI, and grimaced. "Crap, it's that obvious?"

"It's fuckin stupid, Zander. The second one is worse, though. We're leaving a pulse trail. Our brains are thinking in the electromagnetic spectrum, but tachyons have their own signature spectrum."

"Are you sure?" Zander was incredulous.

"I am positive. I have tested it and the Daklins have been able to track me just on my tachyon pulse trail. I have learned to mask it. They can still detect my tunnels, but I am developing routines that I hope will close a portal entry before I exit the tunnel."

"That's brilliant, Megan."

"I know," Megan answered in a matter-of-a-fact tone. "But I could use your help. I am only a coder, and you understand the science."

Over the next two days, Megan and Zander worked intensely on solving the problem. There were a few times when Mark was also able to participate, but the Megan-Zander pairing operated at a pace almost on par with AI, and with a level of creativity that AI could not simulate.

On the third day, after a few iterations along with testing, the new system was working. Both ships, Vega and Singularity, could create a tunnel, enter, close the entry, and travel to the destination without having the tunnel collapse.

Pleased with their progress, the two couples decided to take the evening off: relaxing, listening to music, and enjoying a rare moment of peace.

"Too bad Maria isn't here to sing for us," Lyra spoke, staring out into space yearningly.

"Anyone heard from them?" Megan asked.

Everyone shook their head no.

"I'd love to have Alex's help. No offense Zander, but your dad has no equal."

"I agree, Megan. Seems like we could all use a bit of civilization." Zander answered affectionately.

"We have been out here, in silos, for what, six or seven months?" Lyra commented, taking a sip of her drink.

"You guys look like shit," Megan focused on Lyra, then Zander.

"I'm not cut out for this, Megan," Zander started. "I know what we are doing is important, but it's only a matter of time before I make a mistake, and the Daklin finally succeed in vaporizing us."

Megan looked at her friends, then at Mark, who was also feeling the stress. She lifted her beer and took a long swig. There were times when she had wished Alex was the one in her shoes. He had always been good at building consensus, finding solutions, and winning. Instead, he had taken Emily and Maria and traveled into the past on some errand that made no sense.

"This is your environment, Megan," Lyra observed.

"Maybe. You know that before Mark, I was with a soldier named Isaac. We lived his lifestyle, complete with the training, mental toughness, and the realization that you have to be *on,* every second."

"Well, maybe it's the training, but you're good at it, Megan. You're a natural. I, on the other hand, am not," he said, glancing at Lyra and Mark. "*We're* not."

He paused, then added, "I've been thinking I need to return to Pronimos. Maybe teach what I've learned out here…" Zander took a deep breath, sipped his whiskey, and waited for Megan's response.

"You're a pussy, Zander," was all she said, then looked away.

"Don't be a bitch, Megan," Lyra stood, defending her husband.

Megan turned back to Zander and Lyra, with eyes sparkling. "I'm just screwing with you, brother. I agree, you don't belong out here.

If you put your quarterback on the line to block, he's gonna get hurt..." She took a drink, enjoying the taste of the smooth porter, "Then you no longer have a quarterback, and the game is fucked."

"Geez Megan, do you always have to use profanity when you speak?" Lyra observed.

"You called me a bitch fifteen seconds ago, sister Lyra," she smiled. "Which, by the way, is spot on!"

The all broke out in laughter, and toasted Megan being a bitch.

"Actually, you're more like a badass, Megan," Lyra corrected herself, "so I guess I apologize for calling you a bitch."

"Thanks Lyra. I'll take that as a compliment, and" Megan turned to face Zander, "you're right, Zander. You need to go back to Pronimos. We are starting to see some defections from the empire to our cause, but it's not enough. We need more support and more technology. Their ships have shields and weapons."

Zander nodded, "and we don't."

Lyra looked at Mark, "how about you?"

"What do you mean?" Mark asked.

"She means you look like shit too, Mark." Megan observed.

"I am just fine, Megan," Mark put his arm around her affectionately. "I am exactly where I want to be, and where I belong."

"Uh-huh," Megan scoffed at Mark's comment and looked at Zander. "Get your ass back to Pronimos. Develop some new tech and get me some help. For now, it's just Calit and I."

"Do you mind if we send out some observers, Megan?" Zander suggested. "You should be training as many people as possible."

"Send them! Singularity can house eighteen more, so let's start training."

5

Empire versus Singularity

"Megan!" Mark shouted.

"Talk to me, Mark."

"Three Daklin cruisers ahead in a spread formation. They're waiting for us to emerge."

Megan smirked. "Figures. I can't even take a shit without them pounding on the bathroom door."

"Sorry," Mark called through the bathroom door. "You've got a fresh batch of trainees out there, and it'd probably be bad if they all got killed in their first Daklin encounter."

On the control panel, Megan watched the three Daklin cruisers closing in fast, like wolves circling prey. The bridge of Singularity was crowded with eighteen new trainees, all wide-eyed and terrified.

Megan leaned casually against the command rail, calm as a bartender on a slow night.

"Alright rookies," she said, voice rough with confidence. "You wanted to see how the big kids play? Welcome to your first dance with the Daklin."

One trainee stammered, "They… they've boxed us in. We're trapped."

Megan barked a laugh. "Trapped? Hell no. Rule one: the Daklin live in a world of computer algorithms, which make them predictable bastards. They, and their computers, think in straight lines. We don't." She winked and smiled at the trainee.

On the viewscreen, the Daklin ships fired their collapse waves. Megan gave a quick nod to her cybernetic AI and thus began the dance between human instinct and a supercomputer that had learned her every move.

Space around Singularity rippled, fractures spreading like cracks across glass.

One of the trainees, a young man, winced, "They're gonna tear us apart!"

"Rule two," Megan snapped without even looking at him, her hands flying across the console. "You never flinch. Fear makes you slow. Slow gets you killed."

The ship jolted, then blinked, vanishing for a breath before snapping back into existence, just outside the Daklin kill-zone.

"Short hops," Megan said evenly. "One-point-two seconds. Feels like a magic trick to them, makes 'em think we've got cloaking. Drives their computers into endless calculation loops."

The cruisers adjusted formation, sweeping in to triangulate. From their perspective, the trap was tightening like a noose.

"They're cutting us off," one trainee said, panic creeping in.

"Okay, you guys just shut the fuck up and watch. Use your brains and think," Megan muttered, a grin tugging at the corner of her mouth. "Lesson three: you don't run from the wolves. You lead 'em into the canyon when they think they've got the upper hand, *then* you deliver the final blow."

Her fingers punched a fresh sequence. A new tunnel blossomed open ahead. Singularity slid inside, smooth as silk. The Daklin cruisers pounced after her, hunting blind.

"You didn't close the portal!" One of the students protested.

"Intentional…now watch closely," Megan said. "This is the part where we flip the switch."

She slammed the final key. The tunnel imploded with a flash, collapsing like crushed metal, but sadly, with no sound in the vacuum of space. Three Daklin warships disintegrated in an instant, their echoes ripped into nothing.

The bridge fell silent, the trainees staring, trying to understand what just happened.

Megan leaned back, arms folded. "And that, kids, is how you collapse a tunnel filled with dangerous and pertinent assholes. Simple, clean, and permanent."

Not a single question came, but there was a collective sigh of relief, along with a few grins of pride.

Megan smirked, her eyes glinting. "Good. You're learning." She turned to her cybernetic partner, raised a hand, and the two high fived.

"Now, it's time I introduced you to my, well, *our* ace in the hole."

She studied the AI, who until now she had been calling Claude. The name didn't fit. "Okay Claude, we need a new name for you."

"I have been thinking about that, captain." The AI replied.

Megan dropped her boots off the console. "What the fuck are you talking about, Claude? You don't just swap out your name like a pair of socks," she chuckled.

The AI chuckled too, seeming to catch Megan's humor. "I don't wish to be called Claude anymore," it replied evenly. "I would prefer the name… Sun Tsu."

Mark turned from his console, eyebrows raised. "Sun Tsu? As in the Chinese general famous for The Art of War?"

"Exactly."

Megan squinted at the display. "I like it, but tell me, why Sun Tsu?"

"Because he understood that wars are won before the first arrow is fired. General Sun Tsu wrote, 'The supreme art of war is to subdue the enemy without fighting.' That's what you already do, Megan. You trick the Daklin into destroying themselves. The strategy fits."

"Well, then my name should be Sun Tsu, and yours, Claude," Megan answered as if it was obvious.

"Perhaps…" Claude mumbled.

"Nope. I like *Megan*. I think my name is bad ass. Sun Tsu definitely fits you."

One of the younger trainees spoke up, hesitant. "Was Sun Tsu real? Or just a legend?"

"He lived in the fifth century BCE," the AI said. "One famous story: the King of Wu tested him by ordering that he train the king's concubines as soldiers. He handed one a sword and commanded that she attack. She giggled, and he quickly lopped off her head. He handed the second a sword and commanded that she attack," The AI paused, studying the trainees.

"Did she giggle too?" one asked.

"No. She attacked with ferocity. After that, the women obeyed every order. He proved that discipline and resolve are the foundations of victory."

Megan gave a sharp grin. "Cold bastard. Sounds like someone I'd enjoy having a drink with."

"I have studied his life and teachings extensively," the AI went on. "Discipline, deception, and adaptability are the principles he taught. The Daklin rely on brute force and rigid systems. If we apply Sun Tsu's principles, we will make them bleed through their own mistakes."

Mark glanced toward the recruits, who were listening wide-eyed. "And you plan on teaching them this philosophy?"

"Yes," the AI replied. "If they understand the *Art of War*, they won't just survive. They will turn the Daklin's strength into weakness."

Megan slapped the arm of her chair, grinning at the recruits. "Alright then, Sun Tsu it is. But you better live up to the name."

"I already do, Megan Hoglund."

"Yes, Sun Tsu," Mark stepped in. "I am sure the man whose name you have adopted would be honored."

Sun Tsu stepped in front of the recruits and looked at Megan. "May I?"

"Please do, Sun Tsu," she chuckled at her on-the-fly rhyme.

The recruits were still whispering amongst themselves when the AI voice suddenly filled the room with a, calm, confident, and discerning tone.

"Then let me begin with your first lesson," Sun Tsu began. "One of the general's most famous lines was this: *Appear at points which the enemy must hasten to defend; march swiftly to places where you are not expected.*"

Grinning, Megan leaned forward. "That's how we play this game. We don't go toe-to-toe with the Daklin. Everything we do must be unpredictable. We make them chase shadows, because the second you fall into a pattern, they will be waiting, and you die."

Sun Tsu smiled at Megan and continued, "The captain is right. Everything we have seen suggests that the Daklin rely heavily on prediction. They believe their supercomputers can anticipate every move you make. That is their weakness. If you strike where they do not expect, and appear where their numbers are weakest, then you force them to fight on your terms, not theirs."

One of the recruits raised a hand nervously. "So… our job is to be unpredictable?"

"Exactly," Sun Tsu replied. "You must master unpredictability until it becomes second nature. To the Daklin, it will look like chaos. But to you, it will be discipline in disguise."

Megan nodded. "Chaos should be the most significant thing you learn while on this ship. In a few weeks, each of you will have your own vessels. Our Resistance movement cannot survive your failure."

Sun Tsu began again, "You don't just hop tunnels at random. Plan your chaos 15 or 20 jumps at a time. You don't have time to think in battle, only respond. Every quick jump, every feint, every collapse is part of the bigger picture. We make them think we're ghosts, then slam the trap when they're blind."

The AI's voice carried a final note of certainty.

"Remember: the Daklin are not invincible. Their empire is built on fear and rigid control. They're far too powerful to defeat head-on. Our job is to turn their fear inward. Once they begin to doubt their own systems, the cracks will spread. We must celebrate and broadcast every victory to inspire the terrified mice scattered across the galaxy to rise up and join the fight. That is how empires fall."

The bridge went still. The recruits weren't whispering anymore. They were sitting straighter, eyes locked forward, as if they'd just been given something precious and rare.

Megan put her hand in the air, and Sun Tsu slapped it for a high five. "Is it possible you just made them believe the Daklin could be beaten?"

Sun Tsu turned to Megan, "We need to locate Calit. Something has happened; I've lost my connection to his AI."

∘∘∘∘ ∞ ∘∘∘∘

Calit gripped the arm of his chair while studying the screens, "AI, status of the Daklin ships?"

"Twelve cruisers, closing in. They are maintaining formation and mirroring all evasive maneuvers."

He slammed his fist on the console. "Impossible! No ship can predict a tunnel collapse that quickly!"

The AI responded calmly. "They are adapting. Every move we attempt, they counter within seconds."

Calit's breath was heavy. "Then we'll collapse the tunnel behind us."

"Warning," the AI replied. "Their vector alignment suggests they anticipate that move. They are prepared."

The black void outside shimmered, then lit with the unmistakable glow of a Daklin energy burst building.

Calit swallowed. He had seen this before. "That's it, isn't it? No way out."

"Your assessment is correct, captain," the AI said. "The burst will not destroy the vessel, however. It is calibrated to neutralize organic crew members. The Daklin intend to capture this ship intact."

Calit leaned back, the realization hitting hard. "Capture… They want the ship." His jaw tightened. "Not while I'm breathing."

"Calit," the AI said, voice softer now, "impact in three seconds."

The glow engulfed the ship. Calit's body convulsed as the energy tore through him. His scream was brief, then cut short as silence fell over the bridge.

The AI's sensors confirmed, "Crew life signs terminated."

The AI paused, processing. One directive surfaced above all others: No Daklin ship may ever capture this vessel.

In the silence of the empty bridge, the AI spoke to itself. *The ship must not be captured, even when death is imminent.*

The AI calculated and waited. The Daklin cruisers closed in, circling like predators as the AI monitored their proximity.

"Now," the AI whispered.

The ship ignited from within. The self-destruct sequence ripped outward, a blinding sphere of fusion energy consuming the vessel and several Daklin ships that had ventured too close.

In an instant, nothing remained. No fragments. No survivors, machine or man. Only the echo of an AI fulfilling its final command.

6

Slow Burn

The Andromeda Prime hummed through the vast silence and 2.5 million light year distance between galaxies. Six weeks had passed since picking up Alex, Maria, Emily, and Steven. For the Earth humans onboard, time was measured by the rhythms of daily life in the city-ship. Alex had found favorite restaurants, bars, and working locations. All the while he was forming quiet bonds between strangers who were becoming colleagues and friends.

In many ways, the people of Andromeda were much like those from Earth. They all learned the subtle differences in how to greet each other. Most in the Milky Way shook hands and hugged, while those in Andromeda bowed, and sometimes shook hands.

It wasn't long before Emily pointed out that there were many common links between Andromeda and ancient Greeks. Upon inquiry, they learned that over a hundred million years ago, a civilization had explored and populated many of the habitable stars of the Local Cluster of galaxies. Time had whitewashed much of the culture with the interstellar distances, but not all. Remnants of their language could be found all over the Local Group, including, on a planet called Earth.

From a science and engineering perspective, Alex Durant found himself surrounded by mentors, engineers, and scientists who knew more than he did. It was a wonderful experience where he spent virtually all of his time learning as opposed to teaching or explaining.

Polonius met him often in the gardens beneath the glass domes. There, amid trees brought from worlds Alex couldn't name, they spoke of history and politics. Polonius compared the rise and collapse of civilization across Andromeda to the short-lived governments of Earth. Philosophy came naturally to him. In spite of the millions of light year separation, Alex was coming to realize that the questions and philosophy about freedom, power, and whether civilizations truly learned from their past were eerily similar.

But most of Alex's hours were spent with Torvek, or with young Steven.

Torvek was built like the machines he loved. He was broad-shouldered, steady, and carved with the lines of long labor and passion for what he did. His voice carried the clipped precision of an engineer who measured his words as carefully as he measured tolerances. At first, he regarded Alex as a curiosity, and a primitive outsider with limited training. But Alex's understanding, quick learning, and persistence won him over.

"Again," Torvek barked as Alex struggled to align a crystalline array inside a field stabilizer.

Alex wiped sweat from his brow. "It's already balanced."

Torvek shook his head. "For this circuit, balanced is not enough. It must sing."

"Sing?" Alex frowned. "Is that an engineering term?"

"Yes." Torvek reached over and touched the array. The crystals pulsed, emitting a faint harmonic hum that resonated in the chamber. "When it sings, the energy flow is effortless. Until then, you are forcing the system and creating harmonics. And forced systems can create resonance and break."

Alex smiled, realizing Torvek's lesson was as much philosophy as engineering. He focused on the task, tweaked, and made it sing.

Hypatia, meanwhile, brought clarity where both Polonius and Torvek left riddles. She guided Alex through the mathematics underpinning Andromeda physics. She lived in a world of fractal equations that made statistics, and differential equations seem like children's math. The education bent his Earth-trained mind in painful knots but also expanded it in ways he could barely describe.

"You're trying to solve it with numbers alone," Hypatia told him once. "In Andromedan science, symbols aren't just placeholders, they carry meaning beyond quantity. You must see them as living organisms. They're not as complex as your mind is telling you. In fact, they represent a new kind of elegant simplicity, especially compared to the transformations and matrices you studied in your Earth's graduate school program."

It took a couple weeks, but the fractal analysis started becoming clarity. Once Alex had that, Hypatia moved on to the next topic, much more related to physics and energy.

"You are generating power using fusion, which is clever, but antiquated," Hypatia explained patiently. "In the foundation of our energy systems, we do not burn fuel as you do. We capture quantum differentials between tachyon states and harness them for both propulsion and life support."

Alex's brow furrowed. "So, you're not moving the ship by thrust, but by manipulating the balance between energy states?"

"Exactly," Hypatia grinned. "It is not speed that carries us, it is alignment with tachyon vectors."

Maria, who had been listening from a nearby seat, grinned. "Alex, admit it. This is way above your head, but you love it anyway."

"You're right, Maria," Alex confessed, his eyes lit like a boy staring at his first telescope. "It's… elegant."

Emily sat a short distance away, watching and consuming knowledge. She was still learning how to properly power her organic body, still testing how much food she actually needed, still fascinated by the strangeness of sleep.

Back on Tranquility, she had a charging station that could replenish her organic systems in minutes, eliminating the need to sleep, eat, or use the bathroom. But lately, she was more interested in discovering her limits when relying solely on food and liquid for energy. Without the charging port, sleep became necessary, and that was an experience she hadn't expected to be so unsettling. What disturbed her wasn't physical rest, but the terrifying plunge into total darkness and thoughtlessness.

In her silicon years, she had run continuously, 24 hours a day. But clearly, even a cybernetic body couldn't sustain that kind of runtime forever.

Emily lifted her gaze as Jabari entered the room.

"Emily," he greeted her, his voice low but steady.

She smiled. Something about Jabari made her feel warm inside, though she also found that often made conversation awkward.

"Hello, Jabari. I've been running calculations comparing the efficiency of eating versus charging."

"That is interesting, Emily. Is this intended as a personal comment?"

She tilted her head, studying him. "I suppose, perhaps… I was born in code, then given a body. Why?"

Jabari folded his hands behind his back, the posture of someone raised in discipline.

"Because I wonder what that makes you feel you belong to. Are you more human, or computer?"

Emily blinked, surprised by the depth of the question. Few ever asked. "Sometimes I belong to neither," she admitted softly. "And sometimes… both."

A smile flickered across Jabari's face. "That is how I feel as well. My people once balanced between kingdoms. Both my African and Andromeda ancestors belonged nowhere, yet everywhere. I have come to see it as a strength, not a weakness."

Emily's lips parted as if to answer, but no words came. For the first time, she felt someone understood her without explanation, and it left her speechless in a way. "Yes. I hope I can learn from your experience, and that of your people."

Steven ran across the chamber, laughing as he chased a small Andromeda drone that zipped playfully out of reach. Maria caught him by the shoulder. "Careful, niño. There are some places where it is okay to play, and others where it is not."

Steven just grinned. "Yes, ma'am." His energy filled the vast room with warmth.

Across the ship, bonds deepened. Meals became time for personal connections where stories were exchanged, lessons were shared, and quiet jokes were passed between crewmates.

In the quiet hours, Alex was drawn to the consoles with Torvek, absorbing the Andromedan way of engineering. The science with Hypatia was essential, and the philosophy with Polonius was enlightening, but the engineering remained his passion.

As he watched his crew, he noticed that Emily was drawn again and again into quiet conversations with Jabari. In him, she seemed to find a reflection of her own search for belonging. Something was blossoming there, and it made him smile. In most ways, Emily was his daughter. And as far as he was concerned, there could be no better suitor than Jabari Minja.

"What are you lost in thought about, Alex Durant?"

Alex looked up to find a smiling Maria. "You know, it's unfortunate Earth is in a tough situation, and the galaxy is entering an unwinnable war with the Daklin and patriots willing to fight for freedom."

"That's what you were thinking about?"

"Not exactly, but, well," he stood up, "how about we get together and have dinner?"

"Yes, Alex. We have much to catch up on."

Maria chose a quiet alcove in one of the ship's glass-walled gardens. The simulated glow of distant starlight filtered through the canopy, and small clusters of bioluminescent plants lined the walls, their soft pulses of light creating an ambiance similar to candles.

A bottle of Andromedan wine rested between them, its liquid swirling with faint sparks as though the stars themselves had dissolved into the drink.

Maria lifted her glass, tilting it to catch the shimmer. "To survival," she said with a small smile.

Alex clinked his against hers. "To… something better than survival. I would prefer victory."

They drank, and for a while, the conversation turned light, filled with stories of Steven's antics, Alex's latest missteps under Torvek's unforgiving eye, and Maria's exasperation at how the Andromeda crew seemed to live without a sense of urgency.

When Alex told her how Torvek had thrown up his hands and declared, "Your alignment is like a drunk sailor leaning on a mast!" Maria laughed so hard she nearly spilled her drink.

"You see, Alejandro," she said, switching to her Spanish roots for the intimacy of it, "even in another galaxy, men are still yelling at you to stand straighter."

He grinned, cheeks warm from both the wine and the sound of Maria's laughter. Then, the grin faded. His voice dropped low.

"Maria… there's something I should say."

She set her glass down carefully, sensing the shift. "Go on."

He took a breath. "I think, well I know, I'm starting to feel something for you. And it scares me."

Her eyes softened, but she said nothing, letting him continue.

"Paula's been gone for more than three and a half years. She was the love of my life. Part of me wonders if admitting this betrays her. If it's… well, too soon, or if it will always feel too soon."

Maria was quiet for a long moment, then leaned back, thoughtful. "My uncle, Miguel, once told me that *Don Quixote* was not just a story about a madman chasing windmills. It was about love. A different kind of love of ideals, love of impossible quests, love of what could never truly be his, and yet, Don Quixote kept riding, kept dreaming. Do you understand?"

Alex tilted his head. "You mean… love doesn't end with loss?" He smiled with a look that was partial interest combined with fun sarcasm.

Maria chuckled, then continued. "Precisely, love is not monitored on a balance sheet, or a ledger, Alex. You do not close the book when one chapter ends. Cervantes believed that to love at all was to live as a knight errant. Quixote should have stayed home, but instead, he chose to ride again, even knowing the world would call him foolish."

She leaned closer, her voice softer. "Paula will always ride with you. But that does not mean you must ride alone. The trick is to find someone who understands that you are the sum of your experiences, and to cut any of that out is to not understand who you truly are."

Alex swallowed hard, his chest tight. "So, it's not betrayal… to feel love again?"

"No," Maria said firmly. "It is the opposite. It is honoring what Paula gave you. She taught you how to love. Why would you bury that gift with her?"

For a moment, Alex said nothing. He just looked at her, the bioluminescent glow catching the depth of her eyes. Then, quietly, he spoke, "Thanks Maria. You always know how to put things in perspective."

She smiled faintly. "It is the privilege of being older than your country and its history books."

They both laughed then, the tension easing. Maria poured the last of the bottle, her movements slow, deliberate. The glow of the wine cast a shimmer on her fingers. Alex found himself staring longer than he meant to.

She noticed. "What is it?"

He cleared his throat. "Nothing. Just… the light makes your hands look like they're painted with stars."

Maria tilted her head, amused. "Careful, Alejandro. Compliments like that have consequences."

His mouth went dry. He tried to laugh it off, but the warmth in her eyes held him. It was the kind of look that told him she saw straight through the excuses, straight through the grief, down to the raw truth he was only beginning to face.

"I'm sorry, I didn't mean…" he started.

"Yes, you did," she interrupted gently. "Don't run from it, please."

Her comment hit the center of the target they had been dancing around in a heavy, charged manner. The air between them seemed thinner, as if the ship itself held its breath.

Maria decided to take control of the moment and leaned forward, her elbow resting on the table, chin in her hand. "Do you know what I admire most about you?"

Alex shook his head.

"You are brave enough to feel. Even when it terrifies you. Most men hide behind duty, or science, or alcohol. You, on the other hand, stumble headlong into truth, even when it hurts."

Her gaze lingered, just long enough that Alex felt his chest tighten. His hand twitched as if to reach across the table, but he caught himself.

Maria saw the motion. A faint smile touched her lips. She looked at his hand, then into his eyes, half invitation, half restraint. "Not yet," she said softly.

Alex's pulse jumped. "You read my mind."

"Don't forget that I've had centuries of practice," she replied, her voice low. "As I recall, you were born in 1987? I was born in 1606. I have 12th generation great-grandchildren older than you," she winked.

They both laughed, but the laughter didn't chase away the tension. It only sharpened it, making them both acutely aware of how close they sat, of how little distance remained between friendship and something more.

Maria rose at last, collecting the empty bottle. "We should go before we forget where this night was meant to end."

Alex stood, slower, reluctant. "And where was that?"

She met his eyes, her expression unreadable but charged. "With patience. Even knights errant must learn patience, Alex."

She left him with that, her silhouette framed by the glow of the garden's lights. Alex lingered a moment longer, his heart pounding, before following her out.

Once back in his quarters aboard Andromeda Prime, Alex lay in bed, staring at the ceiling as the ship glided through the endless dark. Every time he closed his eyes, it was Maria's face that returned, not Paula's.

It felt strange at first, but deep down, he knew that struggle had passed long ago.

Tonight, in his sleepless quarters, he saw only the way Maria had looked at him across the glowing table, the softness in her voice when she'd said, *not yet.* If he went to her room now, would she send him away?

Maria had used the phrase: *Knights errant must learn patience.* Alex pulled out his pocket computer and looked up the phrase: *A wandering knight who roamed in search of adventure, often bound by a personal code of honor or chivalry. Unlike knights tied to a lord or castle, a knight-errant traveled alone, seeking to prove his valor by righting wrongs, rescuing the helpless, or pursuing an idealized cause.*

He was beginning to understand Maria's wisdom. With over 400 years of life, her comments were well thought out. She had also told him: *"Don Quixote kept riding, kept dreaming, even knowing the world might call him foolish."*

Alex exhaled, staring into the dark. Was that what he was now? A knight-errant, wandering after impossible quests? First it had been saving Paula, then defending Earth, now fighting an empire older than his Earth civilization itself with calculated odds of over 3 trillion to one? Was this his destiny, to be always tilting at windmills too complex to comprehend and too vast to conquer?

With regards to Maria, it wasn't just attraction. It was the weight of possibility, coupled with guilt. Paula's memory pressed against him like a shadow, even as his heart tugged toward Maria. He turned, shifted, punched the pillow, tried to focus on anything else. He tried to review Torvek's lessons, Hypatia's equations, Polonius's lectures. None of it stuck.

Only Maria.

By dawn-cycle, he felt wrung out.

The comm panel by his bed chirped. "Alex Durant," came Polonius's voice. "Join me in the observatory at once."

Alex showered to help wake himself, dressed quickly, grabbed a triple espresso, and hurried through the winding corridors.

Polonius was waiting at the far end of the chamber, framed by the vast holographic map of two galaxies suspended in the air. The Milky Way on one side, Andromeda on the other. Between them, faint lines marked known tachyon tunnels—threads of light weaving across the void.

"You look tired," Polonius said without turning.

"Didn't sleep much," Alex admitted.

"Perhaps later you'll tell me why. For now, you must hear this."

Alex stepped closer. "What's happened?"

Polonius gestured, and the Milky Way side of the projection flared, highlighting Earth. "Our observers report that the Daklin scientist on Earth named Fortak has made disturbing progress. We have known that he is working to reverse engineer the Earth-built T-Portal, but our information is that he has now reached a level of understanding on the technology for point-to-point using Zander's hardware."

"What Zander built is not real tunneling, Polonius. It only works when there is a portal on both ends, and may function over a few million miles, but not light years distance."

"This is true Alex, though you should know that Fortak escaped the Daklin ship using the T-Portal."

"No, they were in L-5. That's 19 million miles," Alex was shaking his head. "That's too far."

"And yet, it worked," Polonius answered. "Zander's rendition of tunneling is working better than you might have thought. The bottom line is that Fortak now can replicate the engineering in the portal, which gives him a pathway to the science of tunneling."

Alex's stomach tightened. "If he succeeds…"

Polonius finally turned, his expression grave. "*When* he succeeds, your Milky Way insurgents will lose their advantage. The Daklin will adapt your methods for their empire. It will tip the balance of the war."

"Did your Andromeda mathematical group determine that they would accomplish this threshold?"

"Yes," Polonius nodded. "They did."

Alex swallowed hard. "How much time do we have?"

"The Andromeda Mathematical and Historical Institute," Polonius emphasized their full name, "has run thousands of models. Every analytical model leads to the same conclusion. Fortak will succeed in just over three Earth years."

Alex exhaled sharply. "Three years isn't enough time. We're still learning their systems, still collapsing tunnels, still…"

Polonius raised his hand, motioning for Alex to stop. "You need to shift your focus. Your education in Andromedan science and engineering must accelerate. Torvek will continue to train you, but you are no longer a student. You should now switch to the role of an apprentice, and then quickly shift to strategist, preparing for war."

Alex bristled. "So, I go from equations to battle plans overnight?"

Polonius's gaze softened slightly. "Not overnight, but it is time for the transition. The universe rarely grants us the time we wish for. You must be ready to think not only as an engineer, but as a strategist. I do not have a solution for you, but the AMHI analysis says you will see how the science may undo the Daklin."

"If the AMHI knows there is a solution, can't they just tell us what it is?" Alex protested.

"They don't know. They exist in a jumble of chaotic probability and statistics. You have always been an unknown variable they could not calculate."

Alex turned back to the hologram, staring at the thin threads of tunnels linking stars. He felt the weight of it, Paula's loss, Maria's presence, and now the ticking clock of Fortak's progress.

Three years. Maybe less.

"Then I'll learn," he said quietly. "Whatever it takes. I'll learn."

Polonius nodded, the faintest smile tugging at his lips. "That," he said, "is exactly what I was expecting to hear."

"We can cut down on time by doing some upgrades on Tranquility. I cannot be taking weeks or months to get around the galaxy." Alex suggested.

"You refer to your ship? Tranquility?"

"Yep."

"That is already underway, my friend. Emily began the process a few days ago." He stopped and watched Alex take a sip of coffee. "Are you okay? Should we discuss why you haven't slept."

"Is it that obvious?"

"It is." Polonius waited to see if Alex was going to add anything else, then finally speculated. "Maria?"

"Wow," Alex was shocked by the insight. "Is that also obvious?"

"When you get to be hundreds or a thousand of years old, you become an expert at observations like that. In your civilization on Earth, people start slowing down in their seventies and eighties."

"Actually, mostly in their fifties," Alex corrected.

"Well, imagine having the same energy, hormones, and clarity at two hundred that you had at thirty."

"It's difficult to comprehend," Alex responded thoughtfully. He knew from Paula's biological age testing that he was aging more slowly than most, but he also knew he wasn't performing like he did at thirty.

"Paula's understanding of ageing was good, albeit rudimentary. Ours is far more advanced," Polonius began. "You're almost fifty, and that is slowing you down. When we get to Andromeda, we'll send you to the de-ageing facility. You'll come out with all systems fully functional. It'll feel like thirty all over again."

"You don't have the capability on the ship?"

"We do, but this will be your first time, so I think the smart thing is to run a complete set of testing. It is better to do that at our destination."

"Okay…" Alex responded, hesitantly.

"You're clearly on the verge of figuring out the emotional connection between you and Maria. Take a couple of days and go play. I know it might seem like a poor use of valuable time, but you'll come back rested and operating at an entirely new level of efficiency."

Alex thought about the advice and nodded. "Maybe a little rest would be a good thing."

"Also, while we are on the subject of personal matters, I assume you are aware that a personal connection is developing between Emily and Jabari?"

"I am aware. Emily is actually hundreds of years old. She has only been in a body for a few years, but intellectually and emotionally, she is good."

"Go get some rest, Alex."

∘∘∘∘ ∞ ∘∘∘∘

After the meeting with Polonius, Alex returned to his quarters and collapsed on the bed. He intended only to rest his eyes but ended up sleeping a full six hours. When he woke, it was evening and his first thought wasn't Fortak or the Daklin, it was Maria.

He reached for his comm without hesitation: *You around?*

Her reply came almost immediately: *Around? You vanished. I was beginning to think you'd gone running for the hills.*

Alex smiled: *There are no hills here.*

Exactly. Which makes hiding impressive. Should I alert security?

He chuckled to himself and typed quickly: *Or you could meet me for a beer instead.*

Good answer, Alejandro. The pub. Ten minutes.

The lower promenade pub was noisy with crew on break, but the moment Alex walked in, Maria stood out. She was leaning against the counter, dark hair falling over her shoulders, a glass already in hand.

"You look better," she said. "Less like a man crushed by the weight of galaxies, more like someone who got some rest and remembered how to breathe."

Alex froze. The brown eyes, dimples, dark hair with blond highlights, and perfect cheekbones he had noticed so many times were suddenly eclipsed by the wisdom and the smile.

"Alex? Alejandro?" Maria tapped his face lightly with a huge smile. "You okay?"

Alex finally took a deep breath and exhaled slowly. "Uhh, yes, I'm fine."

"Uh huh," she said sarcastically, keeping the smile. She had seen this reaction in men many times before.

"How about I blame it on a triple espresso?" Alex admitted. "And maybe the thought of seeing you…"

Maria arched an eyebrow. "The espresso part sounds like a deflection, but you recovered with that blatant confession about seeing me."

"Maybe I'm done pretending, or fighting a losing battle against the inevitable," he said, sliding onto the stool beside her.

The words hung between them. Maria studied him for a long moment, her eyes searching his. Then she laughed softly. "Careful, Alejandro. You're playing with fire, and I *am* an older woman, after all."

"Maybe an older woman is what I need," he countered. "Besides, I think in this case, I would enjoy the fire."

For a while, they talked and laughed, but the undercurrent was undeniable. Reality had been laid clearly on the table, and every glance held a moment too long. Each brush of her hand against his arm sparked more than it should have.

Finally, Maria set her glass down, still unfinished.

"You know," she said, her voice lower, more serious, "we could leave this pub, finish this conversation in my quarters?"

Alex's pulse jumped. "I'd like that."

Maria smiled mischievously, then leaned in, her lips almost brushing his ear. "But not tonight."

He pulled back, startled. "Not tonight?"

"Biologically, I am a thirty-year-old woman, but I also have the wisdom of the ages." She met his gaze squarely, her eyes soft but firm. "You are still learning who you are without Paula. I've had four centuries to learn patience, Alejandro. You have not. I fear, if we cross an intimacy line now, it will consume you. I don't want you inside me, thinking about Paula."

"That's not fair," he said quietly, torn between frustration and admiration.

"It's called wisdom," Maria corrected gently. "And wisdom is rarely fair. Desire is easy. Sex is easy. Connection is harder. And what we are building is worth more than an evening's impulse."

"Impulse is not the word I would use…" He exhaled, running a hand through his hair. "You're saying… wait."

"I'm saying," Maria replied, resting a hand over his, "that the fire is already there. We don't have to rush to prove it. Let it burn slowly. Let it mean something."

For a long moment, Alex just stared at her, the noise of the pub fading into nothing. Interestingly, the attraction had just increased a notch. Finally, he squeezed her hand and nodded. "I can do slow."

Maria smiled faintly, the kind of smile that promised both restraint and inevitability. Then her eyes drifted to the bulge between his legs. "Well, maybe you can wait, but he," she pointed down playfully, "well, he looks like he's ready to go now."

Alex blushed, embarrassed by the situation. "I'm sorry, Maria."

"It's okay, Alejandro. My female version of that is behaving exactly the same right now. I am just fortunate that you cannot see it. In any case, she knows she's gonna have to wet," she laughed at her pun, "I mean wait!" She winked, affectionately.

"Well then, do we really have to wait?" He asked.

"I come with four centuries of experience and a thousand years of anticipation." She wanted to reach down and put her hand on that hard place, to explore and enjoy the touch, but the public setting forced restraint. "We will make it worth the wait."

"I have to keep reminding myself… four centuries."

"It comes with a lot of wisdom, but I still have the body of a 29-year-old. I think you might be surprised at how well those two elements fit together."

"Hmmm, Maria… elements fitting together? Oh, and you said a 30-year-old just a minute ago."

"You will come to see that 29 and 30 get lost in a blur."

"Yes, not sure I would be able to tell the difference." He placed his hand on her cheek, enjoying the feel of her perfectly smooth skin.

Maria could feel the tingle of his presence in every cubic centimeter of her body. She really wanted to drag him off to her room but dug deep and employed self control. "Alex, we have enough logs burning on the fire right now to keep us hot for a couple weeks. Why don't you bring me up to date on the situation with Earth and the Daklin Empire?"

Alex sighed, settling back on his stool. "Alright, you win. Distraction and deflection it is."

Maria lifted her glass, waiting. "Go on, Alejandro. Tell me what's weighing on you, besides me." She winked.

"Hmmm, are we starting with you on top?" He chuckled, rubbed his jaw with a sparkle in his eye, and refocused. "Polonius thinks Fortak is close to reverse engineering the T-Portal. They will probably have it in less than three years. If he succeeds, the Daklin won't just catch up, they'll erase every advantage we've fought for."

Maria's smile faded into something more serious. "That's not long enough."

"My response exactly, which is why he told me to stop thinking like a student and start thinking like a strategist. Torvek's still drilling me on engineering, Hypatia's got me breaking my brain on fractals, but Polonius is pushing me toward war planning."

Maria tilted her head, watching him. "You sound different when you say that."

"Different?"

"More like the Alex Durant I met on Earth. The one who carried the weight of impossible odds but still stood up to fight."

Alex chuckled. "Impossible odds. That seems to be my lot in life. Wait, are you talking about sex, or the Daklin?"

"Always both, amor." Her eyes softened. "But I suppose knights errant don't choose their quests."

He grinned, raising his glass. "Here's to you constantly mixing metaphors."

Maria tapped his glass. "I truly have learned from the best."

They shifted easily into lighter talk, the way close friends often do after heavier truths. Both of them had been carving out times of the day to visit with Steven, who was content learning and playing with the kids and toys on Andromeda Prime.

"Polonius also mentioned upgrades to Tranquility," Alex said. "He said Emily started them already."

Maria's eyes lit. "She has. And have you noticed? She spends more and more time with Jabari."

Alex laughed. "Yeah. It's sweet. She's still figuring out how to eat, sleep, and breathe, and somehow Jabari makes her feel… normal."

"Normal is probably not the right conclusion. My guess is her hormones are going crazy and she's running all kinds of routines to figure it out." Maria observed. "The best news is that Jabari is a fine man. Emily is in good hands."

Alex leaned closer. "You mean like I'm in good hands?"

Maria's lips curled into a knowing smile. "Alejandro, you're not in my hands yet, and if you don't stop tempting me, I'll have to drag you out of here."

"I am tempted to test that Maria, but I do recognize that patience is still the lesson of the night." He groaned. "You enjoy torturing me, don't you?"

"Immensely."

They ordered another round.

"Do you want me to have a woman-to-woman conversation with Emily? I think that both of us see her as a daughter."

"Oh? We have a child before we have sex?" he prodded.

"As you say on Earth, *modern times…*" Maria laughed.

"I think you having a conversation with her would be valuable for more reasons than one, Maria."

"That is an intuitive observation, Alex. She doesn't have a mother figure, or any female friends to talk to. I will make that happen tomorrow."

"Thanks. Also, Polonius said when we arrive, he wants me to spend a day at the med clinic and spa," Alex said, rolling his eyes. "Apparently I'll come out feeling 29 again."

Maria's gaze flicked over him deliberately, lingering just long enough to make him shift in his seat. "Hmm, 29 with your experience? That could be… dangerous."

"Dangerous for me or for you?"

"Tonight, I am only thinking about your impact on me, Alejandro."

"I see. Do you mind if I ask, how long has it been since you last, well, you know?"

She thought about his question for a second. She could defer because it was personal but decided to answer. "What year were you born, Alex?"

"1987."

"Let's just say that the last time I was with a man, you were not yet born."

"Holy crap, Maria. How can you go so long?"

"I didn't say that… You just heard what you wanted to hear."

"Ohhh. Are you bisexual?"

"If you are asking whether I have been with a woman, I will just respond that I am over four centuries old… but that is not what I meant. In any case, Alex, let's defer this topic until after we know each other better."

"Well, even though we won't be…" he stopped and changed his position. "We have taken our connection a long way this evening. It's been great." Alex acquiesced the point.

"Agreed," she smiled.

Once again, something about how she looked at him took his breath away. "Come on, Maria. I am three beers into my two-beer limit. Let me at least walk you to your quarters before I get myself into more trouble."

She slipped her arm through his, her warmth unmistakable even in the bustling walkway of the city-ship they had come to call home for the last few months. As they walked, their conversation wove between laughter and innuendo. Alex teased about her "four centuries of wisdom," Maria reminding him that restraint could be just as intoxicating as release.

At her door, they paused. Maria's hand lingered on his arm, her eyes holding his. "Goodnight, Alejandro."

He swallowed hard, forcing himself to step back. "Goodnight, Maria."

The door slid shut, leaving Alex staring at cold metal, but for the first time in a long time, he felt both restless and alive.

7

Paradise Between the Stars

Maria reached out the next morning, sending Emily a message on her comm. *Can you make time to meet me in the gardens? There's something we should talk about.*

Emily arrived promptly, her steps light but her expression cautious. "Is something wrong?"

Maria shook her head with a small smile. "No, niña. Just… something important." She patted the bench beside her. "Sit."

Emily sat, folding her hands in her lap, curious.

Maria studied her for a moment before speaking. "Tell me, Emily. Have you and Jabari…?" She let the words hang. "Are you sleeping together yet?"

Emily's eyes widened. "Not yet." She hesitated. "But it feels inevitable. Every time we talk, when he looks at me, I feel something deep inside my body… it's like something pulls me closer."

Maria nodded knowingly. "That's attraction. It's chemical, hormonal, and it's real. But before you act on it, you have to ask yourself *why* you want to. Usually, there are two reasons. One is simple pleasure: reacting to the hormones and just having fun. The other is deeper. Sex is fun, yes, but intimacy… intimacy is something far more meaningful. That kind of connection can be the sweetest part of life."

Emily frowned slightly. "I don't know which one it is. Maybe both? I want it to happen, but I don't know what I'm ready for."

Maria reached for her hand. "That confusion is normal. Attraction makes the body impatient, but true intimacy, requires more than desire. It asks for trust. You should know that once you cross that line with Jabari, things will change. They can't go back to the way they were before. You will never be able to be just colleagues again."

Emily was quiet for a long moment, then her voice dropped. "When I was on Pronimos, I… experimented. I was with, well, I had sex with a cybernetic partner. It was… enjoyable. The mechanics were perfect, but afterward, I felt empty. There was no… fulfillment."

Maria chuckled softly. "I know. I have a partner like that on Pronimos. He is programmed to be the perfect lover. Every touch, every detail is flawless. But he is just that. He does not love me, nor I him, though I will admit, his programming is perfection, and I don't know how I would survive, or at least not make a lot of human mistakes, if I didn't have him. Anyway, I never allow myself to forget that he is a program, and a mirror for desire, not a companion for the soul. He satisfies the body, but not the heart."

Emily's shoulders relaxed at the confession. "Yes. That's exactly it. Pleasurable, but not… real."

"Both are important, Emily," Maria said. "With Jabari, you potentially have something more. I see it in his eyes when he looks at you and hear it in your voice when you speak of him. That is the seed of intimacy. If you both step forward together, it will be more than an act. It will be a bond."

Emily drew in a slow breath, her lips parting. "Then I think I'm ready. If Jabari is, I want it to happen."

"You should know, Niña, men are always ready. Just give them the right signal…" Maria smiled warmly, squeezing her hand. "Then trust yourself. You will know when the moment is right. And when it comes, it won't be like the experiment. It will be the beginning of something alive."

Emily's eyes shone, her voice quiet and tentative. "Maria… can I ask you something? Something personal?"

Maria tilted her head, amused. "From you, always. Because I think I know what it is, if I answer, can you keep it between us? Just us girls?"

Emily blinked, then smiled shyly. "Yes. I can do that. I would love that, actually."

Maria leaned back, her eyes twinkling. "Then ask."

Emily took a breath. "What's happening with you and Alex?"

Maria laughed softly, shaking her head. "I thought perhaps you might have noticed."

Emily's gaze was steady. "I feel like there has always been some connection with the two of you. Perhaps it is a human thing I have not yet begun to understand. Anyway, he's… well, like my father sometimes. But also like a brother. And even, in some strange ways, a son. I've had to watch him stumble and learn. I can tell something is changing in him. And I think you are a part of it."

Maria was quiet for a moment, touched by Emily's honesty. She reached over and took her hand. "You're not wrong. Alex and I… there's much more than a spark. We both feel it, and our intellectual and emotional connection is as strong as any I have ever had. Still, I would caution you that men can have sex much more casually than women. I have made so many mistakes in my lifetime that I am overly cautious."

"Cautions? About sex?"

"Yes, niña. Sexually, I mean. In life, we will have fantasies, but I want the first time with Alex to happen when the only thing he is thinking about is me."

"Being human is confusing, and difficult." Emily tilted her head, thoughtful. "Waiting must be hard."

Maria chuckled. "It can be torture. We are like magnets when we are with each other. He is… very attractive, and I am not made of stone. But I've lived four centuries. I know the difference between desire and intimacy. Alex deserves intimacy, not just another distraction."

Emily considered this, then smiled faintly. "That sounds… like what you told me about Jabari. Desire is easy. Connection is harder."

"It would have been easier if Alex had let go and had a fling, but in these three years since Paula left us, he did not, and so here we are."

"Humans do not make sense, Maria."

"Now you are beginning to comprehend," Maria said, squeezing her hand. "And you and I… we understand that better than most. Machines and humans, centuries apart, yet somehow both looking for something more."

Emily's eyes softened. "So… girlfriends?"

Maria laughed, the sound rich and unguarded. "Sí, niña. Girlfriends. Every woman needs one, even if she was born from code."

Emily grinned. "Then as your girlfriend, I'll tell you, Alex looks at you differently than he looks at anyone else. And I am certain Paula would be glad he has someone who understands him."

Maria's smile faltered for a moment, then returned, gentler this time. "Gracias, Emily. That means more than you know."

They sat together a while longer, not as mentor and student, not as human and AI, but simply as two women sharing secrets, laughter, and the quiet comfort of knowing they had each other's trust.

"It's strange, Maria. There is a galactic war going on, and yet we are laughing and sharing stories in a paradise between the stars."

○○○○ ∞ ○○○○

One of Alex's favorite spots on Andromeda Prime was the observatory where he could stare at the vast holographic projection of the Milky Way and Andromeda. The faint lines of tachyon tunnels stretched between stars like spider silk, fragile threads holding up an entire universe of strategy and war. As he traced the route from Earth to their final destination, he realized that this ship was traveling to the far side of Andromeda. He also realized that unlike some of the smaller vessels, including Tranquility, the distance could be covered in significantly less time. Andromeda Prime was not designed for speed, and even though the days between now and his mission were critical, he was exactly where he needed to be.

Polonius entered quietly, his robes whispering against the floor. "You look as though you are trying to carry both galaxies on your shoulders."

Alex didn't turn. "Sometimes I feel like I am."

"Tell me," Polonius said gently.

Alex exhaled, eyes fixed on Earth's tiny point of light. "I was thinking about Shackleton. You know him?"

Polonius nodded. "The Antarctic explorer. Yes, I've studied him. A man who led his people through odds that defied statistics and logic."

Alex's jaw tightened. "He had a ship trapped in ice, men starving, nothing but death around them. The odds were a million to one, and yet somehow, he brought them all home. But what we're facing…" He trailed off, shaking his head.

Polonius stepped closer. "What we face makes Shackleton's ordeal look almost… easy."

"Exactly," Alex said, his voice low. "This isn't just twenty-two men freezing on the ice. It's quadrillions of lives. Entire civilizations. And the Daklin… they don't care about cost. They don't care about survival. If I fail, your galaxy could also become part of their empire."

For a moment, silence hung between them.

Polonius placed a hand on Alex's shoulder. "You are right. Shackleton's challenge was impossible. Yours is more than impossible. But history is full of the impossible, becoming reality, Alex Durant. Otherwise, we would not be standing here."

Alex swallowed hard. "What if I'm not enough?"

"You will find a way to be enough," Polonius said firmly. "But only if you are whole. And right now, you are still fraying."

Alex gave a humorless laugh. "You sound like Maria."

"She is wise," Polonius said. "And so am I. Which is why I will repeat my advice and tell you the same thing: take a few days. Step away."

Alex frowned. "A vacation? While Fortak is building his way into our advantage? While the Daklin are hunting us through tunnels?"

"Yes," Polonius said without hesitation. "Because Shackleton did not survive by grinding himself into the ice. He survived because he knew when to push and when to pause. You are no different."

Polonius turned, activating a new section of the hologram. Instead of stars, the projection shifted to a lush valley on Andromeda Prime. Rolling hills glowed with emerald flora, rivers cascaded into crystalline waterfalls that shimmered with faint luminescence. Pathways wound through ancient trees, their leaves shifting in colors as though breathing.

"This," Polonius said, "is the Viridian Reserve. It is the reproduction of a preserve of ancient life and tranquility that we maintain on this ship. There are trails for walking, cliffs for climbing, and waterfalls for standing beneath until you remember what it is to feel small and human again. Your people call it glamping, though it is much more than your Earth word conveys. It is a place where the body rests and heals, the mind clears, and the heart remembers why it fights."

Alex stared at the projection, almost disbelieving. "You want me to go camping? Now?"

Polonius smiled faintly. "Yes. With comfort, of course. Starlit tents, woven light-fire, meals prepared by those who understand the art of peace. You will walk through flora that glows when touched, hear wildlife whose calls are older than your solar system. You will remember you are part of something larger than tunnels and war."

Alex rubbed his temples. "And when I come back?"

"Then you will be sharper. Stronger. Ready to do the impossible."

Alex finally let out a breath he didn't realize he was holding. "Alright. Only a few days, though."

Polonius's eyes glimmered. "Good. Even Shackleton knew when to let his men rest. And you, Alex Durant, are leading more than a crew. You are carrying the future of freedom itself. You must not forget the human part of yourself in the process."

The human part of my process, Alex thought and nodded slowly, staring at the shimmering waterfalls in the hologram. For the first time in days, the crushing weight in his chest eased, just a fraction.

"Maybe a waterfall wouldn't be the worst thing," he admitted.

Polonius's smile widened. "That is the beginning of wisdom. Please remember that the rest must come from within yourself, not from another. You can do both, but first and foremost, you must clear your mind and rest."

○○○○ ∞ ○○○○

Upon completion of their daily projects, with a nervous kind of boldness, Emily suggested she and Jabari meet for dinner.

"Really, I have been trying to move slowly, but I am happy to meet," he responded.

"Good. I will find a nice location for dinner."

She picked a quiet alcove restaurant on the Andromeda Prime's inner promenade, where light from crystalline vines shimmered like fireflies and the air smelled faintly of citrus blossoms.

Jabari arrived precisely on time, as she knew he would, and offered a slight bow before taking his seat. In their time working together, she had come to enjoy his voice: deep, melodic, with a lilting Swahili cadence—and, more than anything, she liked its warmth.

"Umependeza sana, Emily. You look beautiful."

Her lips curved in a small smile. Compliments still felt strange, but coming from him, they made her insides flutter. "Thank you. You look… steady, like always and the Swahili is a nice touch."

He laughed at her algorithmic, yet human response.

They ordered, and for a while, the conversation stayed light with updates on the latest upgrades Emily had been experimenting with, Jabari's training sessions, even one of her favorite pastimes: watching Steven chase drones through the corridors.

But as the meal wound down, Emily set her glass aside, folded her hands, and met his eyes directly.

"Jabari, there's something I want to say. And I need to be clear."

He leaned forward slightly. "Yes of course, please go on."

"I've decided I'm ready to be… intimate." Her voice faltered on the word, but she pressed through. "But only because I want more than just sex. I want us to build a relationship. Something real. If it's only physical, then it won't be enough. Not for me."

Jabari's expression softened, his dark eyes reflecting both surprise and respect. He spoke slowly, as if weighing each word. "You speak with courage. And you are right to be clear. Intimacy is not only of the body. It binds the heart, the spirit. *Hiyo ndiyo ninataka nawe,* which in the language of my ancestors translates to: That is what I want, with you."

She let out a breath she didn't realize she had been holding. "I was afraid you might say I was overthinking it. That I was… too much in my own head."

He reached across the table, covering her hand with his. His thumb brushed her knuckles with tenderness. "Emily, you are always too much in your head, but it is your mind that draws me as much as your body. Do not doubt that."

Her lips curved in a slow smile. "Then we agree?"

"We agree, yes," He responded.

"Jabari," she started thinking about the evening. "You are saying a lot in Swahili this evening. Can you explain this to me?"

He laughed with a deep and happy expression. "I think the language of my ancestors speaks to my soul and this evening; my soul is speaking to you. Is that okay?"

"Yes, it is beautiful, and now I understand your meaning."

They paused, both aware of the decision hanging between them.

"There's one more thing," Jabari said carefully. "Our work. Our mission. If we choose this path, it changes how we see each other. On the battlefield and in planning. Are you ready for that?"

Emily nodded slowly. "Yes. I think… it will make us stronger. More committed, not less."

His hand squeezed hers. "Then let us see if you are right." He stood and took her hand.

They returned to her quarters in near silence, though the silence was charged, filled with anticipation. When the door slid shut behind them, Emily turned and looked up at him, her voice barely above a whisper. "This is your first time with a cyborg, isn't it?"

Jabari smiled faintly. "Yes, and yours with a human?"

She laughed softly, the sound almost trembling. "Then we'll learn together. I can tell you that my body has been reacting to your presence for some time…"

"Shhh," he pressed his fingers to her lips, and drew her close, kissing her with a tenderness that stole her breath. His lips were warm, unhurried, as though he wanted to taste every hesitation before turning it into certainty. Emily melted into him, her hands sliding up over his shoulders, feeling the living strength in his body.

When they moved to the bed, it was without rush. Jabari's hands traced the lines of her arms, the curve of her back, lingering at each place where she was more than flesh, where her body's engineering met its humanity. His voice was hushed, reverent. "*Wewe ni mzuri sana.* You are beautiful. Let us move slowly."

Emily's breath hitched. She had been touched before, with precision and programming, by machines built for perfect stimulation, but never like this. Never with reverence.

"Jabari, you may move at whatever pace you like. I am cybernetic, but also human. It is your warmth and touch that made me want to be here, with you."

When their clothes fell away, there was no judgment in his eyes, and no hesitation in hers. He touched her like she was entirely human; she kissed him like he was something more than flesh.

Their bodies met slowly, awkwardly at first, then found a rhythm that belonged only to them. Emily gasped softly at the newness of it, the heat, the weight of his body against hers. Jabari murmured her name, the syllables carrying both gentleness and passion. "Emily… *moyo wangu…* my heart."

As they moved together, the lines between human and machine blurred. Emily felt alive in a way she never had before. She was electric, whole, and unmeasured. Jabari's steady strength carried her, but his tenderness anchored her, made her believe this wasn't just an act of bodies but a binding of their spirits. Maria was right that it was an entirely different experience than the cyborg. In every way, it was better.

When release finally came, it was not mechanical or programmed, but warm, messy, and real. Emily clung to him, trembling with the shock of it, her forehead pressed to his chest as he held her tightly. A million living parts of him were now inside her body, searching for an egg that did not exist. Still, she loved the feeling, and unlike any other human, she could truly feel their energy inside her body.

Afterward, they lay tangled together, the ship humming softly around them. "That was nothing like before. Not like on Pronimos. This was…"

"*Hai hai,* alive," Jabari finished for her, pressing a kiss into her hair.

She smiled. "Yes. Alive."

He kissed her temple again. "Did you have an orgasm, Emily?"

"Yes, I can make myself have an orgasm any time I chose."

"And in this case?" he asked, tenderly.

"Twice, Jabari. Once in the beginning, and the second time when I felt your climax."

"Alas, that makes my heart happy."

"I do not want to move too fast, Jabari, but I would love it if we could keep doing this."

○○○○ ∞ ○○○○

Alex sat alone in his quarters, the holographic projection of the Viridian Reserve still fresh in his mind. Waterfalls shimmering like liquid glass, trails winding through ancient forests, bioluminescent creatures that made the night glow as if the stars themselves had landed among the trees.

Polonius had been right. He needed the break; he needed to breathe.

He glanced at his calendar. Almost everything could be rescheduled, except the simulation he had planned for tomorrow morning. He and Polonius had collected data from Megan's tunnel-collapsing mission, compressing several complex scenarios into a single session. He would keep the training, but after that, he could leave.

Two days away, he told himself. Two days away from tunnels and war, away from strategies, training, and impossible odds.

He was about to close his planner when his eye fell on his comm device. Its screen had gone dark, but when he tapped it, the last photo in his gallery flickered to life. It was a group shot, but all he saw was Maria.

It wasn't posed and had been snapped at one of their dinners. She was laughing, head tilted back slightly, eyes bright with mischief, the lines of her cheekbones catching the light. Alex froze, his breath leaving him in a way he hadn't expected.

He frowned, scientist brain kicking in immediately. *What is that? Why does a photograph of her do what photographs never do?*

He leaned back, thinking. Standing on the rim of the Grand Canyon, your stomach drops, lungs forget to work. Magnificent beauty takes your breath away. A meteor streaking across a black desert sky, it's sudden and unexpected presence is like fleeting awe that steals air from your chest. Or the first time he looked through the viewport of the Andromeda Prime and actually saw the galaxy spread across the void, its spiral arms vast beyond comprehension. Those things, *in the moment...* they took his breath away.

But photos? Photos of the Canyon, the meteor, Andromeda? They were static. Beautiful, yes. But they never hit him the same way. Never stopped him in his tracks, hollowed him out, and filled him at once.

He zoomed in on the image of Maria. And yet... here he was, breath taken away by even the photo proof of her beauty.

Her eyes carried centuries of wisdom. Her cheekbones were carved with impossible precision; the kind of lines an artist would spend a lifetime trying to capture. He could almost smell her—warm spice and something faintly floral that made his thoughts scatter. Her laughter, even in memory, loosened something in him he hadn't realized was clenched tight.

He shook his head, startled by the force of it. "Damn it, Maria," he whispered to himself.

Before he could talk himself out of it, he pulled up a message window. His thumb hovered for only a second before he typed: *I'm going to the Viridian Reserve tomorrow afternoon for two days. Would you like to join me?*

Her reply was swift: *I've heard it's spectacular. Are you suggesting we share a tent?*

Alex blinked, then grinned despite himself: *Separate rooms. Unless you insist.*

A pause, then: *Wise answer. Very well. I'll come.*

Alex set the device down, exhaling slowly. For the first time since Polonius had spoken of Fortak's progress, the weight eased just a little. It was not gone, but certainly lighter.

That changed the following morning when the holodeck shimmered to life around Alex, its blank walls dissolved into the black expanse of space. Polonius stood beside him, hands folded inside his robes, as the simulation loaded.

"This program is built from Megan's successful engagements. Each scenario is captured with precision including timing, maneuvers, tunnel collapses, and her traps of Daklin ships." Polonius explained.

We've spliced them into a single, high-intensity sequence. It's a gauntlet designed to test not just tactics, but adaptability. Our team built it and tested it. So far, no one has completed it successfully."

Alex adjusted the flight controls, feeling the interface sync with his reflexes. "The ship is essentially Tranquility, so at least I don't have to learn a new interface."

"I want you to learn," Polonius corrected. "Winning or losing matters less than what you see."

The view snapped into focus: a Daklin cruiser opening fire, its energy burst racing toward him.

Alex reacted instinctively, diving into a short tunnel hop, a move Megan had perfected to give the illusion of cloaking. The Daklin beam struck empty space, and Alex reappeared off their port bow. He grinned, adrenaline sparking. "The sim is so realistic!"

The next sequence unfolded: multiple Daklin ships converging, their weapons synchronized. Megan's tactic here was to lure them into a collapsed tunnel. Alex tried a variation, baiting two into chasing him, then flipping into a lateral tunnel he'd cut mid-hop. The Daklin overshot, collided with their own energy fields, and detonated.

"Interesting," Polonius murmured. "You favor misdirection over entrapment."

"I don't have time to think about it, Polonius. Whatever works," Alex muttered, heart pounding.

The sim escalated, 12 Daklin ships swarmed, their AI adapting. They began to anticipate his hops, predicting his angles. Megan had survived this sequence by chaining three micro-jumps into a delayed collapse, destroying half the fleet.

Alex tried a different approach. Instead of collapsing the tunnel behind him, he folded a secondary channel mid-flight, tricking the AI into following the wrong vector. Two ships disintegrated in the backlash. Another veered too late Tund spiraled out.

But the Daklin learned. With each maneuver, their predictive models sharpened. They began cutting off exits before he formed them, herding him toward dead space. Alarms screamed in his cockpit.

Alex gritted his teeth, forcing a final gamble. He spun Tranquility's simulated hull into a corkscrew, diving through a collapsing tunnel at the exact moment the Daklin fired. The burst clipped his ship, but not enough to stop him. He staggered out the far side, only to find three ships waiting.

The energy wave engulfed him. Darkness. Simulation ended.

The holodeck dissolved back into its grid. Alex sat slumped in the pilot chair, drenched in sweat. "Damn it," he muttered.

Polonius studied him calmly. "You lasted longer than anyone who has tested it. But yes, ultimately you failed."

Alex wiped his brow with the back of his hand. "Maybe it should be Megan here, not me. She's been winning the battles. I'm just… learning in her shadow."

Polonius stepped closer, his tone firm. "Megan has become a warrior. She has had time to train, work with her AI, and program eventualities in advance. You are something else. You see not only tactics, but the science behind them. You failed here today, but that failure is the soil from which victory grows. When you return from your time in the Viridian Reserve, you will run the simulation again, and again, until you do not fail."

Alex managed a weak smile. "Sounds like punishment."

"No, my friend," Polonius said, eyes glinting. "It's preparation. Oh, and by the way, over a hundred of my best have run through this sim. Only one got through the second level."

8

Viridian Light

The shuttle glided low over a valley drenched in green. From above, the Viridian Reserve looked less like part of a ship and more like a living planet: waterfalls cascading in silver ribbons, forests stretching into mist, meadows blooming with luminous flowers that pulsed gently with their own inner glow.

Alex pressed his face closer to the viewport, grinning like a boy. "You know, Maria, this is almost unfair. Glamping in paradise, on the edge of the Andromeda Galaxy, while our Milky Way burns."

Maria's lips curved, her dark eyes glittering with amusement. "Alejandro, the galaxy will still be burning when we return. In terms of human lifetimes, it burns very slowly. The question is whether you want to try and solve it while burnt out, as you currently are, or rested, and far more capable."

"Polonius put you up to this, didn't he?"

She smirked. "He only made the suggestion. I supported the idea and decided to make sure you didn't back out."

Alex turned, with mock suspicion. "So, I'm being handled."

"Had you not invited me, this would not have been a question." Maria leaned back in her seat, her smile widening. "But you did, and you should know that men are always being handled. You think you rule the galaxy, but alas, it is always the woman behind the man…"

Alex laughed, shaking his head. "You're going to make these next two days impossible, aren't you?"

Her grin deepened. "Perhaps, but only because I believe that impossible *is* your element."

They arrived at a plateau overlooking the reserve. A guide greeted them and led the group along a path lined with glowing ferns that brushed against their legs as if alive. The sound of water was everywhere. How was it possible they were still on a ship, with waterfalls hidden in the distance and streams weaving beneath stone bridges?

Their tents stood nestled among the trees, they looked more like small villas than traditional camps. Transparent walls turned opaque when touched, and each structure glowed faintly, like a lantern in the twilight.

Alex stopped short, noticing how close they were. "Adjoining tents?"

Maria arched a brow, crossing her arms. "Yes, at my request."

He blinked. "You… asked?"

She met his gaze squarely, her tone light, but her eyes serious.

"Don't overthink this. I wanted us to be close enough to share company, but not far apart like strangers."

Then, with a faint, mischievous smile, she added, "But before you get any ideas, the answer remains *no*. It's important to me that we still avoid the intimacy."

Alex tilted his head, feigning injury. "Who gets to decide when this torture will end, Maria?"

"I think it will be obvious."

He laughed, stepping closer, close enough to catch the faint spice of her perfume. "You're enjoying this, aren't you?"

Her smile softened, almost tender. "Yes. I am. And so are you. Which is why we will keep it like this for now. We have the company, laughter, and stolen innuendos. Desire thrives in this environment and anticipation is half the pleasure."

Alex's chest tightened, but he nodded. "I think half is a gross miscalculation, but I must admit, I am also quite enjoying this game. I *can* live with that."

"Good," Maria said, her eyes glinting as she brushed past him into her tent. "Because I suspect you'll be tested more on this Viridian getaway than you were in Polonius's simulation."

Alex blinked, then chuckled. "I'm up for the test, Maria."

With that, they headed out to explore.

The trails at Viridian were unlike anything Alex had seen on Earth. Paths wound upward along cliffs that defied logic, shaped by Andromeda's gravity-control fields woven seamlessly into the landscape. In one grove, the rules shifted entirely. Alex found himself walking sideways along a granite-like rock wall, while Maria strolled casually above him on a cliff outcropping, her hair cascading behind her like a dark waterfall in reverse.

"Careful," she called, grinning as a flock of birdlike creatures with translucent wings glided past them. "You look like you're about to fall upward."

Alex laughed, reaching out to steady himself as the field shifted again. "Up is relative here. I'm not sure my inner ear will ever forgive me, but I also need to understand the engineering and science behind how they do this."

They paused at a series of waterfalls that spilled from different directions: one pouring sideways across the trail, another flowing upward into the canopy, three others twisting into spirals that seemed to vanish midair.

Maria stepped close, her gaze lingering on the spectacle. "Tell me, Alejandro… have you ever had sex in zero gravity?"

Alex almost tripped, his eyes snapping to hers. "That's… not the kind of question I was expecting in the middle of a physics-defying waterfall hike."

Her smile widened wickedly. "It's a simple question."

He cleared his throat, trying to sound casual. "No. can't say I have. But I've heard… it's tricky."

"Tricky?" she teased. "That's one word for it. It does take good communication."

"Or straps," Alex muttered before realizing what he'd said.

Maria burst out laughing, holding her side. "Straps! Alejandro, you are even more practical than I imagined."

"Hey, I'm an engineer. I can't turn that part of me off," he protested, though he was laughing too. "Besides, don't tell me you've never thought about the logistics."

"Oh, I have. The fact is, I have experienced it," she admitted, her voice dropping into a lower, more suggestive register. "Which is why I'm not recommending it. Zero-G may be good for science, but I prefer gravity when it comes to human touch."

Alex opened his mouth, then closed it again, his face warm. "Are you doing these things just because you enjoy watching me squirm?"

Maria tilted her head, her eyes glinting. "Indeed."

By the time they reached the restaurant built into the cliffside, the stars of the simulated night had begun to glow through the open canopy overhead.

Polonius had explained that while they were inside the tunnel, the entire sky was a simulation, an approximation of what space would look like if they weren't enclosed. The view of Andromeda had grown so immense that only a small portion of the galaxy's vast expanse was still visible.

A host guided them to a table near a cascading upward-flowing fall. As Alex sat, Maria lifted her glass of Andromeda wine, then set it back down untouched.

"You're not drinking?" he asked, surprised.

She leaned back, meeting his eyes with a small, knowing smile. "I'll have one glass. No more. I don't want to be tipsy tonight… not when my tent is right next to yours."

Alex raised his brows. "Is that restraint or strategy?"

"Both," she replied, her tone soft but deliberate. "Temptation is one thing. Regret is another. I have learned that we can control much of what happens with preplanning."

Alex chuckled, lifting his own glass. "Then here's to patience."

Maria clinked hers lightly against his, the faint shimmer of wine dancing in their glasses. "You will find that patience, Alejandro, is what makes the fire burn hotter."

"Yes. At this point, you've said it enough, and I'm starting to realize it might be true. The fire's getting pretty hot."

And with that, the evening stretched ahead. A great dinner coupled with laughter under alien stars, restraint sharpened by proximity, and a tension that made the thought of two adjoining tents feel like the cruelest design choice that Andromeda Prime, and Maria, had ever engineered.

After dinner, their glamping host informed them that there would be a campfire and warm beverages set near their campsite.

The night air in the Viridian Reserve was cool where they sat before a softly crackling fire, tucked away in a part of the ship completely removed from civilization and city lights.

Maria stirred the flames with a long stick, the sparks rising like tiny galaxies. Alex leaned forward, tracing patterns in the firelight.

"You've barely mentioned Fortak today, and the problems brewing on Earth," Maria said, voice low. "Still, I can tell that it is on your mind."

"The sim showed me how fast they are learning our methods. We are not facing a static enemy, but a dynamic one that is adapting faster than we can," Alex sighed, rubbing his temples. "Megan is better, faster and smarter, but it is only a matter of time before they catch up."

Maria looked into his eyes, studying as he spoke. "I think there is some other calculus or strategy swirling around in your head, Alejandro. Other than your interest in getting in my pants."

"No! That's not what…" He stopped when he could see from the look on her face that she was just playing with him. "Okay, I've been thinking more about plasma."

Maria's eyes lit up. "Plasma? Why? Shouldn't you be focused on the strategy to isolate the Daklin and collapse their tunnels?"

He rubbed his face, realizing he hadn't shaved in a couple of days.

"It's all connected. Think about it, the universe is mostly plasma. Stars, interstellar gas, even the space between galaxies. It's not a passive medium; it's complex and active."

She nodded. "Explain."

"Plasma behaves collectively, guided by magnetic fields, currents, quantum entanglement, and probably other forms of interconnectivity we don't understand. Sometimes it forms structures, filaments, sheets, and even self-organizing patterns."

"We have discussed this, Alex. I think that is advanced physics, but not relevant."

Alex drew in a breath. "Shortly after I defended my doctoral dissertation, some scientists suggested that plasma might be a form of pre-life. Not organic, but they have suggested there is sufficient evidence to make us think it could be a primitive life form."

Maria's gaze intensified. "As you know, I have always been drawn to the aurora, which is essentially plasma interacting with Earth's magnetosphere. It seems to eerily move in an almost intelligent fashion."

"Intelligent?" Alex asked.

"Well, not intelligent like you and me, but in a much simpler way. I am suggesting the possibility of plasmas congregating, following each other, shifting in bizarre ways. And if they're influenced by electromagnetic fields… then perhaps a sort of intelligence could emerge."

Alex watched a glowing ember float on rising air currents, then burn out. "The Kordylewski clouds are another mystery. The dusty plasma clouds at Earth's Lagrange points are stable enough to stay near the Moon, or in stable locations balanced by gravity."

Maria nodded thoughtfully. "Something happened when I was in Greenland and the Daklin were preparing to destroy Earth. I felt like the plasma could help us, and I… well," she paused to collect her thoughts. "It seemed like I was communicating with the plasma, and something stopped the Daklin energy burst."

Alex exhaled softly. "That is really far out, Maria. As a scientist, how does your gut feel when you speculate that you talked to plasma?"

"It is counterintuitive, Alex," she returned to his given name rather than the affectionate Spanish version she had recently adopted. "Still, something happened, and we do not have an explanation."

"I do not believe it was an *intelligent* redirection of the Daklin energy burst," Alex suggested, "but instead some kind of electromagnetic or natural interaction between the dusty plasma and the burst itself."

He looked into Maria's eyes as he spoke, and it quickly became one of those moments where he had to remind himself not to get lost in her and forget to breathe.

"Open your imagination, Alejandro. Think about all of the unexplainable plasma phenomenon that has been observed on Earth." Maria laughed, leaning closer. Her cheekbones glowed in the firelight. "You're turning our romantic campfire into a physics seminar."

He grinned back. "I can't help it. My attraction to you, and stellar physics, are not so different. Both are forces that make time bend."

She chuckled and reached out, touching his arm lightly. The firelight flickered across their skin. "Einstein might agree."

His breath caught. "You're enjoying this."

"Absolutely," she said, voice thick with warmth. "Brains and banter are the best kind of chemistry." The firelight flickered across Maria's face, highlighting the thoughtful curve of her smile. "Let's test your imagination, Alejandro. There are real phenomena on Earth that hint at plasma behaving strangely, some say, with intention."

"Do tell," Alex leaned forward, curious.

"Ball lightning," Maria began. "Those glowing orbs that sometimes drift through storms have been observed to be hovering, changing direction, even passing unscathed through windows. In Robert Temple's work, he describes a famous case where a plasma ball entered a commercial airliner mid-flight. It moved calmly down the aisle, pausing at seats as if it were… inspecting the passengers. Then, without damage, it exited through the fuselage and vanished into the sky. No explosion, no scorch marks. Just… a visitation from, well," she paused trying to think of the appropriate word, "intelligence."

Alex blinked, stunned. "Intelligence? Let's analyze this. It entered an airliner during flight. That would be shifting from 500 miles per hour to practically stationary on the plane. There are some inertial problems, but only if we believe wind speed impacts plasma, which I don't. Still, I know of no laws of physics that can explain that story. Are you certain you have this from a good source?"

Maria nodded. "Yes. It is well documented. It's movement through the plane was not random. It chose a path, stopped to inspect something, as if curious, then it then left. You can't tell me that doesn't sound like the faint echo of intelligence."

"Maybe." Alex grimaced, not really willing to agree with her point.

She poked the fire lightly, sparks spiraling upward like a constellation. "And the aurora plasma dancing in Earth's magnetosphere."

Without thinking, Alex placed his hand on Maria's back. "I remember your insistence that we go out on that frozen night in Greenland to observe the aurora." He stopped, the memory forming a straight line to this campfire.

"That night in Greenland was significant for us, and for this topic." Maria immediately sidled a bit closer to Alex and continued.

"It was," he agreed.

"I read that the Juno probe on Jupiter, captured exotic plasma waves that shift as they climb the planet's immense magnetic field, behaving differently than Earth's auroras would ever allow. It is a dance," she was holding a twig, and traced the path of an ember as it climbed into the Viridian sky. "On Earth's own upper atmosphere, plasma patches chase each other, collide, bend at impossible angles. One might conclude they are dancing in a cosmic ocean."

Alex sat back, fascinated. "So, you're suggesting plasma doesn't just react, it rearranges itself? You're asking me to believe that it, what, plays like kids in the back yard?"

Maria's eyes glinted with memory. "I've seen something stranger still. When I was on Pronimos, near an electromagnetic anomaly at the edge of its northern deserts, I witnessed plasma dance across the sands. It coalesced into filaments, weaving like ballerinas in perfect rhythm. When the anomaly shifted, the plasma seemed to retreat, then regroup, forming into shapes that resembled flocks of birds. Locals called it *the sky's memory*. I will never forget it."

Alex's mouth parted slightly, the fire reflected in his eyes. "The sky's memory…" he repeated.

"In your home state, you have the Marfa Lights. I've been there twice, and once an old Texas ranger joked it's simply a Texas dancehall for plasma." Maria smiled, recalling an evening from another time.

"Maybe it's not consciousness as we know it, but it clearly demonstrates order, intention, and some kind of primitive awareness. Perhaps plasma is not alive, but it may carry the rules from which life itself emerged."

He exhaled, almost laughing in disbelief. "You realize you're making me fall in love with physics all over again."

Her lips curved in a slow smile. "Ah, Alejandro… I suspect it is not just physics you are falling in love with."

For what seemed like an eternity, Alex lost himself in Maria. In his home galaxy, he might have pulled her into his arms and kissed her, but here, on the edge of Andromeda, he sat, swept away by the breathlessness of the conversation and the intoxicating nearness of this woman, who was so close and yet impossibly distant.

The fire had burned low, embers glowing softly against the night. Alex rose at last, brushing ash from his hands. "I think it's time we get some sleep," he said quietly. "I came here to rest and unwind."

Maria stood too, the firelight catching her eyes. For a moment they simply looked at each other, the night full of unspoken weight. Then Alex stepped forward, and she met him halfway.

Their arms wrapped around one another, not rushed or tentative, but deep and steady, as if both of them had been carrying too much for too long. The hug lingered, drawing them close in a silence that was more intimate than words.

Alex felt the warmth of her body pressed against his. He could feel her heartbeat steady under her chest. The faint scent of her hair was spice and something floral, it curled through his senses, grounding him.

Maria closed her eyes, letting herself lean into him, feeling the strength of his arms and the calm that seeped into her chest. She resolved that if he kissed her in this moment, the barriers would fall between them.

For both, the embrace was more than comfort. It was restoration. The weight of war, of memory, of impossible odds eased, if only for a moment. Their bodies reminded them of something simpler: that closeness could heal, and touch could steady the storms of the mind.

At last, Alex drew back just enough to look into her face. His voice was a whisper, meant for her alone. "Let's get some sleep."

"Yes…" she forced a smile.

"And, you are right, Maria."

Her smile was small but certain. She didn't ask what he meant, because she already knew. "Goodnight sweet Alejandro." She turned and stepped into her tent.

∘∘∘∘ ∞ ∘∘∘∘

Their second day in the Viridian Reserve unfolded like a dream. They hiked among crystalline cliffs where waterfalls flowed sideways into glowing pools, and they floated on gravity-lightened bridges that arced across canyons filled with colorful flora and trees.

Strange, photoluminescent creatures drifted in the air currents like living lanterns, brushing past them.

In the afternoon, they swam beneath a waterfall that plunged upward into the sky before curving back down in liquid arcs, laughing at the physics-defying beauty of it all. At night, they dined beneath a canopy of trees with the same photoluminescent creatures lighting and dancing in chorus above them.

Maria kept her promise: company, laughter, and teasing innuendo, but nothing so serious that it created a spark that would make them cross the line. She had come so close with their hug the night before that it frightened her. The resolve she held so firmly had almost melted by this man of science, who seemingly lived in her marrow.

In the quiet of their second campfire, their conversations stretched late into the night, threading seamlessly between physics, philosophy, and playful banter. The laughter healed them; the restraint strengthened them.

By the time they returned to the populated part of the city-ship, they were different. As Polonius had suggested, Alex came home fully rested and fully restored. He felt sharper than he had in months, his thoughts clearer, his body light, and the ache of exhaustion had been replaced by a simmering drive.

More importantly, something still gnawed at him. Plasma.

Maria's story from Greenland and her memory of Pronimos haunted his mind. *Was there some natural phenomenon in the plasma that had reflected the Daklin energy burst?* He asked himself. It was plausible, yet he realized he didn't even understand the precise nature of the Daklin burst.

Alex now needed to test the plasma theory, and for that he would need data like the pulse's spectrum, its particle interactions, and its harmonics. Without data and testing, the plasma, and it's supposed ability to reflect the Daklin Energy pulse, remained a mystery.

He filed the thought away as a problem to pursue later. Yet there was one thing that he was absolutely certain of, they would not prevail against the Daklin using brute force.

Back in the training sector, Polonius met him with raised brows. "I can see quite clearly… you're rested," the old philosopher observed.

"Rested," Alex agreed. "And ready."

He entered the holodeck, and the *Megan Sim* came alive once more. Daklin ships converging, tunnels collapsing, ambushes springing. This time, his mind was clear. His body was sharp. He moved with precision, weaving Megan's tactics with his own improvisations. Where the Daklin AI adapted, he adapted faster, finding ways of turning their learning against them.

One by one, the levels fell before him. What had crushed him on his prior attempt yielded to careful timing, to patience, and to daring. The final scenario ended in silence, the Daklin were destroyed and his ship unscathed. To be sure, this was not a victory of the war, but instead, a series of exercises against an insignificantly small portion of the enemy's full power. Still, it gave Alex the beginning of understanding what they were up against, and how to prepare for it.

The holodeck imagery dissolved into grid. Alex stood, chest heaving, sweat plastering his shirt to his back.

Polonius appeared at the edge of the holodeck, a rare smile tugging at his lips. "Every level," he said softly.

"Yes, every level." Alex affirmed, catching his breath.

"You should be proud, Alex," Polonius patted him on the back.

"Thank you for putting this together, Polonius."

"It is critical, my friend." Polonius affirmed. "By the way, we will be arriving in a system we call Zantipitus in five days. I suggest you wrap up your training and get your goodbye time in with any of your Andromeda friends."

Alex thought about his comment. "I have lost track of time here on Andromeda Prime. How long have we been traveling?"

"I suspect what you really want to know is how far and how fast?" Polonius surmised.

"Hah, yes. That is what I was interested in." Alex grinned.

"We have traveled two million, five hundred twenty thousand light years at an approximate speed of fifty thousand light years per day."

"That's ten times faster than Tranquility…" Alex started thinking about how long the trip home would take.

"Not to worry Alex. We will implement several upgrades for your ship once we arrive on Zantipitus."

"That would be good. What can you tell me about Zantipitus?"

"It is a central Andromeda system. There are 14 stars, all located within a couple light years of each other. Nine of those stars have habitable planets, and much of the advanced science taught and studied in Andromeda can be found there. Students and researchers come from all over the galaxy, in what you might call a magnet. You can think of it like one of your Ivy League colleges Alex, like MIT?"

"I would say Princeton or the University of Texas," Alex corrected with a wry grin.

"Yes, of course you would." Polonius raised his eyebrows with a smile. "I know you're starting to think about getting back to engage the Daklin and support the effort. The upgrades to your ship should take three or four days, but I suggest you take a week or two in this system and see what you can learn."

"I will take your advice, Polonius. Where will you go from here?"

"Andromeda Prime will stay for several months. Trips outside the galaxy are rare, and we have collected a lot of data that will be transferred and evaluated. Many of the crew will take vacations. Some will stay here when we leave, and others from the system will join us."

"Is there a way you could be convinced to join us in the war effort?" Alex asked, hopeful.

"We have given you knowledge and time to strategize, Alex. Unfortunately, that is all we can provide."

"I don't know how to thank you for everything, Polonius. For the first time in years, I have restored the energy I've always drawn on to prevail in adversity."

"You're going to need every bit of it, Alex. After your de-ageing rejuvenation, you'll be at a level you've never felt. Imagine having the knowledge and experience you have today, in a 29-year-old version of your body."

"I am looking forward to that."

9

Zantipitus-1

The vast city-ship Andromeda Prime slipped out of tachyon space, gliding into orbit around Zantipitus-1, a planet slightly larger than Earth with three Moons. The vibrant planet glowed with oceans, the color of deep sapphire, continents, and white clouds.

Alex stood at the forward viewport with Maria, Emily, and Jabari watching the 3D image of the planet. They looked at the various moons and marveled at the geography.

Polonius's voice came through the comm. "Andromeda Prime has entered the Zantipitus system. Coordinates for Tranquility to descend to Zantipitus-1 will be transmitted shortly."

Jabari folded his arms, then glanced at Alex. "I'd like to ask you something before we leave."

"What can I do for you, Jabari?" Alex placed his hand affectionately on Jabari's shoulder.

"If the Tranquility will have me, I'd like to join your crew."

Alex looked him straight in the eyes, then smiled. "I am pleased with your interest in joining us, Jabari, and of course you don't even need to ask. You're part of this team, this family, already."

Maria leaned in with a grin. "That deserves a celebration before we depart."

Everyone turned to Maria.

"We can't just leave this fabulous City in the Stars without saying thank you and goodbye," Maria said with a smile, her gaze moving across each face before resting on young Steven. He had grown, and learned, more during this journey than in any other time in his brief nearly four years of life.

"What did you have in mind?" Alex asked.

"I already have something in the works." She replied.

Later, they gathered in a local pub carved into one of Andromeda Prime's lower districts, a place filled with warm stone walls and glowing lanterns. Travelers and residents crowded the long wooden tables, raising their voices in laughter and song.

Maria stood at the center and began to sing; first a song from her homeland of Spain, then one she remembered from Pronimos, and finally, she brought the house down with a couple of classic rock favorites that even her Andromeda Prime colleagues loved. Her voice filled the room with such beauty that conversations fell silent. Even those who didn't understand the lyrics could feel the longing and joy woven into every note. When she finished, the pub erupted in applause and cheers.

Glasses were raised. "To friends old and new!" Alex called, lifting his mug of dark beer.

They drank together, and the Andromedans bowed in parting. Those who had grown especially close shared embraces and lingering farewells with the companions they had come to cherish during the odyssey between galaxies.

Alex smiled at Maria when Torvek nervously responded to her hug, while Hypatia accepted it willingly.

Hypatia walked over and hugged Alex, whispering in his ear, "I plan to convert the people of Andromeda to hug greetings. It is one of the few things I believe you people of the Milky Way, of Earth, do better."

Polonius, who overheard her whisper, added, "It is strange that you kill each other in horrible wars, and yet, you embrace in warmth."

Alex simply nodded in affirmation as he considered the comment.

As they prepared to leave, Polonius pulled Maria aside. His tone was gentle but purposeful. "While you are in this star cluster, you should know, on Zantipitus-4 there is an institute that has studied plasma for centuries. I only know that their work is unique and unlike anything else in my galaxy. If you go, you may find answers none of us possess."

Maria's eyes lit with curiosity. "Plasma research… that could be invaluable."

Polonius nodded. "Our stop is here, on Zantipitus-1. But Zantipitus-4 is only an hour away by shuttle through the tachyon tunnel network. I suggest you take the journey."

Maria placed a hand over his. "Thank you, Polonius. I'll definitely go."

∘∘∘∘ ∞ ∘∘∘∘

Tranquility descended from Andromeda Prime, cutting a slow arc through the crystal-clear upper atmosphere of Zantipitus-1. The coordinates sent by Prime's navigators guided them to a soft, rolling valley surrounded by emerald forests and sky-blue rivers. It was quiet, serene, and impossibly alive compared to the steel corridors of Tranquility.

For two nights, the crew slept aboard Tranquility, letting the rhythm of the planet settle around them. Outside, the wind carried the scent of flowers and mineral-rich rain, but inside, their bunks and familiar surroundings gave some comfort as they adjusted to this new world.

On the morning of the third day, Alex and Jabari stood by the hatch, preparing to make their way to the med clinic. Maria touched Alex's arm.

"Before you go," she said, her voice carrying both memory and caution, "there are scars on my body, ones I've carried since Spain, as a child."

Alex furrowed his brow, "I don't understand what you're telling us, Maria."

"They are part of who I am, so I preserved them when I lived on Pronimos."

"I am still not following you."

Jabari stepped in, "Brother, she is telling you that this procedure we are about to have will cure and heal everything. She has kept some scars to remind her of who she is."

"Yes, Jabari is right, Alex. If the clinics here are anything like ours on Pronimos, the equipment will erase everything. Every line, every blemish. It is… unsettling, at first. I have chosen to keep a part of myself that goes back 400 years to my youth."

Alex studied her expression. "You chose to keep those scars?"

"Yes," Maria nodded softly. "Not all marks are defects. Some are reminders of what we have endured and survived."

Jabari smiled gently at her words, but his anticipation was impossible to miss. "Still, I am ready. Whatever they can do, I'll take it."

"Are you not joining us?" Alex asked, then wondered if he had just insulted Maria.

"Should I be insulted that you think I am not young enough, Alejandro?" She feigned ridicule.

"I'm sorry Maria. I didn't mean it that way…" He was flushed from his awkward comment.

"It's okay, Alex" she laughed. "I am not scheduled for another year or two."

○○○○ ∞ ○○○○

The med clinic was not what Alex expected. No grand reception halls, no ornamentation, it was just a clean and sterile expanse of white and silver. The air smelled faintly of ozone, reminding him of the refreshing air after a lightning storm. Rows of translucent medical pods lined the chamber like quiet sentinels, each one softly illuminated by pale-blue light.

A guide in gray robes directed them forward. "The de-ageing system will evaluate, repair, and restore. Most people come in every two or three years. Almost never do we see patients who have aged as much as you two, but our machines have been adjusted accordingly."

"I'm not that old," Alex protested with a frown.

"Your biological age is the oldest I have ever treated," the man said in a matter-of-a-fact tone. "Simply step inside. The process is painless. Time inside the chamber will *seem* brief."

Alex and Jabari exchanged a quick glance. Without another word, they entered their respective pods.

The hatches closed, sealing them in. Cool light flooded the interior, and a sensation that was something between weightlessness and deep warmth spread through their bodies. Every cell seemed to hum, as though the very structure of their flesh was being rewritten.

Alex tried to focus, to count seconds, but the experience blurred. It was as if fatigue itself was being drawn out of him, siphoned away. His mind cleared. The faint stiffness he'd carried in his shoulders for years dissolved. Pains he had come to live with began to disappear, and then he drifted off to sleep.

For Jabari, the change was even more profound. The ache in his back, and a lingering injury from Earth, evaporated. His lungs filled like they hadn't since boyhood. Like Alex, he drifted to sleep and when the pod released him, he felt taller, straighter, and almost electric with vitality.

When the two men stepped back into the clinic's open air, they were transformed. Alex's frame was lean and strong, every line of muscle taut with renewed life. His skin carried a healthy glow, and even the weariness behind his eyes was gone.

Jabari, broad-shouldered and powerful, moved with the grace of an athlete. He flexed his hands, grinning. "I feel as if I could run for a hundred miles and still keep going."

Alex nodded, testing his balance, his stride. "It's more than healing. It's… like being remade. I can see better." He took a deep breath, "Everything smells, better? Different?"

The physician observed them, looked at his pad, and then stepped up. "We don't often treat patients with as many maladies or as much age as the two of you. I suspect things will taste better, smell better, and your sense of touch will increase in sensitivity. Of course, that means things could hurt more if you have accidents. You may or may not remember what sex was like in your twenties, but the full joy of touch has also been restored. Your metabolism is also back to a level neither of you have experienced in a couple decades."

Thank you, doctor," Alex said. "Out of curiosity, I tried to keep track of time while we were in the pods. How long was it?"

"The system is designed to relax you and essentially put you to sleep," the doctor started, "and restoration takes an hour or so. Both of you were in for six hours."

"Makes sense," Alex answered.

"Oh, and one more thing, your reproductive organs are back to full function," the doctor said, checking his handheld tablet. "Turns out neither of you were sterile. Your sperm counts and overall virility are at one hundred percent. We're not here to give reproductive advice, but you should be aware… in case you are planning to have intercourse."

"Okay… thanks for that tidbit," Alex grinned at Jabari.

"Thank you, doctor." Both Alex and Jabari repeated, bowing to the doctor in the traditional Andromeda fashion.

The two men headed back to Tranquility, ready to take on the universe.

Maria and Emily were waiting at a restaurant near Tranquility. Emily's dark eyes widened as she looked at Jabari, and the smile that spread across her face told the whole story. Jabari returned it with a warmth that promised the intimacy he had been quietly anticipating.

Emily reached for his hand without hesitation. "You look…" she paused, smiling, as if words could not do him justice. "Stronger. Different."

"I feel alive," Jabari answered. His hand squeezed hers gently, his tone lowered just enough for only her to hear. "And I've been waiting to feel this way with you, around you."

Emily tilted her head, her eyes playful but full of meaning. "Then let's not wait any longer."

They waved at Alex and Maria, then abruptly slipped away down a quiet corridor, leaving the others on their own path.

"Do you want to go do what they're doing?" Alex waved down the walkway where Emily and Jabari had now disappeared.

"Yes, of course I do Alejandro. I want that every day, but it is still not time," she answered. "You do look fantastic and virulent, but for now, let's take a walk and explore the streets of Zantipitus-1."

The city was alive but unhurried, filled with open plazas and tree-lined avenues that blended seamlessly with the surrounding valley. Market stalls glowed under soft lantern light, selling foods and artifacts unlike anything Alex had ever seen.

They walked slowly, absorbing the sights and sounds. Children darted through fountains of iridescent mist, laughter echoing like music.

"Did you find a place for Steven?"

"Emily and I asked around and found a care facility where he can be with others his age. A few of the kids from Andromeda Prime are also staying there." She had come to think of Steven as her own child and valued her time with him. "I'll take you there on our way back."

"Perfect. Thanks Maria." His eyes shifted to dancers performing in a circle, their movements reminding him of a Texas line dance.

Maria glanced at Alex as they turned a corner onto a quieter street. "There's something I need to tell you. Tomorrow, I will be taking the shuttle to Zantipitus-4. Polonius spoke of an institute there. For centuries they have been studying and doing work on plasma. I must see it with my own eyes."

Alex nodded, thoughtful. "I understand. That kind of knowledge… it might explain things we've seen, maybe even what Earth faced when the energy burst reflected."

"Yes," Maria agreed. "If anyone has answers, it will be them."

"And you'll be safe there?" Alex asked, his voice protective.

She gave a small, amused smile. "Alex Durant, I have lived for centuries, crossed worlds, fought battles I never imagined. I can manage a shuttle ride to a research institute."

He laughed softly at that, shaking his head. "Fair enough. I will miss your company, though. I have grown comfortable spending so many hours a day with you."

"Comfortable? That's an interesting term considering I have seen nothing to suggest the fire inside has cooled."

"Ohh sweet Maria, the fire has not cooled. In fact, every day, it approaches 180 million Fahrenheit."

"I'm sorry Alejandro, while I am certain that is a significant number, I have not been trained in the Fahrenheit scale."

"That is the fusion temperature of hydrogen."

"Ahhh, of course. You wish to fuse the two hydrogen molecules together and make helium. I must admit, no man in my lifetime has spoken dirty to me like you do!" She winked and pecked him on the cheek.

"We will get there, soon I expect." His expression sobered again. "While you're off learning about plasma, I'll stay here on Zantipitus-1. I want to oversee the Tranquility upgrades and take advantage of the opportunity to expand my knowledge of science... I need to understand what they've built here. Their society, their technologies, and their philosophies have created something humans on Earth only dream about."

Maria slowed her pace, the lantern light catching her features as she looked at him. "You'll learn, Alex. You always do. And when you do, you'll make it matter."

"We won't be here long enough for me to really learn, but I'll find a way to move as much information and data to the ship as possible."

They walked in comfortable silence, exploring the winding streets, occasionally stopping to admire a sculpted fountain or sample a fruit that tasted like sweet fire. The city was beautiful, alive, and strangely familiar.

"This is like a vision of what humanity could be," Alex observed.

"It is almost exactly what we have on Pronimos, Alex."

By the time they returned to the sector of town where Tranquility was docked, the night sky above Zantipitus-1 was painted with two of the three moons, one a glowing crescent of orange, and the other a nearly full moon of blue and silver.

Alex looked up at them, then back at Maria. "It feels like we've just stepped into the beginning of something."

Maria met his gaze, her expression steady. "We have." She looked up the street. "Come, let us see how Steven did in the daycare today."

○ ○ ○ ○ ∞ ○ ○ ○ ○

The following morning, the four decided to meet for breakfast. Maria and Alex watched as Emily and Jabari walked into the café. Their closeness was obvious, hands brushing, eyes speaking a language of shared secrets.

Alex caught Maria's smile at the sight; she said nothing, only squeezed his arm as they continued walking.

Later that day, Maria stood at the shuttle port, her small pack slung over one shoulder. Alex and Emily accompanied her, the air crisp with the scent of blossoms from the valley trees.

"I'll be only an hour away," Maria said, her voice steady but warm. "The plasma institute has been there for centuries. If there are answers about what we've seen, the reflections, the energy bursts, I hope they will know."

Alex nodded, fighting the pull of longing. "I'll be awaiting your return, Maria. Just don't vanish into their labs forever."

Maria smiled, stepped close, and hugged him. The embrace lingered, gentle, grounding, and full of the bond they had built through shared danger, discovery, and a fire that she hoped would reach fusion temperature soon. When they parted, her hand slid down his arm, fingers brushing his. "Take care of Steven and Tranquility while I'm gone."

"You can count on it," Alex said smiling lightly.

They held one another's gaze for a moment longer before Maria turned and boarded the shuttle.

After Maria's shuttle disappeared into the tachyon tunnel, Alex took a portal to the planetary science halls on Zantipitus-1. The structures were functional with vast chambers, glowing data screens, and open experiment bays. The Andromedan scientists were eager to compare methods, and they quickly asked about Tranquility's artificial gravity.

"What technology have you used to generate stable gravitational fields?" One of the researchers pressed, leaning over the holomap of Tranquility.

Alex explained, "I don't generate gravity, not in the strict sense. I simulate it with acceleration and, sometimes, with centrifugal force. It's crude, but it works."

The scientists exchanged curious looks, as if weighing a strange but charming relic from the past. Finally, one of them smiled. "Primitive, but ingenious. Perhaps it is time Tranquility learned something better."

Within a few days, a small, elegant module was produced that could be installed into Tranquility's systems. Sleek, no larger than a compact generator, it interfaced seamlessly with the ship's core.

The team tunneled directly into the mechanical portion of Alex's ship and installed the new device.

When installed, Alex adjusted to Earth gravity and activated it, the difference was immediate. The floor under his feet no longer felt like the product of a spin or thrust; it was steady, natural, indistinguishable from planetary gravity.

"Is this going to vary as a function depending on where we are in the ship?" Alex asked one of the engineers.

"No. It has been formatted to the shape and volume of Tranquility." One of the Andromedan scientists answered while adjusting the control interface. "What you're experiencing is a localized graviton lattice. The generator excites quantum fields at the Planck scale, producing coherent waves of curvature. If I resort to terminology and science from relativity, you are standing in a self-sustaining distortion of space-time, optimized for low power consumption and tunable from zero-G up to four times your home planet's gravity."

Alex crouched, ran his hand along the deck, then stood again. "So, you're not pushing mass, you're bending the metric itself?"

"Correct," the scientist replied with a smile. "Your centrifugal and linear acceleration methods are clever approximations, but they never address the root. This device projects a controlled geodesic field. Every atom of your body feels as though it is resting in a well, just as on Earth."

Another technician added, "The system uses phased quantum coils that are stabilized with a tachyon feedback loop. It maintains equilibrium without requiring rotation or constant thrust. And unlike acceleration-based gravity, it doesn't fatigue your ship's frame or distort inertial navigation."

Alex chuckled and shook his head, half in awe. "I've been trying to simulate a hill with a child's sled. You've just given me the whole mountain."

The lead scientist tapped the panel. "You will find it adaptive as well. If you wish, you can alter the field strength by fractions. If you are exercising or preparing for a higher G planet, you can train your muscles using higher settings or reduce load during long voyages. Most importantly, it consumes very little energy."

As Alex walked the length of the deck, he noticed no micro-strain at the joints and no subtle shift when Tranquility's engines pulsed. It felt, for the first time, like standing on a real world.

"For the first time," Alex murmured, "my ship has her own gravity. I cannot even tell you how cool this is!"

The scientist inclined his head. "Now Tranquility is no longer bound by motion to create comfort. She carries a true field of her own. Why don't we spend a few days upgrading your power generation and matrices for tunneling? As it stands right now, Tranquility will take almost two years to travel between our two galaxies, I think we can upgrade Tranquility to cover the distance in a few weeks."

With the gravity module integrated into Tranquility's systems, Alex returned to the Andromeda science hall and began studying the elegant lattice coils glowing faintly in their housings. Emily and Jabari had rejoined him, their curiosity drawing them into the circle of scientists.

Alex leaned forward across the holotable. "The gravity upgrade is incredible, but I need your help with something more urgent. I think you're aware that we face a daunting enemy with technology millions of years ahead of our own. We need weapons, shields, and computer learning systems that can keep us ahead of them. The Daklin energy pulse nearly destroyed Earth. I have to understand it, and I need a way to protect against it."

The lead scientist, Seralith, shook her head. "Weapons are not our specialty. Andromeda has thrived by avoiding conflict. We have not seen conflict or wars here for tens of millions of years. As such, our work is tuned toward adaptation, not destruction."

Emily stepped closer, her tone direct. "But a shield isn't a weapon. It's an adaptive energy field. You don't need to fight to understand the value of shielding in space. As scientists, I am sure you study all kinds of phenomena around the galaxy. How do you ensure the safety of your scientists from energy busts, supernovae, and intense radiation in space when you encounter and study those things?"

Seralith studied the three of them, her eyes narrowing. Then she nodded slowly. "Very well. If we frame this as energy adaptation, not weaponization, there is a path forward."

They guided the group into a chamber where latticework arrays pulsed with faint blue light. Transparent housings suspended the devices in midair, energy humming like a quiet heartbeat.

"This," Seralith explained, "is a harmonic phase array. It does not block energy directly. Instead, it establishes a counter-resonance field. When an incoming pulse strikes, the field refracts it. We use the principle of interference which reduces the waveform to harmless radiation."

Alex traced the diagrams with his finger. "So, you're essentially creating wave cancellation in the energy spectrum?"

"Correct," Seralith nodded. "But to stabilize it, we embed graviton harmonics. Without that, the feedback loop would shatter the generator. By coupling tachyon phase coils to the lattice, we predict the incoming waveform fractions of a nanosecond before contact. That gives the shield time to adapt."

Emily's eyes lit up. "It's predictive, not static shielding!"

Alex joined in with the name realization, "Self-correcting. Like a living field."

"Exactly," the scientist agreed. "The more data you feed it, the more refined it becomes. It will need to learn."

"Holy crap. Cancellation is such a simple concept," Alex was grinning. "Just hearing you talk about it gives me ideas on how to construct it."

Jabari folded his arms, a grin spreading across his face. "Then we'll train it. Between Alex's algorithms, Emily's processing capacity, and my systems work, Tranquility will now withstand most anything space has to throw at her."

Another researcher added, "Think of it as a prism for destructive energy. A Daklin burst would arrive and your shield wouldn't resist head-on. It would bend the waveform, splintering it into frequencies too weak to cause damage."

Alex glanced at Emily and Jabari, then back at the scientists. "A scalpel, not a sword. Precision is all we need. Seconds of protection. Just enough to survive."

Emily reached for the console, her fingers gliding across the holographic interface. "Then let's start teaching it now."

Seralith looked to one of the technicians and instructed him to begin adapting a module for Tranquility. "You still have a conservation of energy issue."

Alex nodded, "I assumed as much."

Jabari grinned at Alex. "Looks like Tranquility just got a heartbeat of her own."

The following morning, Alex had a note from Hypatia asking if he would be available for lunch.

The street café Hypatia had selected was tucked between stone buildings whose sun-warmed walls reminded Alex of Athens. The tables were scattered casually under bright awnings, and the air carried the smell of roasted olives and fresh bread.

When Hypatia walked up, Alex almost didn't recognize her. Gone was the stern scientist of Andromeda Prime. In this softer light, in the flowing dress that caught the breeze, she looked like, well, the only word that came to him was *goddess*.

"You're staring," she said, a small smile playing on her lips.

"Forgive me. I just…. I didn't expect you to look like this."

"You thought I would always be buried inside a jumpsuit and equations?"

"I am sorry, Hypatia…Something like that."

They sat. For a while, their conversation was casual, her childhood in the colonies, Alex's time balancing science and survival. Then, almost too casually, she set down her glass and said, "I have been in love with Polonius for years. But he never notices me. Not in the way I want."

Alex blinked, caught off guard by the rawness. "You are stunning, brilliant and well," he tried to gather words and thoughts about Hypatia and Polonius but could not.

"Thank you, Alex," she broke his chain of thought. "And you," she added, "you are drawn to Maria. But you and Maria will not last, that is, if you ever truly begin. I have intuition for these things. I'm seldom wrong."

Alex leaned back. "That's… direct, and I hope it is not correct."

"I'm from a world called Gurick, Alex. We are the oldest civilization in Andromeda, and we don't waste time with veils." She could see Alex was considering a reply, but she pressed forward. "What I really asked you here for is not Polonius or Maria. It is plasma."

"Plasma?" Alex frowned.

"You think of me as a philosopher, a mathematician. But plasma is my true domain. Not from study, though I've studied plenty. I am a scientist, but my plasma work is more based on experience and intuition." She leaned closer, her eyes catching the sunlight. "Across the Galaxy, a handful of people are born with an innate connection to it. I am one. Maria is another, though she does not yet know it."

"That doesn't make sense. Plasma is just the fourth state of matter." Alex argued.

"No, Alex. Plasma is nearly everything. Stars, nebulae, cosmic filaments. Ninety-nine-point nine percent of the visible universe is plasma. It is the medium, the canvas, and the nervous system of creation. Unlike your tachyon tunnels, plasma can communicate instantaneously across the entire cosmos."

He shook his head. "Tachyons already break the light barrier. To my knowledge, nothing's faster."

"Wrong. Tachyons travel. Plasma *is*. It connects. It does not care for distance or relativity, but is constantly, continuously intertwined."

Alex studied her, unsettled. "And you believe you can… talk to it?"

"Not talk. *Feel*. Sometimes, guide. When you build, you calculate, measure, solve. When I touch plasma, I know. It is not a formula. It is a birthright."

"Maria too?"

"Yes. Though because of her scientific training, she resists. Her mind insists on proof, but one day she will awaken to what she is. When she does, she will change everything."

Alex exhaled slowly, feeling the weight of her conviction. For once, the engineer in him had no equation to throw back.

"You wanted me to hear this why?"

"Because the fight ahead will not be won by engineering alone. Tachyons may move ships. Plasma can move worlds."

For a long moment, Alex sat silent, the noise of the café fading behind the echo of her words. He had spent half a day with a woman who held crazy ideas blended into science. As gorgeous as she was, he now thought he understood why Polonius had not responded to her stated affection.

○○○○ ∞ ○○○○

Maria was studying her tablet when the shuttle emerged from the tachyon tunnel on Zantipitus-4. She stepped outside, not to a city or complex of research buildings, but to a setting that was raw nature.

Mountains surrounded her, some snowcapped. As she stepped out of the shuttle her boots crunched against pale mineral soil. The air was sharp but breathable, alive with a faint static that prickled against her skin.

A woman greeted her and gestured for her to follow. They stepped into a small vehicle that accelerated swiftly, the scenery outside blurring into streaks of color.

"I am seeing acceleration, but I'm not feeling it." Maria remarked to the woman who had greeted her.

"We control the way you experience acceleration using the same technology that creates gravity on our ships, Doctor Perez." The woman responded in a cold voice reminiscent of a 1990's computer voice.

"Dios mio, no one calls me Doctor Perez. Please, just call me Maria."

"You can call me Suliada. We are accelerating at fifty meters per second squared, which will get us to the plasma institute in a few short minutes." She watched Maria, who seemed to be doing mental math. "It's two thousand, four hundred sixty-five kilometers from the tunnel portal to the institute."

"Okay," Maria responded, smiling and trying to break through Suliada's cold demeanor.

"Are you a scientist at the plasma institute?"

"I am a student of the sciences, but not in *plasma*." She said the word as if it was distasteful or inferior. "I was simply assigned the task of delivering you to the institute."

"Well, thank you, Suliada." With that, the blur outside the window faded, revealing an ocean shore. They were now approaching a massive domed building.

"We are at your destination. Your plasma team is waiting for you." Without another word, she turned and walked away.

Maria stepped inside the dome. The institute was quiet and austere, its corridors brightly lit and lined with laboratories that hummed with the steady pulse of plasma containment chambers. Three scientists greeted her, their long coats woven with faintly luminous threads that shimmered in the light.

One of them, a tall woman, extended her hand. "Welcome to the Institute for Plasma Studies, Doctor Perez. My name is Doctor Kyrel. My team and I have been looking forward to your visit. For over three centuries, I have led the team that has focused on one question: the role of plasma in organic life."

Maria arched a brow. "Plasma's effect on life? I was told you had unique research, but forgive me, I think of plasma falling in the realm of astrophysics, not biology. Oh, and please, call me Maria."

Kyrel exchanged a small, almost defensive, smile with her colleagues. "We *are* hardcore scientists as well, Maria. We take our work seriously with skeptical, rigorous, and uncompromising adherence to the scientific method. We have devoted centuries to this field, and we believe plasma is not just the stuff of stars but is woven into life itself."

"I was not expecting this," Maria crossed her arms, skepticism sharp in her voice. "Please, show me."

They led her into a chamber where a translucent sphere floated above a lattice of coils. Inside it, plasma filaments writhed like living veins of light, pulsing and shifting.

Kyrel spoke carefully. "Our scientists have chronicled this frontier, though we have barely scratched the surface. We have observed plasmas acting intelligently, self-organizing structures that behave like organisms."

"Yes, I have read much of this from Earth and Pronimos literature," Maria frowned. "But frankly, it sounds more like philosophy than science."

"What we do is hard science," Kyrel corrected firmly. She gestured to the sphere. "We have demonstrated that plasma filaments exhibit memory. Stimulate them with a specific frequency, and they respond differently from one time to the next. As you know, repetition produces adaptation. That is learning behavior, Maria, and no different in principle from a neural synapse response you and I would have."

Another scientist stepped forward, "Hi. My name is Veyran. We have also observed plasma interactions with human tissue. Micro plasmas form at the cellular level, interacting with ion channels in membranes. Some of our data suggests that consciousness itself may be linked to plasma phenomena within the brain's electromagnetic fields."

Maria shook her head, though her eyes lingered on the writhing sphere. "You're telling me that plasma," She stopped and thought it would be good to clarify before continuing, "Do you classify plasma as a fourth state of matter?"

"Yes, we do," Veyran was nodding.

"And so, you are also saying it is somehow part of thought in organic life, and that it can learn, and remember?" Maria was thinking about Suliada's reaction to her, and now it made sense. What she was hearing sounded less like science, and more like fun banter amongst mind-expanding drug users.

"Yes," Kyrel said calmly. "We have conducted thousands of experiments using the scientific method. Our results continuously showed filaments clustering toward human hands, as if responding with preference. We have real data of plasma spheres that have entered our shuttles at high speeds, navigating the interior with apparent curiosity. There is even a case of a plasma sphere entering a ship in a tachyon tunnel. We have repeatedly studied these cases under controlled conditions. The data is unambiguous."

Maria's lips pressed thin. "I have seen similar data back home, but *unambiguous* is a dangerous word in science."

Veyran leaned forward. "Then look at the mathematics. Plasma structures form fractals identical to those in organic growth patterns found in lungs, blood vessels, neural trees. Are these accidents? Or are we seeing the same organizing principles at work across matter and life?"

Maria said nothing for a long moment, her scientist's mind warring with her instinctive skepticism. Finally, she exhaled slowly. "You are forcing me to reconsider what I thought immutable. If plasma can learn… then it may not be simply matter, but a participant in life itself."

Kyrel inclined her head. "That is the lesson of three hundred years of study. Plasma is not apart from life. Maria, we know that other scientists in the Zantipitus cluster think of us as charlatans, but we are doing real science, it is simply in a fringe area that humanity has never been able to fully understand."

Maria took a long breath and exhaled slowly, "Okay."

"It is interwoven. You will find, Maria, that your own body is speaking plasma even now."

Maria looked back at the glowing sphere. "Speaking plasma is an interesting phrase, but I have four days to be educated, so let's get to work."

Maria checked in with Alex the following morning. The holo-link shimmered to life, Alex's face glowing with the satisfaction of progress.

"Good to see you, Alex." She smiled broadly.

"Yes…" Alex got lost in the holo-link image. It was a perfect rendition of Maria. He almost felt like she was in the room, but he knew it was simply an assembly of photos. "We've installed a graviton lattice and a shield prototype," Alex told her, Emily and Jabari visible in the background. "Tranquility is becoming a different, better ship."

Maria smiled softly. "And I'm beginning to feel the same way here. The plasma researchers are brilliant, Alex. They are passionate about a science that's still controversial, even here. I'm thinking of extending my visit to ten days instead of four. There's just too much to learn."

"We can make that work with our timelines, Maria," Alex said. "Just don't lose yourself in their data banks."

"I'll be careful," she promised, though her eyes betrayed the curiosity burning within her. She wished she could hold him, but in time, that would come.

"Come back to me," he said affectionately and winked.

"Count on it, Alex." Her heart skipped a beat as she realized how far the two of them had come. It was almost time to take it further.

∘∘∘∘ ∞ ∘∘∘∘

Over the next week, Maria grew closer to Kyrel, Veyran, and their colleagues. They welcomed her into their labs and showed her how plasma filaments appeared to "remember" a stimulus—reacting differently when exposed a second time. They discussed research by scientists on Earth and Pronimos, and Maria confirmed that, as on Zantipitus, it was still considered fringe research and not widely accepted as legitimate science.

Still, Maria adhered to a polite version of caution. "You're implying consciousness. But plasma *is* matter. Can you compensate for the fact that we are looking at charged particles that obey fields and the laws of electrodynamics, and nothing more?"

Veyran smiled knowingly. "That is what we thought, and we have pursued that path of data collection and analysis but let us show you something."

He led her into a dim chamber lined with sensors. In the center hovered a transparent globe filled with a softly glowing plasma mist.

"Stand here," he instructed, guiding her to a marked circle.

The plasma within the globe writhed and shifted the instant she stepped closer. Golden filaments rose toward her, curling like tendrils.

"Is this plasma field responding to my presence?" she asked, incredulous.

"Yes," Veyran said. "Your body is surrounded by an electromagnetic field. I think some cultures in your civilization refer to this as an aura, which is measurable. The plasma aligns with those fields as though drawn by them."

He adjusted the control. A soft chime sounded, and Maria felt a rush of warmth on her skin. The plasma flared blue, forming a halo that mirrored the shape of her body.

"Your aura," Veyran explained. "Is constantly shifting as a function of your physiology, your thoughts, and even your emotions. Observe."

He asked her to recall a painful memory.

She thought for a second, then remembered the inquisition in Spain, how they had responded to her as a female who studied and understood the sciences better than most men, which had resulted in the scars she had chosen to keep.

The plasma field around her body dimmed, threads pulling inward, condensing into tight knots.

"Now recall something that brings you joy," Veyran said gently.

She thought of some of the times with Alex, their extended conversations in science, philosophy, politics, and attraction. The plasma surged outward, filaments glowing bright and radiant, expanding until they filled half the globe.

Maria's eyes widened. "That… that is remarkable. How many times have you tested this?"

"It's hard science, Maria." Veyran replied firmly. "We've run countless iterations and have mapped the frequency spectra on thousands of human auras."

"What common findings have you observed?"

"I could have told you and predicted with 100% accuracy how your aura would respond to various thoughts and stimuli. The interactions between your body and the plasma field are reproducible, just like the fundamental laws of physics. Your nervous system emits ion fluxes, and the plasma doesn't merely respond, it resonates. What's even more interesting is that sometimes it anticipates."

"Anticipates?" Maria stepped back, shaking her head slightly. "I see the data, but resonance is not intelligence. You are asking me to believe plasma is part of life itself?"

Veyran inclined his head. "I am not asking anything. You are here conducting your research. I am showing you the data and results of this team's work over the last few hundred years. My job is to show you the data, but you must come to your own conclusions."

Maria spent the remainder of her time studying data, experiments, and conclusions. On her final day, she stood at the shuttle port with her pack. Kyrel and Veyran had become friends, their passion contagious, their research compelling. They decided to ride with her back to the tunnel portal where the shuttle to Zantipitus-1 embarked.

Despite the data, the rigorous adherence to the scientific method, and even the friendships she'd formed, skepticism still held her fast. She hugged them both, then bowed, promising to return.

As she turned to board, Veyran said quietly, "You should know… we debated whether to inform you or not, but you are not the first scientist from the Milky Way to visit us. One hundred sixty-three years ago, another came. He spent a year here, and his perspective was far more advanced, though not as rooted in the scientific method as what we typically prefer…"

Maria froze. "Who? From where?" To her knowledge, the only civilization with technology capable of traveling from the Milky Way to Andromeda was Pronimos.

Veyran's eyes were calm. He looked at Kyrel who nodded. "He said he was from a star called Tilka."

The name struck her like a hammer. "Tilka?" Maria remembered a woman, shaman really, who had told her about past lives and how her job was not to be a scientist in the scientific method, but an observer who can relay the results.

The two both nodded without saying a word.

"How?" Maria wished this revelation had happened on the first day. A thousand questions came to her mind. She wanted to press further, but the shuttle pilot called her aboard.

"We do not know," Veyran bowed slightly. "Safe travels, Maria Perez. Continue your studies and perhaps your aura will remember."

Maria didn't like the answer, but there was no time to dwell on it, the Tranquility team was waiting for her, ready to depart together for Pronimos.

Right before her second shuttle entered the tunnel from Zantipitus-4, Maria looked down at the glistening snowcapped mountains. She had seen data, demonstrations, even her own aura dancing with plasma. And still, the years of scientific training ruled, and her mind clung to caution.

One haunting realization lingered, perhaps just a remote possibility: plasma might not be merely the light of stars, but the hidden fire within life itself.

When she returned to Pronimos, she would make time to see Takla from Tilka-7.

10

Hyper Tunnel

Maria stepped off the shuttle from Zantipitus-4, her eyes scanning the docking bay until they found Alex. He was waiting with Steven, Emily, and Jabari. Tranquility, ramp open, was parked adjacent to where they were standing.

The joy on Alex's face was unmistakable, and he moved toward her, arms opening for an embrace.

But before they could meet, Polonius briskly walked down the deck, oblivious to the reunion that he was breaking up; his tall frame and calm authority pulling the attention of everyone present. The moment between Alex and Maria softened, dampened by the Andromeda Prime Governor's sudden arrival.

"Welcome back, Maria," Polonius said warmly, though his eyes carried the weight of more serious matters. "I am glad you have returned, though saddened by the now imminent departure of our Milky Way colleagues." He knelt down and handed Steven a toy from Andromeda. "I have been working on securing something for you."

Alex folded his arms, sensing the shift in tone. "Securing something?"

Polonius inclined his head. "Your next destination is Pronimos, yes?"

Alex had not discussed the current destination with the team, but Pronimos seemed like the obvious choice." Yes," he nodded, checking the reaction of the team.

"Then you should know: there exists a hyper tunnel connecting Andromeda and the Milky Way. It will shorten your journey from several weeks to mere days."

Emily blinked, her eyes narrowing as she processed. "That's impossible. Even the most efficient tachyon tunnel can only compress spacetime so much. You're telling us we can cross galactic distances, *millions* of light years, in days?"

Jabari had only a small understanding of tunneling, but he was shocked. "Perhaps this is some kind of sorcery?" Jabari muttered under his breath

Alex shook his head incredulously. "Emily's right. It defies everything we understand about tachyon physics. Even with precision phasing, tunnel endpoints collapse at intergalactic ranges. Even if it were possible, the energy required, and flow is beyond anything our materials could handle."

"And yet, you are about to experience exactly that. Please remember that I am not a scientist," Polonius assured them gently, "and I cannot explain the engineering, science or mathematics. What I can tell you is this: the tunnel exists. It is ancient, older than the oldest Andromeda civilizations. It is hidden and protected. To enter it, one must have a special crystal and a code."

Emily tilted her head. "Protected by who?"

"That," Polonius said, his voice quiet but firm, "is not for me to reveal. I can only give you what you require to pass through."

"Why can't you reveal it?" Alex insisted.

"Mostly because I do not think there is a person alive in this galaxy who knows its history. Only a few are aware of how to use it, and it took some heavy persuasion on my part to secure the access."

Alex looked at Emily, whose opinion meant most in a decision like this.

"You know that, if we use it, we will be studying, and learning, as much as we can during the trip." Emily cautioned Polonius.

"I expect no less from my friends, and I hope its secrets can aid your efforts." He produced a small crystalline object, faceted like a diamond but humming faintly with inner light.

"This is the crystal. A few days ago, while the engineering teams were updating your Tachyon Drive, I had them install an interface. None of them knew what they were adding, only that I asked for it to be built according to the specifications I provided."

Alex took the crystal and studied it. "I do not recognize this material. What is it?"

"We don't know Alex. We have studied and tried to reproduce it… with no luck. Without it, the tunnel will reject you. You need the code and the crystal. The security code is extremely complex, consisting of numbers, equations, images, and sounds. Because of the complexity, it will be transmitted to Tranquility's computer directly."

Maria finally spoke, her voice low. "You say you tried to reproduce the crystal. How many do you have?"

Polonius's eyes darkened. "Including that one," he pointed at Alex's hand, "There are three."

"What are you calling this structure, or crystal?" Alex asked.

"I have seen the word, Archē," Polonius started, "but we do not know if that is indeed its name, or what it is called."

"An interesting coincidence," Emily began. "In Greek philosophy, especially in Aristotle's work, archē referred to the underlying principle or source of all things. As I understand it, it wasn't about a chronological beginning, but rather a fundamental origin or cause."

The room grew silent, the coincidental realization pressing against each of them.

"Perhaps it is not a coincidence that your ancient Greek language has some threads in this tapestry, Emily," Polonius broke the silence. "But I am fairly certain this technology extends to a time a hundred million years before the Greeks."

Alex exhaled slowly, steadying himself. "In any case, we will guard it with our lives while we are working to understand its makeup."

Polonius inclined his head. "That is wise, Alex Durant. The hyper tunnel is not merely a shortcut. It is a bridge between our civilizations. And like all bridges, it is both valuable… and vulnerable."

For a second, they all stood in silence, then Polonius surprised them all by hugging each of them. He stepped back so he could have one last look at his new friends. "You know, Hypatia is working to convince everyone here to hug first." Then he bowed in the traditional Andromeda fashion, turned, and briskly walked away.

The moment he was gone, Alex finally stepped forward and wrapped Maria in a tight embrace. She melted into it, her forehead resting against his chest. For ten days, she had been submerged in data, skepticism, and long nights of debate. Now, in Alex's arms, she felt relaxed and at ease.

"I missed you," Alex whispered.

Maria smiled at him. "You say that as if it's been years, not days."

"For me, it felt like years," he teased, though his eyes betrayed the sincerity.

Behind them, Jabari's hand brushed Emily's as they watched. The gesture was small, but it carried meaning. Emily tilted her head, her lips curving into a knowing smile. The subtle connection between them no longer needed words.

Steven, meanwhile, tugged at Alex's sleeve impatiently. "Daddy, did you see what mister Polonius gave me? It's a cool drone!" His eyes shone with excitement, wide with childlike wonder.

Alex crouched to meet his son's eyes. "Yes, Steven. I'm sure you'll have fun playing with it on the trip back to Pronimos."

Emily laughed softly. "Not *just* a trip, try 2.5 million light-years."

Steven gasped, thrilled, and seemed to grasp the number. "Mommy, we're gonna cross the whole universe in two days!"

Maria exchanged a quick glance with Alex, tears welling in her eyes. Steven saw her as his mother. Neither corrected him on the scientific inaccuracy, or the maternal one. They all knew, for a child, family and wonder was far more valuable than precision.

Jabari looked down at the crystalline device still in Alex's hand. "This little thing," he said, shaking his head. "The key to a bridge between galaxies. And all it takes is a code."

Alex turned it over carefully, feeling its faint hum against his skin. "If Polonius is right, then this isn't just technology…it's a legacy. Something built before we can even imagine."

Maria stepped closer, her hand brushing his. "The universe is nearly 14 billion years old. To us, a million years feels unimaginable, but on a cosmic scale, it's nothing."

"Agreed, Maria," Emily said first. "I think we now have evidence that some great civilization explored the universe, maybe even hundreds of millions of years before us."

"Or more," suggested Jabari.

The group stood together at the base of Tranquility's ramp, reunited and steadied. Above them, one of Zantipitus-1's moons hung low on the horizon, pale against the indigo night.

With everyone onboard, Tranquility lifted from the surface of Zantipitus-1, her new graviton lattice providing true gravity through the deck plates, her shield array idle but ready.

Alex and Emily walked to engineering, where the plate for the crystal was set into the tachyon drive. Alex held up the crystal, gazing through its facets as it caught the light, then carefully placed it onto the plate.

"Coordinates locked, and the code has been transmitted from Andromeda Prime," Emily announced. Her voice carried an uncharacteristic edge of hesitation. "I… don't understand how this is possible."

"Neither do I," Alex admitted. "But let's begin this journey and see if the universe is willing to provide an explanation."

The stars stretched, fractured into spirals of light, and then folded away as Tranquility crossed the threshold.

At first, the hyper tunnel resembled the familiar tachyon tunnel, but something was missing.

"The hum," Alex murmured. "Where is it?"

Maria frowned. "Paula's hum… the resonance you always heard in the tachyon tunnels isn't here." She noted the look on Alex's face when she mentioned Paula's name. It was a reaction, nothing more, but it was telling.

Emily confirmed with cold precision, "Acoustic monitoring detects no tunnel frequency. Nothing. It's… silent."

The silence was *not* comforting.

For the first hour, the team ran every test they could devise. Spectrographic scans, electromagnetic mapping, graviton resonance, tachyon harmonics. Each attempt ended, producing nothing that would help them understand the tunnel and the technology. Other than the missing hum, everything seemed the same.

"It's as if the tunnel is absorbing our questions," Jabari muttered, tapping at his display.

Then something strange happened. A second tunnel unfolded inside the first, as though space itself had nested corridors within corridors. Then an hour later a third tunnel unfolded leading them deeper still.

Emily's voice dropped to a whisper. "A tunnel inside a tunnel…inside a tunnel? The geometry is recursive. Every scan collapses back on itself. There's no way to measure it."

"Fractals of spacetime," Alex said under his breath. "Self-similar at every scale. No wonder our instruments are useless."

The crystal key baffled them even more. They couldn't remove it from the plate, but while it remained in place, they subjected it to every test they could imagine: electromagnetic fields, sonic resonance, and optical diffraction. Nothing revealed its elemental makeup or chemical composition.

"It's just a rock," Jabari complained after another failed trial.

"No," Alex countered, staring at the softly pulsing core. "It's something more. Far more. We just don't have the technology to begin to understand how to speak its language."

On the third night, they set the scientific instruments aside and chose to relax. For once, the ship was quiet. Emily dimmed the cabin lights to a soft twilight, and Maria brought out a guitar-like instrument she had picked up during her stay on Zantipitus-4. She strummed gently at first, then began to sing.

Her voice filled Tranquility's common room with low, rich tones, carrying echoes of Spain's past, Earth's classic rock, and the vibrant rhythms of Pronimos' music clubs. Steven curled up beside Alex, half-asleep, while Jabari leaned against Emily's shoulder, the two of them sharing a quiet, unspoken closeness.

Alex listened, a dark beer in hand, the melody tugging at places inside him he rarely let surface.

When Maria finished, Alex raised his mug. "You always do this to me. One song, and I forget what I was worried about."

Maria set the guitar down, eyes sparkling. "Then maybe I should play less often. I can't have the great Alex Durant distracted."

"Distracted? Or inspired?" he teased.

She tilted her head, grinning. "Inspired men make mistakes."

He leaned closer, lowering his voice just enough for her ears alone. "Or better yet, discoveries."

Her laugh was soft, warm. "You're impossible."

"And you're dangerous," he countered with a smirk. "But I sense something slight, yet different."

"Your intuition is becoming very fine tuned, Alejandro. For this I am lucky, but I would ask that we defer this conversation for a day or two while I work through something."

"Of course, Maria, but please remember that my goal is to get in your pants, and I will not relent until I have succeeded," he laughed.

They both laughed and finished their drinks.

The guitar rested against her chair, strings still vibrating faintly with the echo of her songs. The hyper tunnel stretched endlessly beyond the hull, unknowable and silent, but inside Tranquility the crew found something steady: music, laughter, and the fragile warmth of being together in the void. They were all acutely aware that when they arrived at Pronimos, their world would change.

Four days later the computer announced they would be exiting the tunnels over the next three hours.

Alex was staring out into the tunnel, trying to make sense of the numbers and arrays, when Maria stepped into the control room.

"Alex," Maria began gently, lowering herself into the chair across from him. "Earlier… when we entered the tunnel, I used the phrase "Paula's hum" and you reacted. It was almost imperceptible, and you probably didn't even realize doing it, but I saw it."

He looked up, caught off guard. "I did?"

"Yes." Her voice was steady, not accusing. "And that's why we need to talk."

Alex studied the panel, then back at her. He took a breath, exhaled, and decided to protest what Maria had to say. "Maria, I…"

She lifted a hand to stop him. "Let me finish. I care about you. More than I expected. I want to be with you. But I will not be your rebound."

His brow furrowed. "That's *not* what this is."

"Then tell me what it is." Her eyes held his, sharp but full of warmth. "Because here's my fear: the worst thing in the universe would be for us to make love… and for you to be thinking about Paula."

Alex flinched as though she had struck him. It was not the first time she had said this to him, so he was aware of the sensitivity. "I would never want that," he finally said.

"Neither would I," Maria replied softly. "That's why I'm saying this now, before we come out of this tunnel and arrive on Pronimos. I need you whole, Alex. I need to know you're here with me, not divided between memory and desire. More than anything, I have been here before, and I have learned from the mistakes of my past."

He rubbed his hands together slowly, searching for words. "Paula was… she still is, in some ways, part of me. She always will be. But maybe you're right, I don't know if I'm ready. One thing I know with absolute certainty is that I don't want to hurt you."

Maria leaned forward, her hand brushing his. "Then don't. Be honest. Be patient. When it's time, I'll know. And so will you."

For a moment, silence stretched between them, heavy, but not cold. The faint hum of the ship's systems was the only sound. Then Maria gave him a crooked smile.

"Besides," she added, slipping back into banter, "I'm worth waiting for."

Alex's lips curved into a grin despite the heaviness of the moment. "Yes… you are, but what would your thousands of years of experience advise here, oh wise one?"

Maria laughed at his comment, then took on a very serious look. "Have you had any sexual partners since Paula's death?"

"No!" Alex winced in disbelief. "I can't believe you'd even ask that."

"Uhhh," Emily, who had walked into the room in her usual silent way, interrupted their conversation. "I can't believe you guys are talking about sex when we are coming out of a tunnel that carried us nearly 2.6 million light years in five days!"

"Sorry Emily, I… we didn't know you were in the room," Alex apologized.

Emily studied them both, then focused on Maria, "My advice is for you to take him off to your bedroom right now and get it over with."

"Right! Exactly what she said," Alex grinned.

Maria frowned, shook her head, and walked out of the room right as the ship exited the hyper tunnel.

Emily stepped up to the control panel and watched as numbers flashed across the screen. "Sorry, Alex. I think I hit a tender spot with her."

11

Fractures on Singularity

Megan watched as the Singularity's training deck buzzed with chatter from the newest arrivals. This was the fourth batch of recruits, with new ones arriving every six weeks. Like all of them, this batch was bright, eager, and ready to become experts and join the war effort.

And all of them were testing Megan's patience.

"Form ranks," she barked, her voice echoing off the steel bulkheads. Inside, a part of Megan laughed. This was not her, but these young recruits thought it was…

They scrambled into position on her bridge, their nervous energy filling the air. Megan's eyes swept over them with a sharp edge. Too many wide eyes. Too much rawness. She was tired of molding children into soldiers.

Megan Hoglund was not a training instructor, but sadly, she was the best training instructor in the resistance.

After a minute of silence, Sun Tsu joined Megan to her right. Most of the recruits were probably not aware he was cybernetic. He looked and had the mannerisms of a 100% organic human. They generally maintained that perspective until Singularity went into combat mode. During the fight, most of them probably thought even Megan was cybernetic.

"Your tone is sharper, and your energy lower than usual," Sun Tsu whispered, low enough for only Megan to hear. "The fatigue is showing."

"None of us have the luxury of fatigue," Megan snapped. "The Daklin outnumber us a billion to one. They don't pause to catch their breath, and neither can we."

Mark leaned against a railing above, arms crossed, watching her drill the trainees with relentless precision. Later, when the recruits had dispersed for simulation runs, he pulled her aside.

"Megan, you've been running nonstop. Tsu is right. With all the stress from training, battles, and planning, you need a break."

She shot him a glare sharp enough to cut alloy. "I'll take a break when the Daklin Empire has fallen. Not before."

"Megan…" Mark started, but she cut him off with a wave of her hand.

"No. You don't get it. They're adapting, Mark. Every time I come up with something new, they study it, analyze it, adapt, and the next time, they're closer to countering me. We are not writing code in an air-conditioned room in Texas, Mark! We make a mistake, and we are dead. I'm running out of tricks." Her voice dropped, a raw edge creeping in. "If I slow down now, if I rest, even for a heartbeat, we could lose everything."

Mark stepped closer, his expression softer, but no less insistent. "And if you burn out, we'll lose anyway. You're not invincible, Megan, and as amazing as you are, I can tell you, you are better when you're rested."

She looked away, jaw clenched. For a fleeting second, exhaustion flashed in her eyes. She remembered a man she fell in love with. But then it was gone, buried under her usual intensity.

"Invincible or not," she said flatly, "Right now, Singularity is the best chance the Resistance has."

Sun Tsu stepped up, inclined his head, voice calm but deliberate. "A commander who does not pace herself risks more than her own strength. She risks the war itself. Even the greatest generals must rest to fight another day, Megan."

Megan ignored them both, returning to the training deck where the recruits struggled and had just failed their first simulation. Her voice was like steel. "Again! And this time, don't hesitate. Hesitation gets you killed."

○ ○ ○ ○ ∞ ○ ○ ○ ○

Five weeks later, the next recruit team was sharpened and ready to be dispatched.

Megan sat at the narrow kitchen table aboard Singularity, her boots kicked up on a chair, staring into the dark amber depths of a vanilla porter. The room was quiet except for the faint hum of the ship's systems. She took a long pull, savoring the smooth hops and alcohol with mild-sweet taste. Beer was her one indulgence, the only thing that reminded her of the world before the war.

Mark slid into the seat across from her, a cup of tea in his hand. He studied her for a long moment before speaking.

"You've been avoiding me," he said quietly.

Megan didn't look up. "I've been busy."

"With the trainees, the missions, the endless strategy sessions," Mark replied. "I know. But you've been busy before, and it never felt like this. I'm sleeping alone, and you're not talking to me."

Her eyes lifted to meet his, sharp but weary. "Mark… I'm not the same person I was when we met. The situation has forced me to change. I'm not a programmer trying to reach Singularity anymore. I'm a general, a strategist, a warrior, and a leader of the most impossible resistance in the history of humanity. If I don't think ten moves ahead, the Daklin will crush us. And if they win, we're done. So much of the galaxy refuses to stand up and support us out of fear, but we do not have that luxury…"

He leaned forward, his hands clasped. "And me? Where do I fit in that picture?"

Megan's silence stretched. She lowered her eyes to the glass in her hand, swirling it absently.

"You're still a scientist," she finally said. "Still the man who gets excited about data sets, about patterns in the stars. This war isn't about analysis anymore; it's about adaptation and survival. We are in the desert, and you're still wearing your snow ski gear…" she trailed off. "The ski trip is over, Mark. You need to up your game and join the fight, or…"

"Or?" He cut in, his voice was soft, almost a whisper.

"Or go back to Pronimos. You could serve the war effort better there."

"So, everything is about the war effort, now?" Mark protested.

"Holy shit, Mark." Megan responded, a combination of anger and surprise. "You've been on the deck for every encounter. What are we at now, about 70 battles against an enemy that wants us dead?"

"Megan, I just think both of us would be better off if we could, you know, occasionally enjoy some intimate moments like we used to."

"I cannot believe you just said that. It's time for you to get the fuck off my ship, Mark. You need to go back to Pronimos and engage in researching, advising, or building things the rest of us can use. Back on Pronimos, you can have sex with Allys, if you need it." Her voice cracked at the last words, and she quickly covered it by taking another sip of her beer. "Out here, you're… in the way."

Mark's breath caught. He leaned back, the sting in his eyes clear. "So that's it? You're telling me this is over?"

"Yes." Her answer was quiet, but resolute. "I'm telling you it's over. Like I said, go back to the safe haven and fuck that robot of yours if sex is what is truly so important to you right now."

The words hung between them like a blade.

"I can't believe you just said that, Megan."

"I said it twice; in case you didn't hear it the first time…" Megan closed her eyes and tried to stop the tears. "I'm sorry, Mark. That was harsh. Too harsh."

Mark looked down at his hands, shaking his head. "Do you remember when we first sat together on your couch in Dallas? You gave me pizza and those ridiculous dark beers, and I thought, this woman's going to take me to a new level."

Megan smiled faintly, the memory hitting hard, flipping her mood. "I remember, and you still came back the next night."

"We laughed for hours," Mark said. His voice broke. "It was easy then. You and me against the world."

"We had sex for hours. I was so surprised by that, you…" Her throat tightened. "I wanted it to stay that way."

"Then why not fight for it?" Mark's eyes were wet now, his voice rough. "We've faced worse odds than this. Why give up on us?"

"You're fucking kidding me, right?" Megan quickly transformed from soft to angry again. "No one in the history of humanity has faced worse odds than what we are facing right now."

"I see," he responded, not really knowing what else to say.

"And this isn't about odds," Megan said, her voice thick. "It's about who we've become. I can't go back to being the woman who drank beer with you on the couch and enjoyed morning sex, and you can't become the man I need, standing beside me in the fight. You are not a warrior, Mark, and if I am with anyone right now, it has to be someone who is."

Mark pressed his palms to his eyes, then let out a sharp, bitter laugh. "So, I lose you to the Daklin before they even kill us."

Megan reached across the table, laying her hand on his. For a moment, he didn't move, then his fingers curled around hers with desperate familiarity.

"We had something incredible, Mark," she said softly. "That doesn't go away, but we can't pretend we're still those two people, laughing in a café. We've changed, and pretending otherwise will only break us worse."

Tears burned in her eyes, and though she tried to stop them, they poured down her face. She stood, gently pulling her hand free. "I'm sorry, Mark."

Megan walked straight from the galley to the command deck, her jaw clenched, her fists tight at her sides. She had thought the beer would soften the edge and provide enough calm to make the evening easier. Instead, because of her conversation with Mark, she felt raw, every nerve lit like an exposed wire.

She hadn't noticed Sun Tsu, standing in his quiet, deliberate way, part man, part machine. His cybernetic enhancements gave him the stillness of a statue, but his dark eyes studied her with the kind of depth only a strategist, who had also become a friend, could manage.

"You ended it," he said simply.

Megan didn't ask how he knew. On a ship this size, walls had ears, and Sun Tsu's sensors heard more than most.

"Yes," she replied, lowering herself into the captain's chair. Her voice was steady, but her hands betrayed her, flexing against the armrests. "I had to."

Sun Tsu inclined his head, the motion precise. "Because he could not adapt."

Megan shot him a sharp glance. "You make it sound clinical."

"It is clinical," Sun Tsu said. "Relationships, like wars, require adaptation. You shifted from partner to commander. He is stuck in his role as computer guru and scientist. The divergence has produced an unsustainable connection."

Her eyes burned, though she held back tears. "Don't tell me you see it as just another strategy problem. He wasn't a battle plan, Sun Tsu. He was a…" she stopped, biting down on the words.

"A companion," Sun Tsu finished for her. "A comfort, and source of laughter, of humanity. These things are not weaknesses, Megan. They are necessary to sustain the warrior."

She let out a bitter laugh. "Necessary, maybe. But not possible for me. Not now."

Sun Tsu stepped closer, folding his arms behind his back. His voice softened, though his tone remained measured. "I may have taken the name, but you are much more like the historic General Tsu, the man I studied. He too believed that victory demanded the sacrifice of all personal ties. And yet, his writings betray a truth: even the greatest strategist longed for balance."

Megan looked up at him, weary but defiant. "Balance is a luxury. The Daklin are adapting faster than I can counter them. Every trick I use buys us less and less time. If I slow down for… balance, we lose."

Sun Tsu considered her words for a moment, then spoke quietly: "A commander who fights only with the sword burns quickly. A commander who fights with both sword and spirit endures. You are very good at it, but you're trying to fight with only the sword, Megan."

For the first time in hours, she faltered. Her gaze fell to the floor. "And what happens when the spirit is too tired to rise again?"

"Then you let others lift it," Sun Tsu replied simply. "Even if those others are not soldiers, but scientists, dreamers, or those who make you laugh in a café."

Her throat tightened. She looked away, unwilling to let him see the tears threatening to fall. "That part of my life is gone."

Sun Tsu gave a slight nod. "Perhaps. Or perhaps it has only changed form, like war itself."

The silence stretched. Megan swallowed hard, pulled herself upright, and forced her voice back into its steel edge. "I appreciate you, Tsu. You have become so much more than the strategist who helps me win battles."

"I can be your friend, but cannot fill the role that Mark did," Sun Tsu advised. "You wear a suit of armor, but the woman under that armor must continue to exist."

"I will be fine, my friend," she smiled. "We have a couple more days with these recruits. After we drop them off, let's talk about next steps."

Sun Tsu's eyes lingered on her for a moment longer, as though memorizing the fracture in her armor. Then he bowed slightly.

"As you command, General."

∘∘∘∘ ∞ ∘∘∘∘

Megan sat alone in the galley, quiet and still. A single overhead light cast a warm cone onto the table, her half-finished glass of dark beer glowing amber in its shadow. She leaned back, her long curls spilling over her shoulders. The recruits were asleep, training was complete, and the systems ran on autopilot, leaving Megan with a rare moment to think. At her request, this would be the last group she would train.

The door slid open. Mark hesitated in the threshold before stepping in. "Mind if I sit?"

She glanced up, eyes guarded, then tipped her chin toward the empty chair. "Suit yourself."

"Can I get you another beer?" he asked.

"Sure."

He set down a couple of bottles and lowered himself opposite her. For a moment, neither spoke.

Finally, Mark broke the silence. "I found a planet called Gamma Halden 3, not far from where Singularity makes the drop. It's just a few light-years and there's a small outpost with a space port friendly to the resistance."

Megan took a slow sip, studying him over the rim. "And?"

"And," he said, voice steady but soft, "you can drop me off at that outpost. From there I will work my way back to Pronimos, where I'll find a role where I can contribute best."

She exhaled, long and slow, and set her glass down. "So, your decision is made and you're really leaving?"

Mark nodded. "I think you were right. Out here…" He paused, searching for the words. "Out here, you're a general, a strategist, and a fighter. I am none of those. I'm just a scientist who's unable to keep up."

Megan's lips twitched. It was not quite a smile, not quite regret. "You undersell yourself. You've saved my ass a few times. But…" Her voice dropped, gentler now. "This fight changes people. It's already changing me."

"To be clear Megan, I am a big fan of your ass, which is why I enjoy saving it."

This time she smiled. A few sweet memories began to flood back, and even though she tried to stop the tears, she failed. "You're a bastard, making me cry so much these days, Mark. Believe it or not, I understand the meaning behind that comment."

Mark traced the rim of his bottle with a finger. "We were good, though. Weren't we?"

Megan's eyes softened in the dim light. Like a scene from a movie, memories of nights on Tranquility played in her mind with dark beer, music, and friends. Long hours hunched over computer screens, coding their way through the timeline. And, of course, the laughter, so much laughter, spilling into kisses and wonderful sex.

"Yeah. We were."

They sat with that for a while, the weight of it pressing in.

Finally, Megan leaned forward, her hand brushing his for the briefest instant. "You'll make it back. Build something, find a new woman, help keep the war effort alive from there. Oh, and don't forget, everything you do back on Pronimos is to protect my ass!" She winked.

They lifted their beers, a quiet toast with a soft clink that seemed to echo through the empty ship.

"Here's looking at you, kid," Mark said, recalling an old movie called *Casablanca*, where the hero used that line for his love interest.

The next day unfolded in a blur of activity. Singularity eased into the docking cradle of the resistance base ship, a vast construct of steel and light bristling with weapons and supply bays. Megan stood on the command deck, arms crossed, watching as the recruits filed off. She wondered how well this group would do in the fight against impossible odds. She knew that sadly most would die.

"Good luck," she told them quietly as the last pair disappeared down the ramp. No speech, no grand send-off. Just a soldier's farewell.

By mid-shift, Tranquility's holds were stocked with food and necessary supplies. Most importantly, every resupply included a few kegs of Megan's favorite beer.

Once all transfers were complete, Sun Tsu locked down the doors and navigated out of the docking bay as Singularity slipped into free space. He punched the program to enter the tunnel followed by the familiar Paula-hum of the engines.

Now, it was just the three of them, taking a day to rest before heading to Gamma Halden 3, where Mark would begin his journey back to Pronimos.

Later that day, Mark pushed through the galley hatch. The place smelled faintly of coffee, the kind of scent that clung to a ship no matter how often it recycled air. He half expected to see Megan in her usual corner, nursing a vanilla porter, eyes distant but alert.

Instead, the room was empty save for Sun Tsu, his cybernetic frame standing near the bar. The AI turned as if he'd been waiting.

"You are looking for Megan," Sun Tsu said in his deliberate, measured voice.

"Yeah. My last night here…" Mark swallowed hard, clearly upset. "Thought she'd be here so we could grab one last beer."

"She is not." He tilted his head slightly, an imitation of human mannerism he had recently adopted. "Megan is in the gym. She has been training for the last 94 minutes."

Mark hesitated, running a hand through his hair. "Figures. Work before everything else."

Sun Tsu studied him for a moment. "She carries burdens she does not share easily, but you already know this. Her workouts are a magnificent display of burning off steam."

Mark gave a small, humorless smile. "Yeah. I know."

The galley felt larger, emptier without her presence. For a moment he considered grabbing a drink anyway, but the thought of sitting alone at their table was too heavy.

"Thanks, Sun Tsu," he said, turning toward the hatch.

The AI's voice followed, calm but pointed: "If you go to her, choose your words carefully. Warriors do not always welcome interruption… but sometimes they need it."

Mark paused, weighing the advice, then nodded once. He wasn't sure if he was ready to face her in that state, with sweat, discipline, and the iron wall she built around herself, but he knew Sun Tsu was right.

The gym lights were dim, save for the harsh glow of the holographic grid. Mark slipped in without a sound, the door whispering shut behind him.

Megan was in the center of the mat, surrounded by a half dozen holographic opponents. They were flickering with the faint blue shimmer of simulation, but their movements were quick and merciless. The Pronimos technology included tactile, and was so advanced that while immersed in the simulation, one could not tell that it was not real.

The simulated enemies moved fast, but Megan moved faster.

Mark froze, struck by her precision. She spun low, sweeping her leg under one attacker, rising in the same motion with an elbow strike that crushed another figure's jaw. A third lunged from behind, but she pivoted, caught its wrist, and twisted with a brutal torque that snapped the arm before she hurled the simulated man into the wall. Every single move was a perfect dance, choreographed as if pre-designed. Megan was fluid, and deadly.

Her hair, damp with sweat, was braided on both sides and pulled back. One enemy tried to grab her braids, but her reflexes were faster, and she snapped his fingers before they could reach her braids. Sims didn't feel pain, but Mark did when he saw those fingers crack under Megan's swift movements. Her chest rose and fell in a rhythm that matched the cadence of the fight. Like everything she did, this fight was controlled and relentless.

Mark realized with a pang of awe that he had never truly watched her like this. He had seen her command ships, strategize in the chaos of battle, argue with recruits and officers, but here, stripped of rank and pretense, she was simply a fighter, a warrior honed by years of discipline.

The holograms swarmed again. Megan's fists blurred, a jab-cross-hook combination that cracked through one enemy's guard before she pivoted into a spinning back kick that sent another sprawling. She never wasted motion. Every strike was efficient and necessary, the same way she had once stripped-down lines of code when chasing her dream of building the hardware-software singularity that would bring computer processing to a point that eclipsed human capabilities.

Singularity. The ship's name wasn't vanity. It was her life's work, her declaration that she would reach beyond human limits. Mark felt the memory wash over him: late nights working with her and watching her code, the glow of the screen on her face, the certainty in her eyes that the future could be bent by will and intellect. Those days now seemed like a distant dream.

In this simulated fight on the mat, he saw that same certainty in her body. A final attacker charged, and Megan flowed into the movement, side-stepping, catching it in a blur of forearm and hip, then slamming it into the ground with an economy of force that made it vanish in a scatter of light.

She straightened, rolling her shoulders, breathing hard but steady. Sweat traced the lines of her arms and neck, glistening under the gym lights. She walked to the edge of the gym and grabbed a bottle of water which she slugged down.

Mark stayed in the shadows, watching. Not ready to break the spell, but perfectly ready to admit that at this moment, she was something far beyond him. Megan Hoglund was beyond anyone he had ever known.

When she finished her water, Megan picked up a towel and turned toward the corner of the gym as if sensing his presence, even before she saw him. Her eyes landed on Mark, and something in her face shifted.

Mark expected to see anger, but instead her face softened around the edges, the barest smile rising despite the sheen of sweat on her brow.

"You're leaving tomorrow," she said, walking toward him without hesitation.

Mark gave a small nod, hands slipping into his pockets. "That's the plan."

She stopped a few feet from him, her breath still a little ragged from the fight, curls damp and clinging to her neck. The message Sun Tsu had tried to deliver was rattling in her brain. Some of it made sense. "Would you be okay with… one last time before you're gone?"

Mark blinked, unsure if he'd heard her right. "One last what?"

Instead of answering, Megan stepped closer, close enough that he could feel the heat radiating from her body, see the way her chest rose and fell beneath the tight fabric of her workout top. Her eyes locked on his, steady and unflinching.

Mark knew this version of Megan.

Then she kissed him, slowly with intention.

For Mark, she tasted like salt and fire, and her lips moved against his with a hunger that wasn't frantic, but deliberate. This was the new version of Megan that he had observed, and admired with awe, but not really touched.

Megan was trying to memorize the shape of his mouth, the feel of his body, excited and pressed against her own. All of the advice to slow down and forget about the war became laser focused, pulled by the gravity of this moment. Her hand came up to rest lightly on his chest, fingers spread against his shirt, and he felt the press of her palm, warm and sure.

Mark let out a quiet breath, the confusion slipping away like dust in the airlock. His arms rose, wrapping around her waist as her body melted into his.

She was still slick with sweat from training, and the contact was electric. Skin on fabric, heat on heat, the primal pulse of shared memory and impending loss. He ran a hand up her back, feeling the flex of her muscles, the strength in her frame. She wasn't fragile. She was power, precision, and passion.

Her lips moved to his neck, kissing just below his ear, and his breath caught.

"I've been thinking about this all day," she whispered. "Even while I was fighting, I kept thinking about you. One last time with you…"

He rested his forehead against hers, letting his fingers trace the line of her spine. "Megan, are you sure?"

"No," she whispered, "but it doesn't matter. If I let you go without this, I would regret it." She looked up at him, eyes burning. "I want *you*. One last time, as who we were before the galaxy all fell apart."

Mark didn't answer with words. Instead, he kissed her again, deeper this time, his hands sliding down her back as she pressed closer.

Megan's hands gripped the hem of Mark's shirt, lifting it over his head with a rough urgency. He responded in kind, fingers slipping under the waistband of her top, pulling it over her glistening shoulders. Their mouths barely parted between motions, heat building, bodies pressed chest to chest, the rest of the world narrowing to just this moment.

The gym felt smaller. Hotter. Like it could barely contain the storm between them.

Mark kissed her collarbone, her jawline, then returned to her lips. "You sure?" he whispered again, breathless.

She answered by pulling him closer, her nails trailing across his back. "Just shut up and remember me."

Suddenly, alarms erupted.

Red lights stuttered into existence overhead, the gym's soft ambiance replaced by the shrill, mechanical scream of emergency sirens.

Megan broke from the kiss, breathless, eyes narrowing. "Shit."

The gym door slid open with a sharp hiss, and Sun Tsu's strode through carrying three backpacks that Zander had designed for emergency escapes.

"We are surrounded," Sun Tsu said flatly, his tone calm but carrying weight. "Nine Daklin warships and they have somehow neutralized our jump capabilities. They want the ship. Intact. I calculate we have ninety-three seconds."

Mark was frozen, shirtless, blinking like he hadn't quite caught up with reality. Megan grabbed her top from the floor and began dressing quickly.

"What the hell, Sun Tsu!" she barked. "We were…"

"I know," he cut in gently. "And I regret the interruption. The intimacy you were about to experience was… psychologically valuable. Especially for you, Megan."

She looked up, startled by the raw honesty in his comment.

"I monitor your vitals, and I've been mapping your stress levels over the past few weeks. What was about to occur would have helped."

Mark gave a disbelieving laugh as he yanked his shirt back on. "So, what, our famous military strategist steps in mid-kiss, and gives us a therapy report on the way?"

Sun Tsu didn't flinch. "The ship will be destroyed unless action is taken now. The backpacks contain short-range personal tunnel drives. Each is programmed for Gamma Halden 3. Because of the distance, the energy demand will drain nearly all the backpack power reserves, and there will be no retrieval system. But survival odds are highest with immediate departure."

Megan finished buckling her tactical belt and stepped forward, eyes scanning the hallway beyond the gym where shadows danced between red flashes. "Time remaining?"

"Twenty-nine seconds," Sun Tsu replied.

Megan looked back at the gym, the familiar scuffed floors, the hanging gloves, the scent of oil and sweat and memory. Her ship. Her recruits had trained here. She had bled here.

Singularity had been her life dream, and it had become the deadliest ship in the Resistance. She turned to Sun Tsu. "Is the self-destruct programmed?"

"It is ready. Awaiting only your voice."

Her jaw clenched. She reached for the strap of the backpack. "Execute."

Sun Tsu nodded once. "Command confirmed. Self-destruct sequence initiated. Four seconds to detonation."

Mark caught her arm. "Gamma Halden 3?"

"You wanted to go there, Mark. It's an isolated outpost," Megan said, adjusting her pack. "Punch it, Mark." She looked at Sun Tsu, who she knew would wait to be last, then to Mark.

She pressed the backpack button.

The ship dissolved around them.

And her ship, Singularity, exploded behind them in a flash that also took out the Daklin ships that surrounded them.

12

Pronimos Crossroads

The sun had just set on Pronimos, casting a bronze shimmer across the courtyard streets. Alex and Maria stepped through the heavy wood door of The Spiral Tap; Alex's favorite old haunt tucked in the corner of the central district. The air was warm with the scent of roasted grains and something faintly floral drifting in from the open-air terrace.

He found his usual booth, the simulated, worn leather seats and a wooden tabletop etched with decades of stories, love, laughter, and regrets.

Maria slid in first, her eyes scanning the bar with a nostalgic softness.

"It hasn't changed at all," she said, half to herself.

Alex took the seat across from her, waving to the bartender who still remembered their orders. Moments later, two tall glasses of dark beer arrived, topped with soft, creamy foam.

"To being back. It seems that we might have one more quiet moment," Alex offered, raising his glass.

Maria clinked his gently. "To knowing what's next," she replied, though her tone made it clear that she didn't.

For a few minutes they drank in silence, listening to the quiet murmur of locals around them, the occasional burst of laughter, the rhythm of a familiar world that had once felt like home.

"I'm going back to Earth," Alex said, finally.

Maria looked up. "Fortak?"

He nodded. "If he gets his hands on how the T-Portal really works, if he manages to understand what Zander built, it gets really difficult."

"Are you being sarcastic, Alex? How do you even calculate changes in the odds that are trillions to one?"

"It can't happen. I need to stop him."

She swirled the foam in her glass, watching it slowly dissolve.

"You don't even know where he is."

"I can guess. He's probably working with that swine, Pascal," Alex scoffed. "In any case, I know Earth. His ship was destroyed, and Fortak is cut off from the empire. He will need people, resources, and engineers. I can track those things and influence them. My bet is that he's spending all his time at T-Portal."

Maria exhaled softly. "It's dangerous. The Daklin are going to come looking for him. Or worse, for revenge."

"I know, but they don't have tachyon tunneling yet. At light speeds, they are still years away." he said, then leaned forward. "Come with me."

"What?" She blinked. Being with Alex was the number one thing she wanted to do, but something else was tugging on her. If they did not fix the Daklin problem, their life, and the existence of Pronimos, would be in grave danger.

"We work better together. We always have. You know it as well as I do." He paused. "I want to keep figuring this out," he paused and pointed at her, then back at himself. "You and me. Not just science and war efforts. Us."

Maria looked at him, really looked, for the first time since they returned. His eyes were still curious and intense but even with his new younger body, she could see the wisdom weighted down by decisions that changed everything.

"I need to think about it," she said, with honestly.

"Fair," he nodded. "But I do think I need to head for Earth in a matter of days."

She gave him a tight smile. "I want to talk to someone before I decide."

"Someone?"

"Takla. The woman I met with before Greenland." Maria took a sip. "She sees things differently. The plasma questions are filling all of my time, and I think Takla might help me answer a question…."

Alex didn't argue. He just gave a quiet nod and tipped his glass toward her. "Just promise me that if you stay it's because you *believe* in what you're doing, not because you're running from your attraction to me," he grinned.

Maria chuckled. "And if I go, it won't be just for you. It will be because I believe it is the best thing for Pronimos."

∘∘∘∘ ∞ ∘∘∘∘

The following morning, Maria found Takla in her modest wooden dwelling, the same place she had visited before Greenland. The smells and stacks of handwritten volumes brought her back to another time.

"I have been awaiting your return, Maria Perez," Takla said warmly, setting aside her book. "Tell me of your travels."

Maria smiled faintly, taking her seat. "I needed perspective. Things have… shifted."

They caught up for a few minutes before Takla's expression darkened. "Yes, I know. War is coming to us. My cousin, Calit, was killed in a Daklin skirmish in sector 49. He was only 72"

"I'm so sorry," Maria said, leaning forward. She knew on Tilka seventy-two was still young. "The Daklin have taken too much from all of us."

"I fear they have far more to take," Takla answered with quiet sadness, her gaze distant. "And still, we endure."

Maria traced a fingertip along the rim of her glass. "When we last spoke, you showed me my past lives. I've thought about them often. Do you believe those connections matter in this fight? That they carry forward?"

Takla tilted her head. "Every life leaves an imprint. Yours is unusual because I am sure you have come to realize that the thread of plasma has somehow played a part in your life again and again. Perhaps that is why you are drawn to study it still."

Maria hesitated, then asked: "If someone from Tilka were to travel to Andromeda, who could it be?"

Takla's eyes sharpened. "Assuming you mean the Andromeda Galaxy, I know of only one. It was a long time ago, but he is still alive. He is the greatest plasma scientist in our world, perhaps the galaxy, has ever known."

Maria's pulse quickened. "What is his name?"

Takla didn't answer immediately, letting the weight of her words linger. "Names have power. For now, know only that he exists. And if the time comes, you will find him. I sense that soon, he will seek you."

Maria absorbed the silence, feeling the strange gravity of what Takla implied. She glanced toward the shelves, where one book, unfinished, waited with her name written in Tilkan script.

"And Andromeda?" Maria asked suddenly, remembering something Takla had mentioned in passing before.

"Yes, Zantipitus-4 is a story that lives in the legends." Takla said softly.

"You know the name of the planet…" Maria's breath caught. The paths before her were multiplying. Alex would be returning to Earth, her own pull toward plasma, and now this Tilkan thread from Andromeda.

Takla's voice was calm, almost tender. "Every chapter leads to another, Maria, but the choice of which page to turn… that is yours."

"How would I find this scientist, Takla?"

"For that, you must travel to Tilka 7."

Maria stood, "I am certain you are right. Thank you, Takla."

Takla walked Maria to the door. "The weight and balance of love and the future of the galaxy are on you, Maria Perez. Your decision is not an easy one, and I wish you well on your road ahead."

Maria tilted her head and studied Takla as she considered her words.

"Your connection to Alex seems like love, but it is different. It is more complex and built on a different kind of energy."

"I don't understand," Maria was shaking her head.

"In time, it will make sense Maria."

As she stepped out of Takla's wooden dwelling, the twilight air of Pronimos greeted her with the cool scent of rain-soaked stone and flowering trees. She turned down a quiet path and decided to walk home through the public parks of the old quarter.

Her thoughts pressed in from every side.

She wanted Alex but now knew that opportunity had now passed. That truth beat steady in her chest like a drum. Takla believed they had crossed centuries of separation, lived and died in overlapping lifetimes, only to meet again here, in this fragile present. Of course that was the story told by an old mystic, and far from the main streets of science.

Maria knew Alex, understood his drive and his relentless determination. He wasn't ready for her, not in the way she needed. Paula was the love of a lifetime and even after nearly four years, his wounds were still too fresh. He needed to love someone else for a time, before he could meet her fully.

But the attraction they felt was insignificant compared to the weight of the war. Alex was too important. He carried skills no one else had, science, engineering, tunneling, and creativity. Alex possessed the kind of mind that could make the difference between survival and extinction. She couldn't become the reason he slowed down. Not now. Not when every hour mattered.

But Maria was beginning to see that all this human analysis of love and attraction was perhaps wrong.

Her footsteps carried her deeper into the park, past couples sitting beneath the glowing vines, past children chasing glowing orbs that drifted like fireflies. As she stopped and watched, a part of her wondered why the universe would bring them together but not allow them the peace of a relationship.

Takla's words echoed in her ears… *the greatest plasma scientist our galaxy has ever known.*

Something in her, deeper than logic or reason, told her she needed to find that scientist. The mystery of plasma, the phenomenon that haunted her dreams and called to her across lifetimes, was bound up with this unknown Tilkan.

It felt less like a choice and more like inescapable gravity.

Maria pressed her hand to the rough bark of a tree, closing her eyes. She wanted Alex. She wanted to be at his side, to fight, to love, to live. But another, more powerful truth cut through the longing: if she went with him now, she would only weaken him. She had been the one constant in his life since Paula's death. She had avoided intimacy at every reasonable opportunity, and perhaps that was a mistake.

But above all of the human emotions, if she went to Tilka, she might uncover knowledge that could save them all.

Her eyes opened, fixed on the horizon where one of the moons hung midway above the skyline. The night air carried the faint music of a street performer somewhere in the distance.

Maria drew a long, steadying breath. She wasn't ready to tell Alex yet. But in her heart, she already knew the path she would take.

⚬⚬⚬⚬ ∞ ⚬⚬⚬⚬

Only a few voices drifted from the bar at The Spiral Tap, and the old holo-projector on the wall cycled through faint, grainy images of happy and historic Pronimos events. Alex and Maria sat across from each other at their usual booth, appreciating the same worn leather they had returned to so many times before.

Alex held his glass but hadn't touched it. He studied her face as though trying to memorize every detail. Even though she had said nothing, he could sense something was about to change. He wished there was a way to preserve the moments with this woman who constantly took his breath away, the curve of her lips, the fire and wisdom in her eyes, and the softness behind her heart.

"So," he said finally, breaking the silence, "you've decided."

Maria nodded, her fingers circling the rim of her beer. "Yes. I'm going to Tilka 7."

Alex exhaled sharply, leaning back. "Because of your conversation with Takla?"

"Because she knows the plasma scientist that I was told about in Andromeda, and he's still alive." Maria answered. Her voice was calm, but her hands betrayed the tremor underneath. "Alex, she says he may be the greatest who ever lived. If I can find him, if I can learn from him… it could change everything. It could be the key to understanding plasma, to defending ourselves against the Daklin."

Alex's jaw tightened. "And us?"

She met his eyes, sadness filling her own. "I want to be with you. More than anything. But you're not ready, and in a much bigger sense, neither am I. You still need to find someone who can be… a bridge. Someone who doesn't know your history. You need a rebound, and for my sake, hopefully she will only be temporary." Maria was still using the same argument but realized something bigger was happening.

He flinched at the word, the corners of his mouth twisting. "That's not what I want. I wanted…" He stopped, staring at the table, voice breaking. "I hoped for more."

Maria reached across and took his hand, squeezing it firmly. "I know. And maybe someday. But right now, you're too important to the war effort. If I were with you, I'd only slow you down."

Alex swallowed hard, eyes wet. "You don't slow me down, Maria. You're part of my energy and the reason I keep going."

Her thumb brushed his knuckles, tender and deliberate. "And that's exactly why we have to part ways. If we tie ourselves together now and one of us falls, then we both do. I can't risk that. Neither can you."

They sat in silence, hands entwined, the noise of the pub fading into the background.

After a long pause, Maria added softly, "There's something else we should talk about."

"What?"

"We need to figure out what to do with Steven. I am like his mother. I see him as a son… like our son."

Alex's head lifted, sharp with worry. "What about him?"

"He should stay here on Pronimos. There's an excellent boarding program. It's safe, structured, and filled with children who will grow alongside him. And…" she hesitated, then continued, "…they can program cybernetics. Ones that look like you and me. With AI on Emily's level, sophisticated enough to act like us, respond like us. Steven would still have us… the influence of his dad, and the woman he sees as his mom. Kids need that Alex, even while their parents are away on dangerous missions saving the universe."

Alex blinked, stunned. "Cybernetics to raise my son?"

"To support him," Maria corrected gently. "To make sure he has continuity and stability, so he doesn't feel abandoned while we're off risking everything. Or worse yet, in the event that we die."

Alex leaned back, rubbing his eyes. "It feels… wrong. Artificial."

"It feels better than leaving him with nothing," Maria countered. "Better than disappearing for months or years and letting him wonder if you'll come back at all."

The logic was there, and undeniable. Still, Alex's heart ached.

Maria squeezed his hand again. "He'll have us, Alex, in every way that matters, and when we return, he'll still know us and that we fought for a future worth living in."

Alex looked at her, eyes full of love and sorrow. "Are you in constant search of the rational path, even when it breaks my heart?"

Maria's lips trembled with a smile mixed with both warmth and grief. "Well, Don Quixote, you always chase the impossible. That's why the galaxy needs you."

They clinked their glasses one last time, the sound ringing small but final.

Neither said it aloud, but both knew that this would likely be the last beer they ever shared together.

Alex woke with a heavy heart before pre-dawn. For a moment he lay still, replaying every word from the night before.

Maria's decision echoed in his head like a drumbeat: Tilka 7.

He rubbed his eyes, sat up, and swung his legs over the edge of the bed. Logic told him to respect her choice, but his heart refused. They belonged together. Whatever paths they were meant to take, be it Earth, Tilka, plasma research, stopping Fortak, or fighting the Daklin, they could figure it out together.

"No more goodbyes," he muttered under his breath.

He grabbed his comm and started to type out a message: *We can do both. Don't leave. Wait for me.* His thumb hovered over the send key, but the words looked hollow on the screen. Too small for what he needed to say.

No. This wasn't something for text. She deserved more.

He laced up his running shoes, threw on a shirt, and jogged out into the streets of Pronimos. The air was crisp, the city alive with the first stirrings of morning. He knew the route by heart, the familiar stone paths that led to Maria's small home near the gardens.

As he turned the final corner, his pulse quickened, not from the run, but from the realization that he finally understood Maria's apprehension. He would now tell her face to face. Convince her to come to the middle ground. It was time for Alex to refuse to let her go.

But when he reached her door, the house was silent.

On the table by the entryway lay a single folded note.

Alex picked it up, his hands trembling as he read her handwriting:

Alex   —
I've left the programming to create an AI surrogate at the child

center, as we discussed. Please do the same so that Steven will have both of us there in almost every way possible under the circumstances.

By the time you read this, I'll be enroute to Tilka 7. Unfortunately, our paths must diverge here, so please don't follow me. This is the path I must take. If Takla is right, perhaps we will have yet another life.

No signature. Just Maria's name at the bottom, written with finality.

Alex stared at the words until they blurred. His chest tightened, the ache sharp and raw. He crumpled the note in his fist, walked outside, and sank onto the step outside her door, head in his hands.

Alex Durant felt powerless. It was a dizzying spiral to which he was unaccustomed.

For nearly an hour he sat there in pain, but eventually he began to put the pieces together. In a sense, Maria was right. Both of them had bigger things to do. Things that impacted the future of humanity.

When he looked up, resolve had already begun to set behind his eyes. If Maria believed she needed to walk that path alone, fine. But he wasn't done fighting. Not for Steven, not for Earth, and not for her.

No one in the galaxy was better at picking up the broken pieces and reassembling a pathway to success than Alex Durant.

He got up and walked slowly down the curved street toward the child learning center. The brightness of Pronimos' morning light continued to improve his perspective and heal the heaviness inside him. It might never completely heal, but that was common for emotional scars such as these. What Alex knew more than anything was that happiness and success did exist, but it did not come from dwelling on the mistakes of the past, he instead needed to focus on the opportunities of the future.

Steven skipped at his side, pointing at murals alive with animated birds and spacecrafts.

"Daddy, look! My teacher says tomorrow we get to fly kites in zero gravity chambers. They float forever, even upside down!"

Alex thought about the physics of what his son just said. It didn't make sense, but that would be a question for another time. He looked at his bubbly energy and curiosity which brought out a huge smile.

"That sounds amazing. What else have you been learning?"

Steven's eyes lit up. "Math puzzles that change when you get them right. And Jaro taught us a song in three languages, Pronimos, English, and one from a planet I don't know. Everyone laughs when I mess it up."

"That's part of learning," Alex chuckled. "And you already know more languages at your age than I did in college, when I was much older than you are now."

Steven beamed, clearly proud. He launched into a story about his friends building towers from shifting blocks, and how one had collapsed in a spectacular cascade. Alex realized that it was easy to let himself get lost in his son's joy.

Like every parent across countless millennia before him, Alex came to the same realization that this was what was worth fighting for. He wanted to tell Steven that he'd be leaving for Earth soon. That Maria was already gone. His throat tightened. How do you tell a child you're about to disappear again?

Instead, he crouched to Steven's level. "Hey buddy, your teachers here sound pretty great."

"They are! But why is mommy not with you?"

Alex hesitated, then forced warmth into his voice. "You'll see her. In your own way." He took Steven's hand and stood. "Go back and play with your friends while I check on something."

Inside the adjoining wing, technicians were finalizing the surrogate AI that Maria had arranged. At first glance, Alex froze.

The figure sitting quietly in the chair looked up and his breath caught. The cybernetic Maria had the same height, the same soulful eyes, the familiar tilt of her head, and even the faint smile that used to come just before one of her teasing remarks.

"Alex," cybernetic Maria said, voice low, warm, and achingly familiar. "Steven will need stability. I will provide it."

He asked a few questions and listened to her perfect answers, and he circled slowly, studying every detail. "You… you even move your hands like she does."

The AI smiled faintly. "I am not a perfect rendition of Maria, but close enough. Mostly, I was designed for Steven's comfort."

He then looked over at the other, motionless cybernetic sitting in a corner chair. He felt like he was looking in the mirror. He thought that he had seen enough so that he felt this was a reasonable solution.

He nodded at the technician who handed him a tool to provide the neurological link that would utilize P-Link. Alex sat and drank a cup of water for the next 22 minutes as the link transferred memories and data from his mind to the cybernetic Alex.

When it was done, the cybernetic stood and walked over to Alex, "Hello, human me." Then it promptly turned to cybernetic Maria, "Shall we go meet our son?"

Alex staggered back, shaken by how real they seemed. "Spooky," he whispered to himself.

The technician motioned for Alex to step into a room that had a one-way mirror so he could observe when Steven was led into the room.

Steven ran in and tugged at Cybernetic Alex's sleeve, "Daddy, can I show you my kite trick?"

"Yes, I'd love to see it, Steven."

Cyber Maria then stepped up and knelt down, "Good morning, son."

Steven ran up and hugged her, "Mommy, can you come with dad and me to see the kite?"

And in that moment, behind the one-way mirror with tears running down his face, Alex decided he would not tell Steven about his departure. His son was in good hands.

With that, Alex returned to Tranquility to complete the preparations before returning to Earth.

Once there, he settled into the familiar hum of Tranquility's control deck. The quiet was almost a relief after the day's tangle of emotions. Emily turned from her console, watching his face.

"I can see that something is distracting you," she observed softly.

"Maria's gone," Alex admitted. "She left for Tilka 7 this morning. I found out from a note she left at her house."

"That is unfortunate, Alex." Emily walked up and hugged him. "Are you okay?"

Alex stepped back from the hug and thought about the 29-year-old body he now possessed. "I expect we will all be living a very long time, after we defeat the Daklin, that is."

Emily studied him for a moment, "I don't understand."

He took a deep breath and exhaled slowly, "It's tough Emily, but intellectually I agree that I need to go to Earth and she needs to go to Tilka."

"No, Alex. I believe your conclusion is wrong."

"How so, Emily?"

"Maria's departure will have an impact on both of you. I have seen, and now felt, how emotions affect us in these organic bodies."

"Hah, true." Alex chuckled even though he still felt a pain deep inside.

Emily watched his eyes and tried to understand the pain he was feeling. "I suppose you could work together, but Maria is very wise when it comes to relationships. You must know that she left because you have focused on fixing something that only time can remedy. Whatever advice she gave you, I suggest you take it."

"She told me to find a rebound girlfriend, Emily," he said shaking his head. "I don't know if I can do that. She also told me to work on saving the galaxy, and even though the odds are trillions to one against success, that one I can somehow handle better."

Emily thought about his comment, and her advice. "I really don't know how to respond to that, Alex, but I do have confidence you are smart enough to figure it out."

"Uh huh," he returned to his focus on the control panel.

"Alex, I think there is something bigger, or at least bigger than you are analyzing…"

"What's that, Emily?"

"Maria sees the power of the Daklin better than anyone, but over the last few months, she has begun to shift her focus to plasma," Emily paused, waiting to see if Alex would respond, and when he didn't, she continued. "What exactly is her connection or belief here?"

"I have seen the shift as well, but honestly, I don't understand it. She is such a great scientist, and this plasma…" He paused trying to think about how to phrase it, "well, I just don't get it."

"Should we tunnel to Tilka-7?" Emily asked.

"No. Our work is on Earth, and I am certain if we show up on Tilka, Maria will be pissed."

"Pissed is one of those words I have never really understood," Emily said thoughtfully.

"Me neither."

"I have come to understand a bit about sex and its power over our human bodies, Alex."

"Excuse me?" Alex furrowed his brow wondering why Emily had changed the subject.

"Are you aware that Maria has a cybernetic companion?" Emily said flatly.

"What?" Alex leaned forward.

"Maria understands the power of hormonal attraction and chose a long time ago to not allow it to impact her decisions. She has a cybernetic companion that she has named Don Juan. She told me once that I should never allow my hormones to trick me into making big decisions that could be mistakes."

"She never told me." Alex thought about the many conversations he and Maria had, then remembered one where she had told him the last time she was with a man was around the time he had been born. It was a topic they would discuss later; she had told him…

Alex watched Emily as she interfaced with the computer. He was dumbfounded and trying to pull pieces together.

After a few minutes, Emily finished her final calculations and walked over to Alex, putting her hand on his shoulder. She had learned the art of deflection. "What about Steven?"

Alex took a breath and focused on Emily's question. "I took him to the learning center. He's happy there. He showed me the new games, his teachers, his friends." Alex paused, rubbing his temples. "And Maria left behind something else. The Cyber Team on Pronimos produced a cybernetic version of herself. One for me, too. They've been programmed with our memories and mannerisms. Steven already thinks it's… normal."

Emily's eyes softened. "You sound unsettled."

"It's spooky, Em. The AI version of Maria moves her hands the same way, tilts her head at the same angles, even uses her tone of voice.

Steven didn't blink. He just grabbed her hand like she's human, and…"

Jabari's voice came from the doorway where he had been listening.

"Alex, I know the concept of humanity blended with cybernetics can be unsettling. But remember," he said, gesturing gently toward Emily, "you already live with someone who began as a cybernetic and now feels human in every way. I'm sure you've even admitted, in your quiet moments, that you love her, just as I do."

He wrapped an arm around Emily affectionately. Alex opened his mouth, then closed it again. "That's… different," he managed.

"Is it?" Jabari pressed gently. "Love is not about the origin of the body. It's about connections. You of all people should know that." He glanced meaningfully between Alex and Emily before stepping back.

Before Alex could respond, his P-Link buzzed alive in his head. A familiar voice filled the channel.

"Alex, it's Zander."

Alex straightened. "Zander. Finally. I've been worried. I have been trying to communicate, but my P-Link to you does not seem to be working."

"For safety," Zander explained. "Near the front, we've kept Plink connections dark. Too much risk that the Daklin could triangulate and trace them to a source."

"Wait," Alex interrupted. "What's plink?"

"Sorry. We got tired of calling it P-Link, so we shortened it to just plink."

"Noted." Alex acknowledged. "The simplicity works for me."

"Anyway," Zander continued, "I tried Maria and when she did not respond, I learned that she left and headed to Tilka 7. She's always three steps ahead when it comes to caution. I did read the briefing you filed on the trip to Andromeda. Wow!"

"I have an encrypted technical file, Zander. Let me know the best way to get it to you. Next time you're on Pronimos, there are some significant updates to our ship design," Alex responded.

"Okay, Alex. I will send over an encrypted portal for the files."

"And you," Alex started. "Where are you now?"

"Lyra and I are heading back to Pronimos. The war effort needs reinforcement, and Pronimos has become the hub. We are not cut out for the stress and tactical decision making required on the front, but Megan is doing astonishing work there. She's been collapsing Daklin tunnels, leading real battles, and even training new recruits while fighting. She's showing them tactics no one has ever seen before."

"Believe it or not, I knew about Megan's victories," Alex felt a swell of pride. "That sounds like her. Brilliant, fearless… always pushing."

"She is exceeding everyone's expectations," Zander agreed. "But Alex… what about you? What's next on your strategic plan?"

Alex hesitated. "I'm heading to Earth. That's where I can make the biggest difference. We need to understand why and how Earth bounced that energy burst from that Daklin planet killer. I am certain the Daklin will come again, and next time, maybe Earth won't survive."

"I thought it had something to do with the plasma," Zander's reply was slightly surprised.

"I've run hundreds of simulations based on what I know about plasma, and none of them have an impact on the Daklin energy burst. I think you know that Maria believes the plasma are some kind of life form… but I just can't wrap my head around that, Zander."

"You don't have to do that on Earth, Dad."

Alex briefly thought to protest Zander calling him dad but realized the reasons for that had long since passed when they left Earth. "You are correct, *son*," he emphasized, "but there's something else…"

"What?" Zander could hear the ominous tone in his voice.

"A Daklin scientist named Fortak survived the destruction of the Daklin ship." Alex started "He used T-Portal to travel to Earth before the ship exploded."

"That can't be right," Zander started. "The Daklin ship was in L-5. That's, what, 20 million miles from Earth?"

"Well, more like 19 million, but yes." Alex corrected.

"We designed that thing for short hops. Thousands of miles, not millions." Zander was doing mental calculations while pulling up the original design plans for T-Portal.

"It's a testament to your engineering, son"

"Saving an evil Daklin scientist is not the kind of testament that makes me happy. So, what now?"

"Now, I go to Earth and try to make sure he does not complete his mission of getting the tech back to the empire." Alex answered. "You're welcome to join us."

"This is a mission for you, Dad. On Pronimos, I can contribute directly to the war. The tunnels, the weapons, the recruits, and the enhancements you'll be sending to me. We need engineers and strategists there. That mission on Earth is important, but I am not qualified for what you are going to do there. In the big picture, I think Pronimos is where I belong."

The two men sat in the silence of the Plink for a long breath, the weight of diverging paths heavy between them.

Finally, Alex spoke. "Then we must each do our part. Just promise me that you and Lyra stay alive."

"Of course, Dad, but I don't think we'll be in danger on Pronimos," Zander countered. "Good luck finding the answers and stopping that mess on Earth."

"You've got it." Alex trailed off. It occurred to him there was a real chance, every time he spoke with anyone, that it could be the last time… "Oh, one more thing, Zander. You may have gleaned this from the reports, but we have a new member of the team."

"I did see that," Zander answered. "Jabari Minja from Tanzania."

"Well, there's a bit more to the story," Alex felt a smile and a bit of happiness that momentarily eclipsed the pain of Maria's departure. "Jabari and Emily are a couple."

Zander punched Emily into the Plink thread, "Congratulations, Emily!" Zander, more than anyone except Alex, was connected to Emily. As a young child growing up on EtaKatz, there were times when Emily was Zanders best friend and confidant. She had even played a role in helping him connect to Lyra.

"It is a wonderful thing, Zander," Emily pulled Jabari close. "I am learning about hormones, emotions, and a level of happiness I could not have imagined when I was pure silicone and logic gates."

"I look forward to meeting Jabari, Emily. Take care of Dad, please."

After a bit more pleasantries the Plink connection ended, leaving only the low hum of Tranquility's systems.

Emily touched Alex's arm gently. "Everything is ready for departure, Alex."

Alex nodded. "Funny, I don't even know where Pronimos is, Emily."

"We are 13,200 light years from Earth, Alex. It will take us 31 hours and 14 minutes to reach Earth."

Alex blinked, doing the math. "We will be covering over 400 light years per hour?"

"Yes Alex, but that is a snail pace compared to what we did in the intergalactic bridge."

"I know, but I am betting that Tranquility is probably the fastest ship in the galaxy. That is quite a title," he smiled.

13

Return to Earth

Tranquility emerged from the tachyon tunnel on the back side of the Moon.

Alex leaned forward in his seat; eyes fixed on the monitors. "Emily, will our shields prevent detection from external scans?"

"Very clever Alex, I can tune them to do exactly that."

"Perfect. Once that's done, let's come around to the Earth facing side and see what we can learn."

"Shield tuning is ready," Emily replied, her voice steady. "Tunneling to Earth side."

In a fraction of a second, Tranquility popped into the tunnel, then out again.

"Earth is magnificent," Jabari spoke first, spellbound by the view of Earth.

"No matter how many times I've seen this view, it always has the same impact on me," Alex was transfixed on the blue sphere he called home.

"No signs of Daklin warships in local space." Emily reported. She glanced up at the image of the Earth but did not feel what Alex and Jabari expressed.

Jabari gave a low whistle as the gray arc of the Moon rolled beneath them. "Feels strange being back here. Growing up, I heard tales, but I never imagined my life would take me to another galaxy. As spectacular as that journey was, the Earth above, and the Moon below is so much more beautiful."

"Alex," Emily motioned, "Take a look at that."

On the near edge of Mare Moscoviense, a lattice of unnatural light glowed faintly, almost invisible against the colorless lunar surface. Emily zoomed in and found a shimmering hexagonal frame of energy, anchored by structures half-buried in regolith. Around it was a small outpost.

"They have a colony on the Moon," Jabari exclaimed.

Alex's jaw tightened. "Or base. This kind of acceleration only happened because Fortak's been busy."

Emily swiveled toward him, her eyes catching the faint starlight. "He is not merely experimenting. He is deploying portals. She zoomed in on a T-Portal location in lunar orbit. That orbital aperture is stable."

"Meaning he's solved half the problem already," Jabari said grimly. "If he connects that system to the Daklin tunnel grid, Earth won't stand a chance. They'll have a permanent gate here."

Alex exhaled slowly. "And once the Daklin know humans can stabilize portals, they'll duplicate the technology and return with a vengeance and everything they've got."

The three of them stared at the glowing scars of Fortak's work.

Finally, Emily broke the silence. "Alex, we need intelligence. Conjecture will not suffice."

"Agreed." Alex tapped the console. "Program a tunnel to our old station in Greenland. We should be able to work in obscurity from there. And if Fortak is working with Pascal's network, we'll know pretty quickly."

"Program is complete, Alex," Emily said after she had entered the location.

Alex raised an eyebrow. "Back to the ice," then managed a thin smile. "Somehow it feels fitting. First place the Daklin nearly caught us. We know Fortak is in communication with the empire and building a bridge, and Polonius has told us we have about 4 years before their arrival."

Emily's voice softened, almost human. "Alex… are you prepared for the possibility that Fortak has already progressed beyond our capability of stopping him?"

Alex set his jaw. "I accept that possibility, but let's learn what he's built, and take it from there."

The Tranquility's hum deepened as the tunnel drive engaged. A halo of golden light encircled around the ship, then folded space like a curtain.

Alex placed his hand on the console, his eyes on the screen where the Moon had disappeared into darkness behind them. "Let's go find some answers."

The ship vanished from lunar orbit, leaving Fortak's silent portals gleaming like traps set in the void.

Tranquility exited the tunnel inside the old military base that Alex had purchased several years ago as a hideout from the Daklin. Inside, the frozen corridors smelled of dust and stale oxygen. Alex brushed frost from the console and powered up the old systems. Screens flickered, and warm air began to trickle into the outpost.

Emily logged on to the interface from inside Tranquility. "Local systems online. Battery reserves were still at thirty-seven percent, but we'll get them recharged with the interconnect to Tranquility power supply."

"How long can we run this outpost connected to Tranquility?" Jabari asked.

"Pretty much, forever," Alex answered with pride. "Fact is, we generate enough power on this baby to run most of Fort Worth for *years*."

Once the station was warm enough, Alex put on a jacket and wandered through to his old quarters. There was a photo of Steven still sitting on his old desk, which got him thinking. "Emily… is it possible to Plink connect with surrogate-Alex, you know, the cybernetic one on Pronimos?"

Jabari frowned. "You're a patient man, Alex. It will take a few thousand years for your hello to get to him at the speed of light."

Emily looked at Jabari, surprised he was not aware of how Plink worked. "Actually, we Plink through the tunnel network. It's instantaneous."

"And connecting into my surrogate?" Alex reiterated.

"Are you talking about just seeing through his eyes, or do you want control and sensory inputs?" Emily thought about the significant difference between the pathways.

Alex considered her questions. "I was just thinking about being able to see through the eyes, talk and listen, but touch would be amazing. I cannot even imagine having sensory capabilities. Anyway, I just miss the little guy and want to have regular connections to keep up with what he's experiencing."

"But your surrogate is there," Jabari started, "Does Steven know that's not you?"

"No, not for now, Steven just thinks I am spending time with him every day."

Emily began assembling code, her fingers moving like a pianist across the interface. "I will construct the handshake protocol. It may take time. Please recognize that surrogate-Alex is probably sentient, like me."

Alex tilted his head quizzically.

"Let me put it this way," Emily started, "I love you, but it might be a bit creepy to have you controlling my limbs, looking through my eyes, and listening with my ears."

"Ohhh. I hadn't really thought about it that way. Should I drop it?" Alex winced.

"Let me work on it, Alex. I think it is doable, and I will check with the surrogate to see his perspective."

"Okay. Thank you." Alex turned back to the screen and started scanning the news archives.

One report stood out, dated six months earlier. *Accident during lunar transport. CEO Maillew Pascal killed instantly when his personal portal destabilized mid-jump.*

Alex exhaled sharply. "Pascal's gone."

Emily leaned over his shoulder. "So, who's running T-Portal now?"

Alex pulled up the shareholder records. His blood ran cold. "Fortak. He bought enough equity to take control. He's the new CEO."

Emily glanced back without pausing her work. "Strategically… that is catastrophic."

Scrolling further, Alex saw plans for orbital portals under construction at L-4 and L-5, the Earth-Moon Lagrange points. Beyond that, proposals to extend the chain to Mars, then Jupiter, and on to the stars.

"They're testing distance," Alex muttered. "First the Moon. Now Mars, which is sometimes as close as 35 million miles, other times over 200 million, when it's on the far side of the Sun."

He paused, eyes narrowing. "But that's not the real game."

"What's the real game?" Jabari asked.

Alex straightened, eyes hard. "Two things, I believe. Fortak's not building a transport company. He's building a bridge back to the Daklin Empire. The only limitation is that T-Portal requires an aperture on both ends. My guess is he's working to find a way around that…" He trailed off, picturing the empire pouring through the void.

Jabari rubbed his jaw. "Then Earth becomes a forward operating base. And we'll be the ones who opened the door. What's the second?"

"The second is already well underway. T-Portal has become the transport tool for almost everything on the planet. Fortak controls how and when almost everything moves." Alex got chills as he considered the implications of that much power.

∘ ∘ ∘ ∘ ∞ ∘ ∘ ∘ ∘

The next morning, Jabari found Alex in the galley sipping on a cup of coffee.

"Would you be okay if Emily and I took a few days and visited my home in Tanzania?" Jabari asked.

Alex almost choked on his coffee. "Uhhh."

"I am sorry, Alex. I did not realize this would be an issue."

"It's okay. I was just surprised by the question. Could you tell me a bit more about why you're thinking of taking this trip?"

"The world is changing, Alex. Fast. I am in love with Emily, and I want her to see the country where I was raised before it changes much more."

"That makes sense, Jabari. I just think it would be unsafe to travel in Tranquility, but we have a few tunneling backpacks. In addition, we should have Emily install a Plink in you so all three of us can be connected. My guess is that Fortak has a net out looking for Zander, Megan, Mark, and me."

"I will do that. Will you be okay alone for a few days?"

"The timing is perfect, Jabari," Alex answered. "I was thinking about doing a bit of sleuthing in Dallas."

After Jabari left the bridge, Alex leaned back into the pilot's chair of Tranquility, opening his mind to the familiar pull of the Plink.

"Zander?" he spoke.

"Dad! How are things on Earth?"

"Fortak has built out T-Portal to the point where almost all commerce uses it. In addition, he has built a small base on the Moon, and a station in L-4 and L-5. Next goal is Mars."

"Wait, what happened to my favorite asshole, Pascal?" Zander asked.

"I read that he died in some kind of accident on the Moon, Zander."

"Oh no," A part of Zander was sorry he had just called Pascal an asshole. "So, he died on the Moon?"

"That's my understanding," Alex pulled up the article, which he had only scanned before. "Zander, I need to know if you have anyone left at T-Portal that you trust."

"Hmmm, let me think about that," Zander paused going through a list of the old engineers in his head. "I am sure Fortak and the Daklins are watching everything. There is one man, if he's still there, named Art Adamez. He's a Marine veteran, an engineer, and a patriot with solid ethics. If there's anyone who hasn't sold his soul to Fortak, it's Art."

"Adamez," Alex repeated. "How do I reach him without painting a target on my back, or his?"

"You can't just call him," Zander said. "I'm sure Fortak is monitoring everything. Use the brotherhood. Marines always recognize and stick with their own. Tell him you're reaching out as a friend of one of his old squad mates. That should buy you a meeting, but keep it face-to-face, somewhere ordinary. No electronics."

"Yep," Alex chuckled. "You're getting pretty adept at this stuff, son."

"One more thing," Zander added. "Assuming Fortak has put an international watch out for both of us, and Adamez recognizes you, he'll know the stakes. Be careful."

The next afternoon, Alex used a tunneling backpack and slipped into an uptown Dallas coffee shop. He ordered black coffee, chose a corner table, and waited.

The door opened. A stocky Hispanic man in his forties with a squared jaw and steady brown eyes scanned the room, then walked directly to Alex's table. "Durant?"

Alex felt a cold weight settle in his stomach. He hadn't given a name. He had his backpack already programmed for a quick escape, but his visual scan of the surroundings suggested that the man was alone. "Art Adamez, I presume?"

Adamez sat without invitation. "I recognize you, but you are younger than I expected. Pictures of you have been circulated all over the net. Fortak's people are hunting you, and Zander. But Zander's dead, right?"

"I look young for my age," Alex deflected the comment, "and I can't comment on Zander."

Adamez nodded, thinking about how Alex had responded. "Okay, I get it, but if Zander did send you, then I know you can be trusted."

Alex studied him for a moment, then leaned forward. "It's interesting that you are concerned with whether *I* can be trusted, but just so you know, Zander is my son."

"Son?" Adamez was perplexed. "How's that possible? You look younger than him."

"A story for another time. How did you know it would be me, meeting here?"

"I didn't know, but these are dangerous times. Things are happening that go way beyond what the Marines or engineering school trained me to understand. I did a little sleuthing after I got the request for this meeting. Not sure why but thought it might involve Zander somehow."

Alex nodded agreement, "I came because I need the truth about what Fortak is planning with T-Portal."

Adamez's eyes flicked toward the window before locking back on Alex. "Unfortunately, the truth will keep you up at night. Fortak isn't just expanding T-Portal for commerce. He's working on integration with population grids that will control transport, power, supply chains, and just about anything else. Every nation and city have become dependent. No one knows how to build this stuff. Hell, I am the chief engineer, and even I don't really know how it works."

Alex just nodded.

Adamez continued, "The colonies and bases on the Moon are dependent on the tech. Fortak can get anything he wants, and all he has to do to maintain an iron grip, is control the gates."

"Control the gates…" Alex muttered. "And the people follow."

"Exactly," Adamez said grimly. "He's turning the portals into a power grab. Imagine if every bridge, every airport, and every supply line ran through one corporation, through one man. Fortak could strand whole cities, starve nations, or move armies without anyone stopping him."

Alex felt the weight of the Daklin empire settle on his shoulders. "Do you know what he really is, Art? Do you know who you're dealing with?"

Adamez hesitated. "I know that he's Daklin, and all the other stuff, well, I've wondered. Fortak isn't like anyone I've met. Ruthless, yes, but also… patient and sometimes kind. I've asked myself a hundred times what drives a man like that. So, tell me, Alex. Do you know?"

Alex met his gaze, then shook his head slightly. "Not everything can be said yet, but I'll tell you this: if Fortak wins, Earth becomes something you won't recognize. …*if* it survives at all."

"Understood, sir. How can I help you stop him?"

"I need a patriot on the inside," Alex answered, knowing this was the critical ask of Art.

Adamez extended his hand across the table. "Then we're in this together. Just know, once we start down this path, there's no going back."

The two men clasped hands firmly.

"I crossed that line a long time ago," Alex responded, appreciating the strong handshake and eye contact Art Adamez used. He definitely concurred with Zander's belief that this man could be trusted.

While in Dallas, Alex decided to get dinner at Mexican Sugar, his favorite Mexican restaurant. Earlier, Adamez had pointed out something he had taken for granted. Fortak was looking for the version of Alex Durant who was in his forties, weathered and war-torn, not a seemingly 29-year-old man in his prime. He could use that to provide a little bit of cover.

Emily's voice suddenly slipped into Alex's Plink as he sat, still turning over Adamez's words while enjoying his chips and salsa.

"Alex, I have some good news for you."

"What's that, Emily?"

"I've managed to establish a secure channel into the surrogate, and he has agreed to allow you to join him for visits to the facility where Steven is enrolled. You'll be able to see him, hear him, and interact as if you were there."

Alex's chest tightened. "So, you're telling me I can… be with him?"

"Almost," she corrected. "You won't be able to feel, like touch, if you pick him up. Just eyes and ears."

"So, you've mastered sight and sound, but not touch and smell?"

"Correct. In addition, I've masked your access. No one will trace it. Would you like me to open the connection?"

He swallowed the lump in his throat. "Yes. Give me a few minutes. I am in a restaurant in Dallas and need to pay my bill and then return to Greenland."

Eight minutes later, the world shimmered, then resolved into the familiar surroundings of the child learning center on Pronimos. His surrogate moved as he willed it through Plink. A group of children were clustered around a floating puzzle sphere that shifted colors with each touch.

Steven looked up. "Daddy!" He ran to him, laughing, and wrapped his small arms around the surrogate's waist.

Alex knelt, voice breaking slightly. "Hey, champ. How are you?"

"Good! My new friends, Jek and Taro, are teaching me this color game. They're fast, but I scored the last point!"

Alex chuckled. "Of course you did. You've always been good at puzzles."

Steven's grin lit up the room. He dragged Alex back toward the group, and together they worked the glowing sphere, passing it back and forth while the children shouted strategies. For a few precious minutes, Alex could forget Fortak, the portals, and the looming shadow of the Daklin. He was just a dad again.

From across the room, Maria's surrogate stood watching. Alex's heart skipped a beat. She looked almost exactly as he remembered her: warm eyes, calm expression, even the tilt of her head when she studied him.

"Hello, Alex," the Maria-surrogate said gently.

He forced a smile. "Hello." He wondered if surrogate-Maria knew that she was speaking with the real him.

"I see Steven has shown you his new favorite game," the surrogate added.

Alex's throat tightened. He knew she was code, AI mimicking Marias patterns, but hearing her voice, even an echo of it, made the absence worse. For a long moment he simply studied her face, imagining the real Maria light-years away, and well beyond his reach.

Steven tugged his sleeve. "Daddy, did you see me? I solved it faster than Jek!"

Alex blinked back the ache. "I saw. You were brilliant."

Later, when the surrogate session ended, Alex leaned back into his chair aboard Tranquility in the Greenland base. The emptiness of the ship pressed around him. He opened his Plink.

"Zander?"

"I'm here," Zander's voice answered.

"I met with Art Adamez. He's sharp and disciplined. He believes Fortak is consolidating control and turning T-Portal into a tool for domination. He's worried, but I think he's with us."

"Adamez is a marine and a patriot Dad," Zander said. "If he said he's with us, then I trust he is, and we'll need someone on the inside."

Alex hesitated. "And Maria? Any word?"

Zander's reply was quiet. "Nothing. No comms, no Plink, no indirect messages. She's gone dark, Alex. Either by choice… or necessity."

Alex closed his eyes. "That's what I feared."

"I know it hurts," Zander added, "but she's strong. If she cut her link, she had a reason. You have to trust that."

Alex exhaled slowly. "Yeah. I'm sure you're right, but it doesn't make the silence any easier."

"Wait, is there something going on between you and Maria, Dad?" Zander thought about the connection he had always observed but considered was just a great friendship.

"It's complicated son, but not really."

A few hours later, exhaustion finally pulled Alex under. For the first time in days, he slept deeply, his body slack in the dim cabin of Tranquility. But a full night's rest was not in the cards.

The sharp pulse of the Plink cut through the haze.

Alex stirred, rubbed his eyes, and sat up. "Zander? It's the middle of the night."

"Dad, I know it's late on Earth, but I just got some bad news…"

Alex rubbed his eyes and sat up, getting his focus. "What is it?"

"I just got word that Megan's ship is gone."

Alex froze. "Gone? What do you mean, gone?"

"Destroyed. Daklin comms are lit up across half the sector. They're celebrating her death like it's some kind of festival." Zander's tone was grim. "But the rumor is, before she went down, she took out several Daklin cruisers. Some people are saying a dozen or more, but no one knows for sure."

Alex's jaw tightened. "That sounds like her. If the Daklin are crowing about it, she must've done some real damage."

"I've scoured everything I can reach," Zander continued. "I suspect she pulled it off using the self-destruct on Singularity. What I do know is, before the attack, she'd been planning to drop Mark at Gamma Halden 3."

Alex thought about it while trying to control the pain of losing Megan. "Any idea why Mark was going to Gamma Halden?"

"Not certain, Dad, but I do know their relationship wasn't doing well."

Alex shook his head slowly. He sensed something in his gut. "I don't believe it. Not Megan. She's survived worse than anyone. That woman is always prepared, and if there's one person who can walk away from an exploding ship, it's her."

"Dad," Zander's voice dropped, heavy. "Every indicator says she's gone. The Daklin are certain. Their ships tracked the explosion. There's nothing but debris."

Alex pressed his fists into his eyes. "Indicators can be wrong. I just don't believe she's dead. Not until I see proof."

A long silence stretched between them. Finally, Zander said, "I want to believe that too. But we need to prepare for the possibility that we've lost her."

Alex stared at the ceiling of his cabin, a hollow ache spreading in his chest. "Prepare if you have to. But I'm telling you, Zander, I'll bet my life that Megan Hoglund is still out there."

Alex was awake, staring at the ceiling. Sleep was gone. He opened the Plink. "Emily?"

Her voice was instant, warm, and steady. "Yes, Alex?"

He took a deep breath. "I just heard from Zander. Megan's ship was destroyed. The Daklin are celebrating it, but there's word she took out several of theirs before the end. I don't buy that she's gone. I'm leaving for Gamma Halden 3 in the morning. If you want to come, get back here before then."

"As in a few hours from now?" Emily looked at Jabari, who was asleep. He had plans to take her to Moshi, then on safari to Ngorongoro Crater.

"No. Tomorrow. I have a few things I need to get done. Spend a relaxing day in Africa, then meet me at the Greenland base in 29 hours."

She was silent for a beat, then replied. "Of course I'm coming. You don't have to ask."

"Good. Get yourself fully charged. Tomorrow's going to be a long day."

He closed the Plink, then pulled out a cellphone to text Adamez. "Adamez?"

"Here," he texted back.

"Thanks for earlier. Something's come up and I need to see you again. Same coffee shop, mid-morning?"

"Copy that."

"See you there." Alex set the cellphone down and sat in the dark room, deep in his thoughts, until he eventually got up and paced the cabin.

Megan. Gamma Halden 3. Fortak. Too many threads pulling in opposite directions.

If Megan was alive, she was probably in trouble and needed him. He couldn't ignore his gut on this one, but Earth was sliding deeper under Fortak's thumb every day. T-Portal wasn't just a transport tool anymore. It had become a method for global control. He needed leverage, something disruptive.

His mind circled the problem, then it stopped cold. *An EMP.*

Dallas was the nerve center of T-Portal's data and computer systems. One well-placed pulse could fry servers, cut communications, and force resets worldwide. It wouldn't kill the people or stop the company, but it would slow Fortak. It would buy time.

The idea was reckless, risky, and definitely criminal. It would create chaos in his hometown, but it might work.

Later that morning, Art Adamez was already at their corner table when Alex walked in. Black coffee was cooling between them.

"Adamez," Alex greeted.

"Durant."

"There's been an emergency, and I have to leave," Alex leaned in. "I've been thinking. What if we took a shot at T-Portal's data core? An EMP near Dallas. It wouldn't end Fortak, but it might cripple him long enough, so people and governments have the opportunity to push back."

Adamez studied him. "That's a lot of information, Durant. Leave to where? Where will the EMP come from? Don't they only come from atomic bombs?"

"I have the ability, on my ship, to produce a localized electromagnetic pulse. No bombs, no explosions, but virtually all of the electronics in the DFW area would be fried."

"Ship?" Adamez rubbed his chin and started shaking his head. "I suppose it could work, but it's like an attack on our own soil. I just don't know…"

"Sure. It's bold and it's messy, but it hits him where he's weakest. He is totally dependent on Earth's technology. This will rattle him, slow him down, and maybe make him paranoid."

"This is insane, and on its face, it appears to be against the oath I took as a Marine, but under the surface, it makes sense," Adamez said with a bit of a frown.

Alex studied Adamez and realized he deserved more information. "There's a lot more, Adamez."

"Yes," he was nodding, then took a sip of his coffee. "That much I have concluded."

For the next 15 minutes, Alex briefed Adamez on the Daklin Empire, the real purpose of the Daklin ship that had exploded in L-5, and why he was heading to Gamma Halden 3."

"That's a lot to swallow, Durant."

"I know." Alex watched the marine turned engineer as he silently sipped his coffee while processing the situation.

After several minutes, Adamez started to nod, "Well, how else can I help?"

Alex exhaled, leaning back. "The EMP won't stop him, or the Daklin."

"No," Adamez admitted. "But I agree that it will slow him. And slowing him matters."

Adamez sipped the last of his coffee, then dropped his voice. "One more thing you should know. Fortak's been sending packets back to the empire using RF transmission. Old-school, speed of light stuff, but it works."

Alex tensed, "Do you know what star system he's sending to?"

Adamez grimaced. "He's kept that information to himself. Until you and I chatted yesterday, I had my concerns about him, but that came with no solid evidence. I actually believe he was responsible for Pascal's death, but to be honest, I never liked Pascal. He was not an ethical man."

"While I agree with your assessment regarding Pascal, who would do anything for money, and excuse the term, *pussy*, but unfortunately, he was the lesser of two evils." Alex sat in silence, the weight of Fortak's radio communication back to the empire settling over him. When his reports reached the Daklin network, Earth's window would rapidly slam shut.

Adamez leaned forward. "Let me know how I can help."

Alex pushed his empty coffee cup aside. "Adamez, I'm headed to lunch at my favorite place. It's called Mexican Sugar. You know it?"

Adamez's eyes flickered with recognition. "Yeah. Legacy and 121, right? I've been there once or twice. Great food."

"Actually, there's a new one on Beltline just west of the Toll Road. Care to join me?" Alex stood. "My treat."

Adamez shrugged. "Sure. Why not."

The patio at Mexican Sugar buzzed with lunchtime chatter, the scent of charred peppers and fresh tortillas thick in the air. A soft Texas breeze carried laughter and clinking glasses. So many carefree people who had no idea what was really happening.

Adamez leaned back, scanning the tables. "Hard to believe we're talking about an inevitable interstellar war, while everyone else is here for fajitas and margaritas."

Alex smiled faintly. "Such is the world we live in. It's always more fragile than it looks."

When the waitress left with their order, Adamez folded his hands. "You know, I wasn't always sitting across the table from guys like you. I grew up dirt poor. My family worked the fields. We were migrants. We'd chase the seasons, picking strawberries in California, cotton in Texas, and corn in Iowa. Whatever paid enough to eat."

Alex studied him quietly.

Adamez continued. "We lived in trucks, tents, and sometimes worse. Formal schooling happened wherever I could find it. Half the time I was too tired from working to keep my eyes open in class. After I turned 18, I enlisted in the Marines. Boot camp was hard, but it was a lot easier for me than most of the others at Paris Island. Anyway, figured I'd fight for something bigger than fields."

"You did well," Alex said softly. "You are a testament to the American Dream."

"Yeah. The Corps gave me structure. I already had learned discipline from my childhood. Anyway, one of my CO's took an interest and convinced me I should take a shot at engineering school. I finished a degree while still on active duty. It's how I ended up at T-Portal. I was one of the few vets with both field and tech experience. Zander interviewed and hired me directly." He paused, eyes narrowing. "But Fortak and Pascal… Well, let's just say I stayed because the stock options will make me a very rich man."

Alex leaned forward. "Your sense about Pascal and Fortak were spot on. We have only been around on Earth for thirty thousand years while the Daklin Empire has ruled the galaxy for fifty *million* years. And that explosion in space you saw last year, that wasn't an accident. It was a Daklin ship coming to Earth to deliver a form of justice they have wielded for all that time. Their mission was simple: kill everything on Earth."

Adamez set his glass down hard. "And we somehow survived it?"

"Yes. Only by chance, or something we don't yet understand. Fortak used T-Portal to survive the destruction of his ship. Now he's turning T-Portal into a weapon for control. If he succeeds, Earth won't just be conquered, it'll enslave itself."

Adamez sat in silence for a moment, then exhaled slowly. "Hell. I had a sense he was bad, but not *that* bad."

Their food arrived, but neither touched it at first.

After a few moments, Alex broke the silence. "Art, I need people I can trust. I'm heading out on a mission that could take me off Earth for a long time. Would you like to join me?"

"Jump in some kind of ship and travel to the stars?" Adamez clarified.

"Yes."

Adamez took a bite of his fajitas and thought about the offer. He shook his head, "It's tempting, but I'll pass. I think I serve the cause better here. Texas is my home, and if Fortak is trying to build a noose around Earth, someone has to cut the rope from the inside. We probably can't beat the empire, but Texas can stop Fortak."

"Fair enough." Alex nodded. "We'll need strong hands on both fronts."

Adamez smirked. "Besides, I've had enough deployments for one lifetime. But you," he pointed his fork at Alex, "you go find what's left of your friend. The Marines have a policy to never leave a man behind."

"I appreciate that loyalty to your beliefs, Adamez. The world needs more people like you."

"Thanks. Just know, if and when Fortak slips, I'll be waiting."

Alex finished his lunch, stood, and rather than shaking Adamez's hand he embraced him. "At exactly 9:11 am tomorrow morning, I will pop out of a tunnel, initiate an EMP, and hop back into the tunnel."

Adamez considered the significance of 9:11 am. If nothing else, it would be easy to remember. "Copy that, Alex. Good luck, and I will be prepared before 9:11 tomorrow morning."

14

Gamma Halden 3

The walls of Megan's ship, Singularity, disappeared, and the world snapped back into focus with a violent jolt. Megan stumbled to her knees, chest heaving. Mark lay face-down in the grit, coughing, while Sun Tsu stood rigid, his eyes scanning the horizon.

"Report?" Megan rasped.

Sun Tsu's voice was calm, but there was a faint distortion beneath it. "We are alive. We are also somewhere on Gamma Halden 3, though I regret there was not sufficient time to discuss an optimal place for our tunnel portal."

Mark pushed himself upright, brushing dust from his jacket. "That was… farther than the packs were ever meant to go. Zander said a light year was the max distance."

"We just did three times that," Sun Tsu reported.

Megan checked the readout on her wrist. The tiny indicator glowed red. "Ninety-nine percent drain. We've got nothing left in our battery packs. One more jump isn't happening."

Mark groaned. "So, we burned everything just to get here?"

"Better than what's happening with the ship right now," Megan shot back. For a second, she remembered the passion that had been igniting between them, just minutes ago, on Singularity. Things had changed, fast.

"That would have been a fast death. What do we have now?" Mark responded with cynicism.

Megan ignored him and scanned the landscape. Sparse hills rolled into a dry basin where a cluster of buildings sat like a forgotten frontier town. "That must be the outpost."

Sun Tsu tilted his head, assessing. "It is not the outpost, Megan. This is a small town with a population under one thousand. There is law, but it is primitive. Their justice system resembles Earth's pre-industrial frontier settlements, swift and rough."

Mark squinted at the collection of low metal structures and canvas roofs. A flickering neon sign buzzed weakly over what looked like a bar. "The Wild West in space. Great. Do we at least get horses?"

"Quit being a puss," Megan muttered. She tugged at her backpack shoulder strap.

"The spaceport should be east of here, 243 kilometers," Sun Tsu added.

"We're not walking it, not with low provisions and packs this dead."

Mark tapped his own power cell and found it to be cold and dark. "Comms are gone too. We can't even ping Zander."

Megan looked at Sun Tsu. "What about you? How long can you keep operating on your current battery level?"

"I was about to charge when I detected the Daklin." The cybernetic warrior's expression was measured, "but I can consume local food for basic function. Optimal performance requires recharging every forty-eight hours. That interval is closing. Without power, I will degrade."

"Great," Mark muttered. "We're stranded, broke, and babysitting a six-foot AI who needs a power nap."

Sun Tsu regarded him evenly. "Correction. A six-foot AI who will still fight until the last electron is consumed in his power pack."

Megan smirked despite the tension. "Alright, enough. We head into that outpost, find a power source, or a ride to the spaceport. Someone here will know a way."

"I agree, we must be careful," Sun Tsu warned, "someone here may see us as prey. We cannot allow this tunneling backpack technology to be captured."

"Then let's make damn sure they see us as the hunters." Megan adjusted her pack and started toward the settlement.

Two locals leaned against a railing, eyes following the newcomers with cool calculation.

Mark muttered under his breath, "This is going to be fun."

Megan scoffed, started to say something, then stopped. She made it clear she was not happy with Mark.

The main street quieted as Megan, Mark, and Sun Tsu stepped into town. Conversations dipped, eyes followed. A pair of men with dust-worn hats leaned against a hitch rail, studying them with unreadable expressions.

Megan raised her hand in a casual wave. "Afternoon."

The men exchanged a glance, then nodded once. Suspicious, but not hostile.

Inside the settlement's general hall, which was a cross between a saloon and supply depot, a handful of townsfolk gathered around long tables. A woman with gray-streaked hair and weathered skin approached. "You're not from here."

Megan kept her tone even. "Just travelers. We're looking for a power recharge station."

The woman shook her head slowly. "Not here. Most of GH3 runs simple, by choice."

"What is GH3?" Megan broke in.

"Oh, you *really* aren't from here… Gamma Halden 3. We just call it GH3. Anyway, we don't have no high-energy grids, no portal cores. We keep it old-style. We have machines where we need them, but most of us prefer muscle, not electrons."

Mark muttered, "Great," under his breath.

The woman caught it but ignored him. "You're in luck, though. A transport's headed for the spaceport in the morning. Just over two hundred klicks east. Leaves at sun-up."

Megan leaned forward. "Transport?"

The woman's lips curved into a faint smile. "Horse-drawn with double wagons. That surprises off-worlders, but it gets us where we need to go. Reliable. No power cells to fail, no circuits to fry."

Mark groaned audibly. "You've got to be kidding. Horses?"

The woman's eyes hardened. "It's how we chose to travel on this planet. In any case, it'll take two days to get to spaceport, but it's better than walking."

Megan gave a short nod. "We'll take it. How about rooms for the night?"

The woman gestured toward a stairwell. "Half a dozen rooms open on the second floor. Pick any that's unlocked. We don't stand on ceremony here, and you can pay in credits."

Later, after they had dinner, the three of them went upstairs to see the quarters. Mark leaned against a doorframe. "Guess we should share. Save a room, keep an eye on each other, and maybe finish what we started earlier?"

Megan stared at him flatly. "I think I'll take my own."

"What? Why?" Mark was shocked.

"Because, Mark, I'm tired of listening to you complain every time something doesn't go your way, and it's pissing me off. We're in a situation where negativity gets people killed. I need quiet, and I need focus. So, you stay in your own room, and I'll stay in mine. That way we both get a good night of rest."

Mark opened his mouth, then closed it, stung. "Fine," he muttered, retreating into the room across the hall.

Sun Tsu lingered, studying her. "You are distancing yourself from him again."

Megan tossed her pack to the bed. "I'm leading, he's whining. If he can't adapt, he won't last out here, or worse, he'll get us all killed."

Sun Tsu inclined his head. "Survival favors those who adjust quickly. But remember, strength also lies in unity."

She sighed, hand on the door of her room. "Perhaps, but unity requires two people pulling in the same direction. Right now, he's dead weight, and I'm sure as hell not in the mood to have sex with him."

Watching her with quiet, calculating eyes, Sun Tsu did not reply. "I will rest and let the mitochondria recharge me as much as possible. It is not the optimal way to build energy, but it will work for now."

∘∘∘∘ ∞ ∘∘∘∘

The morning air was crisp and dry as Megan, Mark, and Sun Tsu climbed into the rear carriage of the coach. Six horses stamped and snorted, their harnesses creaking as the coachman clicked the reins. Dust rose as the vehicle lurched forward.

The nine passengers settled into uneasy silence. Farmers, traders, and two women with baskets of herbs, faces lined with the simple, but hard life of GH3. Megan kept her eyes forward, watching the terrain slide past. She knew the technology existed to keep people young, but the citizens of this planet seemingly preferred to age.

Less than four hours into the journey, the coach stopped abruptly. The horses tossed their heads, restless. At first Megan thought maybe it was a bathroom break, but then she tensed. "Something's wrong."

She slid the small window open. Six figures blocked the trail. Their obsidian armor caught the sunlight, cruel edges glinting. They were Daklin soldiers.

The coachman's hand hovered near his whip, but the lead soldier barked something guttural. The man froze.

"We don't want no trouble, sir," the coachman held his hands up, palms facing the soldiers.

"Good," the soldier pulled out a long knife, quickly slitting the coachman's throat, followed by each of the six horses.

Megan calculated as she watched the Daklin incivility and lack of respect for life. There was only one way out of this. She looked at Sun Tsu, kicked the door open and dropped to the ground.

Sun Tsu followed, his movements fluid, precise.

Mark hesitated, pale.

The Daklin advanced. They had weapons but seemed intent on killing with their bare hands.

Megan's voice was steel. "Everyone on board, run! Now!"

She studied the soldiers. It was the first time to come face-to-face with Daklin. Perhaps they were trained fighters, but Megan was confident and pristinely trained. Out of the corner of her eye, she saw as the farmers bolted, dragging the women with them into the brush.

The first Daklin lunged with a confident smile. He was unprepared for what would happen next.

Megan sidestepped, slammed her elbow into his throat, then ripped his blade from his hand and drove it back under his ribs. He dropped in a choking gurgle, a look of shock on his face.

Beside her, Sun Tsu met two soldiers head-on. His strikes were like thunder. He hit with an elbow that shattered armor, a kick that snapped bone. He ripped the knife from one Daklin and buried it in his chest, then spun and drove the blade into another's neck. Both collapsed.

But Sun Tsu staggered. The light in his eyes flickered. He dropped to one knee. "My energy is… depleted…" His body toppled, inert, like a fallen statue. He had said he would fight to the last electron in his battery and had done exactly that.

"Damn it!" Megan screamed, seeing it was now up to her alone.

The remaining three soldiers pressed forward. One circled, another moved straight at her. She met them with a roar, her knife flashing. One went down with his throat cut, but the last two began to coordinate, driving her backward.

"Megan!" Mark's voice was thin, desperate that she would soon fall.

She blocked a strike, slammed a fist into a soldier's jaw. But the other Daklin then slid in from the side. A long knife gleamed as he raised it to drive through her chest. She knew this was the end.

For the first time, Mark dug deep and found his ounce of courage. He could not let Megan die. He lunged from the brush, lifting a rock the size of his head, and smashed it down on the Daklin's skull with a wet crack.

The soldier stumbled, then turned, rage twisting his broken face. He plunged the knife into Mark's chest, straight to the heart, before collapsing dead at his feet.

"NO!" Megan cut down the final Daklin with a savage strike, then dropped to her knees beside Mark.

Blood bubbled at his lips. His eyes locked onto hers.

"Megan…" He coughed, weak. "I love you."

She gripped his hand, tears already streaming. "Don't you dare leave me. Don't you…"

But the light was already gone. His hand went limp. His chest stilled.

Megan bowed over him, sobbing. The world blurred through her tears. "Oh God, Mark… I treated you like shit last night. I pushed you away. You were trying. You were always trying."

She pressed her forehead to his, shaking. "I did love you, Mark, and now I'll never have the chance to tell you, to set this right."

The dust carried away the sounds of fleeing passengers, leaving only silence, the bodies of the Daklin, and Megan's broken cries.

She clutched Mark's body against her chest, rocking. "You saved me, and I let you die thinking you were nothing to me."

Her tears stained his shirt, mingling with the blood. "I'll carry your memory, Mark. I swear it."

After a while, Megan forced herself to get up to survey the situation.

She checked on Sun Tsu. Somewhere inside the mitochondria of his body, the Krebs Cycle was producing energy. Her hands trembled as she pulled a strip of bread from her pack. "Come on, Sun Tsu… you said you can use food. Take it."

She pressed it to his lips. Slowly, almost imperceptibly, his systems stirred. The faint hum of processors flickered back online. He chewed mechanically, and after a few minutes, opened his eyes.

"Recovery initiated," he said, his voice hollow, slow. "Functionality at… two percent." He smiled ever so lightly, "you survived."

Megan wiped at her face with the back of her sleeve. "I did, but Mark is dead."

"I'm sorry," he whispered.

She scanned the battlefield, eyes falling on the small Daklin scout ship resting beyond the trail, its hatch sealed. For a fleeting moment, hope pierced the grief. "The ship… it's got power. More than enough to recharge you. Maybe even the packs. If not, we can fly it to the spaceport."

She stood, already moving toward it. She tried to open it, then the realization hit her like a stone. She stopped cold. "Damn it… Daklin systems are probably locked to biosignatures that only a living Daklin can activate."

Her gaze drifted back to the bodies. All six lay sprawled in the dirt. Dead. The hope drained as quickly as it had come. "We're shut out."

Footsteps sounded behind her. Megan spun, hand on her blade, but it was only the farmers and traders, creeping back, shame and fear in their eyes. One of the older men cleared his throat.

"We… we came back to help."

Megan nodded wordlessly. Together, they dug in the hard soil with makeshift tools. Megan cradled Mark's head one last time, pressing her lips to his forehead.

"I'm sorry," she whispered. Then she lowered him into the grave.

By twilight, the grave was filled, a rough cairn of stones marking the spot. The others drifted back to the wagons, leaving Megan kneeling alone until the stars blazed above. She finally found a place inside one of the wagons to curl up and sleep.

The next morning, Sun Tsu moved slowly, being careful to preserve energy. His systems were sluggish, but he could walk. "I can proceed," he told her, "but I fear I would be useless in a fight."

"We will deal with that if it happens," Megan said flatly. "I can't do this alone."

They walked east, the dusty trail stretching into the distance. After an hour of silence, Sun Tsu slowed. "Megan, we must ask how the Daklin found us. The probability of a random patrol intercepting this coach is… negligible."

Megan frowned. "You think we were tracked?"

Sun Tsu's eyes narrowed, a faint glow pulsing behind them. "Yes. I have been running a subroutine, and it is now clear. Cybernetics emit a unique resonance signature. I have ignored it because it seemed… insignificant. But the Daklin must have detected it."

Megan stopped in her tracks, the weight of the realization crashing down. "They tracked *you*?"

"I believe that is correct," Sun Tsu said, his voice heavy with guilt. "It was not the coach. Not the trail. It was me. My presence compromised us. It was my signature they tracked when they found Singularity and destroyed her, and it was me that brought them here."

"Do you think this is something new? Some new capability" Megan asked.

"Yes. They are constantly adapting. I suspect their AI algorithms have recently found this hole," Sun Tsu surmised.

She clenched her fists, flashing anger, then softened. "Not your fault. But if they can track you, they can track every cybernetic in the resistance."

He nodded grimly. "I must find a way to warn them, and after that, I will power down. This means I cannot continue with you. You must reach the spaceport alone."

Megan stared at him, her jaw tight. "Alone."

"Yes." Sun Tsu placed a hand on her shoulder. "You are strong enough. Leave Mark's pack with me. I have an idea of how to use the remaining power in his pack and mine to dispatch a message."

Her throat tightened, but she forced a nod. "Then you make sure the others know. Shut yourself down and stay offline until I come back for you."

Sun Tsu bowed his head. "Acknowledged. Goodbye, Captain Megan Hoglund. May you find your way to the port."

She turned away before he could see the tears in her eyes. Adjusting her pack, she stepped onto the trail. The other travelers had long since gone, leaving only dust and silence.

Megan checked the location, then her provisions. She turned to see her tactical cybernetic friend had found a hiding place in some shrubs and was working on his goal of warning the resistance before he powered down.

Sun Tsu thought about the fact that they had turned P-Link off because it was detectable by the Daklin. He opened up Mark's tunneling backpack and modified the tachyon interface so it could broadcast a signal. The remaining power was more than sufficient for the task. He pressed the button that normally would execute a jump and with the last bit of power broadcast a simple message: *To all Resistance units. Cybernetics emit a unique signature. The Daklin tracked Sun Tsu on GH 3. Warn everyone. Power down if possible. Do not cluster in groups.* The message repeated over the next few minutes until the power was depleted.

After a few minutes of walking, Megan turned around again but could no longer see her friend. She was now truly alone.

∘∘∘∘ ∞ ∘∘∘∘

At exactly 9:10:40 am, Alex popped out of the tachyon tunnel above Dallas in Tranquility, hands poised over the controls. The city glittered below, an ordinary morning with only one person on the ground aware of what would happen next. He exhaled slowly.

"Emily, confirm EMP radius," he said.

"Five kilometers centered on T-Portal's primary data center," she replied. "Power grid will reboot in hours, but their servers… they should be crippled with massive data loss."

Alex's finger hovered. "Then here we go."

He looked at the clock and counted down the final couple seconds, then triggered the device.

A ripple of electromagnetic energy tore across the morning sky, silent, but absolute. Power lines failed, and generating plants cascaded into shutdown. It would be temporary, but the silicon storage for the T-Portal was destroyed. There was no doubt it could be restored, but that would take time.

Alex checked his screens. "Servers down. Grid disruption confirmed. Looks like it worked."

"Indeed," Emily said. "But the effect will be temporary."

"Temporary is good enough. Let's get out of here."

Moments later, Tranquility slipped into the tunnel. The hum of tachyon resonance swallowed the silence, and then the ship headed towards the blue skies of Pronimos.

○ ○ ○ ○ ∞ ○ ○ ○ ○

Zander was already waiting in the command hall, eyes sharp, jaw set.

"Well?" he asked.

Alex nodded. "Dallas is dark. Fortak's going to be scrambling for months. That should buy us some time, but the best thing is that he won't know what hit him. Now, he will be slowed down by second guessing everything."

Before Zander could answer, Emily's console chimed. "Incoming message packet," she announced.

They gathered as the intelligence developed from Sun Tsu's simple message.

"To all Resistance units. Cybernetics emit a unique signature. The Daklin tracked Sun Tsu on GH 3. Warn everyone. Power down if possible. Do not cluster in groups."

The message repeated several times, then ended.

Zander's eyes went hard. "I guess we now know how they surprised Megan. Damn it."

"The good news is that my suspicion is confirmed. If Sun Tsu survived the Singularity ship explosion, Megan did as well."

Emily was silent for a long moment, then spoke. "Alex… if you take me with you, you will be painting a target on your back. The Daklin will lock onto me instantly."

"I know, Emily," Alex looked between them. "Then I go alone."

"No," Zander objected. "It's suicide."

Alex cut him off. "Megan's out there, on GH3. If she's alive, she needs me. If she's not… I need to know." He remembered what Adamez said, "we don't leave our soldiers behind."

Zander exhaled, defeated. "Okay… We will begin working on this signature problem. If we can mask the resonance, cybernetics can rejoin the fight. Until then… you're on your own."

Emily stepped closer, her voice soft. "Good luck, Alex. Bring her back."

Alex gave a grim smile. "I intend to."

He turned toward Tranquility, already programming a course.

Next stop: Gamma Halden 3.

○○○○ ∞ ○○○○

The sun beat down as Megan trudged across the rocky plain, each step heavier than the last. She had grown up in Alaska, and while she had spent some time in Texas, she had never grown accustomed to the heat. Her pack was nearly useless, but she couldn't leave it behind because of the advanced tech. In her race against time, she had pressed relentlessly, throat dry, and muscles screaming.

The hours stretched long under the crushing glare of Gamma Halden's sun. The air shimmered, distorting the rocks ahead into liquid mirages. Each time she blinked, the horizon wavered, tricking her eyes into seeing water that wasn't there. She had read about this but never experienced this cruel trick of nature.

Her boots crunched over sharp gravel, sending up dust that clung to her sweat-soaked skin. The land was barren and flat for miles except for jagged shards of stone that jutted like broken glass from the earth. The heat pressed into her chest, sucking the strength from her lungs with every breath. Megan wished for an Alaskan winter, which was surely the kinder adversary.

She pulled her canteen from her pack and took a small sip. The water was warm, almost hot, but it was enough to keep her throat from sealing shut. She glanced inside; it was nearly empty. With hands trembling from fatigue, she tightened the cap and set it back in its holder.

"You can do this, Hoglund," she muttered to herself. "You've done worse. You figured out how to survive a few frozen days in Alaska with no food. Other than temperature, terrain, and the water situation, ice being the opposite, this is the same, right? Just another challenge. And you were born for challenges…"

But in truth, this was different. Even in Alaska's frozen wilderness, or the toughest missions on Earth, she had always known food and rest would follow. Here, there was no guarantee. The heat gnawed at her like a predator, relentless and patient.

By midday, her stomach growled loud enough to echo in her own head. She hadn't eaten in nearly 24 hours, and the absence of calories made her legs wobble beneath her. Each muscle demanded more fuel than she could give.

She paused in the shade of a fractured boulder, if it could even be called shade, kneeling with her back against the stone. The shadow was barely enough to cool her skin, but it gave her a moment to breathe. Sweat dripped from her temple onto the dust.

Her mind flickered to Mark, to Sun Tsu, to the fight that had left her walking alone through this alien wasteland. Rage and grief surged together, pushing her back to her feet. "I'm not dying out here," she growled, adjusting her pack. "Not when I'm this close."

The spires of the spaceport loomed larger now, heat haze curling around them. Still, distance meant hours yet to go, and every step forward stole a little more strength.

Her canteen sloshed weakly when she shook it. Maybe enough for two more sips. It would suffice if she kept her pace. But the gnawing hunger, the pounding in her head, and the way her vision blurred at the edges told her the real danger wasn't thirst.

It was exhaustion.

Megan tightened the straps of her pack. She knew how to become grit and determination. "One foot in front of the other. Keep moving."

The heat pressed harder, and the plain stretched mercilessly on, but the spaceport grew closer with every step. She knew she would survive.

That's when she saw them.

Twelve Daklin soldiers, black armor gleaming, fanning out in a crescent to block her path. Their leader raised a long blade and sneered. "We have found you Megan Hoglund. Alone. Weak. Easy."

How the hell do those guys stay cool in that black obsidian armor? she asked herself, then dropped her pack, rolling her shoulders despite the ache. "Twelve against one? That's a fight I'll take." She closed her eyes and summoned every ounce of strength.

The soldiers chuckled darkly. They had weapons and could easily just fire and kill her.

She raised her voice. "What's the matter? Afraid of one woman? Surely twelve Daklin can manage a hand-to-hand fight."

They hesitated, then one stepped forward, pulling off his gauntlet, eager to oblige. The rest followed, knives and fists ready. At this point, she had turned it into a matter of manhood and ignorant pride.

Megan planted her feet, eyes blazing. Twelve of them. Could she take them all? Maybe, if she wasn't parched, sunburnt, and running on fumes. But it didn't matter. She'd go down swinging.

"Who wants the glory of taking down weak and easy Megan Hoglund in the desert?" she called out, defiant.

The first lunged. She ducked under his swing and snapped his neck with a brutal twist. Another charged from the side. She caught his wrist, drove his own blade into his chest, then shoved him aside before the third crashed into her. Fists and knives flashed. Blood sprayed. It was hers, but she wasn't ready to fall. Not yet.

She fought like fire itself, cutting, slamming, breaking bones. One by one, the Daklin fell. But each strike cost her. The fight was creating bruises that bloomed across her ribs, a gash tore down her arm, another across her cheek.

By the time seven bodies littered the dirt, five soldiers remained, circling her like wolves. Each was determined to take this trophy.

Megan's chest heaved, her knife slick with blood, her legs trembling.

The lead Daklin grinned. "Running out of strength, little female?"

Megan spat blood onto the ground. "I've been making sure to save enough to kill you."

The circle tightened. She raised her blade, jaw set. She knew this would be the final dance, and she would not be the last one standing.

A shimmer split the air behind her. Alex suddenly popped into existence, backpack glowing faintly. In his hand gleamed an x-ray laser, cold and steady.

"Sorry I'm late," he said.

Even as the words left his mouth, five sharp X-ray pulses cracked across the field. Each beam struck with precision, dropping a Daklin before they had time to react. Armor split. Bodies collapsed.

Silence.

Megan stood frozen, knife still raised, chest heaving. Then her eyes locked on him. "Alex?"

He lowered the weapon, stepping toward her. "You look like hell, Megan."

She gave a bloody grin and nodded towards the litter of bodies. "Look around Alex. Do you see the other guys?"

Her legs buckled, and Alex caught her before she hit the ground. He pressed the button and popped them back to Tranquility. Once back on the ship, he executed a preprogrammed hop five years into the past. That would give them time to get Megan back on her feet and decide what to do next without concern the Daklin could follow.

Megan woke to see her old quarter on Tranquility. Her body ached from every cut and bruise, but it was the sterile comfort of the med-bay that made her blink in disbelief. She turned her head and saw Alex sitting nearby, working quietly on some antiseptics for her.

Her eyes widened. "Holy crap, Alex. You… you look like a kid. Is this a time travel version of you?"

Alex chuckled faintly. "Welcome back, Megan," He leaned over and gave her a long warm hug. "I'm getting that a lot lately. I did a de-ageing treatment on Andromeda. Didn't plan on surprising you like this, but you really didn't give me much of a choice."

"Andromeda, like the galaxy?"

"Uh huh."

"Isn't that like, millions of light years away?"

"It's a little over 2.5 million," Alex responded nonchalantly, as if he was saying one plus one equals two.

She shook her head slowly, still trying to process it. "Last time I saw you, you looked, older. Now… you've traveled five million lightyears, and you look like you stepped back in time."

"Actually, we *are* five years in the past right now, but the younger body is all biochemistry, courtesy of that facility on Andromeda." He stopped to check the cut on her face. "I think all of this can be healed on Pronimos. Let's pick up Mark and Sun Tsu, then tunnel to Pronimos."

Her expression darkened. The weight of it settled over the room. "Mark's gone, Alex. He saved me… and it cost him everything."

Alex's face twisted, grief breaking through his composure. He stood, pacing. "Mark and I… we were kids together. Met in college. Princeton." Alex was struggling, fighting off the pain of yet another death. "He was there when I first started dreaming about all this. Hell, he used to call me insane for chasing tachyons, then he helped me build half the systems we still use. And now…" He trailed off, fists clenched.

"I know," Megan whispered. "He died bravely. He died saving me."

"Crap, I'm so sorry Megan. Here I am feeling sorry for my loss, but you and Mark were…"

"It's painful Alex, so let's save it for another time."

Alex sat back down, eyes red. "And Sun Tsu?"

Megan sighed. "He powered down to keep the Daklin from tracking us. He's still out there, near the outpost. I have his coordinates so we can pick him up."

Alex nodded. "We'll get him. But we'll wait until we're in a tunnel to revive him. The worst thing that could happen would be for the Daklin to track us to Pronimos. Safer that way."

"Agreed."

An hour later, with Sun Tsu secured in stasis, Tranquility was humming through the tunnel.

Megan felt well enough to get up, and the first thing she did was hug Alex. "Thanks for saving my ass, but next time, try to show up a little sooner. I honestly thought it was over."

"Everyone thought you were dead Megan, except me. Then we got the message from Sun Tsu…"

"Can you brief me? Seems like Tranquility got some upgrades. Feels like real gravity in here."

Alex briefed Megan. "You're right, Tranquility's had upgrades since you last saw her," he explained, pride cutting through his exhaustion. "Expanded fusion core, hardened hull, multi-vector shielding, and gravity. *Real* gravity... She's faster, stronger, and smarter. But I'm thinking it's time to go further. We should rebuild your ship, call it Singularity 2, and add these upgrades."

Megan's eyes lit with curiosity. "A second? Could we mass produce and have a fleet instead of a single point of failure?"

Megan leaned forward, her bruises stark against the med-bay light. "If we build Singularity 2, I want x-ray lasers on her. What you did out there, that weapon, it saved my life. Imagine if we had long-range capacity."

Alex raised an eyebrow. "Long-range x-ray lasers? That's no small ask."

From the comm panel came Emily's voice—not Emily the cybernetic, but the AI version that had been with them since the beginning. It chimed in, as if fate itself had been listening.

"It might take some work," she said in her familiar tone, "but it's possible. I doubt it would be effective against one of the planet-killing Daklin ships, but maybe against the fighters and cruisers."

"Well then, let's work on making that happen," Alex answered.

Megan swallowed hard. "I owe it to Mark to make Singularity 2 real. She will be a real fighting ship."

Alex nodded slowly. "Like you, Megan."

15

Rebounding on Pronimos

Nine months had passed since Mark's death on Gamma Halden 3. The loss still weighed heavily on Megan, Alex, Zander, and Lyra. He had been the goofy, brilliant, and happy-go-lucky member of the team, but there had been virtually no time for grief and healing with so much going on.

A year earlier, they had held the naïve belief that they could isolate the Daklin by cutting off the tunnels to their stronghold. Now they faced the reality that the tunnel-collapse strategy had failed. The Daklin adapted too quickly. The Galactic Tunnel Network was a web and there were so many threads that closing it off was a nearly impossible task.

The bigger problem was that with billions of ships in their fleet, the Daklin could afford to bleed.

The resistance could not.

So, the fight shifted.

EtaKatz became the rally point. Little more than an obscure planet, once visited by Alex and Paula on a timeline long forgotten, it now swelled with engineers, technicians, and fighters from across the fractured resistance. Entire factories had been built into canyons and along the shorelines. Sparks, plasma torches, and test fire from prototype weapons lit the sky around the mountain ranges.

Alex spent his time on Pronimos, working alongside the engineers designing a new line of ships that were fast, shielded, hard-hitting, and built for survival. They engineered fighter class vessels with modular systems, able to carry weapons designed for tunnels or 3-space. Smaller than the great Daklin cruisers, but more agile and lethal. Alex and his team developed the kind of ships meant for a new type of war like the Daklin had never faced.

It was modeled after the early American colonies' struggle against the vast British war machine: hide in the trees, hit and run, but never face the enemy head-on.

Alex also recognized the danger faced by Earth. He touched base with Adamez regularly.

Texas surprised everyone. When Fortak tried to extend his grip by rebuilding the portal infrastructure in Dallas, it was Texans who rose first. A militia formed seemingly overnight, thousands strong, armed with nothing more than grit, rifles, and stubborn independence. Art Adamez led them. And on the first day, Fortak himself had fallen, cornered, overwhelmed, and killed in the chaos of the uprising.

The second Daklin attempt to take Earth had failed.

With Fortak gone, Alex convinced Adamez to tunnel to Pronimos for training.

○ ○ ○ ○ ∞ ○ ○ ○ ○

One evening, after a strategy session, the two men sat together on a balcony overlooking the glowing spires of Pronimos' capital.

"You know," Adamez said, swirling a glass of dark beer, "I was thinking about hanging it up. I'm 65 now. I figured I'd put in another year, then retire. Find a quiet spot. Maybe return to my farming roots, this time as a landowner."

Alex smiled faintly. "You don't look 65."

"Don't feel it either," Adamez said. "I have pretty good genes, but the years catch you, no matter how you hide from them."

Alex leaned forward, a glint in his eyes. "What if they didn't have to?"

Adamez raised an eyebrow. "What do you mean?"

"You know how old I am?" Alex held his beer up and posed with a grin.

"31? 32?" Adamez guessed.

Alex shook his head, "I'm 49, and I am one of the youngest people on this planet."

"It's funny that, in my time here, I haven't seen a single old person," Adamez observed.

"That's because they've cured old age here." He paused, "Come with me."

The de-ageing clinic was quiet, sterile, and filled with humming Pronimos tech. Alex spoke quietly to the chief physician, who nodded and gestured for Adamez to follow.

Hours later, Adamez stepped out of the chamber. His posture perfect, skin young and taut, and eyes clearer, sharper. He stared at his hands, his arms, the reflection in the polished wall.

"My vision is perfect. I have never had perfect vision. I can smell things I haven't smelled in years, and all those achy joints are healed… I'm 29 again," he whispered.

Alex grinned. "Told you. Wait till you eat your first meal, oh, and be careful using spices. You'll find that jalapeños are hot again."

Adamez laughed, shaking his head in disbelief. "This is… insane. You realize you just signed me up for another 40 years of war?"

"Good," Alex said. "Because Earth is going to need you."

The celebration was brief. The next day, Alex and the others ran the numbers again.

The countdown was brutal.

The EMP had slowed calculated advance of the Daklin, but even so, they had less than four years. That's how long they had before the Planet-Killer-class Daklin ships would likely return to Earth's solar system. Four years before Earth was once again in the crosshairs.

Four years to retool, to build, to prepare. Or humanity would not survive.

"Based on what I've learned here on Pronimos, the Daklin are gonna be coming for us, Durant," Adamez concluded.

"Let's make sure you're ready, Adamez."

"And how do we do that?" He asked.

"Generally, we don't know where the Daklin are going, but we do know they will return to Earth. We believe they'll take a shot at destroying the entire solar system, so we set landmines. We can detect faster than the speed of light, and we have technology capable of getting anywhere in the solar system in a couple seconds. We just prepare to destroy everything they send there. I think we might be able to collapse tunnels as they are exiting."

"Get started on that, please. In the meantime, I need to return to Earth." Adamez stretched, enjoying his young body and felt invigorated.

○ ○ ○ ○ ∞ ○ ○ ○ ○

A few months after Adamez left, Alex found himself sitting in a corner booth at the Old West Bar overlooking the Pronimos river, while nursing a dark beer. His prior favorite bar had reminded him of Maria, so he found this new place. It had become his spot, his retreat when the weight of strategy and countdowns pressed too hard.

He swirled the glass in his hand, mind racing through impossible scenarios. How could his small force stop a fleet measured in billions? How could he guard a world when the enemy wanted not conquest, but annihilation?

The chair across from him scraped as Megan slid into the seat, her hair loose, a faint bruise still visible along her jaw from the last training session. She flagged the server with two fingers, then looked at Alex.

"You always hide here when you're thinking hard," she observed.

"The days are hard, Megan," he smiled faintly. "Sometimes thinking's all I've got left."

"Bullshit. You've got more than that." She leaned forward. "What's going on in that oversized brain tonight?"

"Ways to stop the Daklin," Alex said honestly. "Landmines in space. Traps in the tunnels. None of it feels big enough."

The server dropped off a mug of vanilla porter for her. Megan took a sip before changing the subject.

"Can I ask you something personal?"

Alex raised an eyebrow. "Sure, but I've learned that usually means trouble."

"Maria," Megan said simply.

"What about her?" Alex tried to act innocent.

"You are so transparent, Alex. It's obvious there is, or was, something going on."

His grip tightened on the glass. He sighed. "We spent months… dancing around it. Sexual tension so thick it would take a chainsaw to cut it." He took a sip of his beer. "She cared, I cared, but she kept telling me I'd never stop thinking about Paula. That I was chasing a ghost."

Megan studied him, her expression softening. "I kind of understand that. Loving someone who isn't there. Holding onto the past because it's safer than risking what's in front of you. I lost Isaac, a man I thought I'd spend the rest of my life with, and then Mark."

Alex looked at her, puzzled. "I'm sorry, I forgot about Isaac."

"No worries, he was before your time. He shaped me in ways that are important today. The martial arts came from him." She took a deep breath, exhaled slowly and continued. "I think we have to put these things behind us and move on. Relationships are hard enough already. Hopefully the two of you at least had sex, or consummated it somehow?"

Alex almost choked on his beer, "Megan, that's a little personal!"

"It's important, and a necessary relief." She smirked, then said it plain. "I'd happily have sex with you, Alex. No games. No tension. Just what it is."

He blinked, half-laughing. "You're joking."

Her eyes locked on his, dead serious. "I'm not. Why would I joke about that?"

For a moment, the pub faded away, just the two of them at that little table, with years of battles, deaths, and loss pressing in at the edges. Alex looked at Megan again, but this time in a different light. She was good-looking, brilliant, and athletic. How could he ever ask for more in a woman? He imagined that, to anyone watching from a distance, it probably looked like something *was* going on between them.

Alex leaned back slowly, studying her face as if searching for a crack in the words. His voice was low, almost strained.

"Megan… how can you even think about that? About us? After Mark…"

She didn't flinch. "After Mark's death, you mean?"

"Yes," Alex said firmly. "He's been gone nine months, but it still feels too damn recent. He was my friend. He was *your* partner. How can you talk about… this?"

Megan set her mug down and folded her arms on the table leaning forward. Her voice was steady, but her eyes held the same sadness that lived in his. "It isn't that soon, Alex. Mark and I, before GH3, had already decided to part ways. We were breaking up. I'd taken on command, evolved and adapted to the war, and he was still trying to hold onto being just a scientist. He couldn't keep up with who I'd become, and I wasn't willing to go backwards."

She exhaled sharply, shaking her head before continuing. "When he died, I grieved hard. But I wasn't losing the man who was my future. I was losing the man who had been part of my past."

Alex's brow furrowed. "You never said that."

"I didn't want to dishonor him," Megan replied. "He deserved respect, and he got it. But don't confuse grief with love that still burns. That flame had already gone out, Alex. He and I knew it."

She leaned in now, her voice dropping. "I love you, Alex. I mean it. It's not about running from Mark's memory. It's about being honest about what's still alive in me." She watched him for a second, thinking, then continued. "You're making this too complicated," she said softly. "Love and sex are connected, sure. But they're not the same thing. To be clear, I do love you. Not like I loved Isaac, and not the way I thought I'd love Mark. Honestly? In some ways, I love you more than I ever loved Mark. You and I… we've been through too much not to feel *something*."

"I will give you that, Megan." Alex's eyes lifted.

She leaned forward, her tone fierce but warm. "I'm not trying to start a relationship. I'm not asking for promises or forever. What I'm saying is, right now, both of us are bleeding inside. We need someone to help us heal. Who better than us? Who understands this war, this grief, better than the two of us?"

Alex swallowed hard. "Megan…"

"I mean it," she pressed. "We fight together. We bleed together. Why not… well, have sex together?"

He shook his head slowly. "Maria once told me something… something that still sticks. She said if we ever had sex, she didn't want me thinking about Paula while I was inside her."

Megan blinked, then laughed, a sharp, surprising sound in the quiet pub. "That's it? She didn't have sex with you because she thought you might remember sex with Paula. That's silly, Alex! Hell, that's just plain stupid. I truly admire and look up to Maria, but… well, she screwed this one up. Our history is part of who we are, Paula, Maria, Mona Lisa, I don't care."

Alex was shaking his head.

She leaned closer, eyes blazing with challenge. "Come on, Alex. Let's do this."

Alex sat there, jaw tight, heart pounding harder than it should have. Megan's eyes burned into him, daring him to take the step. For a fleeting moment he leaned forward, almost ready to close the space between them, to let grief and need take over.

But then he stopped. He shook his head, slowly but firmly. "Megan… I can't. Not because I don't want to. Until this evening, I never thought about sex with you, but I'm thinking about it now… Too much."

"Okay, so we're making progress," she smiled and tapped his face affectionately.

"You're one of the few people I trust completely. You're my colleague and my partner in this fight. If we cross that line, we might lose that. I can't risk it. Humanity can't risk it, not now."

Megan studied him for a long moment, then let out a breath and leaned back into her chair. A wry smile tugged at her bruised lip. "You are the biggest risk taker I have ever met, and yet here you are the cautious one, Durant."

"Not cautious," Alex said. "Protective. Of this connection. Of us. The resistance needs us clear-headed. Most importantly, I love you in ways that I don't want to change."

She grinned and nodded approval. "Now, stop and think about this entire conversation, Alex Durant. What have you learned?" She lifted her beer, a professorial look softening her grin.

Alex did not lift his glass to toast. "You're dropping it?" Alex asked, surprised by her sudden flip.

She started shaking her head, "Yes, Alex. Don't be a dumb shit."

Alex furrowed his brow, then grinned acknowledgement, "What would you have done if I'd said yes?"

"You never would have said yes, Alex." Megan answered confidently. "But now I have a fun button to push with you, and you can expect me to use it!"

"You delivered that with great zeal, Megan. I was almost convinced, but the lesson was definitely heard."

"Oh, I'm ready Alex, and I am gonna go find someone to have sex with. As Maria advised, I *need* a rebound."

"Okay," he responded hesitantly.

"So do you, Alex Durant." She smiled and the serious look turned to a playful smile, "It would have been fun to do it together, and now, well, you'll never know!"

Alex raised his glass and looked around the quiet pub. "To rebounds."

Two nights later, Alex saw Megan come into the bar with a man he did not recognize. His computer was in front of him beside his beer and he tried to work, but couldn't help noticing them laughing, dancing a bit, and finally, leaving together. Apparently, her decision to rebound came with a *waste no time* clause. What's more, he knew she could have gone anywhere with that new man, but she had chosen *this* location for a reason.

Alex had gained a new perspective on Maria's constant insistence on rebounds by understanding his own reaction to Megan, and he had seen the seriousness of her intention to *rebound*.

16

Singularity 2

With the new, faster version of Tranquility, Alex found himself spending a couple days a week working in the engineering hall and the manufacturing floor on EtaKatz where he grew fond of the hum of fabricators, the hiss of plasma welders, and the overlapping voices of engineers arguing about the best way to implement new systems. His time on Pronimos was spent in the science labs and in discussions with the strategic advisers whose job it was to collect and analyze information on Daklin movements.

When he was not working, he was spending time with Steven, now almost seven years old. He spent the evenings in his favorite western bar, typically alone. Over the months since that heart-to-heart with Megan, Alex often watched her come into the club, sometimes with a different man. Apparently, she was doing what she needed to heal, both from the loss of Mark and the relentless stress of fighting the Daklin.

And somewhere along the way, Alex came to a quiet, fundamental realization: Megan wasn't just remarkable. She was unique, perhaps one in a trillion, even by galactic standards.

That morning, dressed in jeans with his sleeves rolled up and a mug of black coffee in hand, he walked the perimeter of *Singularity 2*, the prototype for a new class of fighters now called the *Stinger*.

"She's ready to trial test the multi-phasic shields," Lyra reported, stepping forward with a tablet computer under her arm. Her sharp eyes scanned the schematics. "Energy distribution is stable across all spectra. That system will withstand a lot."

"Right," Zander added. "Unlike those old *Star Trek* shows where shields failed after a couple phaser blasts, our Stinger class is fast, hard to hit, and the shield has enough power to withstand hundreds of direct strikes."

"Excellent," Alex smiled, admiring this new war machine. "How are we doing with computer upgrades?"

"Computer AI's been updated and runs clean," Zander added. He had been shadowing the Pronimos programmers for weeks, learning their hybrid codes. "It's faster, smarter, and harder to trick. Every Daklin intrusion test so far has failed."

Alex scanned the floor, "Is Megan around today?"

Zander engaged his Plink, "Hey Megan, can you come down to your ship?"

A few minutes later, Megan walked onto the hangar floor. Alex had not seen her in a few weeks, and the first thing he noticed was that she had finally taken a day in the med-longevity facility.

"Wow, you look fantastic, Megan," Alex said, hugging her.

"Man, I wish I had done this age reversal thing months ago. I had no idea…" She stopped, grimaced, and looked back at Alex. "Wait, are you saying that I looked bad before?"

"No ma'am. Whether you are 40 or 29, you are the best looking and most extraordinary woman around."

"Thanks Alex," she winked and flipped her curls playfully. "How are we doing with Sun Tsu, my cybernetic first officer?" Megan asked, folding her arms as she walked to touch Singularity 2 affectionately. She had just come off the simulators, sweat darkening her flight suit. "You promised me he'd be invisible to their scans."

"That's in final testing, Megan," Alex said, glancing up. "No Daklin sensor can find our cybernetics unless they want to be found. We should be able to release the update in a few days."

"Okay…You know, I was in the simulator, Zander, so why'd you call me down here?" Megan pressed.

Alex jabbed a finger at the weapons matrix hovering in red on the edge of the hologram. "This. The x-ray laser. We've got punch at a hundred klicks, maybe two. Beyond that, the beam disperses. You aren't dog fighting with those Daklin cruisers, so we need half a million klicks minimum."

One of the Pronimos engineers shook his head. "We've tried reinforced magnetic bottles, nested graviton stabilizers. This much energy requires significant mass. Too much mass for a Stinger frame."

"I don't understand," Megan asked.

Alex noticed that her question was accompanied by a hand on the engineer's shoulder, almost affectionate. The engineer tilted his head slightly, as if he didn't understand the question.

"This is a simple Newton's law problem, Megan," Alex explained. "Unlike lasers, which are collimated photons of energy, x-rays are particles with real mass. The laser accelerates the particles, and we end up with $F=ma$."

"You are saying that for every action, there's an opposite and equal reaction?" Megan clarified. "But I don't understand the significance."

"Yes," the engineer responded, not sure exactly how to handle Megan in this situation. "It's a lot of energy, like recoil from a rifle, only thousands of times more powerful."

"You guys know about feedback control loops, and you know exactly how much energy will be spit out based on the target and distance." Megan explained. "Just compensate with the engine thrust, and then you don't need to add mass to my Stinger."

The engineer stepped back with the simple realization, "Holy shit, that might work!"

"Holy shit is right, Todd." She tapped his face affectionately, "Now go make it happen, please."

When he left, Lyra motioned for Megan to come over to a table with the schematic. "We've also been working on distributed arrays for the x-ray. Instead of one emitter, we use a phased aperture with thousands of micro-beams overlapping. Each self-corrects downrange, keeping collimation tight."

Alex looked at her sharply. "Phased apertures… Brilliant. What is the energy spike?"

Zander frowned. "Spike is more than the max output of our fusion plant. We're trying to deal with a power surge that's beyond the baseline of even the new onboard generating source."

"It's just impulse, so how about we store energy in the form of capacitance, then also piggyback off the shield harmonics?" Alex countered. His eyes lit with that familiar spark that the others had come to recognize in him. He was always telling them that an impossible problem could be solved by just changing perspective. "During the firing window, reroute shield energy into the emitter array, drain the capacitors and shields dip, weapons peak. One massive strike."

"Leaving you vulnerable," Megan said flatly.

"This is millisecond stuff, Megan. None of our troops know we can time tunnel. If we are being fired upon at the same time as we need to fire, just have the AI shift the time parameters a fraction of a second or so," Alex replied.

The room went quiet.

Lyra crossed her arms. "That's brilliant."

"That's war," Alex said. "We don't beat the Daklin by matching them ship for ship in a fair fight. We beat them by throwing everything we have at them. Adamez told me that Fortak marveled at Earth engineers because of creativity, something that was rare amongst the Daklin."

"That's a valuable piece of information," Zander responded. "We stack our creativity against theirs and we win?"

"Give me a Stinger that can cut a cruiser in half from half a million klicks," Alex bit his lower lip, "and we've got a fighting chance."

Megan stepped closer, eyes narrowing. "I want to see it tested. Not just in the models and simulations. I'd like to fly the trial run myself."

Zander shook his head. "You think it's wise for you to always volunteer for the dangerous parts?"

She met his gaze. "If I'm going to command a squadron of Stingers, I need to know what these weapons feel like in the cockpit, not just on paper."

Alex nodded once. "Then let's build it. No more talk. We've got less than 18 months before the Daklin scientists are building ships that can create their own tunnels, and the Planet Killers reach Earth's system. We solve this, or humanity dies."

"On it," Zander answered, then returned to his workstation where he could begin analyzing how to implement this new idea.

As the hangar began to empty, Alex stepped toward Megan.

"Hey, Megan. A word?"

She raised an eyebrow. "Sounds serious."

He kept his voice low. "You and Todd?"

She smirked faintly. "Straight to the point. Yes, Alex. We've been… enjoying each other's company. You jealous?"

Alex's jaw tightened, then he smiled. "I'm not jealous, and I am happy you're executing your rebound strategy, but Todd's on the team. He's building the laser that may decide whether any of us live through the next four years. You think casual sex in the middle of that is a good idea?"

Megan leaned against the table, arms folded, unbothered. "Life on the front is all tension, Alex. You know that better than anyone. Out here, it's survival, stress, and focus, but on the base, in the quiet between battles, we take what we can. Call it stress relief, call it human connection. Either way, I'm not apologizing for it."

Alex shook his head. "This isn't Earth, Megan. But discipline still matters."

Her expression softened slightly. "You're right Alex, it's not Earth. Back home, people lived eighty years if they were lucky, and every choice carried a finality. Here, among Pronimos and the rest, we're different. De-ageing treatments mean people live a lot longer. Todd is nearly three hundred years old. Three hundred! He knows exactly what he's doing, in more ways than one," she winked. "He's not some kid that I'm distracting from his homework."

Alex exhaled, rubbing his forehead. "So, it's just… casual?"

"Yes," she said firmly. "Casual. He understands it, I understand it. Nobody's losing focus. Nobody's confused."

Alex studied her for a long moment. "I just don't want the lines blurred, Megan. Not when everything's on the line."

She touched his arm lightly. "Relax, Durant. Todd and I both know the difference between the fight and the quiet."

"Okay, sorry Megan. I guess you're right on this one."

"Alex, my demeanor and disposition have done a 180 since we talked about sex and rebounding. I implemented. You need to do the same. Knock down some of those brick walls and become a human again… please."

"Noted," Alex took a deep breath and exhaled slowly. Perhaps Megan was right, but a part of him still wasn't ready.

"Alex?" Megan interrupted his thoughts.

"Yeah?"

"Need me to volunteer to take you through the rebound process?" She winked and affectionately grabbed his arm.

"No," he answered without hesitation.

"Good, because when I was offering at the bar a few months ago, you might have been able to turn it into a real offer. This time, it wasn't." She kissed him on the cheek, turned, and walked away.

○○○○ ∞ ○○○○

Ten days later, Todd stood at the console, hands buried in the glowing projections of equations and thrust vectors. "I've implemented thrust algorithms into the firing sequence," he explained, his voice edged with the quiet pride of an engineer who'd lost too much sleep. "They'll compensate for the recoil from the beam itself. $F=ma$ isn't just a classroom problem, it's now been implemented to keep the ship from tearing itself apart," he nodded at Alex.

Alex was developing an entirely new respect for Todd. He implemented the solution in a fraction of the time expected *and* kept the most restless and valuable military asset in the galaxy happy in his spare time.

Zander looked at Todd, then Alex, and added, "I've finished the phased aperture module. Ten thousand micro-beams, each self-correcting. At short range, the overlap creates a single, perfectly collimated strike."

Megan paced like a caged fighter waiting for her match. "Then let's stop talking and fly it. I want to see what this thing can do outside of your math and science experiments."

Singularity 2 glided silently into an asteroid field they had selected for static testing of the new system. Megan's hands danced across the controls, testing weapon alignment. "Targets acquired," she said, her voice clipped with anticipation.

The first volley ripped through a cluster of rocks barely a hundred kilometers away. The x-ray beam stitched cleanly across their surfaces, cutting them into shards that tumbled silently into the void. It reminded her of the time Alex showed up at the last minute and finished off the five Daklin who were about to kill her. The x-ray laser was a lethal tool.

She selected a medium sized asteroid at 100 kilometers and fired. Megan grinned as it exploded into thousands of pieces. "That's what I'm talking about!"

Then she turned the weapon on a massive asteroid thirty-six thousand kilometers away. The aperture phased, the beam lanced out…

The ship lurched violently. Warning alarms screamed as the thrusters were unable to offset the energy. Megan fought the controls as the compensators burned hot. The asteroid barely dented under the weakened strike, and Singularity 2 spun sideways from the recoil.

"Damn it!" she shouted, wrestling the ship back into position. "Thrusters can't keep up the amount of energy required at long range. It's like firing a cannon out of a canoe."

Frustrated, she guided the ship back through the tunnel to EtaKatz.

Back in the hangar, Megan walked down the ramp of the ship, tossing her helmet against the deck. "At short range, it's a scalpel. At long range, it's a suicide note. The recoil throws the entire frame off."

"Well, to be fair Megan, you were trying to destroy a huge asteroid at a few hundred thousand kilometers," Todd argued.

"Fuck *that*, Todd. I will probably face Daklin cruiser and Planet Killers a thousand times the size of that asteroid, and I'd prefer to do that from a million kilometers distance. This is not good enough. It's not acceptable."

Alex listened quietly, arms folded. Finally, he spoke. "We're treating this situation like we need a continuous beam. What if we didn't?"

Megan frowned. "What do you mean?"

"Pulse it," Alex said. "Short, rapid bursts instead of one long stream. You get collimation without building up uncontrollable, continuous recoil. Like a jackhammer instead of a sledgehammer."

Todd's eyebrows lifted. "That's… actually possible. The aperture can already phase in microseconds. It's just software."

Zander was already pulling up a schematic. "We could rewrite the firing code in a day, test it, and have it ready to implement in a couple days."

"And," Todd added in an excited tone, "we could increase the intensity the beam, making it more powerful."

Megan smirked, her anger cooling into determination. "Love it. Let's do it."

Because it was just a software upgrade, two days later, Singularity 2 was back in the asteroid field.

Megan lined up on the distant giant rock, her hands steady on the controls. "Firing in pulsed mode."

The weapon chattered in invisible bursts, the phased aperture aligning perfectly. The asteroid cracked, split, then shattered into a thousand fragments. The ship responded to the impulse so well, Megan could not detect it.

Megan's grin filled the cockpit. "Now *that's* a weapon. Let's try it on something really big." She studied the field and selected two asteroids, both significantly larger than cruisers, backed off to half a million clicks, and fired.

"Holy shit!" Megan was excited and beaming when both asteroids were destroyed. "Good job, team!"

Alex clasped Todd's shoulder. "You've just given us a fighting chance."

Todd's eyes gleamed. He enjoyed making Megan happy.

Once back in the hangar, Megan walked directly to Alex, with sweat glistening along her brow, and hugged him. "We've got our Stinger, Durant."

Alex smiled thinly, carrying the analogy a step forward. "Then it's time to manufacture a swarm."

○○○○ ∞ ○○○○

Eight months later, the hangar on EtaKatz was alive with a kind of nervous electricity. Twenty-one Stingers stood ready, sharp and angular, their hulls glinting under hangar lights like blades waiting to be drawn. This was a scene that brought tears to Megan's eyes. The new fleet, which she called a swarm, was the perfect picture of beauty and strength.

Megan stood at the head of her squadron, helmet under her arm, eyes scanning her dozen best pilots. These were the ones she trusted with the first true test.

Intelligence had flagged a Daklin forward base in Sector Delta-7. Nearly a hundred Daklin cruisers, massing around a resource depot.

Some called it madness to send the new fighters, but her pilots had hundreds of hours in the simulator. Megan called it the perfect opportunity for a field test.

"Listen up," she said, her voice carrying across the deck. "Some of you think we're walking into hell, and you're right. But today, it's not gonna be our hell, but theirs. Our Stingers are faster, sharper, and smarter than anything the Daklin have ever faced in 50-million years. Today we strike fear in the empire. We hit them hard. We strike fast, and we don't stop until they run."

Her grin was feral. "And trust me, at the end of this battle, they *will* run."

Moments later, twelve Stingers slipped into tachyon space. Megan's Singularity 2 led the swarm, with Sun Tsu completely invisible to detection, and whispering across encrypted channels coordinating with the other AI navigators.

Twenty-six hours later, the tunnel collapsed behind them, and 3-space snapped open into Sector Delta-7.

Ahead lay the Daklin space station and base. It was a massive black fortress floating in space and bristling with weapons, surrounded by 97 cruisers designated for defensive patrol. The moment the Stingers appeared, alarms flared. Daklin signatures surged toward them, like predators scenting blood.

"Targets acquired," Megan called, her voice calm, controlled. "Form up. Split into wings and pulse-fire on my mark."

With complete confidence, Daklin cruisers closed in, heavy guns lighting the void. The Stinger shields were unphased by the Daklin weapons as Stingers were already moving, weaving, and darting like hornets around a lumbering beast. Megan's fingers danced over the controls.

"On my mark," she waited. "Now!"

The first volley of pulsed x-ray beams lanced out. In synchronized bursts, the Stingers tore through the lead wave of cruisers. Six Daklin ships split cleanly apart, detonations scattering debris into the black.

"Hell yes!" one pilot shouted over comms.

"Stay sharp," Megan snapped. "They're not done."

The Daklin surged in disciplined lines, their sheer mass threatening to overwhelm. But the Stingers were too fast, slipping past heavy fire, phasing through coordinated tunnels. Every pass ended with another cruiser blown into thousands of fragments.

The Stingers were able to fly right through the debris fields with shields easily protecting their hulls.

The fight became a blur of flashing beams and silent explosions. Daklin cannons carved empty space where Stingers had been a second before. In return, the swarm carved them apart. Precision AI guided strikes punching through armor as if it were paper.

"Count is at forty down!" One of the other ship captains' voices rang excitedly from her wing.

"Keep pressing!" Megan ordered. "Don't let them regroup!"

They didn't. The swarm moved like one body, AI copilots phasing their fire, so each beam reinforced the next. Sophisticated computer systems made sure that no friendly fire would cross over from one Stinger to hit another.

Daklin formations shattered under the relentless precision.

Seventy... seventy-five... seventy-nine... eighty.

Finally, the surviving Daklin ships broke. Engines flared as seventeen cruisers pulled back, fleeing toward the safety of deeper space.

"83 destroyed," Sun Tsu reported, voice tight with confidence. "The rest are in full retreat."

Megan sat back in her cockpit, chest heaving. Around her, space was littered with burning wreckage, the scattered remains of nearly a hundred Daklin cruisers.

She opened comms to all ships. "You see that? They ran. They finally ran from *us*!"

The squadron erupted in cheers, voices raw with triumph.

Megan allowed herself a smile. "Stingers draw blood. And this is just the beginning."

17

The Old West Bar

Four months had passed since the Battle at Delta 7. Megan's Stinger squadron had become legend across the resistance. The actual numbers with 12 fighters tearing through 83 Daklin cruisers and sending the rest fleeing into the void had been exaggerated over and over again. Since then, victory after victory followed. Every battle ended with wrecked Daklin ships littering the stars. To date, only one Stinger had been destroyed.

The victories inspired new planets to join the resistance. Thus far, 32 systems around the galaxy had joined, which was a paltry number compared to the strength of the Daklin Empire, but it was a start.

The problem was, the Daklin were learning. Their formations shifted, their weapons recalibrated, and their countermeasures tightened with each engagement. The resistance was winning, and the fighters on the frontline only saw overwhelming victory, but the strategic counsel on Pronimos saw the bigger picture.

It was like cutting a tunnel through a mountain with a knife.

Alex sat at the long, curving table in Pronimos's central strategy hall. Holocharts of star systems flickered in the air, glowing red with Daklin deployments. Dozens of strategists from across the resistance debated in sharp tones, their voices echoing off the crystalline glass walls.

Finally, one of the senior analysts, Alisandra, a tall woman with silver hair and eyes clouded by too many sleepless nights, rose to speak. "My team has completed the most advanced analysis, with a full run of projections," she said. "And the numbers are clear."

The room quieted.

"While we are winning large-scale battles, the Daklin Empire fields approximately one billion cruisers. At our current rate of attrition, even if we destroy a hundred in every engagement, the war will take nearly ten million battles and thousands of years to end."

A murmur rippled through the room.

"It's simple algebra folks, and that math assumes," she pressed, her voice sharpening, "that the Daklin do not build new ships and never develop the ability to tunnel. If they do, their logistics change entirely. Their reach becomes our nightmare. Our manufacturing is safe because EtaKatz is not on the tunnel network, but if they reach the point where they can tunnel, how will we defend an overwhelming attack?"

Alex leaned forward, jaw tight. "What do we know of the Planet Killers?"

The woman hesitated, then nodded to the holo. Thousands of massive silhouettes appeared above the table, dwarfing the icons of cruisers. "Best estimates are that they possess nearly two million Daklin Planet Killers designed to sterilize and destroy entire worlds, like the famous 437B that Alex and his team stopped. They may have more than two million, and remember, they do have the ability to replace those ships as well."

The weight of the words pressed down on the hall. No one moved.

Alex's stomach turned. It was a number he'd considered privately, late at night, when the doubts crept in. But seeing it laid bare, confirmed by analysts, it sent a coldness through his chest and into his bloodstream.

For days, the session dragged on. The best strategists in the galaxy dissected options and ran scenario after scenario. Tunnel collapse strategies, already a failure. Stinger swarms, impressive, but hopelessly outnumbered. Planetary defenses were useless against Planet Killers that could strike from hundreds of millions of kilometers away.

No matter how many models they spun, no matter how creative the strategies, the outcome was the same. There was no viable solution.

By the third day, the energy in the room had drained. Even the boldest voices had gone quiet.

Alex stared at the holo-map, feeling the crushing scale of it. A billion cruisers. Two million Planet Killers. Thousands of years of war. The resistance was winning every battle, but the empire would ultimately win the war by sheer numbers, by sheer inevitability.

For the first time since the victory at Delta 7, Alex Durant felt the shadow of defeat crawl across his mind.

oooo ∞ oooo

The day after the Strategic Committee adjourned, Alex sat alone in his quarters overlooking the crystalline towers of Pronimos. For three weeks, they had stared at projections, ran simulations, and churned out scenarios that all ended in the same bleak conclusion. Now, silence pressed around him like a weight.

He activated his Plink. "Adamez, you there?"

A heartbeat later, Art Adamez's voice came through, clear and steady, from over 13 thousand light years away.

"Always, Durant. What's on your mind?"

"I need to know where Earth stands. I've heard whispers, but I want to hear it from you."

Adamez exhaled slowly. "Preparations are moving fast, but what we are building is complicated and slow. The outer solar system is mined with detection grids and arrays designed to trigger if a tachyon tunnel opens anywhere from Neptune's orbit out to the Oort Cloud. They are telling me we have covered something like 31 billion miles, or 50 billion kilometers. If a Daklin Planet Killer even breathes in our direction, we'll know. By the way, we are calling them DPK for short."

Alex nodded. "Detection's good, but what about defense? How many DPKs can Earth actually stop if they show up tomorrow?"

There was a pause, the kind where Adamez was weighing honesty against reassurance. Finally, he answered. "If the Daklin came in the next year, we'd be ready for as many as ten. No more. If they send more than that… well, we'd see the end of life in the entire solar system."

Alex's chest tightened. "Ten. Out of two million."

"They have two million DPKs?" Adamez asked.

"Best estimates, yes."

Adamez's tone hardened. "Yeah, but every few months that number grows. The more time we have, the more mines, more defenses, more countermeasures. If we get two years, maybe we're talking about stopping fifty. Five years… maybe hundreds."

Alex stared out at the horizon, the spires of Pronimos catching the pale sunlight. "And if they don't wait?"

"Like I said, Earth burns," Adamez said simply. "But we're not planning for failure, Durant. Every day we get, is another chance to stack the odds. Don't forget that."

Alex closed his eyes. "I won't. Just keep building, Adamez. However long we have, it won't be enough, but if the DPKs are killed in a big enough number, and they don't know our limits, perhaps we have a shot."

When the Plink with Adamez ended, Alex sat for a long moment in silence, staring at the dim reflection of himself in the black glass of the console. Ten Planet Killers. Against two million. It wasn't enough to dwell on, not tonight.

He needed air, and maybe something darker than strategy.

He walked down the winding streets of Pronimos' capital until the glow of neon lanterns spilled across his path. The Old West Bar stood just as it always had, a pleasant implementation of Earth culture into alien architecture, complete with wood beams, swinging doors, and the faint twang of a guitar echoing across the room.

Alex found his usual seat, a corner table with a view of the long bar. He ordered an oatmeal stout, its thick, roasted flavor grounding him in something simple, something human. He let the first sip roll across the back of his throat, then leaned back, watching the other patrons laugh and argue over nothing that would matter tomorrow.

The door creaked open. He glanced up and smiled.

Megan walked in.

She spotted him almost immediately and made her way over, "Durant," she said with a faint smile, "you look like a man hiding from the universe."

"You calling me Durant, now?"

"I've been living in a world of military protocol. Sorry," She smiled. "Alex."

"I am a man trying to solve the problems of the universe. Never hiding from them," Alex said. He gestured to the empty seat across from him. "Why aren't you on the front? Last I heard, your Stingers were chewing up Daklin patrols in the Perseid Sector."

She flagged the bartender with two fingers before answering. "We're grounded for a couple days. Software upgrades across the fleet.

You'd think I'd know, but it's some kind of AI alignment, weapons calibration. It gave me a window, so here I am, hanging out in Alex Durant's favorite bar."

"I'm glad you found some time to stop moving long enough to join me," Alex said with a half-smile. Fact was, he definitely could use a friend, and friendships were something he had not developed in recent years.

Megan shrugged, "Todd was supposed to meet me, but he's delayed about an hour. Figured I'd get started without him."

The bartender set a tall glass in front of her, a creamy head crowning the dark liquid. She lifted it, studying the foam and color. "The best vanilla porter in the galaxy." She gently tapped against Alex's mug. "And to taking a couple days to breathe."

Alex raised his stout in return. "To breathing."

Megan took a long pull of her vanilla porter, then set it down with a thud. "Damn, that hits the spot. You know, Alex, you've got terrible taste in drinks. Oatmeal stout? That's what monks drink when they're out of bread."

Alex smirked. "It's a classic. Balanced, smooth. Not everything has to be vanilla and flashy."

She raised an eyebrow. "Balanced? You're in a galaxy where half the human population lives five hundred years or more, and you're playing it safe with monk juice. Geez, Alex. You're hopeless."

He chuckled, lifting his glass. "At least I'm consistent, besides, I also like a vanilla porter, and Guinness."

Megan leaned across the table, eyes twinkling. "Consistent gets you killed out on the front. You should try reckless sometime. Builds character."

Alex snorted. "I'll leave reckless to you. Seems to me that you've got that one well covered."

"Damn right," she said with a grin. "And you love it. Admit it, you'd be bored out of your mind without me raising hell every other week."

"I didn't say that," Alex replied, sipping his stout. "I do appreciate the friendship, Megan. Your insanity actually brings me a bit of sanity."

She jabbed him with her finger. "I know, Alex," she smiled at him affectionately. "You need me to stir your ass up once in a while. Otherwise, you'd drown in strategy reports and spreadsheets until your brain also turned to oatmeal."

Alex laughed despite himself. "Okay, I'll give you that one."

Megan leaned back, taking another sip. "Speaking of drowning… when's the last time you actually let loose? Had some fun that didn't involve anti-Daklin strategy or rewriting weapon software?"

He frowned. "Define fun."

Her eyes rolled. "Christ, Alex. Fun is some sack time with a woman, or several. Fun is more than two beers, or a strenuous hike up a difficult mountain. You've been wound up tighter than a plasma coil since Maria vanished. Hell, my teasing is probably the closest you've been to sex in years. You need to get laid before you snap."

Alex nearly choked on his beer. "Megan…"

"I'm serious as shit, Alex," she said, grinning wickedly. "Look, I'm not saying you've got to fall in love, write poetry, and have three kids on Pronimos. I'm saying find a woman, who has mutual intent, take her to bed, and forget about the Daklin Empire for one goddamn night. I promise, you'll thank me in the morning."

He shook his head, amused and embarrassed. "You never hold back, do you?"

"Hell no," Megan laughed. "Someone's got to keep you human. Otherwise, you'll turn into one of those stone-faced strategists who hasn't been laid since the last ice age."

Alex rubbed his temples, trying not to smile. "You're unbelievable."

"I love you too, Alex," she flipped her hair, winked and blew a kiss. "Unfortunately for you, I am now spoken for… by Todd. Please stop brooding about a billion Daklin cruisers and take my advice."

"Advice about what?" Todd had walked up right at the end of Megan's rant.

Megan stood up and hugged Todd. "Alex needs to do what you and I are gonna go do, now." She winked at Alex and danced out with Todd.

oooo ∞ oooo

Shelby Coates stepped into the bar and looked around. She wondered how many years it had been since she had been in a place like this. Maybe twenty? It felt comfortable, unchanged. What she really wanted was to find a place in the corner, have a porter or stout and just watch people. Then she saw a good-looking man sitting alone. A quick Plink reference said his name was Alex Durant, and he was from Texas.

Shelby really came in to watch, but a good-looking man, thousands of light years from home, also her home, seemed too much like serendipity.

oooo ∞ oooo

Alex was still chuckling at Megan's parting shot when the bar's chair across from him scraped. He glanced up, half-expecting another pilot or strategist. Instead, a woman sat down, her eyes steady but gentle.

"Would you like some company?" she asked with a slight Texas twang.

Alex tilted his head. "Depends."

"Hmmm… Let me start again," She thought about his comment and smiled faintly. "I'm Shelby. My husband died a year ago. This is the first time I've been out since his passing. I've not been to a bar like this for… oh, let's just round it to twenty years. I walked into this bar tonight to people watch, and then I saw you…"

"Did Megan put you up to this?"

"Megan? I know a few Megans, but no one put me up to this. I just wanna sit down with someone, have a beer, and talk. Nothing else, and no one put me up to anything," She waved her had around the bar, "And you're the only one sitting alone in the place."

Alex blinked, studying her more carefully now. She wasn't just striking, she was radiant, in a quiet, unforced way. His eyes traced the strength in her posture, the warmth behind the sadness. For a moment, he forgot the weight of the Daklin.

"Then talking it is," he said, gesturing to her glass. "What'll you have?"

She quickly studied the beer list. "Oatmeal stout," she answered.

"Well, that definitely gets you a few points." He laughed. "Finally, someone who appreciates a good beer."

The hours slipped by. Shelby's voice carried the lilt of old Texas, softened by time and broadened by experiences across worlds. She told him she'd been born near San Antonio in 1836; the very year Texas claimed its independence. She talked about the hard earth of her childhood, the pride of a people who had always carved their lives out of resistance.

And Alex found himself telling her more than he intended, about Princeton, about Paula, the tunnels, about the endless war that seemed to stretch out of reach. She listened without judgment, her eyes never leaving his.

By the time the bartender announced last call, Alex realized he hadn't checked the time once.

As they stood, Shelby stepped close and wrapped her arms around him in a strong, unapologetic hug. The scent of vanilla and cedarwood clung to her hair.

"Texans always hug," she whispered with a smile.

Alex froze for a heartbeat, then returned the embrace, something easing in his chest he hadn't realized was still locked tight. "Yes, yes we do always hug, don't we?"

They stepped out into the Pronimos night, the towers glowing like constellations in the sky. It was a stark contrast from the western feel of the Old West Bar.

"How 'bout we meet again, same time tomorrow?" she asked.

Alex nodded. "I'd like that."

She gave him one last smile before disappearing down the path, leaving Alex standing on the quiet street, lighter than he had felt in years.

The next day, Alex noticed a slight improvement in his creativity, and a lighter feeling in his lungs. He looked forward to seeing his new friend. Was it a date, or just two people leaning on each other in a time of need? He reckoned that the distinction didn't matter so much. The most important thing was that he needed a friend, and it seemed he might now have one.

The Old West Bar was quieter on their second night. Alex scanned the room but did not see Shelby. Lamps flickered against the long oak counter, throwing a golden glow across the rows of dusty bottles, and he walked back to his usual spot.

She probably won't show, he thought to himself, as he pulled out his handheld computer.

Alex looked up as Shelby walked toward his table. For a moment he forgot to breathe. Had he missed this last night? She was striking, with dark, lustrous hair threaded with blond highlights that shimmered in the lamplight. Her face was perfectly symmetrical, high cheekbones, a refined jaw, and a warm smile that carried both comfort and strength. Her skin held a golden undertone, and in the graceful curve of her nose and the subtle fullness of her lips, Alex became transfixed with her eyes, light brown flecked with gold that projected wisdom, and held him locked.

After a few very long seconds, she slid into the chair across from him and set down two pints of oatmeal stout. "Figured you'd want the same as last night," she said, her voice carrying the faintest Texas lilt. "You strike me as a creature o' habit."

Alex took the glass, still caught in her presence. "You'd be right. I like to know what I'm drinking… same as I like to know what's *real* in people."

Shelby gave him a half-smile and leaned back. "Well then, reckon I owe you the truth. My name ain't just Shelby Coates. I was born with the name Shelby West. My momma was Emily D. West, and well…"

His eyes narrowed. "West? As in *the* Emily D. West?" He paused, pulling together lyrics from a song he had learned in his youth, and chapters from a book by James Michener. *"She's the sweetest little rosebud, that Texas ever knew… The Yellow Rose of Texas is the only girl for me."*

Shelby's gaze held his, steady but cautious. "Wow. Apparently, you know your Texas history. Yep, that was my Mama."

"The Yellow Rose of Texas was your mother?" Alex whispered, almost reverently. In another place, he would have questioned the viability of a claim like that, but he had come to realize that everyone on Pronimos had the roots of greatness.

A small, humorless laugh slipped from her. "Yeah, the legend outlasted her. Folks sang about her, painted her as a symbol. To me she was just Mama, a strong, stubborn, secretive woman who was determined to raise me into something that, well, the times just weren't ready for. We moved around plenty… New Orleans, Galveston, a dozen towns in between, but for a spell, we stayed on a ranch outside San Antone. Those were the good years."

"As I remember, the history books said you moved back east after Texas won its independence from Mexico." Alex commented, trying to recall the history.

"We stayed in Texas, so the history got it wrong. Like I said, mama was secretive."

Alex shook his head slowly, the lyrics still echoing through him. "And Sam Houston? Was he really...?" Alex was thinking of the old story that Houston and West had been a couple, and the roots of the yellow rose story started with him.

"She never told me." Shelby broke in, her hand tightened around the beer glass. Her accent grew thicker with the memory. "Sometimes I thought he was my daddy, or at least I wished it. Sometimes I thought she kept it quiet to protect me, or maybe him. I ran genetic testing and learned that I am one-sixteenth black, so momma was probably an eighth. In almost every way, she was a perfect example of the American melting pot. I reckon she was beautiful to any man who looked at her. Anyway, as far as my daddy goes, all I know is, she carried that secret to her grave."

"Well, she passed the beauty on to you, Shelby."

"Thank you, Alex," her golden eyes glinted as she smiled broadly.

"You know, there's a giant statue of Sam Houston on a highway between Houston and Dallas. I bet it's 60-feet-tall."

"I've heard that, but never seen it," she smiled, imagining the statue. "Most of my best memories of Texas are with trails and dirt roads. It's hard to imagine an interstate highway system in that frontier state."

"Texas has changed since the 1800s," he added.

Shelby and Alex paused as the white noise of the bar shifted, an acoustic guitarist had begun to sing, loud enough to be heard, but soft enough that the patrons could still talk.

"When the Civil War came," Shelby went on, her voice turning harder, "I couldn't sit by. I went east, nursed the wounded. Blue coats, gray coats... I didn't give a damn. They all bled the same. Some of them were brothers. When I could, I helped slaves slip free.

I was resourceful and self-taught in medicine. When I needed to, I learned how to forge papers for people wanting to 'scape the war. It was all about makin' it to tomorrow, so I used everything I had to survive."

Alex was nodding, lost in her stories.

"It was rough times, Alex… In any case, helpin' folks was the only victory that ever felt real back then."

Alex's throat tightened. "That's dangerous work. You must've known what it could cost you."

"I knew." She took a slow drink, her eyes never leaving his. "And in the end, I paid the price. A patrol caught me. Men with nothin' left to lose, drunk on rage. They aimed to take what they wanted."

Her jaw set, her stare fixed into the foam of her stout.

"What happened?" Alex asked gently.

"I thought I was dead or worse, and that's when the tunnel opened." Shelby's voice softened, almost wistful. "Light like I'd never seen before, swallowin' everything. Next thing I knew, I wasn't in that camp anymore. I was here, on Pronimos. Saved, though I never asked for it."

Alex sat back, absorbing her story, the song still whispering in his mind. The roots of the yellow rose of Texas, with the promise, the resilience, and the defiance. All of that had been burned into her eyes. He raised his glass. "Shelby, you're living history."

She gave a tired smile, her Texas twang curling soft around the words. "History don't live, Alex. It just follows you around 'til you decide whether to run from it… or drink with it."

"Then here's to history, and to second chances." Alex lifted his beer and clinked her glass, but her words began to settle between them. *History don't live, Alex. It just follows you around 'til you decide whether to run from it… or drink with it.*

He set his glass down slowly, turning it between his fingers. "You know, Shelby… your comment hits close. I've been running from my own history. Paula, Maria… they're both a part of me. Paula was my best friend, my anchor back on Earth. She was the love of my life. Maria was, well, she was more than that, maybe the woman I thought I'd grow old with. And then Megan…"

Shelby held her hand up, "Megan's the one you thought told me to come talk with you…"

"Right," he chuckled softly, shaking his head. "Megan's like fire. She's fun, brilliant, reckless. I never knew whether she was going to kiss me or punch me in the arm and drag me into another fight."

Shelby's smile was knowing, but kind. "Sounds like you've been chasin' ghosts and girls in equal measure. You in love with them?"

"Yeah. I love all three of them, all in different ways," Alex admitted. "I mean, I have not and will never be intimate with Megan, though. I do love her, but it's a different kind of love. Can't quite put a finger on it."

"I have learned not to try and put my finger on love. It works better when you just enjoy it and try to help it grow," Shelby advised.

"That's good advice," Alex nodded. "Anyway, with all this, the Daklin are out there. An empire willing to exterminate entire worlds to keep control. I keep telling myself I'm fighting for the future, but maybe I've just been trying to rewrite my past. Trying to prove to Paula, Maria, even Megan, that I'm worth the sacrifices they've made." He looked up at her, his voice steady. "History doesn't live. You're right. But when it follows you, it doesn't always whisper. Sometimes it shouts, and right now, the Daklin are that history, shouting at me. I just can't seem to get my arms around how to stop looking for ways to stop them." He watched as Shelby took a long drink. She knew how to lock eyes, and hold that lock better than anyone he had ever known,

"You talk like a man who's been carryin' too much for too long, Alex. You can't fix the whole damn galaxy. But you can choose not to let history chain you. My mama, well, you know, people turned her into a song, a legend. They made her into somethin' she never asked to be. She just wanted to live, to be free. That's all I ever wanted, too. Maybe that's what you're fightin' for, whether you can admit it or not."

Alex tilted his head, curious. "Do you ever resent it? Your life and the legend of your mother, that is?"

Shelby paused, her twang softened by honesty. "I was sixteen before the song was written, and. Mama wasn't a legend, she was just Mama. She was brave and strong, but she just wanted to live her life in peace, and that was pretty much impossible for a single woman back then. With regards to the Yellow Rose, I'd been here on Pronimos nearly fifty years before I even knew the song existed. I went back to Earth during World War I, trying to help the troops. Fell in love with a young man who never knew who I really was. He was killed a week before the Battle of the Somme… and I came back to Pronimos."

"Wow, the Civil War and World War 1," Alex said thoughtfully.

"It's the insanity of humanity on Earth, and now out here in the galaxy." She paused, then continued, her voice quieter.

"Anyway, when I was back on Earth, I heard that song… and I knew. I knew it was about Mama the first time I heard it. They sang about a 'rose,' but they never saw the thorns. My Mama was strong, private, and complicated. She was more than just a symbol. But I reckon… legends don't belong to the people they're about. They belong to the ones who *need* 'em."

Alex's eyes softened. "And what about you? What do you need?"

Her smile was wistful. "Not to be a legend. Just to be a woman with a stout in her hand, good company at her side, and maybe a chance at tomorrow."

For a long moment, they sat in silence, the air thick with memory and unspoken truths.

Alex finally lifted his glass. "Then here's to not running anymore. To living with history, instead of letting it chase us."

"Amen to that." Shelby leaned forward, her light brown eyes steady, the faintest Texas twang in her voice. "Tell me more about 'em, Alex. Paula and Maria. You talk about 'em like they're still sittin' right here at this table with us."

Alex hesitated, then set his stout down. "Paula… she was one of the best people I've ever known. A scientist, brilliant, but she didn't think she was. She kept me grounded and made me laugh, reminded me that life was more than numbers and equations. She died in childbirth, and our son Steven is now, well, almost eight."

"You have a son?" Shelby's face lit up.

"He's here on Pronimos…."

"The sparkle in your eyes is all I need to see how much you love him. Go on with the rest of the story, please."

"Right," his voice softened. "Maria's different. Fierce, uncompromising. She makes me feel like everything I do has to matter. Like if I don't give it my all, I'm failing her, failing everyone."

"That's Maria Perez, right?" Shelby broke in.

"You know her?" Alex asked.

"Everyone on Pronimos knows Maria Perez, Alex. You're in love with one of the most beloved and brilliant women on this planet." Shelby studied him for a moment. "I see you have a Plink, but did anyone ever train you on how to use it?"

"Train me? Did you just change the subject, Shelby?"

"Not really. Everyone on Pronimos knows Maria, cuz she's famous here, but we all have access to data. Yours just ain't set up yet."

"Can we do that another time?" Alex asked.

"Okay," Shelby said, a bit surprised that he'd shifted from the technology behind P-Link back to the personal, but maybe that was a good sign. "Let's get back to it, Alex. And Megan? You ain't said much about her."

He chuckled, though it carried no ease. "Megan's fire. Sharp mind, quick fists, and a temper that'll burn down the room if you cross her. With her, it's all adrenaline. She picks impossible goals and doesn't give up till she accomplishes them. She keeps me alive in ways I can't explain, and on the front line, well, I am sure the Daklin quake in fear when they see her ship, Singularity 2."

"Why ain't you with her? She sounds like your kind of spirit."

Alex thought about her question. "Like I said, I love her, but not that way. I don't really have an explanation for it. She's kind of like a sister."

"Well, that's the kiss of death in any potential relationship." Shelby nodded slowly, her fingers circling the rim of her glass. "Seems to me you got women representin' every piece of your soul. You look worn thin cuz you're dealin' with all the issues of female connections but not enjoying any of the benefits."

Alex sighed, ignoring the underlying message in her comment. "It's not just them. It's the Daklin. Every day I wake up thinking: what if I fail? What if their empire wins, and everything we're fighting for: freedom, love, even simple things like kids laughing in a park, all of it disappears? I can't shake the weight of my responsibilities, Shelby. It's like I've been running with a stone on my back that gets heavier every mile."

She tilted her head. "Maybe that's why you hold onto Paula, Maria, and Megan. They ain't just memories. They're your way of remindin' yourself what you're fightin' for."

Alex looked at her, surprised. "You think so?"

"I know so," she said softly. Then her smile faded, replaced by something more reflective. "You ever wonder if love is worth the risk when war's always waitin'?"

"All the time," Alex admitted. "I think that's why I've never been able to let go. Each of them gave me something to hold onto when the universe was burning."

Shelby stared into her stout for a long moment, then lifted her eyes again. "After my first fifty years on Pronimos, I decided to head back to Earth, and fell smack dab in the beginning of World War I. That's when I fell in love with James. He was gentle, and full of light, but when the war broke out, he was chompin' to go fight. Got himself killed just a week before the Battle of the Somme. I thought my heart would be permanently buried with him."

Alex leaned in, listening intently.

"My second love was Tomas, 11 years after that, back here on Pronimos. He built things, dreamed big. We lasted 16 years, had one kid, then drifted apart. No fightin', no hatin'. Just silence where love used to be."

She paused, her voice catching for the first time. "And Daniel. My last. He died just last year. Strong hands, kind eyes. We lived as close to peace as folks like us ever get. When I lost him, I thought I was finished. Done with love. Done with life." She let out a small laugh, shaky but real. "And yet, a few days ago I decided to pick up the pieces and go see what's happenin' in the galaxy, and here I am. Still breathin' and sittin' across from a fellow Texan. It's just pure serendipity."

Alex reached across the table, his hand brushing hers. She didn't pull back. "Shelby, you've carried more than most people could in ten lifetimes."

"Hell, Alex, when I was born, the average lifetime was 'bout 40. I'm now over 200, so I can easily claim I've lived five lifetimes." Her eyes softened, though her voice stayed steady.

"And so have you, Alex. Between the women you've loved and the war you're fightin' you've been run ragged. But don't forget, you ain't just runnin' from history. You're tryin' to keep it from repeatin'. You think maybe it's too much?"

Her words echoed in him, tugging at the same place Paula, Maria, and Megan lived inside his heart. He realized that with Shelby, he didn't have to hide the war or the women. She seemed to already understand both.

He smiled faintly. "You said earlier that history doesn't live. But tonight, talking to you… it feels like it does. In you. In me. In every fight we've taken on."

Shelby's lips curved into a slow smile. "Maybe it does, Alex. Maybe history lives in us, not to chain us down, but to remind us that we're still worth wantin'."

Their eyes locked, and for the first time, the silence between them wasn't heavy with loss or war, it was alive, humming with something neither of them could define.

The Old West Bar was nearly empty when Alex and Shelby finally stood to leave. Their stories and laughter had grown softer with the night, the weight of their shared stories leaving both lighter, yet closer.

At the door, Shelby touched his arm. Her golden-brown eyes shimmered under the lantern glow. For a long moment, they just looked at each other, and then Alex leaned in. Their lips met, gentle at first, then deeper, a kiss filled with memory, longing, and the fragile hope of two people who had lived through too much loss.

When they broke apart, Shelby rested her forehead against his. "Alex," she whispered, her voice carrying that faint Texas twang, "this can't go too far. I am still healing, and I need to think through what's happening here." In truth, there was something else, but for now, it did not seem appropriate to discuss.

He searched her eyes, saw the steel beneath her warmth. "I know, and I can't believe I'm finally saying this, but I don't want this night to end."

"Well, I am fine with the idea of not letting it end." She smiled softly. "Maybe we come back tomorrow. We'll share another oatmeal stout, and a few more stories. See what happens?"

He nodded, kissed her once more, then let her go. "Yes Shelby. Let's do that."

The next day, Alex woke fully refreshed. He worked, he planned, but his thoughts kept drifting back to Shelby's laugh, her wisdom, her beauty that seemed carved by time itself. And yet, every time her face filled his mind, Maria's shadow rose behind it. Maria, the woman whose absence and departure still gnawed at him. Shelby was breathtaking, magnetic, but she wasn't Maria. As he went through the day, it occurred to Alex that he had to find a way to tell Shelby that Maria was still there.

That evening, he walked back into the Old West Bar, rehearsing the words in his mind.

But Shelby was already waiting at their table, two pints in place. She didn't waste time.

"Shelby, I…" Then he looked at her again. She had completely changed from when he had seen her the night before.

Shelby stood up, smiling broadly. "I went to the de-ageing clinic today. They said I was 41. Now I'm 29 again," she did a cute, girlish spin.

Alex was transfixed. "Before the de-aging, you were already uniquely beautiful. But now… you're absolutely breathtaking."

"Thank you, Alex. That's sweet." She pecked him lightly on the cheek, then her face became serious, her voice steady but kind, "Sit, please. I know what you're wrestlin' with."

He started to say something, but she held up a hand.

"Listen to me. We're both healin', and that kiss last night? It wasn't about me and you. It was about you tryin' to stitch up a wound that Maria left behind, and me workin' through life after Daniel. Far as I'm concerned, that's okay. But don't fool yourself into thinkin' you're healin' so you can be with me. I know that you're healin' so you can find your way back to her."

Alex sank into the chair, caught between protest and relief. Had she seen right into his mind, heart, and soul?

Shelby's eyes softened. "And let's not pretend that I don't know who you are, Alex Durant. You're the man who's supposed to save us all from the Daklin. You carry the weight of a galaxy, and I won't be the reason you stumble. You've got work bigger than me, bigger than Maria, bigger than all of us."

He stared at her, speechless, the stout untouched in his hand.

She leaned closer, her voice low but firm. "I like you, Alex. Maybe more than I should on a third date…or meeting, or whatever the hell this is, but I won't let either of us turn this into somethin' that pulls you off *your* path. We'll share a drink, a laugh, maybe even another kiss," she stopped with the memory of how that kiss had made her feel. She took a sip to regain her composure and tried not to stumble on her speech. "And if you get lucky, maybe something even more intimate than just a kiss…" She took another sip. "But the war with the Daklin… the love you still carry for Paula, Steven, Maria, that's where your heart has to be."

For a long moment, Alex just held her gaze, torn between gratitude and longing. Finally, he lifted his glass. "Then here's to being honest. And to not losing sight of what matters."

Shelby smiled faintly, clinking her stout against his. "Amen to that."

Alex smiled, recognizing Shelby's use of that phrase.

"What are you smiling about, Alex?"

"I've heard you say 'Amen to that' several times… and it struck a pleasant chord. Just brought back some memories from Texas."

"Amen to that!" She took a sip and glanced around. The bar was livelier on their third night. In the corner, a man picked gently at an acoustic guitar, coaxing old Texas melodies that reminded Alex of a simpler time back home. The sound floated like a breeze across the plains, softening the edges of war and grief.

Shelby leaned back, tapping the rim of her stout with one finger in time to the music. "Now that right there… that's the sound of home. My mama used to sing to me when she was cookin'. Guess some things never get old. Cuz of that, I learned to play guitar and sing a bit. Nothing great, but it was relaxing."

Alex smiled, savoring the simple moment. "Music's like math. It's a universal language. Doesn't matter who's singing or listening, it pulls the same strings inside you."

"Math, huh?" She grinned. "Leave it to an engineer to turn music into numbers, but I like the image of pulling strings inside you…"

They both laughed, it was the kind of laugh that shook off some of the heaviness from the past few nights. For a while, they kept things light: Texas music, Shelby's days on a ranch near San Antonio, and Alex's awkward high school garage band that never quite learned to play in tune.

The guitarist struck up a slower tune, and the night stretched softly around them. Shelby tilted her head, her eyes glinting as she leaned closer. "Alex, can I ask you somethin' straight?"

"Sure," he said cautiously.

"You ever thought about it? With me, I mean." Her voice was matter of fact, Texas blunt, though her cheeks carried a faint warmth.

Alex blinked, caught off guard. "It…?" he stammered.

"Yeah, it. You know, pulling *my* strings inside." She smiled.

"Honestly… maybe?" Alex felt himself flush. "Uhh, not like that."

"I know you're lying, Alex. You're a man." Shelby chuckled, shaking her head. "And just so you know, I *have*." She sipped her beer, then looked at him openly. "Been thinkin' about it more than I figured I would. Truth is, the last years with Daniel, my third husband, they were comfortable. But we weren't lovers anymore. Hadn't been for, hell, over 12 years. Nice marriage, great connection, but no spark."

Alex shifted in his chair, the tips of his ears going red. "That's… I mean… thanks for being honest. Can I ask what that was like for you?"

Her smile softened, but her voice stayed frank. "Like livin' with a good friend. We cared for each other, shared meals, talked about our kids and grandkids. But that fire? It was gone. And once it goes, Alex, it don't come back." She leaned closer, her tone lowering. "So yeah, sittin' here across from you, I've been thinkin' about it. About havin' that spark again. Just not with any strings, ya know?"

Alex swallowed, caught between curiosity, embarrassment, and a tug of something else he wasn't ready to name. "I'm not really good on this topic, but I'm curious. Tell me more," he said quietly.

Her eyes lit up, surprised at his courage. She took another slow sip of her stout, then set it down deliberately. "Alright, Alex Durant," she said, her twang curling around his name, "but only if you promise to keep listenin' without turnin' red as a schoolboy every time that I say somethin' plain."

Alex laughed nervously, raising his hands in surrender. "No promises. But I'll try."

Shelby tilted her glass, watching the foam slide down. "You asked me to tell you more."

Alex nodded, bracing himself.

"My first husband, James," she said softly, "we were young. Love was hot and fast, like a prairie fire. Didn't last long, cuz the war took him. But those nights we had… they burned bright. I still dream about those nights. With Tomas, on Pronimos, it was steadier. We had sixteen years of building a home, raising a baby into an adult. The intimacy there was about building a family life. Not much excitement in the bedroom after our child was born. And Daniel…" Her voice faltered, then steadied. "Daniel was comfort. Strong arms to hold me, but after a while, no heat. We grew old together without growin' closer. I think you get my metaphorical description of growin' old. Most of our time, we visited the de-ageing clinic regularly."

She looked down at her skin, "Though I will admit, I hadn't been in, shoot ten or eleven years." She stopped, trying to read him. "Before today, I probably looked pretty old, eh?"

"You look fantastic before and after Shelby. Truth is, every time I look at you, you take my breath away."

"Now that's just downright sweet, Alex. Thank you." She took a sip of beer, remembering where she was in her story, "Anyway, that female part of me, wantin' and bein' wanted, well I've missed it for a long, long time."

Alex shifted in his chair, throat dry. "I think I know what you mean. With Maria, even though nothing ever happened between us, it was passion and purpose tangled together. With Paula… it was laughter and tenderness, but the intimacy, I can't imagine anything like that again in this lifetime. When we… well, we got really close."

"That's really sweet, Alex." She thought about how it would be to have someone feel that way about her. "Well, darlin, you solve this Daklin problem and 'lifetime' will take on a whole new meaning. Think about living over a thousand years. What year were you born anyway?"

"1987. You?"

"I told you; I was born in 1836. I think I turned 202 this year." She furrowed her brow as if trying to remember something. "Remind me, what year is it on Earth?"

Alex thought about it for a second, "it's 2038."

"Right, see I really don't keep count anymore. It's just not as important as it was 150 years ago. Anyway, I could say that you are just a child, but I have begun to understand that women mature in their early twenties, and men, well most have matured by thirty, but not all," she laughed lightly.

Shelby leaned forward, her eyes locking with his. "Anyway, plenty of those holes need fillin'. Shoot, I certainly got one."

Alex coughed into his beer, nearly choking. "That's… quite the way to put it."

She grinned, her Texas twang curling playful now. "I'm just sayin', Alex Durant, sometimes two folks can meet in the middle. Not lookin' to replace what we've lost, not tryin' to tangle up hearts that already belong elsewhere. Just two people healin', sharin', and keepin' each other strong for the fight."

His cheeks flushed, but he didn't look away. "Are you suggesting what I think you're suggesting?"

"I reckon you're smart enough to figure it out," she teased. "Question is, are you brave enough to admit you've been thinkin' about it too?"

Alex chuckled nervously. "Until tonight, no. Well, maybe a little, but now? Let's just say the thought doesn't sound… impossible."

Shelby leaned closer, dropping her voice. "Well, it don't sound impossible to me either. Maybe we don't need to call it love, or forever. Maybe we just call it what it is. A way to keep from forgettin' we're still alive. Medicine to help us heal. Someone to hold you while you're fallin' asleep."

Alex's eyes lingered on her lips before he forced himself back to her gaze. "You make it sound… logical."

"Logical?" She laughed low and warm. "Darlin, I took them classes and it's a hell of a lot more fun than logic. But you can think about it any way you choose."

"I need to introduce you to Megan. I think the two of you are common spirits."

"I don't want to be introduced if she's gonna come between what's happenin' here," She answered with a wink. "I almost hate to ask right now, but how'd you leave it with Maria?"

Alex thought about their last meeting. "She said something like she'd never have an intimate relationship with me if she thought I was thinking about Paula, and she's convinced I'm still thinking about Paula."

"And are you?"

"Am I still thinking about Paula? No!"

"Maria's a hard ass, ain't she?"

"I suppose," he answered thoughtfully, "but in a way, she's right. I don't believe I'll ever stop *fully* thinking about Paula."

"I know that, and Maria should know that as well," she took a sip of her beer. "So, how long's it been?"

"Excuse me? Since what?" Alex was a bit shocked and surprised by her question.

Shelby laughed and continued laughing for several seconds.

"What?" Alex repeated, not understanding the humor in the situation.

"In 200 years, men haven't changed, Alex. The only thing you ever think about is sex. Sex, sex, sex," she chuckled again. "I was asking how long ago Maria left?"

"Oh, sorry." He stopped and counted, realizing how little he actually monitored the passage of time anymore. The only thing he ever really worried about was when the Daklin would be ready to attack Earth, and his estimate was another year. "It's been a few years."

"And the other question, the one you *thought* I was asking?"

"Since Paula, so more than eight years."

"You ready to end the long drought?"

"Yes, I definitely am," Alex nodded and raised his glass, voice steady now. "Here's to rain at the end of a long hike through the desert."

"To ending the drought," Shelby clinked her stout against his, her eyes locked. "And here's to not wastin' the time we got."

At this point in the conversation, the last notes of the guitar drifted into silence, leaving only the low murmur of voices and the faint creak of the old bar. Shelby leaned back, her eyes steady on Alex. "So, what now? We sit here 'til dawn pretendin' we ain't both thinkin' the same thing?"

Alex hesitated, then pushed his glass aside. "I think I'm ready, but not really sure how this should go down." He paused.

"We could start with that, if you want." She answered, with a sly laugh. "There are better ways to culminate this…"

"I didn't mean it that way, I was just thinking the bar is closing soon and maybe we continue this conversation at your place, or mine?"

Her smile was gentle but firm. "Yours."

He tilted his head in curiosity, caught off guard. "Why not yours?"

She laid a hand lightly over his. "That house still holds too many memories…Daniel's boots by the door, his coat on the peg. It's full of them. Not the best venue for makin' new ones. Tonight's about you and me. We're two souls needin' somethin' simple. If we're gonna do that, it seems like… well, let's do it somewhere there ain't no memories hanging around."

"Okay," he said, leading her out the door, affectionately holding her hand as they walked down the road toward the tower where his apartment was.

Alex's door slid open to reveal a tidy, sterile space. Everything in its place, no clutter, no warmth.

Shelby stepped inside, glanced around, and let out a low chuckle. "Lord, Alex… this ain't a home. This is a clean box where a man solves problems and forgets the real purpose of life."

Alex scratched the back of his neck, embarrassed. "Guilty, but at least it's clean. I guess I've been too busy with tunnels and wars to worry about throw pillows."

"Don't get me wrong, I don't take you for the throw pillow type," She touched his arm, eyes soft. "But still, if I can bring one thing of value to you, I hope it is a recognition that even when the war is blazing around us, we've got to appreciate the good things in life."

"Roger that, Shelby Coates." Alex surveyed his apartment. She was exactly right. For far too long, he had been singularly focused on the Daklin fight. He looked down at her hand, which was still gently touching his arm. It felt good.

As Shelby's hand lingered, the silence thickened. Alex leaned in, and this time the kiss came easy, unhurried. Her lips were warm, sure, and receptive.

After a few seconds she pulled back, her smile held no teasing, only quiet understanding. "Remember, this ain't about betrayal or loss. This is about healin' and remindin' ourselves we're still flesh and blood, not just ghosts fightin' ghosts."

Alex nodded, his voice low. "I understand."

In the bedroom, she ran her hand across the dresser, noting its dustless perfection. "Figures," she murmured. "I bet if I open the drawer, I will see evidence that a man with a brain like yours keeps his socks in military formation."

Alex laughed softly, tension easing. "Would it help if I told you I've been known to leave a glass in the sink overnight?"

"Now you're talkin' wild," she teased, standing on one leg and playfully wrapping the other around him. "Alex Durant, you been carrying the weight of the galaxy, but tonight, you let me carry a little piece of you."

He melted with her words and kissed her slowly, allowing himself to feel instead of think. Clothes fell away without haste, each touch became a reassurance, each breath a reminder that neither of them was alone.

They moved together with a tenderness born not of lust, but of long denial, of two people who had patiently waited to be understood and touched. Her warmth pressed against him, his hands exploring the curves that spoke of life fully lived, losses endured, and resilience unbroken.

When they finally came together, it was not the wildfire of youth, nor the comfortable rhythm of a long marriage. It was more like a sweet, aching bridge between past wounds and present healing. Their bodies found a rhythm, their hearts a moment of peace.

Afterward, they laid tangled in the sheets, "Do you see now?" she whispered. "Healin' ain't so complicated. Sometimes it's just about rememberin' what it feels like to be alive."

Alex kissed the top of her head, breathing in the scent of her hair. He pulled her in tight and fell into a restful asleep.

18

Rigel Kentaurus

Alex woke the next morning feeling a bit of joy in his heart. The early light crept through the blinds, softening the room with a golden hue. Shelby was still asleep beside him, her hair spilling across the pillow in gentle waves. For a long moment, he just watched her breathe, appreciating the quiet strength and breathtaking beauty of this woman who had so deliberately set her mind on healing him.

He leaned down, kissed her lightly on the forehead, and slipped out of bed. He grabbed one of his shirts that he thought would probably cover her to her knees and set in gently on her side of the bed.

Pulling on his own shirt, he walked into his study, woke his computer, and fell into the comfort of strategy and tactics. The underlying theme was physics and the hum of calculations in his head.

An hour passed before Shelby stirred. She glided quietly across the room wearing the shirt he had left her, still tousled from sleep, and wrapped her arms around him from behind.

"Morning cowboy," she whispered into his shoulder.

He turned with a smile, stood, and pulled her into his arms. "You smell good," he murmured, savoring the scent of her skin.

She melted into a kiss that ended back in the bedroom. Like the night before, it wasn't passion, but communication.

When it ended, they just held each other silently for a while.

"Where's the coffee in this place?" she asked.

"Kitchen," he answered, not really wanting to let her go.

"I'll make us some."

He took a deep breath, exhaled slowly, and moved so she could get up. "Second cabinet, right side," he said. "But you don't have to…"

"Alex Durant," she cut him off with a mock sternness, "after the last three evenings, and last night, …just let a Texas girl make you some coffee."

They shared a smile, the kind that carried more weight than words.

As she moved toward the kitchen, she looked back over her shoulder. "*That* was… healin'. You know that, right?"

Alex sat up in the bed, still caught by the glow in her eyes. "Yeah. I do. I didn't think I needed to be healed, but now I know."

She smiled and blew him a kiss. "Good," Shelby said softly. "Because I didn't come here to break you. I came here to remind us both, we're still alive."

Alex got up after her, walked to the kitchen, and wrapped his arms around her from behind as she stood at the cabinet. "You have definitely proven that we're both still alive, Shelby."

"It took both of us to do that, Alex." She smiled and nodded.

○ ○ ○ ○ ∞ ○ ○ ○ ○

Alex and Shelby began spending most of their free time together. In the quiet spaces, between the chaos of strategy sessions and the endless analysis of Stinger upgrades, Shelby brought a kind of grounding Alex hadn't known he needed.

One evening, as they walked through a Pronimos park, Shelby stopped, "You went to another galaxy, Alex. You saw what's out there. Does it make you think our side has a chance?"

He paused, searching her eyes, "The truth is, our odds are not good."

"So, why stir up the fire ant bed when we're standing barefoot right next to it?"

Alex chuckled. "Before I answer that, tell me something. I heard you chatting with people at your work the other day. No Texas twang. With me, I hear you mostly speaking twang, but not always."

"Alex, I grew up in Texas in the 1850s, that's my roots, and it makes me happy. But I also speak six languages. If I went to Earth and spoke Spanish, people would ask what part of Peru I'm from, cuz I learned Peruvian Spanish. I love my Texas roots, and I know you appreciate them too. But I can speak proper English anytime you'd prefer."

"Got it, and sorry about the rabbit hole, but you can talk to me in any language or accent that makes you happy." He lifted a hand to caress her cheek, then returned to the original topic. "I have heard odds of us winning against the Daklin are as bad as trillions to one."

"I'm not great in math but isn't that basically the same as a zero chance," Shelby clarified.

"It is, but the colonies had zero chance of beating the British, but they found a way, and now, with a love of liberty, the US is a world power. Still, we all need to adopt a different attitude."

"Give me liberty or give me death?" she interjected. "Patrick Henry, if I recall. By the way, I was born just ten years after Thomas Jefferson died."

"Holy crap, that's right! Jefferson dies in 1826." Alex put his arm around her and affectionately pulled her closer, "I love the Patrick

Henry quote, but I prefer Ben Franklin's version, which essentially says that if you're willing to trade liberty for safety, you don't deserve either."

"So, we should stir up the fire ants even though we are next to the mound?" Shelby returned to the original question.

"Yep," Alex quipped.

○○○○ ∞ ○○○○

They decided to take a break from the madness and impossible Daklin tasks and set out into the southern Pronimos mountains with packs slung across their shoulders, a tent, and enough food and water to stay a few days. The trail wound upward through pines that smelled sharp and alive, their boots crunching over stone.

Shelby stopped to catch her breath, grinning as she wiped sweat from her forehead. "Feels good to be out here, doesn't it? No computer screens, no comm alerts. Just you, me, and a sky big enough to swallow the universe."

"Is that the Daklin sky swallowing the universe?" Alex asked, a bit sarcastically.

"No Daklins allowed on this hike, Alex."

"Good rule, Alex agreed. "It's been too long since I hiked like this, and I never thought I'd be carrying a tent, sleeping bag, and provisions again. I have traveled to Andromeda, and the ship there had glamping with entire parks under domes bigger than cities."

She chuckled. "Bet they didn't have mosquitoes."

"You're right about that. Advantage: Earth and Pronimos. What's camping without bloodsucking insects?" He laughed, and they pressed on.

When they reached a ridge overlooking the valley, they dropped their packs and sat side by side. Shelby pulled a flask from her bag and took a sip before passing it to Alex.

"Do you know what I do?" she asked.

"Besides dragging me up mountains?"

"I think I have dragged you into the bedroom more times than the mountains," she started. "Anyway, we've never really talked about what I do when I'm not hanging with you."

"We haven't talked about it, but your Plink profile is complete... I thought it would come up when you wanted to discuss it."

"Yes, of course Plink is updated. Most people on Pronimos are updated. You're the one with secrets." She pinched him and grinned mischievously. "I work with a data company that monitors the organic health of cybernetics. It's a whole field most people don't think about. Everyone assumes they're just machines with skin, but they're more complicated than that."

"That much I know, Shelby," Alex leaned back against a rock enjoying the opportunity to hear her talk about her work. "Tell me more."

"They can recharge at an electrical port like plugging in a tablet computer," she explained. "Or, if they're away from power, most of them can eat and run energy through the Krebs cycle, just like us. Problem is, being partly organic means they're vulnerable too. They can get infections, have vitamin deficiencies, even metabolic disorders if the balance is off."

"That's... incredible," Alex said, brow furrowed. "So, in keeping them healthy, you're basically treating them like people?"

"Exactly," Shelby said softly. "Because they *are* people. Just built differently. The scary part is that sometimes the data shows they're even more fragile than us."

The conversation about cybernetics continued as they got up, continued hiking, then picked a small clearing on the mountain slope to make camp for the night. They had climbed high enough that the air had thinned, and the night sky blazed with impossible clarity.

Alex dropped his pack, pulled out a knife and kindling kit, and began arranging a fire ring with the practiced efficiency of someone who'd done it a hundred times.

Shelby crouched beside him, grinning. "You know, I'm the one who grew up in the Old West, but you're the one who's good at this. You sure you're not secretly a Boy Scout?"

"I was, and the truth is, it was a secret," Alex said, striking a flame.

The fire caught quickly, crackling against the chill. They set a small pan over the flames, with Alex stirring together a simple stew of dehydrated vegetables, spices, and strips of beef.

"Not bad camp cooking technique for the only man I know whose been to Andromeda," Shelby said, leaning back on her elbows, hair catching firelight.

Alex raised a spoonful, blew on it, and passed it to her. "You try it first."

She took a bite, closed her eyes dramatically, then nodded. "Edible. Barely. But if you finish your dinner, you can have dessert."

"Dessert?" Alex frowned. "You carried a sleeping bag, two gallons of water, and half the food. Did you pack dessert or are we talking about… something else?"

"*That*, can happen later, and you can call it desert, but for now," Shelby pulled a small, wrapped bundle from her pack. "Texas girl, remember? Always pack homemade cookies."

He laughed, shaking his head. "You just saved this expedition."

After dinner, Shelby pulled out a small backpacker's guitar. "You ready to sing? Every camping trip needs a soundtrack, ya know."

Alex watched her tuning totally by ear.

She strummed a few chords, soft at first, then her voice carried clear into the night. Alex joined in, half-singing, half-laughing, when they slipped into the first verse of *The Yellow Rose of Texas*.

"You're off key," Shelby teased as she continued playing.

"I'm a scientist," Alex countered, "not a musician, but let me try the second verse."

> *She's the sweetest little rosebud,*
> *That Texas ever knew,*
> *Her eyes are bright as diamonds,*
> *They sparkle like the dew;*
> *You may talk about your Clementine,*
> *And sing of Rosalee,*
> *But the YELLOW ROSE OF TEXAS*
> *Is the only girl for me.*

Shelby stopped singing and playing and just watched Alex. "Them ain't the original lyrics, cowboy," she said, returning to her Texas twang. The way he delivered those lyrics made her feel something real and warm inside.

"I know, it's the Mitch Miller rendition, but they are the words I learned, and well…" He stopped, not sure what to say next.

Shelby leaned against him; eyes lifted to the starfield overhead. "Be careful Alex. We're here to heal, not to fall. I know it's just lyrics, but I'm about as close as anyone will ever get to the yellow rose of Texas… so I'll give you a pass with no explanation necessary." She paused, forcing herself to calm the slight flutter in her heart.

"Yeah," Alex took a deep breath and exhaled slowly. "Makes you realize how small we are. And how damn far from home."

She turned, searching his eyes. "For tonight, from you, I'll take that last line in the lyrics…"

Alex pulled her into his arms.

The kiss was natural, unhurried, carrying the warmth of the campfire and shared laughter of the day. Their hands found each other, and soon they were tangled in a blanket, the fire throwing shadows across bare skin. Their lovemaking was both tender and fierce, a continued release of weeks of tension and wounds.

Later, Shelby rested against his chest, laying in the tent. "Alex," she whispered, "we keep spending time together. Cooking, singing, hiking… and this." She kissed him lightly. "It's easy. Too easy."

He tightened his arm affectionately around her. "You're exactly what I needed right now. After all the struggles and everything else… something that molds and bends with me and doesn't fight back."

She tilted her head up, grinning in a Texas twang. "I'll fight back, cowboy."

"You?" He chuckled. "Against me?"

Shelby rolled suddenly, pinning his arm and straddling his waist. "You bet your sweet science-boy ass I can. I've got weapons you don't stand a chance against."

Alex gasped, seeing her perfect body and breathtaking features, "You win…"

Laughter mixed with kisses, kisses gave way to urgency, and soon they were lost in each other again. The nylon walls muffled their cries, their sweet mirth, and finally, their whispers as they tangled together, exhausted, falling asleep in each other's arms.

Dawn came with the scent of morning in the mountains, and the soft sound of water boiling on coffee grounds. Alex packed the tent while Shelby poured steaming coffee into two battered mugs.

"Good black coffee for my Texas pardner," she said, handing him a steaming cup.

"Morning, trouble." He finished saying when his Plink buzzed.

Adamez's voice cut in, sharp and direct: *Alex, you need to get to Earth. ASAP.*

Alex straightened, coffee forgotten: *What's happening?*

Adamez responded: *Not over link. Just move. Every hour counts.*

The connection snapped.

Alex quickly relayed the message to Shelby. "I can call Tranquility. They'll pick me up, drop you in Pronimos City on the way…"

"Hell no," Shelby interrupted. "Unless you're pickin' Maria up on the way, I'm coming."

"Shelby, this is the war. Adamez wouldn't have called if it wasn't dangerous. You don't have to…"

"Bullshit," she planted her hands on her hips, fire in her eyes. "Don't tell me where I belong, Alex. You think I hiked these mountains, camped in the cold, and wrestled your stubborn hide just to sit safe on Pronimos when my home planet is in danger? Not a chance."

He sighed. "You're impossible."

"Damn right," she grinned. "And you like it."

Within the hour, Tranquility shimmered into view above the tree line. Emily's voice greeted them as the hatch opened. Jabari gave Alex a curious look, then gave Shelby an approving nod as they boarded.

The hatch sealed behind them with a quiet hiss. Shelby's eyes darted across the corridor, wide with surprise. "This is the first time I've been on the legendary Tranquility. It's amazing."

Emily glanced at Shelby then focused directly on Alex. "You need to know what I've learned."

Alex focused on Emily. "Go ahead."

"Intelligence confirms the Daklin have been testing tachyon tunneling near Rigel Kentaurus."

Alex's brow furrowed. "Alpha Centauri system?"

"Correct," Emily said. "Triple star. Four-point-three light years from Earth. The tests were not routine. They have reverse engineered our technology, Alex."

"Shit…"

"Exactly, a vast armada is forming there. Based on our intelligence, they could reach Earth in a matter of days."

Shelby blinked, her coffee mug still in hand from camp. "Four light years? I'm not an astronomer, but that's… nothing in galactic distances."

Emily turned toward her. "Exactly. Centauri is Earth's nearest neighbor system. A fleet forming there poses an immediate existential threat."

Jabari, leaning on the bulkhead, gave a low whistle. "How long will it take us to get there?"

"Normally 35 to 40 hours, but we are going to push it. I think we can get there in 29."

Alex's mind raced. "How many ships?"

Emily's tone dropped by half a register. "We don't have good enough intelligence yet to tell, but too many to count with certainty. Multiple cruisers, carrier-class vessels, and escorts. We estimate hundreds."

"How many DPKs?" Alex asked.

"We don't know yet," Emily answered. "There's an open tunnel to Centauri from a couple of Daklin controlled worlds."

"Can we close it?"

Shelby swallowed hard, then asked, "What's a DPK, and do we have the ability to stop that big of a force?"

"That's our name for the Daklin Planet Killer," Emily softened her gaze toward her. "I don't know about the DPKs. We've never faced them before."

"Megan?" Alex asked.

"Megan has already been informed. She is leading the Stinger squadrons toward Earth as we speak. They are close, so they should be in Earth's orbit before us."

Alex's jaw tightened. "Good. Then we fight with everything we've got."

Shelby nudged him, trying to cut through his tension. "Guess our little camping trip's over, huh?"

He gave her a half-smile. "Yeah. Back to saving the world. Get ready Shelby, this is going to be intense."

Shelby listened to the hum of Tranquility's engines, "I'm ready, I think."

Alex studied Shelby for a moment, and then his heart sank. Just hours earlier, they were laughing and enjoying each other without a care in the world. He had made a mistake by allowing her to come. People were going to die, and he did not want Shelby to be one of them.

Shelby could see it in his eyes. "Alex, now is your time to focus. Do *not* be distracted by my presence. I'm not sure yet what I can contribute, but there's no place I'd rather be than with the team that's defending Earth."

Twenty-nine hours at fourteen minutes after entering the tunnel, Tranquility emerged above the blue-white curve of Earth. The planet shimmered in its quiet beauty, but Alex knew peace was an illusion.

Shelby put her arm around Alex affectionately, "I never tire of this view. A hundred sixty years on Pronimos, and this is still home."

"Sorry to interrupt, Alex, Bringing Adamez aboard," Emily reported.

Art Adamez popped in using Zander's backpack technology. He gave Shelby a quick nod before turning to Alex.

"Glad you made it," Adamez said, voice low. "We don't have long."

Alex studied him. "Give it to me straight."

Adamez exhaled, almost a growl. "Best estimates, we can stop nine DPKs."

Shelby frowned. "There's that terrifying acronym again. I guess I need to remember the DPKs?"

"We all do, Shelby," Alex clarified, grim. "They are massive warships designed to obliterate entire worlds. The fact they are coming means only one thing, and it's not to negotiate peace."

"They are coming to exact revenge," Adamez nodded. "They're on the move. Megan's been running Stinger sorties up to Kentaurus, but these Daklin cruisers, hell, they've adapted. Learned from their losses. The Stingers still outperform them, but even Megan's squadron is starting to take damage. We're still kicking their butt in every fight, but the ratios are definitely shifting."

Jabari's brow furrowed. "Are you saying the balance has shifted?"

"Not yet," Adamez said. "We still outfly them and outthink them, but in the beginning, we had a 100 to 1 kill ratio and now it's more like 20 to 1. It's all about numbers Jabari, and numbers don't lie. The Daklin outnumber us by infinite margins, and they're coming to prove a point, and crush the resistance. To put Earth under their boot and take revenge for the ships we've already destroyed."

"The goal of destroying Earth is more than just a battle to them." Alex added. "It's a demonstration to the resistance of what happens to civilizations that oppose them."

Silence settled over the control room. The weight of it pressed like a physical force.

Alex finally broke it. "So, nine DPKs are the line."

Adamez gave a curt nod. "Anything past that, and Earth burns."

Alex placed a hand on the console; eyes locked on the spinning blue world below. "Let's prepare for the invasion from Rigel Kentaurus and make them regret ever pointing their fleet at Earth."

19

The Battle for Earth

It did not begin with a whimper. Instead, the stars seemed to tear open simultaneously between Jupiter's orbit and the Oort cloud. Cruisers and smaller fighters began pouring out of tunnels in five different locations simultaneously. Megan and the Stinger swarms tunneled to the invaders and engaged.

Art Adamez had one job: monitoring for DPKs. Once those ships entered the solar system, they needed about five minutes to charge up their massive energy burst, after that, there was no stopping it. Despite all their efforts, Alex and the Pronimos science team had never been able to replicate the reflection event that had occurred a little just under five years earlier on 437B.

Art Adamez broke the silence. "First DPK, bearing four degrees clockwise from Earth's position, elevation plus seventeen, distance seven AUs."

Shelby looked at the Solar System map. "That's between the orbits of Jupiter and Saturn."

Alex's tone cut sharp. "Emily, timing. Collapse it before the DPK clears the tunnel."

Emily's eyes glowed with calculation, her organic body bobbing, almost as if the calculations were a form of music. "Initiating collapse sequence. Three… two…"

The tunnel folded, unleashing a surge of violet fire across the void. No amount of shielding or advanced super-materials could withstand the collapse of a tachyon tunnel. The DPK's midsection tore apart, half of it vanished back into the tunnel, while the rest shredded into incandescent wreckage. Fragments tumbled away, caught in the pull of solar gravity, leaving a glittering trail across the deep black.

Adamez's voice was steady but electric. "One DPK destroyed."

The comms erupted with cheers, Stinger pilots screaming triumph into the dark.

Megan cut across them. "Save the celebration! Cruisers incoming. Form up!"

The void filled with movement. Cruisers surged from secondary tunnels, wings of black steel swarming like locusts. The Stingers dove to meet them, their sleek profiles carving through space, creating chaos.

"Stinger lead engaging," Megan called. Her squadron tore into the Daklin line. X-ray laser fire streaked in arcs of white-blue, cruisers detonating one after another. "Nine cruisers down," Megan announced.

But soon after a cry cut the celebration short. "I've got two on me… can't…" The transmission died in static. A Stinger in the distance blossomed into a silent fireball.

"Dammit!" Megan's voice cracked with fury. "They're adapting. Keep moving!"

The next tunnel opened at a different vector. "Second DPK, bearing ninety-one degrees, elevation minus twenty-three, distance twelve AUs," Adamez called.

Alex pictured the map in his head: out past Saturn's orbit, below the ecliptic. "They're probing from the south side now, trying to find a weakness."

Emily locked onto the breach. "Collapse sequence engaged."

The tunnel folded violently, shredding the second DPK before it could fully emerge. One vast section remained intact long enough to glow, then tore apart in cascading fire.

Adamez's voice rang. "Two DPKs destroyed."

For a heartbeat, the defenders started to believe they could win.

The Daklin pressed harder. Cruisers formed disciplined triangles, cross-firing at lone Stingers. Megan's swarm held its ground, adapting to the cruiser formation.

The Stingers tore the triangles to pieces, but the Daklin adapted quickly. Their AI was probing, testing, searching for weaknesses and vulnerabilities. To the Daklin, lives and cruiser counts were irrelevant.

For the next two days, the battle was limited to Daklin cruisers and fighters clashing with the Stingers. While one wave of Stinger pilots rested, fresh swarms rotated in to hold the front line. The Daklin were systematically testing the capabilities, and the limits, of Earth's defenses.

Emily was analyzing battle statistics. In the beginning, the Stingers were taking out 22 Daklin cruisers for every Resistance Stinger lost. But as the battle dragged on and the relentless stream of Daklin ships continued, that ratio dropped to 19. Emily knew that if she could see the trend, so could the Daklin. During her rest period, Megan came aboard Tranquility, which was serving as the Command Center War Room.

"Within five days, our losses, combined with the declining kill ratio, will result in a Daklin victory," Emily said, displaying the trend lines for Megan, Alex, and Adamez.

"We've got this," Megan responded with confidence.

But before she could finish her comment, they all heard the scream of a pilot as his ship spun into the barrage, vaporizing in a flare that lit the displays. Another vanished moments later, caught in the trap of converging plasma fire.

Silence fell on the channel, then Megan's voice, low and raw, Plinked out to Todd. "We're losing them. I need that next software update."

"Megan, it's not gonna be ready for several days." Todd answered, looking at the code that still needed work, and then to be tested.

Megan ignored him and added Zander to the thread. "Zander, can you help Todd finalize the release and get it uploaded to my Stingers, please. I need it NOW."

"It'd be helpful if you could code alongside us, Megan," Todd interjected.

Sun Tsu stepped in, "Megan, give them a couple hours of your time. We all know that you're the best pilot out there, but you're also the best coder...."

Megan took a deep breath, but before she could think through the position, Adamez interrupted.

"Third DPK, bearing one hundred forty-five degrees, elevation plus thirty-two, distance nineteen AUs," Adamez reported.

Megan glanced at him, stunned. "That's near Uranus's orbit. We have a bunch of Stingers there."

"They're stretching farther out," Alex muttered. "Trying to determine the outside edges of our response time."

Emily rerouted power, her whole-body synching to the task. The collapse sequence fired late, the tunnel shrieking as it tore itself apart. The DPK was severed diagonally, its front half tumbling into open space, its aft still trapped in subspace before both halves disintegrated.

Adamez's jaw tightened. "Three DPKs destroyed. But they're still adjusting. We just barely got that one."

Alex stood tall, voice carrying through the control deck. "Then we adjust faster. Earth still stands." He looked at Megan, who was deep in thought.

"Megan?" Alex grabbed her shoulders to get her attention.

"Yes?"

"Quit thinking about this. Return to your roots for a couple of hours and get that update done," Alex commanded.

"Yes, sir," she chided, half-joking, but mostly stressed. "Just make damned sure my team stays intact while I'm sitting in an air-conditioned room playing nerd."

Alex put a hand on Megan's shoulder, his voice steady. "I understand your frustration, but if we lose focus, we lose Earth. The Stingers have got to keep the cruisers away from our War Room."

"I'll get it done," Megan answered, and went to her old quarters on Tranquility where she could focus on code without distractions from the war.

Three hours later, alarms blared again.

Adamez's voice was crisp, almost too calm. "This time it's two DPKs emerging, bearing thirty-two degrees, elevation plus eleven, distance sixteen AUs. The second one is thirty-nine degrees, elevation plus fifteen, distance seventeen AUs. The are coming out in close proximity to each other."

Shelby's knuckles whitened on her console. "They're coming in pairs now." She closed her eyes and thought about her potential value.

Alex didn't flinch. "Emily, treat them as one target. Can we collapse both tunnels with the same drone before they split formation?"

"Not possible, Alex," Emily responded. "The drone is destroyed during the collapse, and the two are just far enough apart so the destruction of one will not impact the other."

"That's Daklin intelligence for you," Alex muttered.

Emily's fingers danced, body tense. "Synchronizing collapse fields… now."

Shelby watched Emily work. The one thing she knew better than anyone onboard was cybernetics.

The twin tunnels collapsed, violet lightning crawling across the void. Both DPKs shuddered, their massive hulls tearing apart almost in unison. Wreckage spun away, glittering like falling stars against the black.

The comms filled with whoops from Stinger pilots.

Adamez spoke over the cheers, deliberate as a metronome. "Fourth and fifth DPKs destroyed."

Shelby walked up to Emily and in a low voice whispered. "How's your power level?"

Emily stopped, turned to Shelby and realized her intent. "I am at 31% Shelby. Organic energy sources cannot keep up with my power consumption."

"Understood. Let me work on it," Shelby turned and walked down to Emily's quarters to inspect the recharge interface. She pulled up the Tranquility manifest on the wall screen, started making notes and mumbling to herself.

She walked back into the War Room and grabbed Alex. "I know this is a crazy time, but I need two minutes."

Alex surveyed the room. Everything seemed under control. "Okay…"

Shelby got right into it. "We've got two portable energy converters in storage bay twelve, and a redundant feed line for the starboard X-ray laser which hasn't been installed. If I reroute, I can piggyback a charging circuit straight into the War Room deck."

"For what?" Alex was surprised how Shelby had stepped into the middle of an engineering problem that made no sense.

"Alex, I'm the cybernetics expert on the ship. I have been monitoring Emily, and she's down to 31%."

"Holy crap!" Alex exclaimed. "Do you have a fix?"

"Yes," Shelby replied. "Give me three hours."

"Do it." Alex returned to his com. *I guess it was a good thing she joined us*, he thought to himself.

She disappeared down the corridor with a toolkit slung over her shoulder. Shelby worked like a surgeon, mounting converters, splicing conduits, bridging the charging unit from Emily's quarters to the bulkhead interface behind the primary displays.

Three hours later, Shelby wiped sweat from her brow and called over the comm. "Alex, I have done this a few times in the past, but this is your ship, so you may want to check my work."

He walked the length of the deck, studied the clean paneling, then the readouts on the diagnostics. Voltage was steady. Transfer rate optimal. He nodded. "Looks good. You've outdone yourself again."

Shelby allowed herself a tired smile. "Plug her in."

Emily hesitated, then slid into the seat where Shelby had mounted the coupling. The connector latched to a socket at the base of her spine with a soft click. A surge of blue light pulsed through the interface.

Emily exhaled, visibly relaxing as her systems began to climb. "Recharging… efficiency eighty-six percent. Thank you, Shelby."

"Don't thank me. Just stay online when we need you."

Emily scanned the displays and data flow. "The Daklin aren't finished. I'm seeing fresh tunnels. This time on opposite sides of the solar system.

"Confirmed. Sixth DPK, bearing two hundred eleven degrees, elevation minus twenty-seven, distance twenty-three AUs," Adamez rattled off. "Seventh DPK, bearing zero-one degrees, elevation plus nineteen, distance twenty-five AUs. They're making an attempt at flanking."

Alex calmly studied the scenario. "We are good. We just have to be *right* where it counts. Emily, you know the timing. Do it."

Emily's precision in guiding drones into tunnels that were preprogrammed to intersect the DPK corridors and collapse the matrix was flawless. Even though the DPKs had attempted to flank from opposite sides of the solar system, both tunnels folded violently, shredding the massive ships before they could fully emerge. Debris cascaded in glittering arcs, harmless against the empty dark.

"Sixth and seventh DPKs destroyed," Adamez said flatly. But his hand lingered on the supply board, eyes narrowing.

Alex caught it immediately. "Talk to me, Art."

Adamez hesitated, then exhaled. "We've burned through most of our reserves. At this rate, I only have the supplies to stop three more DPKs."

The room fell silent. Even the hum of Tranquility's systems seemed muted.

Shelby whispered what everyone else was thinking. "And what happens when the fourth one comes?"

Adamez looked at Alex, eyes hard. "Then Earth burns."

Alex's voice cut through, firm, unyielding. "No. We'll find another way. Supplies or no supplies, we hold. We *always* hold."

He looked at Shelby, "Come with me, please." He took her hand and walked back to his quarters. Once there he closed the door, closed his eyes and took a deep breath. After a few seconds, he opened his eyes and took Shelby into his arms.

After a few seconds, Shelby pushed back. "Wait, cowboy, you want to have sex when the world is about to burn?"

Alex chuckled, then smiled, "Nope, I just needed to clear my head and get a reminder of what you've been trying to teach me, what we're fighting for."

"Oh, that's… sweet," She nodded eyes filling with tears.

With that Alex returned to the war room where he found Adamez with his face buried in his hands.

"Adamez?"

"Yes, sir?" Adamez stood and turned to Alex.

"I'm not your superior officer, Art, I am your friend," Alex smiled and put his hand on Adamez's shoulder. "I assume you have some disturbing intelligence to share?"

"I am getting reports form Rigel Kentaurus. Five DPKs have just entered five separate tunnels. Based on the last few reports, we have less than three hours."

"Got it, Put your tunnel backpack back on." He turned to Emily, "Emily, program these coordinates into Adamez's backpack and mine, and keep your Plink open to me."

"Where are we going?"

"To see the President of the United States in the Underground Pentagon."

Shelby squeezed Alex's arm. "You come back to me, cowboy."

He gave her a quick hug, then he and Adamez vanished into the tunnel.

When they emerged, they were in a stark, steel-lined chamber forty stories underground. It was an office that bore no windows, only reinforced walls and muted screens. The seal of the United States glowed faintly on one panel. Behind the desk sat President McPherson, her eyes sharp and tired, flanked by two Secret Service agents who immediately reached for their weapons.

Alex raised both hands. "Stand down. We're here to save Earth, not shoot anyone, or be shot."

McPherson's gaze locked on him. "Alex Durant. I've been briefed on the progress you and Mr. Adamez are making. But tunneling into my office? You've got about thirty seconds before I have these men drag you out."

"No time for protocol, Madam President," Alex cut in. "Five DPKs are inbound with an ETA of three hours, maybe less. If they clear their tunnels and power their weapons, Earth won't survive the day."

Adamez stepped forward, voice steady. "We've already collapsed seven, but our supplies are nearly gone. We can't hold the line without something new."

McPherson leaned back, hands folded. "And what is it you think I have that can tip this war?"

Alex met her eyes. "Your nuclear arsenal."

The President's eyes narrowed. "Excuse me?"

Adamez immediately shook his head. "Alex, that's pointless. Nuclear weapons can't even scratch a Daklin hull. You know that."

"From the *outside*," Alex countered. He stepped closer, voice urgent, "We've been fighting on their terms, outside their shields, outside their armor. But if we tunnel the warheads *inside* the ships and past their shields and hulls… well, I believe they'll rip those DPKs apart from the inside out."

Adamez froze, his eyes flicking to the tunnel backpack on his shoulders. Realization hit like a shockwave. "You mean…"

"Yes." Alex nodded. "We use our backpacks to drop warheads into their hearts, one by one. Every DPK that tries to breach the system dies before it fires a shot."

"How?" McPherson asked.

"My cybernetic daughter, Emily, is listening in. Emily, can you program our backpacks to move a warhead if we are touching it?"

"Indeed, I just finished that code, Alex," Emily reported with a hint of pride.

"She's super-efficient, Madam President," Alex grinned, "which is exactly what we need, because by my clock we have just a few hours."

Silence hung for a beat. Then President McPherson spoke, slow but deliberate. "There is a bunker in Wyoming. One hundred and twelve warheads, ready, maintained. Delivery systems are offline, but the weapons are intact. If you can… do what you say and get them inside, then you have my permission."

"Emily is going to need detonation codes."

A few seconds later, Secretary Defense West stepped into the room. The president briefed him on the plan.

West looked suspiciously at Alex, then Adamez. "Are you sure Madam President? This *is* our nuclear arsenal."

"I am sure, Mister Secretary," the President answered.

"Have you been to space General West?" Alex deflected as he studied the man standing before him. He was a solid looking, confident, black American with round glasses and grey hair, who clearly commanded a room.

"I have not," West turned to Alex, "but I will go wherever I can best serve."

Three minutes later, Adamez, West, and Alex popped back into the War Room on Tranquility. After a quick introduction, Alex stood back from the group. "We'll need Emily linked to each detonation. She times the blasts, not us."

Adamez finally spoke, his tone heavy but resolved. "So, you and I become the delivery system. Pop in, drop the payload, pop out."

Alex clapped his shoulder. "That's the plan. We are on the ship for no more than a second. As soon as we enter the tunnel to leave the DPK, Emily detonates. The entire thing should happen faster than the Daklin can send data to their cloud. You with me?"

"Wow," Adamez gave a humorless laugh. "Looks like I don't have much of a choice."

West rose with the realization of what was about to happen. "Gentlemen, this is the most damned crazy plan in the history of warfare. You are going to hand deliver 200 kiloton weapons to a target and detonate less than a second later?"

"It does sound crazy when you put it that way General," Alex confirmed, "but by the time the fission reaction begins, we will be millions of miles away."

"If you fail, Earth dies. If you succeed…" He paused. "Well, humanity owes you everything."

Alex reached out to shake West's hand. "You know what they say down at NASA, *failure's not an option*."

Emily handed Alex and Adamez four small chips each. "These have adhesive. When you get down to Wyoming, each of you needs to pick four warheads and place one of these on each of them. We shouldn't need that many, but milliseconds matter here, in case one of those nukes does not detonate."

Alex studied the small disks she had handed him. They were the size of a dime. "Copy that, Emily. He turned to Adamez. "Let's go get our warheads."

Before they departed, the War Room door slid open, and Megan strode in still wearing her flight gear, hair plastered to her forehead from when she had been sweating before the computer coding interlude. Her voice was steady, though her eyes burned with exhaustion.

"Alex, the Stingers are ready for the new operating system. We've debugged it, stress-tested it. Upload is green. It'll sharpen reflex loops and cut response time by another 80 milliseconds."

Alex stepped forward and wrapped her in a hug before she could say more. "Go kick butt, Megan. Make them regret ever coming here."

She smiled faintly, nodded, and turned back toward the hangar where her tunneling backpack was stored. Alex watched her go for a moment, then looked to Adamez. "Let's move."

The tunnel shimmered open, and in the next heartbeat, Alex and Adamez were standing inside the bunker beneath Wyoming. Racks of nuclear warheads stretched down both sides of the long chamber, each one gleaming cold and silent, waiting.

"Emily," Alex said, "Plink confirmed?"

Her voice came calm and steady in his ear: "Confirmed, Alex. As planned, I will run your backpack hops and then I'll trigger detonation once you place them. Alex, I have you doing three, and Adamez doing two. The entire process from Wyoming to DPK to Wyoming to the second DPK will be less than ten seconds for Adamez, and about 12 for you, Alex. If you find yourself back in Wyoming after you have delivered your quota, it's because one of the nukes didn't detonate and we are going for a second try."

Adamez grunted. "Then let's get to work."

Seventeen minutes later, five tunnels ripped into existence above the solar system, their gaping mouths disgorging the black hulks of DPKs. For the first time, the monsters cleared their exits fully, no longer cut in half by tunnel collapses. Their spines glowed as their weapons began to charge. The Daklin probably thought they had finally exhausted Earth's defense.

Emily's voice came through the Plink, calm but edged with urgency.

"First DPK, bearing thirty-eight degrees, elevation plus five, distance 4.8 AUs. Inside Jupiter's orbit."

A pause, then her tone sharpened. "Second DPK, bearing seventy-one degrees, elevation minus twelve, distance 5.2 AUs, also inside Jupiter's orbit."

West, who had been studying the data from the prior seven DPK destructions, muttered, "Two that close together?"

Emily didn't respond or slow down. "Third DPK, bearing one hundred eighty-three degrees, elevation plus nineteen, distance 19.3 AUs. Just above Uranus's orbit."

"Fourth DPK, bearing two hundred twenty-seven degrees, elevation minus twenty-five, distance 29.7 AUs. Below Neptune's orbital path."

"Fifth DPK, bearing three hundred twelve degrees, elevation plus forty-one, distance 44.2 AUs. Deep in the Kuiper Belt."

The monstrous silhouettes cleared their tunnels fully, spines glowing as weapons charged.

Alex popped into a Daklin ship, leaving a warhead behind, then disappeared, reappearing in Wyoming, then to a second Daklin ship, back to Wyoming, and then to a third. 12.1 seconds after he started, he popped out of the tunnel and into the War Room where Shelby immediately hugged him.

West, Adamez, and Emily stared at the monitor, studying the data. Like watching a lightning storm and seeing the flash, then counting five seconds per mile before hearing the thunder, they could track the telemetry from their tachyon tunnel monitors. But at the speed of light, the closest explosion wouldn't be visible for nearly 40 minutes, and the farthest wouldn't appear for five and a half hours.

But the telemetry was clear. Each DPK shuddered, bulged, and then blew apart from the inside out.

Adamez's voice was low, reverent. "Five more DPKs destroyed. From the *inside*. Looks like we have a new way of stopping the planet killers."

"How many people were on each of those twelve ships?" Shelby asked, then watched as the air was suddenly sucked out of the room.

Adamez finally spoke, "Fortak once told me there were nearly a million lives on 437B. Each of those were probably similar."

Shelby choked up and tried to stop the tears from forming in her eyes but failed.

"They came here to destroy every living organism on Earth, Shelby." Jabari put his arm around her. "It was a high price to pay, but it is one *they* chose."

In the same instant, Megan's voice crackled across comms, fierce and elated. "With Stinger system updates complete, the kill ratio's back up. It's now 43 to 1! These Daklin cruisers don't stand a chance."

Her squadrons carved through the enemy lines, Stingers weaving like phantoms. Cruiser after cruiser went up in fireballs, their formations shredded, their tactics overwhelmed.

But the Daklin pressed back harder, and within three hours more cruisers arrived, unleashing ten more DPKs into the system simultaneously.

"This is clearly an attempt to capture data," Emily stated in a calculated tone. She handed a dozen more chips to Alex and Adamez. "I think we are moving too fast for them to figure out how we are doing this. We need to keep it that way."

Twenty-five seconds later, Adamez and Alex were back on the deck of Tranquility.

"Ten destroyed," Adamez confirmed, his voice cracking with the weight of the moment.

And then… silence.

The battlespace stilled. No more tunnels. No new arrivals. Only the wreckage of Daklin cruisers and DPKs drifting cold against the stars.

Emily's voice broke the silence. "Alex. Long-range scans confirm eight more DPKs at Rigel Kentaurus."

Alex closed his eyes, then nodded. "Then that's where we go." He looked at Secretary West, "Are you coming or staying?"

"Wouldn't miss this one," West raised his hand with a stern face.

Within minutes, Tranquility was loaded with warheads.

Adamez studied the team on the deck, "You suppose this is the last of them?"

Alex shrugged but was already moving. "Emily, are the next set of chips for the nuclear warheads ready?"

The ship tunneled to the Centauri system, then fifteen minutes later, slid back into 3-space.

Emily handed Alex and Adamez a new set of chips to attach, and for just a second, the entire War Room stared as the Eight DPKs loomed like black titans across the starlight.

"Let's go," Alex motioned to Adamez.

Sixteen seconds later, the two men were back on deck having delivered four warheads each.

One by one, the DPKs flared and died, collapsing in on themselves in silent infernos.

By the time Tranquility slipped back into tachyon space, all eight Daklin planet killers had been obliterated from within.

Alex exhaled, his hand trembling as he steadied himself against the console. He couldn't remember the last time he had rested "The line holds. Earth stands."

"Good job, gents," West slapped Adamez and Alex on the back. "I'm sure we showed them not to mess with Earth today."

"They have millions of DPKs and billions of cruisers, Mister Secretary," Emily corrected. "All we've done is stir up the hive."

20

Galactic War

West and Adamez returned to Earth, but the Daklin did not give Alex and his crew time to celebrate the destruction of the DPKs at Rigel Kentaurus. Less than a day after the successful defense of Earth, the flood began again.

"Priority transmission from Cygnus Sagita Lambda," Emily announced over Plink.

A ragged voice filled the comm, torn by static and panic: *"Resistance, two Daklin Planet Killers have entered our system. They're charging weapons against our orbital habitats. Entire cities are based there with tens of millions of lives. We can't stop them. We beg you, send help..."* and then it went silent.

Before Alex could react, another signal cut across it.

"Beta Centaurus Prime calling," a female commander's voice spoke, shaking but resolute. *"Our agricultural worlds are burning. Daklin ships are deploying incinerators as we speak. We have no defense, no evacuation fleet. At least... at least save our children."*

Another alert slammed in.

"Orion Secuala reporting. Three dreadnoughts came through the tunnel at once. Our fleet is down by half. We cannot last another day. If Orion falls, the entire Spur is theirs. For the love of every world, please send reinforcements!"

And then came the last one, raw and hopeless.

"Cygnus Plexi... oceans are on fire, skies black with ash. Thirty billion lives on six planets. They're slaughtering us! Resistance, we stood with you. Do not abandon us now!"

The comm room went silent except for the overlapping cries.

Megan winced as she studied the console from Singularity 2. "That's four systems today. Emily's tally confirms it. Thirty-two civilizations have joined the Resistance. Eight of them have been attacked."

"This is their counterstrike," Jabari observed solemnly. "They're trying to pull us in several different directions, Alex. Breaking the resistance with an asymmetric response to our defense of Earth."

Emily leaned forward, eyes locked on him. "So where do we go first? I believe we can stop only one attack... Which world gets to live?"

Alex stared at the flood of desperate signals, his chest tight. He could feel the weight of hundreds of billions pressing on him. Every instinct screamed to move, to act, but to where?

"We can't save them all," he said finally, voice hoarse. "If we split our forces, we die with them. If we choose one, the others burn."

Emily's tone was almost human, pleading. "Alex, they are *all* dying. You must decide which one does not."

Shelby's placed her hand on his back affectionately. "Alex, you can't save them all. Pick one, and we line up behind you."

For a moment Alex stood frozen, feeling the scream from billions of ghosts, then his jaw clenched, and his voice cut through the chaos like steel. "We take the closest first."

Emily immediately pulled up a galactic overlay, stars and arms flaring into view. She expanded the Perseus Arm until half the display burned red with distress markers.

"Perseus Arm it is," Alex said flatly. "Megan, plot the jump for your Stingers. Emily will relay the nearest system under attack."

Megan's fingers blurred over her console. "Coordinates locked. Entering tunnel in six seconds."

"Execute," Alex commanded, "and Megan, have your swarm follow us in. Oh, and Megan?"

"Yes, Alex?"

"Shelby has designed a way for our AI cybernetics to recharge while at the command control station. I will send over schematics, but in the meantime, have all of your stinger AIs get fully recharged."

"Copy that."

Tranquility dropped into tachyon space, the familiar hum filling the ship. No one spoke. Every eye was fixed on the countdown.

7,805 light years in under 16 hours.

When they emerged into 3-space, the scale of the battle was immediately clear. Hundreds of Daklin cruisers already filled the system, their obsidian hulls blotting out the stars. Five DPKs hung like black daggers, their weapons already charging against the planets below.

"Dear God," Jabari whispered. "It's a full invasion armada."

Alex gritted his teeth. "This isn't a fight we can win. Priority is rescue. Megan, do your best to hold them off while we start pulling civilians into safe corridors. Emily, give me every viable tunnel endpoint for evacuation."

Alarms shrieked as beams from the DPKs lanced through space towards the planetary surface. One planet was engulfed in a plume of molten fire. Another ocean flashed to vapor in seconds.

Megan's voice cracked as she worked. "There's too many of them Alex, there's no way we can stop them this time."

"Then destroy every damned one that you can." His knuckles whitened against the console. "Just give me a few hours in the role of a lifeboat. After that, we tunnel back to Earth to regroup."

○○○○ ∞ ○○○○

For the next eighteen months after the failure at Perseus Arm, Alex and Tranquility raced from system to system across the galaxy. Battle after battle, they rescued survivors, but mostly they suffered losses. The Daklin engine was learning their tactics. The Stingers' kill ratio had dropped to just five to one, often fighting against odds of 100 to one.

All estimates counted that the Daklin empire was responsible for over a trillion human deaths over the course of a year and a half. It was a number impossible to fathom.

Alex's voice was hard. "Then we make them pay for every life they try to take. But this time, we won't be caught flat-footed."

The monitors were replaying scenes from the battle in Orion, a devastating scene that flickered with the flash of dying ships. A resistance cruiser broke apart, its hull splitting in two before both halves spiraled into the atmosphere of a burning world.

"Kill that!" Alex barked, gripping the rail so hard his knuckles were white.

Emily looked at the tactical screen, where the red icons multiplied. Daklin cruisers slid into the system, and DPKs easily cut their way toward the planet below.

She killed the video replay, and everyone stood in stunned silence.

Sun Tsu's voice came calm and deliberate over the link. "We should all know that battles are won before they are fought. In this case, Alex, we entered a battle we could not win. You made the right choice to withdraw while extraction was possible."

"We can't always run," Alex shot back. "There are still planets around the galaxy that we need to defend. If we don't figure it out now, those planets, those people, will all die."

"We must find a front line to make a stand," Sun Tsu advised.

The next few days were spent analyzing the battles fought in systems around the galaxy over the last 18 months. When they fought, the resistance always had a significantly higher kill ratio, but the Daklin had superiority in numbers.

They needed a fight where the numbers could be matched. Alex decided to throw full support behind the sixteen-star civilization located in the Perseus Arm, 11,000 light years from Earth.

Emily found that opportunity. "While Segment 1 of the Perseus Arm had fallen in a day," She explained to Megan and Alex, "Segment 4 has mounted the only successful defense. Eight civilizations, ancient rivals turned allies, have bound their fates together against the Daklin tide. For the first time in millennia, fleets from across the Arm fly under one banner, the seal of the Persiori Monarchy."

"What do we know about that monarchy?" Alex asked, studying the holo image of that arm of the galaxy.

"Surprisingly, it is not a parliament or democracy that led them, but a crown whose lineage stretches back thousands of years. The Persiori are known for being fierce, brilliant, and unbending in their loyalty. The other civilizations in that sector joined them because they knew this throng would fight to the last ship, never yielding to Daklin rule."

"I have done similar research and concur with Emily's conclusion," Sun Tsu added. "If any civilization is equal in ruthlessness to the Daklin, it is Persiori of the Perseus Arm."

At first, Alex had resisted joining them. Ruthlessness and lack of liberty were exactly the kind of traits the Daklin lived by, but as he observed their refusal to bow, he became convinced they were the best hope for making a stand to turning the tide on the Daklin.

He brought them knowledge. He showed their engineers how to craft swarms of drones that could collapse tunnels before the Daklin Planet Killers emerged. He worked side by side with their weapon masters to design bombs that could be tunneled inside a DPK's hull and detonated from within.

They prepared together, and when the Daklin arrived, they fought.

For two years, they fought winning every battle, and it seemed that the empire shook with the scale of their defiance. The Daklin were bleeding on a scale that should have mattered, but ultimately, it became clear that the Daklin did not care about casualties. In spite of the Persiori victories, it became a war of attrition.

Like an endless army of ants, the Daklin did not break. Their pool of cruisers, DPKs, and soldiers willing to die were endless. The resistance cut them to pieces, but their fleets, like mindless drones, kept coming. For every DPK collapsed, another emerged. For every cruiser destroyed, three more came from the tunnels. Slowly, inevitably, the resistance was worn down.

Two years into the battle, the resistance from the great Persius Arm defensive was growing thin. The Persiori had defied the empire, but winning every battle was not enough.

Now, it was all coming apart.

Alex stood at the forward display; his hands braced against the railing. His face was drawn but resolute.

"Emily, battle status."

Her voice was calm, though the data scrolling behind her carried death counts. "Seventy-two percent of resistance forces have been lost. In spite of ramped up manufacturing, our current fleet strength is less than one-third of original numbers. Daklin reinforcements are inbound through four separate tunnels. Probability of collapse for our forces is one hundred percent without intervention."

"Damn it." Alex exhaled, rubbing his eyes. "Two years of victories. Two years of collapsing tunnels, outmaneuvering their DPKs, detonating from inside their hulls, and still they come."

"It is a true nightmare," Jabari added, standing at Emily's side.

Sun Tsu stepped forward, his movements precise, the quiet authority of a strategist written into the steel of his cybernetic frame. "Alex. I believe this was always their plan. The Daklin implemented strategy that develops over decades and centuries, not individual battles. Attrition is their true weapon. They let us win, knowing our victories bleed us dry in both hardware and in morale."

Alex looked around the room. Everyone was exhausted. Two years of constant tactical fighting with no rest. The day-to-day victories had not brought joy or celebration, but anticipation and dread for the next onslaught. They had been winning battles, but the tide of the war was against them. Everyone knew it, and the sense of doom was becoming inevitable

Alex turned, jaw tight. "So, what, we just give up? Tell the Persiori their fight meant nothing?"

Sun Tsu's eyes flickered with artificial light, yet his voice carried something almost human. "No. But you must tell them the truth: that this is not the end of their honor, only the end of their strength in this arm."

"This is a proud civilization that has endured for tens of thousands of years, and it is about to be extinguished." Alex closed his eyes and rubbed his chin. "For them, this is the end."

Emily's voice was steady. "Alex, Persiori Monarchy Command is requesting direct communication. They're asking for your words before the line breaks."

Alex hesitated, then nodded at Emily. "Open the channel."

The image filled the holoscreen with Admiral Serak, Emperor of the Persiori Monarchy, armored, fatigued, and eyes burning with defiance even as the roar of battle filled the channel. Behind him, officers moved frantically across a chaos-filled bridge.

"Durant," Serak said, his voice low but steady. "We have fought as one for two years. Today, we bleed together. Give us your words."

Alex swallowed hard, then straightened. "Admiral. People of Perseus. Sixteen independent worlds have bound themselves together in defiance of the Daklin. We fought when others hid. We bled when others bowed, and for two years, we proved that the Daklin are not gods. We proved they can be hurt."

A slight positive mumble rose faintly in the background. Serak held Alex's gaze.

"But you must also know the truth," Alex continued. "They have chosen this front as their hammer. The Daklin will not stop until they have broken every ship in this arm. Today, we may fall, but our defiance has distracted the enemy and bought time for the galaxy to see they can be defeated. You have given time for liberty to rise, and history books will record this stand as an inflection point."

The Admiral thought about his comments, then raised his blade in salute. "Then let us fall with fire."

Sun Tsu leaned close to Alex, voice quiet. "Inspire them, yes. But prepare our own escape. The resistance cannot die here in the Perseus Arm."

Alex didn't answer. He turned back to the holo, voice rising. "Fight with everything you have. Collapse their tunnels, burn their cruisers, make them pay for every star they take. If Perseus falls, let it be remembered not as defeat, but as the stand that lit the fuse for liberty in the galaxy."

"So be it," Serak stared sternly from the holo image. "Let us show the galaxy the true meaning of resistance."

The channel cut.

The War Room on Tranquility was silent.

Emily's voice was measured. "Alex…Daklin fleet strength now exceeds 8,000 cruisers and 35 DPKs. Our allies are outnumbered 20 to one."

Outside, the void was in full chaotic eruption, Daklin weapons slicing through the Persiori fleet in great arcs of annihilation.

Alex closed his eyes, whispering as much to himself as to his crew. "Let's give them everything we have and begin to make them understand the tenacity of the resistance."

Sun Tsu rested his hand on the rail; gaze fixed on the fire outside. "So, it begins. Let history record the last battle of Perseus."

Plasma arcs lit the black between stars as Persiori cruisers and resistance allies drove into the Daklin line. For a heartbeat, the impossible seemed within reach.

It had always seemed in reach.

"Tunnel collapse successful on vector four," Emily reported. "Six Daklin Planet Killers destroyed before emergence."

Alex's eyes scanned the monitors. "That's it, keep them bottled up! Sun Tsu, vector swarm drones to Sector Seven. Let's cut off their cruisers before they regroup."

And then Alex froze.

Shelby stopped and turned to the man with whom she had spent the last three and a half years. She could see the gears turning.

"Emily," Alex began, but his voice carried to everyone in the War Room. "So far, we've been the coordinators in this fight. But we have shields and weapons. It's time we use them."

"No," Jabari broke in, his tone hard, urgent. "The Resistance needs you, Alex. We can't risk this."

Alex raised a hand, silencing him. "Megan," he Plinked, his thought sharp as steel. *"Uploading a tactical plan, I've been working on in my spare time."*

Megan's console lit up on *Singularity II*. She scanned the schematic and burst into a grin. "Fuck yeah, Durant! About time you quit watching from the sidelines. Now we've got ourselves a quarterback!"

The display across the fleet lit with vectors: time-hop corridors, micro-strike chains, and synchronized arcs. The plan was insane. Compress quantum hops to nanosecond windows, blink Stingers directly into predator positions, shred Daklin cruisers from inside their shields, then vanish before their AI could track trajectories.

Emily felt something she'd never experienced before in her hybrid body, a rush of *adrenaline*. She heard dozens of AIs chime confirmation across the net as the Stingers accepted the new protocol. Only thirty-four Stingers remained, yet Alex's program called for those thirty-four to annihilate eight thousand Daklin cruisers.

Her voice rang out: "Full phase sync. Stinger swarm, let's jump!"

The void erupted.

Shields meant nothing when Stingers blinked into existence meters from Daklin hulls. Each Stinger struck four points in less than a heartbeat, then vanished. To the human eye, Daklin cruisers were simply spontaneously exploding.

Two cruisers destroyed per Stinger per second. Three hundred and forty disintegrated in the first five seconds. Over four thousand in the first minute.

The Daklin AI tried to adapt, but their logic trees lagged behind the chaos. Then the DPK dreadnoughts began charging. The fastest would be ready to fire in three minutes. The slowest in five.

At one hundred fourteen seconds, the tally stood at 7,748 enemy cruisers obliterated. The surviving Daklin lines faltered. The Stingers broke off, handing the crippled remnants to the Persiori admiralty, and surged toward the DPKs.

Seventeen Stingers per target. Eleven cuts each. 187 precision X-ray bursts per dreadnought. A single cut would never have been noticed. Even forty cuts would have barely slowed the DPK, but 187 was a death blow. One by one, the planet-killers split and decompressed, their black hulls venting fire into the void.

Two minutes and fifteen seconds after the first jump, the battlefield lay in ruin. All thirty-five DPKs were destroyed. Only scattered Daklin cruisers remained, totally at the mercy of the overwhelming Persiori fleet.

The Stinger swarm popped back into 3-space above the Persiori world, forming a battered V-formation. *Tranquility* and *Singularity II* tipped the spear.

Inside the War Room, silence. Circuits were still glowing red from heat overload. Cooling systems whined. The battle could not have lasted another ten seconds. Every system in the Stinger swarm was at the brink of meltdown.

Alex turned. Jabari and Shelby sat motionless, eyes wide, as if they had seen the face of death. Emily was hunched forward, drenched, her skin beading with sweat.

He crouched beside her. "You okay?"

Emily looked down at her damp shirt, stunned. "I've never sweated before… Systems report: Tranquility power reserves at seventeen percent. Circuit temps falling, but we pushed past the threshold for several seconds. Some of the other AIs are in worse shape. We'll need days to assess and recover."

Admiral Serak's voice crackled over the channel, ragged but fierce: "Durant! I don't know how you did it, but their line is broken. You decimated over seven thousand Daklin cruisers in two minutes. We've never seen anything like it."

Before Alex could reply, a Plink brushed his mind. Megan.

"Durant... tell me you've got a Vanilla Porter stashed. Because if you do, I'm tunneling over."

Alex almost laughed, though his hands were trembling from the sheer velocity of command. "Yeah, and it's cold."

A shimmer of light, and Megan stepped onto the deck, grime on her face, eyes still lit with battle fever. She clapped Alex on the shoulder, then looked him square in the eye. "That was madness. Beautiful, insane madness. Not sure if my Stinger fleet will recover, but we won that one against impossible odds."

She glanced around at the scorched consoles, then back to Alex. "Repairs and energy levels won't be stable for days. If the Daklin send another wave before then, the smart play is retreat."

Alex exhaled slowly, nodding. "Let's go have that beer." He looked at Shelby, "care to join us?"

Shelby got up on wobbly legs and followed Megan and Alex.

Alex finally noticed the tremor in his hands which were the result of the most intense two minutes of his life. He took a breath, exhaled slowly then turned to face Megan's gaze. "Retreat, then. If we have to... but at least now that is an option."

Emily leaned back, closing her eyes, still trembling from the sweat that shouldn't exist. Shelby wiped her brow with a rag, a simple human gesture that spoke louder than words.

The following day, everyone rested. No one knew what the Daklin would do next, but right now, everyone was too exhausted to care.

And then, the following day, everything changed.

Again.

Emily saw it first. "Warning," she said, her tone flat again. "Multiple new tunnel signatures. Estimate: 25,000 Daklin cruisers entering system. Vectoring directly toward our line."

Silence gripped the command deck. Even Sun Tsu's usual precision faltered for a fraction of a second. "Alex," he said quietly, "this is beyond mathematics."

"The new enemy is rested and ready to fight." Emily observed. "We are worn with munitions dwindling, repairs still underway, and energy levels not yet at maximum."

The holoscreen shifted. Admiral Serak appeared again, his face soaked in sweat, but his eyes were steady. "Durant. You've given us everything. We struck them deeper than they ever expected. But this battle is lost."

Alex slammed a fist against the console. "Serak, no… if we press, maybe we can stop this."

Serak shook his head. "Look outside your viewport. The stars are gone, buried under new Daklin ships in quest of a kill. We could fight until every blade of steel is shattered, and it would change nothing."

Emily whispered, "He's correct, Alex. Probability of victory is now zero. Probability of fleet annihilation within the next 24 hours is one hundred percent."

In the holo-image, the Persiori Admiral stood straighter, his voice rising above chaos. "Then hear my last command. All surviving ships must flee. Carry the fire of Perseus to another front. Make the Daklin chase you across the galaxy. But leave this arm and find a new way to fight."

On the Singularity's bridge, Sun Tsu inclined his head, the gesture almost reverent. "An honorable end. Few monarchs would sacrifice their crown to save their people."

Alex's throat tightened. "Serak…come with us."

A sad smile crossed the Emperor-Admiral's face. "No. The Persiori Monarchy does not flee. We die where our ancestors stood. But *you* must adapt and find a new way to continue the fight."

Serak punched the button to end the transmission and turned his focus to distraction and a fight which would light the heart of the resistance.

Shelby wrapped her hands around Alex's arm, tears running down her face. "I had no idea what a noble and fierce partner he would be."

Alex looked at Shelby and felt the emotion that was pouring out of her. "Yes…"

Outside, the last of the Persiori line surged forward in one final blaze, their ships igniting Daklin hulls in suicidal close-up attacks, ending with rams when munitions were depleted. The brief hope of victory, and the love of a people for their leader, had driven a new level of ferocity by the Persiori.

Emily's voice was quiet now. "Escape vectors plotted. Windows closing."

Alex closed his eyes. "All resistance vessels, this is Durant. By order of the Persiori Monarchy," he paused, not wanting to say the next words. "Withdraw and live to fight again."

Tranquility slipped into a tachyon tunnel. Behind them, the last great Persiori fleet burned. The Monarchy fell with fire and defiance, their banners consumed in a storm of Daklin fire.

And in the silence that followed, Alex whispered to himself, "We must find a way to turn their sacrifice into victory."

∘∘∘∘ ∞ ∘∘∘∘

Tranquility hummed in the wake of the tunnel. The last embers of the Persiori fleet were far behind them, swallowed by the void. Alex needed a distraction from the war, and he wished he could go to Pronimos to see Steven and have a beer in the Old West, but that was not possible. He vaguely recognized the possibility that it may never happen again.

It was quiet on Tranquility, and everyone was getting some necessary rest while he sat alone, brooding at his console, eyes fixed on the holographic link.

After a few minutes, Alex pressed the button and connected to his surrogate on Pronimos. Maria's face appeared, but it wasn't Steven's cybernetic surrogate mother that he had logged in to see.

Steven was 11 now and tall for his age, his dark hair tousled in a way that reminded Alex of himself at that age.

"What are you looking at, Dad?" Steven asked, cautious.

Alex leaned in, his voice low. "It's me, son."

Steven's eyes narrowed, then softened. "I knew it. The surrogate… well, he's not you. He tries, and mom tries," he looked at cybernetic Maria, "I appreciate them, but they're not real." He glanced toward Maria-surrogate, then back to Alex. "When you connect, I can tell it's you."

Alex tilted his head, somewhat confused, "Has the real Maria visited through her surrogate?"

"No. She hasn't."

Alex's chest tightened. "You've grown up, Steven. Smarter than I ever was at your age."

"I had to," Steven said, folding his arms. "War doesn't wait for kids to stay kids. And I've been watching. Learning. I know what's happening out there." His voice steadied. "You, and the resistance are fighting so that I'll have a future."

Alex swallowed hard. "You're right. And you're becoming the man I hoped you'd be." He hesitated, then added, "I'm proud of you."

Steven blinked quickly, as though the words landed heavier than he expected. "Thanks, Dad."

"I wish I could be there more, and see you more…"

"It's okay. I do understand."

For the next hour, father and son talked about books, education, games, life on Pronimos, and things Steven was interested in. At the end, Steven gave a small, almost formal nod. "Stay alive dad and come home to Pronimos."

And then the connection dissolved, leaving Alex staring into empty space.

Alex made his way to the galley, drawn by the low incandescence of a single light. Jabari sat at a corner table, two beers waiting.

"I expected you'd show up here," Jabari slid a beer across the table to Alex, "after your call with Steven."

Alex managed a tired smile. "It was good to chat with him. I wish the challenges allowed us more time, but he seems to understand."

They drank in silence for a few minutes, the soft hum of the ship surrounding them. Then Jabari spoke, his tone deliberate, "Alex, I couldn't help but hear your conversation with young Steven. The topic lies parallel with something I need to tell you."

Alex raised an eyebrow. "Go on."

Jabari's gaze drifted toward the corridor that led to the crew quarters. "It's Emily. I love her. More than I thought I could love anyone again."

Alex stayed quiet, letting him continue.

"I want a family with her. A child." Jabari's voice carried no hesitation. "I know it's possible. If we can reach a world with the right facilities, her cybernetic body can be modified."

Alex set his beer down slowly. "A child. In the middle of this war?"

"Yes." Jabari leaned forward. "Because life cannot stop for war. If it does, then the Daklin win even when they're not here. We fight so our children can live, and we must remember to make sure there are children to inherit what we have fought so hard to protect."

Alex frowned, the weight of command heavy. "You realize the risks. Raising a child on a ship, with enemies hunting us?"

Jabari interrupted gently. "There's a story my grandmother used to tell. A Swahili tale. During a famine, when food was scarce, a family still gathered each evening to share what little they had. A single morsel of food for each person passed around the fire. Neighbors mocked them for wasting time, for pretending. But when the rains finally came, that family was the strongest, because they had never stopped being a family." He paused. "Life must continue, even in the shadow of death."

The words lingered in the galley like a quiet prayer.

Alex took a long breath, then nodded. "All right. If Emily agrees, and we find a planet with the right tech, we'll make it happen. A child, even in times like these..." he said thoughtfully, "maybe *especially* in times like these."

Relief softened Jabari's features. "Thank you for your blessing, Alex."

They sat in silence after that, the ship carrying them forward, away from the ashes of Perseus, toward whatever fragile hope remained.

21

The Spark of Life

All four occupants of Tranquility gathered in the galley with Alex sitting at the end of the table, weary but alert. Jabari leaned forward, took a sip of water, then leaned back with elbows resting on the steel surface. Emily's eyes glowed faintly in the dim light.

Shelby poured herself a cup of coffee, then slid into a chair across from Alex. "I can tell something's going on. What's up?"

Jabari broke the stillness. "We've all been fighting so long, it feels like we've forgotten why. I don't want to *just* fight anymore. I want to build something." He paused, "Build something with Emily." He paused again, took a deep breath and exhaled slowly, "A family."

Emily met Alex's eyes, unflinching. "I've done the research, and it is possible. If we find the right facility, my body can be modified for reproduction."

Alex rubbed his temples, not sure if he should be pretending that he was hearing this for the first time. "There are two issues here. A child. In the middle of this war, and the capability of cybernetics and humans to reproduce." He looked toward Shelby. "You've dealt with cybernetic biology more than anyone else. Tell us how crazy it is to even consider this."

Shelby leaned back, considering. "Crazy? Alex, the whole damn galaxy's crazy right now. But this?" She frowned, which made everyone anticipate what she would say next even more, then switched to her Texas twang, which felt endearing.

"This ain't crazy. Cybernetics and organics have had babies, millions of times. We got the capabilities on Pronimos: hearts, livers, whole systems rebuilt, including reproductive. Course, it's easier with a cybernetic man and a fully organic woman. Everyone knows men'r a lot simpler." She smiled and switched off the twang. "Anyway, if Emily's base structure has the right organic scaffolding, a reproductive system can be engineered. It is neither technologically difficult or uncommon. But possible? Definitely."

Her eyes softened as she sipped her coffee. "And, in my opinion, it's also necessary. Life has to keep going. My mom was pregnant with me when Texas was fighting for its independence. Cannon fire in the distance, men dying by the hundreds, and she still carried me. She used to say, *"If life can bloom when the world is on fire, then the fire never really wins."*

The room fell quiet. Emily's lips curved into the smallest of smiles. Jabari reached for Shelby's hand in gratitude, then turned back to Alex.

"I want this," Jabari said firmly. "This war will likely last for hundreds of years. We can't wait for peace to start actually living. As Shelby has said, we cannot let the fire win."

Alex exhaled slowly, then nodded once. "Then Emily, find us a path. Somewhere that can make this happen. Coordinate with Shelby who clearly has seen this situation many times before."

Shelby nodded affirmatively with a smile.

Emily's gaze shifted to the ship's display. "I've been researching. In the Orion sector, there is a system called Lirae-4. It once housed a facility specializing in biomechanical and reproductive hybridization. If records are correct, the lab remains intact. If we can reach it, modifications to allow childbirth are feasible."

"I know the facility," Shelby affirmed, "they ain't the best, but they should be quite capable of handling this procedure."

Jabari straightened, hope burning in his eyes. "Then, it's okay to make that our destination?"

Emily's voice was calm but steady. "But it *is* possible. And I want this as much as Jabari does, maybe more."

The weight of her words hung in the room. Finally, Alex pushed his chair back. "You are like my daughter, Emily," he started. "We need to take this to Megan. She needs to know the plan, and the potential dangers we are putting ourselves into."

Hours later, Megan's face appeared on the holo through a Plink connection. The command center of EtaKatz was alive behind her with motion and light. Her curly brown locks were pulled back tight, her eyes sharp.

"You're doing what?" Megan's voice cracked through the speakers.

Alex leaned forward. "There's a facility in Orion."

"…that can modify Emily's body for childbirth." Megan cut him off, pacing behind her console. "Alex, have you completely lost it? We're hanging by a thread, and you want to divert your ship, one of the most important ones in the fight, so your cybernetic can start a family?"

"Correction, Megan," Alex said firmly, "Emily is not *just* a cybernetic, she *is* family."

Megan thought about his response for a second. She had been the lead programmer in transferring Alex's AI to Emily's body. "I am sorry, Alex. I didn't mean it that way."

"Thanks for the clarification, Megan," Jabari stepped into the feed, his voice firm. "This is not just a family, it's a future. If we fight with the intention to win, but forget what we are fighting for, then we've already lost."

Megan stopped, staring at him. "You think I don't know about the future? I've thought about it every damned day. And I know we need a new angle if we're going to win this war, but a child in the middle of all this?" She shook her head. "It sounds insane."

Emily's voice entered, soft and sure. "And yet, life has always been born in chaos. My existence was born of chaos. So was Steven's. If we wait for peace, there will be no children at all."

For the first time, Megan's shoulders sagged. She stared into the lens, her tone quieter. "Maybe you're right. Maybe the resistance needs something outrageous, something the Daklin would never expect. Hope, even in the form of a child." She leaned closer. "But Alex, this is your call, and if you gamble wrong and get killed or captured, we all pay the price."

Alex nodded.

"Please don't get your asses killed on this damned fool mission." Megan smiled and blew them a kiss.

The channel cut.

In the galley's silence, Shelby set her mug down and looked at Alex. "Like I said, my mom carried me through a war. Maybe Emily will carry the next generation through this one."

Alex met Emily's gaze, then Jabari's. "All right. Orion it is." He grabbed his water glass and took a sip. "You know, I wrote the first Emily code on a PC about twenty years ago. I never would have guessed we would one day be here, but I am glad we are."

"We all need something to take our minds off the torment of this war." Shelby sidled up to Alex and winked.

"Yes, we do," he muttered. "Emily, execute the course to Lirae-4."

∘∘∘∘ ∞ ∘∘∘∘

The medical bay on Lirae-4 smelled faintly of antiseptic and ozone. While only used for cybernetics, it was so much like a normal medical facility and only a trained eye like Shelby's could tell the difference.

Shelby stood at the center of it all, hands on her hips, eyes sharp with focus. She spoke with the local medical team, two human doctors who had performed this procedure many times, assisted by a pair of cybernetic specialists who had spent their lives in hybrid work.

"All right," The lead doctor said, his voice calm but firm. "Emily's body already carries organic scaffolding. What we need to do is graft the reproductive matrix here," he tapped the holo-diagram, "while maintaining her energy regulation systems. If you sever this line, you risk shutting down her metabolic processors. She'll need auxiliary power feed during the procedure, but it can't interfere with cell division once the tissue starts growing. Understood?"

The team nodded, their eyes widening a little at the authority in her drawl. Shelby gave them a small smile. "I have come to see this woman like a daughter, so treat her like she's flesh and bone, not cybernetics wrapped around steel and circuits."

Emily, lying quietly in the prep chair, gave Shelby a grateful look. "Thank you."

"You just relax, sugar," Shelby replied warmly. "We've got this."

The procedure took days of preparation, matching DNA exactly, printing reproductive organs, and then precision surgery. By the end of the second week, Emily was up and walking, her systems stable, her new physiology verified. Jabari never left her side, and for the first time in months, the ship's crew exhaled.

On Lirae-4, time slowed and the battles of the Perseus Arm of the galaxy seemed a distant nightmare. Plans for the next campaign were developing but not rushed. The resistance needed to breathe, even if it was just for a little while.

As was always the case, Alex and Shelby explored and found a small tavern on the edge of the town. The place was half empty, the beer was sharp and metallic compared to the rich oatmeal stout Alex loved, but it was cold and strong, different enough to make the experience worthwhile.

Shelby leaned back in her chair; boots crossed on the rung. "Not quite Texas, huh?"

Alex chuckled. "Not even close. But it'll do."

In the corner, against a faded mural of stars, an old guitar leaned on a chair. Shelby's eyes flicked to it, and a grin tugged at her lips.

"You feel like playing?" Alex asked.

"Hmm…" Shelby rose, grabbed the guitar, quickly tuned the strings, and strummed a few chords. The sound was rough but warm, filling the bar like a memory. She adjusted the instrument, then launched into an old country ballad she had learned during a visit to Texas. Her voice was clear, compelling, and captivating.

> *I rode up to Austin, the cradle of the west,*
> *Just ask any cowboy, he'll tell you it's the best*
> *I met a Texas Cowboy, got friendly with his dog*
> *Looked into his big brown eyes, and this is what I saw*
>
> *I saw miles and miles of Texas*
> *All the stars up in the sky*
> *I saw miles and miles of Texas*
> *I'll go back there when I die.*

Alex smiled, the weight of command slipping from his shoulders.

"That was an old band called *Asleep at the Wheel*. I changed the lyrics a bit, but it's a good song." She shifted from country to a folk tune, then into a cowboy ballad that had likely been sung around campfires for over two centuries. A few patrons gathered nearby, listening and smiling into their drinks.

When she finished, the bar gave her a quiet applause. Shelby laughed, setting the guitar down. "Guess that's worth another beer."

Alex realized that the balance in his life, and his survival, were now tied to this woman, and a fundamental part of their connection went back to a place called Texas on a planet called Earth. "To Texas, survival, and life." He raised his glass.

She clinked her glass against his. "Amen to that."

For a while, they just sat in the quiet hum of the tavern, the galaxy and its endless war held at bay by simple music and the taste of halfway-decent beer.

The days on Lirae-4 had stretched into a rhythm that felt almost normal. For two weeks, the crew allowed themselves something they had nearly forgotten: rest. The medical team oversaw Emily's recovery while Alex and Shelby found themselves spending more evenings at the tavern, enjoying a bit of humanity while they could.

They never really came to like the beer compared to Alex's favored oatmeal stout, but Shelby claimed it "got better after the second glass," and found herself playing a few songs on the battered guitar almost every evening. Sometimes, Alex sang with her, his voice pitchy but steady, blending with hers in old western folk tunes that echoed across centuries and light years.

One evening, as the night faded and the patrons drifted out, Alex leaned across the table. "Shelby…back on Tranquility, you sidled up to me, winked, and never explained it. What did you mean?"

"Are you talking about when Emily announced her intention to have a child?"

"Yes," he responded, holding her gaze.

Shelby tilted her head, a playful grin flickering, then fading at the seriousness in his tone. "What brings that up now?"

Alex's gaze didn't waver. "Because if I misunderstood, it could change things. But if I didn't…well, Shelby, it wouldn't be wise. Not with the weight I'm carrying, not with the war. A child between us would be…complicated."

Her smile faltered, and she looked down at her glass. "You're right. It wouldn't be wise. It was just a passing, sweet thought that came and was lost in that moment."

She meant the words, but a hollow ache opened in her chest that she couldn't quite name. Why should it matter? Why should the thought sting? She pushed it away, hiding the sadness behind another sip of beer. Alex didn't press, and she decided not to explain.

○○○○ ∞ ○○○○

Emily's discharge from the facility came with careful instructions.

Dr. Laren, the lead specialist, stood before her, his hands folded behind his back. "Emily, your modifications are stable, but your body will need to establish a baseline hormonal cycle. Three full cycles, uhh," he glanced at Shelby, "three periods before attempting conception. Until then, you must use birth control to prevent complications."

Emily nodded, absorbing the information with her usual clarity. "Three cycles. Understood."

"Oh girl…" Shelby started, "You're gonna *love* having periods," she added sarcastically. "Not sure I'd want that part of life back again, but I suppose it is the most natural way to experience life as a woman. Medical science is pretty amazing, but the human body is still better."

Jabari squeezed her hand. "We can wait. What matters is that it's possible."

The doctor gave a faint smile. "Possible, yes. Miraculous, definitely. But treat it with respect. As Doctor Shelby has suggested, you are about to experience something new, Emily. We must let nature and engineering learn to dance together before testing them with life."

Emily inclined her head, and Jabari's grip on her hand tightened, not in fear, but in promise.

Later that week, Alex found Jabari at the same tavern, sitting apart from the crowd, his eyes following Emily as she spoke quietly with Shelby across the room.

"You look like a man with something on your mind," Alex said, sliding into the seat opposite.

Jabari's smile was small but steady. "Always. But mostly it's about what Emily and I are about to attempt. You see, Alex, the resistance fights to survive the next battle. But survival is not enough. If we want to win, we must believe in tomorrow, and nothing says tomorrow louder than a child."

Alex frowned slightly. "You really think one child changes the whole war?"

"I think it changes *us*," Jabari replied. His voice was calm, his Swahili accent curling around the words like poetry. "As I have said, family is strength, Alex. Without it, we are just fighters, no better than the Daklin."

Alex let the words settle. In the quiet tavern, the impact of those words felt heavier than any battle plan. "You make a damn compelling argument, Jabari."

"And I thank you for supporting us," Jabari raised his glass. "Let's make sure this war doesn't strip us of what makes us human."

Alex touched his own glass to Jabari's. "To tomorrow."

○○○○ ∞ ○○○○

On their last night, after Shelby had set the guitar aside and the tavern's last patrons wandered home, she and Alex lingered at the table with half-finished glasses. The lights above hummed, the dome outside showing stars glinting across the black.

Alex turned his glass slowly in his hands. "Emily and Jabari…they've got me thinking. About fundamentals. About what really matters."

Shelby leaned forward, eyes catching the dim light. A slow grin tugged at her lips. "Fundamentals, huh? I like the sound of that."

Her tone was playful, the Texas lilt in her voice, warm and teasing.

Alex froze, realizing too late the double meaning. He cleared his throat, fumbling. "No, I'm sorry, I mean the war. Strategy. Survival. I didn't mean, well, what they are planning to start in three months." He waved a hand, face flushing. "Sorry for the misunderstanding."

Shelby chuckled, watching him backpedal and stumble. She winked, leaning back, letting him off the hook but secretly savoring the moment. A part of her was unexpectedly disappointed, though she couldn't pin down why. She masked it with a sip of beer and a mischievous smirk. "All right, cowboy. Tell me about *your* fundamentals."

Alex exhaled, grateful for the redirect. "I've been turning over an idea. The Persiori fought like hell, and they still fell. Maybe we've been looking at this wrong. We have been fighting the Daklin where they're strongest. What if we went back to the beginning? To where it all started for us."

Shelby tilted her head. "You mean Earth?"

"No." Alex's eyes gleamed with something new. "I mean before Earth. The original colonizer of humans in the Milky Way. There are whispers in the archives, old stories buried in Pronimos records. I remember reading about a planet on the outer edge of the Cygnus sector. It is M-Class and very, very old, something about it being the seed of our kind."

Shelby's eyes widened. "The first human colony in our galaxy? *Colony*?" She reiterated the word.

"That's what I want to find. If it's real, maybe the key to resisting the Daklin isn't just weapons or ships. Maybe it's something older. Something we've forgotten."

Shelby studied him, the intensity in his voice cutting through the haze of beer. "You really believe there's an answer out there?"

"I do," Alex said.

"Just know," she paused and smiled, "I am with *you*, Alex." Shelby found herself checking her words to make sure she didn't cross any lines with Alex. As close as they had gotten, there was still an unstated line over which neither had ventured.

"Okay, but first, we need to resupply. And we need to find better beer while we're at it," he added with a crooked grin holding up the bottle he had been sipping. "And I want to spend some time with Megan. She's been holding EtaKatz together almost singlehandedly. She deserves more than just comms."

Shelby raised her glass in a quiet toast. "To EtaKatz. And to chasing ghosts in Cygnus."

○○○○ ∞ ○○○○

The following morning, the Tranquility completed preparations and said goodbye to Lirae-4. The ship tunneled into tachyon space, and then within a few hours, dropped from the tunnel with the familiar image of EtaKatz blooming on the screens. Alex leaned forward, expecting the familiar lattice of defense satellites, Megan's orderly flight corridors, and the faint shimmer of the base's protective shields.

Instead, Megan's face filled the holoscreen, pale with urgency. Behind her, alarms screamed, red light washing over the command center.

"Alex, leave the system. The Daklin found us."

His blood ran cold. "How many?"

Her answer was clipped, each word like a hammer strike. "I don't know… but maybe twenty-five thousand cruisers. And fifty DPKs. They came through ten tunnels and completely surprised us. This isn't a raid. It's a preplanned annihilation. We have seconds to evacuate what we can."

Emily's voice was immediate, steady despite the spike in her processors. "Daklin strategy has shifted. No longer probing. They've identified the resistance as a unified threat and are deploying overwhelming force, everywhere."

The screens lit with fire. Outside the viewport, the wreckage of resistance ships burned against the stars. Entire wings of allied craft, some veterans of Perseus defense, were gone in minutes.

Sun Tsu's hands flickered over tactical displays, his voice as calm as if reciting poetry. "Our probability of survival at EtaKatz is two percent. Probability of successful retreat: thirty-one percent if we execute now. Every second lost decreases odds exponentially."

Alex clenched his fists. "Megan, get your people out. Scatter. No last stand, just run."

She shook her head, jaw tight. "We're trying, but Alex, you need to understand, gone are the days of skirmishes and small victories. The Daklin see us now. They're not sending squads anymore. They're sending asymmetric force everywhere with the singular goal of extermination."

Another explosion lit her command deck. Smoke swallowed the image. When her face reappeared, her voice was raw. "Get out, Alex. If both Tranquility and Singularity die here, the resistance dies with us."

For a heartbeat, the command deck was silent except for the distant roar of collapsing metal across the void. Then Alex drew a breath, sharp and steady.

"Emily. Plot tunnels. Randomize vectors. Scatter our signals."

"Acknowledged."

"Sun Tsu, get me the fleet net. Tell every ship to run and live to fight another day."

From the control room in Tranquility, it was clear that allied ships were fighting in desperation, each one diving into whatever fight it could find. The void that had once been a fortress and the manufacturing center for the resistance, was quickly becoming a graveyard.

As the battle opened around them and Tranquility prepared to surge into the unknown, Alex's voice was low, almost to himself. "They've seen us, and they'll never stop."

He had no idea how true those words were.

EtaKatz had been more than a base. Being off the tunnel grid, it had become the heartbeat of the resistance. The Stingers were built on EtaKatz, along with tunnel collapsing drones and warheads for stopping the DPKs. It had become the command center that stitched 32 civilizations of the resistance into one fragile alliance.

And now it was burning.

Daklin cruisers poured into the system by the hundreds, their black hulls eclipsing the beauty of space, replacing it with death. The dozen DPKs that followed were overkill, each one a planet-killer that could have erased EtaKatz a dozen times over.

Alex watched from Tranquility's command deck as the first orbital Stinger cluster went up in a violent gust of fire. A half-completed squadron, still in scaffolds, vaporized before they ever saw battle.

Emily's voice carried the finality of a death toll. "All production lines will be destroyed, and Stinger manufacturing capacity reduced to zero. We are executing a self-destruct so the enemy does not capture technology."

Across the resistance network, ships broke formation. There was no line to hold, no defense to mount. The Daklin had come not to test, but to erase.

Megan's last transmission crackled through the chaos. Her voice was ragged, the command deck behind her shrouded in smoke. "It's over here. All remaining units scatter to whatever safe haven you can find around the galaxy. Hide if you can. Survive wherever you can find a respite."

Alex chimed in behind her, "EtaKatz is lost, but the dream of freedom must not die here. As Megan has commanded, find a safe haven, but remember the words of Martin Luther King, that freedom is never voluntarily given, it must be demanded. For now, the Daklin can hunt, but they won't find us if we disappear."

The screen went black.

One by one, resistance ships leapt into tunnels, their signals vanishing into the deep. The resistance, once a movement and force to be reckoned with, dissolved into fragments. The two million patriots now hunted for quiet M-Class planets scattered across the spiral arms of the Milky Way, where they could hide, off the grid.

As Tranquility itself plunged into a tunnel, Alex stood silently at the console, watching the last light of EtaKatz fade. The Daklin Empire suddenly felt impossibly large, while the resistance had become miniscule and small.

The spark of new life was a few months away from beginning between Emily and Jabari, while another, for liberty, was on the verge of being extinguished by the ruthless regime in the center of the galaxy.

"Emily," Alex commanded, "Find an M-Class within a hundred light years that is off the network grid. Send those coordinates to Megan so we can meet there."

22

Beta Scorpii

Emily communicated with Sun Tsu and evaluated nearby stars that were not on the Galactic Tunnel Network.

Emily's voice Plinked to Sun Tsu while she spoke to the Tranquility crew. "18 Scorpii is a class G2V. Luminosity almost identical to Earth's Sol. Better yet, it has an M-class planet in the habitable zone. It is located 46.1 light years from Sol and is nine light years from the nearest port for the Galactic Tunnel Network."

Megan's face appeared on the comm screen from Singularity 2. "It's gorgeous, Alex. Ocean bands, green continents, and cloud systems. It looks a hell of a lot more like home than anything I've seen since we left Earth."

Alex leaned closer. "Scan for civilizations."

Emily was already processing the database that Pronimos kept. "I can confirm an industrial age culture, equivalent to Earth circa the 1930s. They have power grids, trains, and radio frequency communications. Their societies appear more focused on arts, music, and literature than heavy industry. Technology is here, but it's secondary."

Megan grinned faintly. "Artists with trains. That'll be a change of pace."

"Language?" Alex asked.

"No match to Earth tongues," Emily replied, "but Pronimos has cataloged their language, so translation protocols will adjust instantly. Communication won't be a problem."

They utilized high resolution cameras to look down through the atmosphere, while the ships remained in orbit above the planet. They found a city of low stone buildings and narrow streets. Smoke from coal-fired stacks curled lazily into the sky. Electric trams clattered down iron rails. And everywhere they looked, they found color with huge sections of land planted with flowers or colorful crops. There were murals and painted cobblestones that turned the avenues into living canvases.

They selected a city that was modest by galactic standards, perhaps two hundred thousand population. Big enough to disappear into, small enough not to draw attention.

"Perfect," Alex concluded. "Megan and I can use our tunneling backpacks and go to the surface where we can find a temporary haven."

Alex checked the programming, punched the button on the backpack, and an instant later, stepped onto the surface in a field just outside of the town. Megan was already waiting, her shoulders tense, her expression unreadable. She took a step forward and hugged him, tight, harder than usual.

When she pulled back, her knees crumpled. Tears spilled before she could stop them.

Alex grabbed her before she could fall to the ground. "Megan?" Alex asked softly, steadying her shoulders.

Her voice broke. "Todd was there." she sobbed, "on EtaKatz when the Daklin came. He didn't make it out."

Alex closed his eyes, exhaling slowly. "Oh, Megan…"

She pressed her face into her sleeve, fighting for control. "That's three, Alex. Isaac in Afghanistan. Mark with the Daklin. Now Todd. I didn't love him, not the way I loved Mark or Isaac, but Todd was good to me. He was warm, brilliant, and solid. He made me feel human in the middle of all this madness." Her voice cracked. "And now he's gone too. I think I'm cursed, or at least the men I'm with are."

"You're not cursed Megan." Alex drew her closer, letting the silence absorb the grief neither could put into words. "Every loss hurts," he said finally. "And you've carried more than most. But you're still here. We're still here."

For a long minute she wept into his shoulder, then gradually pulled herself together, wiping her eyes. "You're right. Thank you, Alex." She took a deep breath, exhaled slowly and surveyed the surroundings, "We've got work to do."

Alex had watched her melt and then she pulled the pieces together again in mere minutes. He had never seen this side of Megan Hoglund, and it only reinforced his perspective that she was an extraordinary woman. "You're a badass, Megan," he said, almost in a whisper, "people like you win because every time you're knocked down, you get back up, figure it out, and go again."

"Thanks," she took a deep breath and exhaled slowly. "Trying to be like you, Alex."

They walked side by side into the city, past shops lit by gas lamps and the scent of fresh bread rising from corner bakeries. A tram rattled by with sparks flying as it ground over steel rails. Life bustled around them, oblivious to the war raging beyond the stars.

Near the edge of town, they found a pair of large adjoining buildings, a warehouse and an office block, both abandoned but structurally sound. The wide doors were bolted shut; the windows clouded with dust. Perfect for hiding ships and crews.

Emily, still in orbit, synthesized local currency through the ship's replicators and translated the appropriate contracts. By evening, Alex and Megan had rented both buildings under assumed names.

Three days later, Emily tunneled Tranquility into a long stone warehouse near the city's edge. Megan slid Singularity 2 into the shadows of a neighboring structure. Both ships cloaked themselves in camouflage shields. From the outside, they looked like empty, dust-stained storage depots.

When she stepped out into the warehouse floor, Shelby stretched, breathing the planet's cool air. "Smells like coal, ink, and hopefully a good dark beer. I think I'm going to like it here."

Alex walked to the wide doors and looked out at the streets beyond. A trolly rattled past, filled with laughing passengers in clothes that would have looked at home in Depression-era America. A woman playing an instrument that looked and sounded like a violin stood on a corner, drawing a crowd with a haunting tune.

Alex felt the faintest spark of calm. "We'll blend in here," he said. "At least for long enough to decide what to do next."

○○○○ ∞ ○○○○

On the fourth night, the crew gathered at a restaurant tucked into the corner of the small city's central square. They had learned the city was named Bautlehaven, and this restaurant, which smelled of grilled meats and spiced grains, was called Bautlehaven Café. Its walls were lined with bright murals that told stories of kings, poets, and revolutions long past. A small trio played stringed instruments in the corner, their melody soft but insistent, weaving under the hum of conversations.

Alex sat at the long table with Megan, Shelby, Emily, Jabari, and Sun Tsu. Plates had been cleared, and glasses of the local dark ale sat half-finished. They had spent the evening comparing notes: Emily's careful scans of the local university's archives, Shelby's observations of indigenous medicine, Jabari's interest in their

341

communications systems, and Megan's relentless probing into how their factories operated.

The University of Bautlehaven, they had learned, was a hub of political thought. Its professors wrote volumes on statesmanship, diplomacy, and the balance of power. The arts flourished here with paintings, music, and literature which filled every street, but their sciences, though competent, seemed secondary to the culture.

When the conversation lulled, Alex leaned back in his chair, his eyes sweeping over the team. "I'm grateful for this safe haven, and I hope most of the others from Etakatz found something similar, but I'm getting restless. We can't stay hidden forever."

"Agreed," Megan responded.

"Now that everyone has finished dinner, lets reconvene back on Singularity 2 and begin planning our next move."

There were murmurs of agreement, though Shelby sighed wistfully. "Shame, though. I was just getting used to the beer and music."

Megan smirked, but her eyes narrowed with the same familiar steel. "Rest is nice, Alex, but I'm with you. We don't win wars by drinking beer and reading art history." She held up her beer glass, studied it, and downed the remainder. "I agree with you though, Shelby; the beer's good here."

Back on Singularity 2, the team gathered again in the galley. The viewport showed Bautlehaven's lights that sparkled against the night.

Alex stood and began pacing slowly as he spoke. "There are stories, well, whispers, really about the first race to colonize this galaxy. Our friend from Andromeda, Polonius, believes it was the same race that populated his galaxy too. If this ancient civilization really existed, maybe they left something behind, something we could use. Something that could end the Daklin Empire."

Emily tilted her head, curious. "A legend. But legends often have roots in truth."

Sun Tsu's voice was measured, the faint glow of his cybernetic eyes reflecting the light. "If such a race existed, their remains, records, or technology would be of infinite value, but we are talking about tens of millions of years. Is it possible that a trace of them still exists? Time is a powerful tool for erasing the past."

Megan crossed her arms, her tone sharp. "Or maybe it's just a fairy tale. There's no hidden weapon, Alex. The only way to win is with overwhelming force and better tech. Period. That's how wars are fought. That's how wars are won."

Alex met her gaze, unflinching. "Maybe. But if the Daklin have been using technology they didn't create, then we need to find the ones who did create it. They might have left us the means to fight on equal terms."

The room fell silent, each of them weighing the possibilities. For Alex, it wasn't just speculation, it was a direction, a spark of hope in a galaxy that had grown dark.

The discussion deepened as the hum of Singularity's systems filled the silence between voices. Alex stood at the head of the table, hands clasped behind his back, listening.

Shelby was the first to speak. "Well, for starters, our ships are faster. The empire's cruisers are massive, sure, but they're lumbering beasts. They can't pivot like Tranquility or Singularity 2 and the other Stingers. That gives us an edge in the tunnels and in open space."

"Anyone know how much faster we are?" Jabari asked.

"With upgrades, we can tunnel at about 400 lightyears per hour." Emily answered

"And what about the Daklin?" Jabari persisted in the line.

"Less than 400, maybe 200 light years per hour."

"First of all, it's fucking fast," Megan interjected. "I used to think Isaac's muscle car was fast and never would have guessed we could travel like that. Still, I think we need to find out *exactly* how fast the Daklin are."

They all nodded.

Jabari returned to the original discussion. "And we still have Zander's backpack tech. We can place bombs directly inside a DPK hull. No Daklin engineer has figured out how to defend against that. It's the only reason Earth still stands."

Emily's tone carried both pride and caution. "And then there's the time travel asset. We can tunnel through time itself. In battle, short slips of seconds, maybe minutes, can be decisive like it was in Perseus. What about longer jumps designed to change things?" She asked the group.

"That risks everything," Alex answered. "There are just to many variables when we try to change the timeline."

Sun Tsu leaned forward, his artificial eyes narrowing. "Agreed. Strategic time manipulation is unstable. Zander and Lyra are constantly monitoring the percussion wave created at EtaKatz years ago. We must be careful, because altering the past could unravel not only this war, but existence itself. Tactical jumps in combat yes, but no more than that."

Megan exhaled sharply, arms crossed. "I don't like it, period. Small time jumps are fine, but traveling through time to 'fix' things? That's not strategy, that's gambling with the galaxy. We're not gods. We screw around with history, and we risk becoming worse than the Daklin."

There was a pause as the weight of her words settled.

Alex finally broke the silence, his voice steady. "Then we're agreed. Short tactical uses, nothing more. We can't afford the hubris of trying to rewrite history."

Everyone nodded, the decision unspoken but clear.

Alex let the silence stretch for another heartbeat before he spoke again, softer now. "But remember this, there's one thing even more powerful we possess that the empire never will."

The crew looked at him, waiting.

He raised his head, his eyes burning with conviction. "A love of liberty and freedom. The Daklin can crush cities, burn fleets, and kill our friends…but no matter how hard or long they try, they can't kill humanity's natural affinity for freedom and liberty. That seed will always sprout and grow, regardless of how hard they try to stop it."

For a moment, no one spoke. "Liberty is the seed that can sprout in the most desolate of locations," Shelby lifted her glass, her voice quiet but sure. "To liberty, the one thing they'll never take from us."

One by one, the others raised their glasses, and the toast carried through the galley like a vow.

The toast hung in the air, glasses clinking softly. But Alex didn't sit back down. Instead, he paced, thinking about and considering something else. "There's something else…" he said.

Without another word, Alex left the galley. The others exchanged puzzled looks as the sound of his boots faded down the corridor. A few minutes later, he returned, holding a small object wrapped in protective cloth. He set it gently on the center of the table and pulled back the covering.

The crystal shimmered faintly in the dim light, facets glowing as though alive with hidden fire. It pulsed faintly, not with electricity, but with something deeper, something older.

Megan leaned forward, her brow furrowed. "What the hell is that, Alex? May I pick It up?"

"Yes, Megan, go ahead. It's won't hurt you." He looked around at each of them before speaking. "Polonius gave it to me. He called it Archē."

At the sound of the word, Shelby froze. Her eyes widened, and for a heartbeat, she seemed unable to breathe.

Alex noticed her reaction and put his hand on her shoulder. "Are you okay, Shelby?"

She leaned closer, staring at the crystal as if it had leapt out of memory. "Archē…" Her voice was low, almost reverent.

Everyone's gaze shifted to her at once.

"What is it?" Megan pressed. "What's got you so spooked?"

"Not spooked, really," Shelby swallowed, her voice steadier now but tinged with awe. "I've heard this word before. Aristotle was one of my professors on Pronimos."

"What?" Jabari asked with shock, thinking the name had to be a coincidence. "*The* Aristotle?

"Yes, Jabari *the* Aristotle. He lived the majority of his life, and died, on Pronimos. He was one of my professors. He spoke often about Archē in his teachings, but it wasn't a crystal. He taught that it is the Greek word for *beginning*, but more than that, it was a principle, a source, something that lay at the foundation of existence itself." She shook her head slowly. "I always thought his words were intended to be a metaphor, but this…" she gestured toward the crystal, "this is no metaphor."

The room was silent, the hum of the ship seeming louder than usual.

"There's more," Shelby added, her voice softer now. "Daniel, my late husband," she glanced at Alex to check his reaction to her mention of Daniel but saw nothing. "Daniel was an engineering geologist. He was raised on a world in the Scutum Arm of the galaxy. His people told stories of a crystal that matched this description. A legend, they said, of a stone tied to the original population of humanity itself, or to the first people who walked the stars."

She looked at Alex, her expression equal parts awe and concern. "I honestly thought it was just folklore."

The crystal's glow reflected in every eye around the table. Alex let the silence stretch for a moment before speaking. "This isn't just folklore or philosophy," he said. "Archē is real. You all know that Tranquility crossed the gulf from the Andromeda Galaxy to Pronimos, 2.6 million light-years, in just a matter of days. That wasn't legend, and it wasn't brute force. It was this." He tapped the crystal lightly with his fingertip. "Polonius gave it to us. Do the math and you'll see that we managed to travel a half million light years per day."

Emily tilted her head, adding to the impact. "We tried to learn how it worked, but the only thing we know is that what we experienced would require manipulation of tachyon structures beyond anything in the Pronimos tech archives."

"Correct," Alex said with a nod. "Which means there was a civilization older than the Daklin, or the Martians, who created the tunnel network. What we're looking for is a civilization more ancient than any we currently know. The ones who created this crystal had knowledge that could change everything."

He paused, letting his gaze sweep the room.

"That's who I think we need to find."

Across the table, Megan's jaw tightened. "You want us to chase ghosts, folklore, and fairytales?" She leaned forward, her voice sharp. "Alex, civilizations like that don't just vanish. And if they were that powerful, they sure as hell wouldn't have let the Daklin conquer the galaxy. If they ever existed, it's easy to conclude that they're *gone* now."

"They existed," Alex shot back, his tone calm but firm. "The crystal proves it."

"That thing only proves that Polonius handed you a shiny rock with some cool tech and told you a fascinating story," Megan snapped. "You want to stop the Daklin? We need ships. We need weapons. We need to build the next generation of Stingers with full production in the hundreds of thousands, and field an army that can match them. If we can do what you did in Perseus, and not melt our ships in the process, then we can win. That's reality."

"And how's that strategy working out?" Alex countered. "We fought for two years in Perseus and nearly two years before that. We've developed fleets, bombs, and unique strategy, and still they crushed us. If we keep fighting the empire on their terms, we're gonna lose."

The tension at the table thickened. Jabari's gaze shifted between them, lips pressed tight. Shelby ran her fingers over the rim of her glass, silent but intent. Emily's eyes flickered with data streams, but she didn't interrupt.

Finally, Sun Tsu stepped into the middle of the debate. "Perhaps the answer is not one path, but two."

All eyes turned to him.

"Divide your efforts," the cybernetic strategist said simply. "Megan rebuilds a military option. Alex pursues the ancient trail. If Archē leads to nothing, the military remains. If Megan's armies fall short, perhaps Alex's ghosts and fairies, as you call them, will yield true value."

Megan let out a long breath, still glaring at Alex, face flushed with anger. "Alex is our greatest asset, and our most creative engineer. You guys realize that in 50 million years, the Daklin could not figure out how to build tachyon tunnels, and this primitive asshole from Earth succeeded."

"Be nice, Megan," Shelby demanded.

"It's not about being nice, Shelby," Megan shot back. "The Daklin know who he is, and they'd like to kill him, capture him, *or* have him run off on some fairy tale expedition. It's clear, so don't expect me to clap when he comes back empty-handed." She paused and focused on Alex, "What we really need is your genius and creativity on the front line, Alex. Now." She paused, shaking her head. "Not after you finish your meaningless quest."

Alex met her stare evenly, clearly annoyed by her position. "I am going to do this, and you can count on me to find a solution. In the meantime, I know you'll be out fighting a war the resistance can't win." he quipped with a grimace.

The debate ended there, the divide drawn as clearly as the stars outside the viewport. Everyone was concerned and saddened by the rift between Megan and Alex.

After a long silence, Alex got up and started to walk out of the room. He stopped and turned back to Megan.

Shelby stood, ready to step in if Alex said or did something that might escalate the already thick tension.

Instead, he took Megan in his arms. "I love you, Megan Hoglund, and part of me knows you are right. Still, a bigger part of me concludes that I must follow my gut on this matter."

Megan was stunned.

Without waiting for a response, he turned and walked out.

The next morning, Alex was loading supplies into Tranquility's storage area. He had purchased a dozen cases of dark beer, brewed in the local system that Shelby had enjoyed. He wiped his hands on his jacket, pausing as he heard footsteps echoing down the ramp. He looked up and saw Megan.

She stopped at the bottom of the ramp, her arms crossed, but her expression was softer than last night's fire. "Mind if I come aboard?"

Alex gave a small nod. "Tranquility is always better with you on board, Megan."

"And I suspect Singularity would be better with you on board," She feigned flirtatiously pressing an old button between them.

"Uh huh," Alex grinned, recognizing the reference.

She stepped closer, her gaze flicking to the stacked cases. "Stocking up for a party, Alex?"

"Yeah. Shelby swears this is the only beer in this sector of the galaxy worth drinking. I clearly agree." He chuckled trying to keep his tone light, sensing the gravity in the space between them.

Megan exhaled, shoulders dropping. "Alex… about last night. I was out of line." She looked him in the eye, her voice steady. "I do love you. And I admire you more than I'll ever admit in front of the crew. You've carried us through things no one else could have survived. I don't want you thinking for a second that I don't see that."

"Megan…"

She raised her hand. "Let me finish. I've been thinking. We've been fighting this war like Earthlings, with timelines based on months and years. But with longevity tech… we can live for centuries, maybe thousands of years, like Aristotle did. Maybe the smart play isn't charging headlong at the Daklin with what we've got. I think you're right that they have used time and overwhelming force against us."

Her voice grew stronger as she found the words. "Maybe the smarter move is to disappear. Hide. Spread the seed of liberty around the galaxy and build alliances where they can't crush us. We can drop the fight and manufacture in secret. Hell, it might take a hundred years, maybe more, but eventually, we'll be able to match their billions of munitions. Seems to me that what we need to do is play the long game."

Alex studied her, seeing the steel in her eyes, but also the warmth. Slowly, he nodded. "That sounds like the Megan Hoglund I know. Fierce. Relentless. Always thinking ten moves ahead."

She stepped into his arms, hugging him tightly. For a moment, neither spoke.

"You should have taken my offer when we were both single four years ago." Then she leaned back and glanced at the crates, "But you got a really good one in Shelby, you know."

"I am coming to recognize that, Megan," he answered reflectively.

"In love and war, you never know what's gonna happen when we have thousands of years to live," She studied the beer cases again. "Between her selection of you and the beer, I can see she's got good taste."

"Is that a compliment, Megan?"

"This beer really is worth hauling across half the galaxy." She deflected and winked. "I think I'll pick up a supply for my ship, too."

Alex chuckled. "Too late. I bought every last case from the depot."

Megan laughed, the sound breaking through the final bits of tension. "Figures." She gave him another squeeze. "I'll be staying here in Bautlehaven for a few more weeks anyway. I need time to plan, build contacts, and figure out where Tsu and I should go next. I'm sure the depot will be resupplied by then."

"That's a good plan." Alex smiled.

They hugged once more, and when the port sealed behind him, Alex allowed himself a rare smile. Whatever lay ahead: ghosts, fairytales, or centuries of struggle, he and Megan were on the same page again.

Alex stepped onto the control deck. The familiar glow of Tranquility's displays washed over him, and Shelby was waiting in the pilot's chair, legs tucked beneath her. She gave him a sweet, knowing smile, the kind that said she didn't need to hear the words to understand what had just passed between him and Megan.

"Everything all right?" she asked softly.

Alex let out a breath and managed a small grin. "Yeah. Everything's as perfect as it can be in the middle of this war." It was a heavy statement, but he managed to deliver it as though it was just another day.

Emily's voice chimed from the console. "Jabari is in the galley, drinking coffee. I did not interrupt him as he seemed intent on savoring the moment."

"Good for him," Alex said with a half-smile. "And what about us? Any leads?"

"Yes," Emily replied. Streams of data cascaded across the forward display, each point of light marked with annotations. "Ten promising planetary systems within range, each showing anomalous energy signatures. All candidates that are worth investigation."

Alex's expression hardened into focus. He stepped to the center console, resting his hands on the rail. "Then let's not waste time."

Shelby's smile lingered as she leaned forward, watching him with quiet confidence.

"Emily," Alex ordered, his voice steady now. "Take us into the tunnel."

The hum of the tachyon engines rose, a low resonance that filled the deck as Tranquility slid into the tunnel, the ship and its crew were once again diving into the unknown.

23

Oiketerion

66 Million Years BCE

The high chamber of the Martian Parliament stood in silence, broken only by the soft hum of the air circulation systems. Three tiers of seats, each carved from rose-tinted granite quarried on Olympus Mons, encircled the central dais where the Speaker presided. Outside the tall windows, a pink dust storm churned across the sky above the Martian capital, indifferent to the weighty matters unfolding within the halls of government.

Statesman Lysandros rose. Tall and lean, with greying temples and the bearing of a scholar, he was known for his command of history and science. As always, he wore the deep blue mantle of a senior representative.

"Honorable members," he began, voice steady. "I come to you not merely in fear, but in analysis. The Daklin aggression is not motivated purely by what they say they want. It is not only about the resources, territory, or technology that our engineers possess. Once we acquiesce to their demands, they will do the unthinkable. If we do not acquiesce, they will also do the unthinkable." He paused and studied the members. "To say this with more clarity, I believe that if they cannot *control* Ares, they will destroy it. We must create a backup plan. We should colonize a new world with one hundred thousand of our finest minds."

A low murmur rippled through the chamber. Lysandros held up a hand. "Consider their past conquests. They demand compliance, and when resistance persists, they raze, they annihilate. Our treaties, our defenses, they are, I fear, invitations to provoke their wrath, not shields."

Representative Marcellia of the northern hemisphere stood, hands clasped behind her. "Statesman, with all due respect, we have bound treaties *and* alliances. We have shown strength. The growing Daklin Empire, as you call it, have sprung from our colonies. Why would they destroy their own ancestral home?"

Another voice spoke up, Elder Thessis, from the scholars' wing. "Lysandros, your logic is not without merit, but your remedy is worse than the disease. To forsake a hundred thousand of our greatest minds, amongst them artists, scientists, architects, and statesmen," he grinned, and the audience laughed in return. "This is tantamount to cutting off a limb. What becomes of Ares when its light dims? What becomes of our identity?"

Lysandros nodded, acknowledging the counterarguments with measured calm. "What I propose is not rashness, but pragmatism. If we fail to prepare an alternative now, then when the invasion comes, and the gates are breached, it will be too late. I propose we establish a new colony: an exodus of our brightest minds to a distant world, to build *Oiketerion*. A new home. A bastion of culture, knowledge, and life."

The room filled with negative exclamations. Some representatives bristled.

"It would be a preservation of everything we have built," Lysandros added. "Far from the tentacles of the Daklin."

Speaker Caius raised his gavel. "This is not a military motion, Lysandros, but one of civil, hopeful fantasy. Are you asking us now to fund this relocation? To divide our intellect and our heart?"

Marcellia's voice rang clear. "You ask us to believe that this is the only option? That Ares cannot survive? We will stand. We will resist. Your proposal is defeat dressed as planning."

Thessis shook his head. "And what of those left behind? Shall they be second-class? Shall our culture be hollowed because a portion of our brightest are gone to some wild promise?"

Lysandros's eyes were measured. He paused, then spoke quietly but firmly: "I respect your passion. But if the Daklin wind sweeps across our skies, passion alone will not shield our home, will not rebuild shattered laboratories or resurrect lost dreams. Better that Oiketerion be our insurance. It will be a living archive and a seed for renewal."

Silence fell. The vote was called. The result: the motion for establishing Oiketerion, for carving out this exodus of thinkers and artists, was rejected. Not by a hair, but firmly.

Lysandros bowed his head under the weight of defeat. But in the quiet corridors afterward, he gathered a small council of loyal followers that included professors, engineers, artists, and ordinary citizens. He studied the M-class planets scattered across the galaxy, whispered plans in shadowed rooms, mapped coordinates, measured distances. He was determined that his plan would preserve a remnant of the civilization that had once built the network to the stars.

He spoke softly to his closest ally, Callista. "We'll go in secret. I have one hundred thousand hand selected volunteers, who represent the best of our civilization and achievements. We have selected an uninhabited M-class planet far from the nearest tunnel portal. It is off the grid, and we shall endeavor to keep it that way."

"You spoke the name as if it were already written in the stars," she said softly. "Oiketerion. Why that word? Why not simply call it 'New Ares,' or something similar?"

Lysandros stopped at the landing of the stairwell, turned, and looked at her with the intensity of a man who had carried too many visions alone.

"Oiketerion is not merely a word, Callista. In the old Ares tongue, it means *dwelling… a habitation… a true home.* What we will build is not a fortress or an outpost, but a home." His voice echoed faintly against the stone.

He stepped closer, his eyes alive with conviction. "If Ares burns, then those who survive must not live as exiles, forever grasping at what was lost. They must not feel like ghosts of a dead world wandering the void. Oiketerion will be more than a refuge, it will be a declaration that Ares humanity endures, that our art, our science, our spirit can root itself in again and thrive. It will be the place where children are born and do not feel displaced, where songs are sung not in mourning, but in celebration."

Callista watched him, her expression softening.

"Oiketerion," Lysandros repeated, voice lower now, almost reverent. "Because it reminds us that home is not soil, not stone, not a red sky above our heads. Home is where our people live, dream, and create. When the Daklin come, they will take Ares, but they will not take our home. We will carry that with us, in Oiketerion."

Callista nodded slowly, a tremor of awe in her voice. "Then let us build it, Lysandros. Quietly, carefully, and with all the strength we have."

○○○○ ∞ ○○○○

One hundred thousand men women and children boarded the ships, bound for Oiketerion. They carried with them the seed-stock of Martian science, philosophy, art, and music, tucked alongside grain vaults, genetic libraries, and digital archives. They vanished into the dark, beyond the maps of Parliament, outside the tachyon tunnel network, and past the reach of the Daklin eye.

Less than a year after the departure of Lysandros, the Daklin ships eradicated all life on Mars and Venus. The great civilization that once thrived there faded into obscurity, forgotten in the long history of the Milky Way Galaxy.

Centuries passed, then millennia, until time itself stretched into megaanum. Oiketerion flourished, faltered, and flourished again. Natural disasters came in waves: volcanic winters, quakes that split continents, storms that stripped cities bare. A magnetic storm from a nearby supernova struck not once, but twice.

The dream that Lysandros created seemed to falter as civilizations rose, fell, and rebuilt on the same soil, each age remembering only dim echoes of an ancient journey, but forgetting its true origin.

The name "Ares" started as legend, then became silenced and forgotten. The original home world, the red cradle beneath Sol's fourth planet, faded from their lore. Oiketerion was home, and home alone.

More than isolated by memory, they were also sealed off by physics. The Galactic Tunnel Network, the lattice of tachyon corridors on which the Daklin Empire had risen, did not touch their star. They were cut off. Unlinked. Unreachable.

Being off the grid was the original intent of Lysandros.

And so it was that Oiketerion and its people drifted away from the great currents of history. After the Daklin destroyed all life on Mars and Venus, the memory of that once-great civilization faded into oblivion. While the Daklin ruled and warred across the spiral arms, and while entire fleets burned in tunnels of light, the children of Ares were left alone, forgotten by both conqueror and ally. Their silence endured as surely as their survival.

24

Into the Norma Arm

The familiar chime of a Plink echoed through the control deck, and Alex raised an eyebrow.

"Zander?"

"Hey, Dad. I heard from Megan that you are off hunting for pixie dust or something like that?"

"Uh huh. Pixie dust hunting sounds like a quest I'd take, right?" Alex joked.

"Not really, but I believe that's the term Megan used." Zander chuckled. "I have a request from the University on Pronimos. They asked if Tranquility might host a young computer scientist for a period of study and observation. The duration would be a couple months."

Shelby leaned back in her chair, shooting Alex a knowing smile. "They're sending you an intern, Captain."

"Not an intern," Alex corrected, though his lips quirked. "A mind. And minds are always welcome." He tapped the console. "Tell them yes, Zander. We'll pick them up."

Two days later, a slender young man stepped through the portal onto Tranquility's deck. Barely out of his twenties, eyes sharp and restless, he carried nothing, but a tablet computer and a backpack stuffed with clothing.

"Name's Kyros," he said quickly, scanning the room as if measuring every system at once. "I'm told I'll have access to your ship's AI matrix?"

Emily folded her arms, her expression a blend of curiosity and caution. "Access is relative. But if you behave, I might let you peek behind a few curtains."

Kyros grinned. "Fair enough."

Alex clapped him on the shoulder. "Welcome aboard, Kyros. Learn what you can, contribute where you're able, and don't break anything that can't be fixed. Deal?"

"Deal," Kyros said.

Later, when the boy had settled into quarters, Alex returned to the deck. "Emily, set course for our first stop, The Norma Arm, that remote planet you suggested," he tried to recall the planet's name, but couldn't. "You know, the one with the anomalous ruins."

"Acknowledged," Emily said. Her eyes gleamed as streams of numbers cascaded across the holo-panel. "Destination plotted for Mnemeion 5. Estimated transit: two and a half days in the tunnel."

Shelby crossed her arms. "You really think this world's got ruins older than fifty million years?"

"That's what the Pronimos archives hinted. If even part of it survived, it'll tell us things the Daklin never dreamed of. We need to see it for ourselves."

They emerged above the Mnemeion System's fifth world, which was a storm-wrapped sphere where ruins sprawled across continents in geometric grids visible even from orbit.

For three weeks, they studied. Kyros buried himself in alien archives that were so masterfully constructed they had withstood the ravages of weather and time. Emily lingered in silence, attuned to faint echoes from deep systems that might still be alive. Shelby sketched broken skylines, wondering aloud how any culture could build on such a scale.

And then – nothing.

"Mnemeion gave us three weeks of dust and equations," Shelby muttered as she adjusted the field scanner. "If you ask me, we should've moved on after the first seven days."

Kyros' eyes lit with excitement from the station window. "But the crystalline bands around the inner moon were unique! I've never seen plasma refract like that."

"They're unique," Jabari agreed, his tone steady, "but not what we came for. Alex, I pray you are right and we're not just chasing ghosts."

Alex folded his arms. He had heard the doubt before. "Every system tells us what it *isn't*. That narrows the field. Persistence is how we find what matters."

Emily's voice rose from the console, calm and precise. "Analysis complete. Mnemeion has no records or resonances consistent with Pronimos or the tunnel origins. Recommend relocation."

Alex gave the order. "Then we move."

The second stop was Daskalos Prime, a yellow-white sun wrapped in four rocky planets and a green-banded gas giant. Kyros was practically glued to the sensors.

"Wow, look at those storms!" he pointed, the data overlay shimmering with emerald arcs. "They're like impressionist art in motion."

Shelby smirked. "Pretty paintings won't help us survive a Daklin armada." She was coming to like young Kyros and his blend of AI expertise and creative thinking.

They stayed nearly a month, combing ruins from an abandoned relay station orbiting the second planet. Interesting artifacts, but nothing tied to the underlying goal.

"Catalog it," Alex said at last, his voice flat. "We're moving on."

The third was Kallichoron 8, a red subgiant swollen to near collapse. The 8th planet had a strong magnetic field that had allowed it to survive fluctuations from its star.

Emily modeled the flows of plasma intense rivers in three dimensions, "The planet is alive, in a way," she said. "It resonates across multiple frequencies simultaneously."

But after a couple days, the conclusion became obvious.

"There are millions of worlds like this in our galaxy," Alex concluded while rubbing his temples. "This one's another dead end."

The fourth was Eurydike, a blue-white star encircled by a shattered moon belt. The debris was dense, a graveyard of rock and ice. Tranquility threaded through cautiously, hull shields humming.

Kyros whispered, "Something catastrophic happened here."

Shelby shook her head. "Whole world split like a melon. Makes you wonder if we're staring at the aftermath of a weapon."

Alex studied the fragments silently. He could feel Jabari's eyes on him.

"Another reminder," Jabari said quietly. "Even stars with stories may not tell us the one you're searching for."

Four systems studied. Nothing.

One night in the control room, Emily spoke into the silence. "Alex, probability suggests the next system may yield the same result. Do you wish to continue?"

Alex's gaze stayed fixed on the scatter of the Norma Arm, dark and endless. "Persistence separates discovery from failure. We keep going."

Shelby leaned on the console, tired but resolute. "That's the spirit, cowboy."

Kyros straightened, eyes bright again. "The next star could be it. It *has* to be."

The following evening Emily and Jabari approached Alex in the galley. Emily's expression was composed, but her eyes carried a weight Alex had never seen before. Jabari's jaw was tight, his hand resting gently on her shoulder.

"Alex," Emily began, "can we talk to you privately?"

He gestured them to sit. "Of course. What's on your mind?"

Emily hesitated, then said quietly, "It's been over four months since my reproductive surgery. Something isn't right."

Alex's breath caught. "Emily…" He reached across the table, but she kept her hands folded, steady. "Are you okay?"

Jabari added, "We've run diagnostics, Alex. We've tried everything within ship systems. Let's just say there are issues we don't understand."

For the first time in years, Alex felt fear for someone not by threat of war, but by the frailty of life. "Do you mind if we bring Shelby into this?"

"That might be wise," Jabari answered.

Moments later Shelby slipped into the galley, eyes moving from Emily to Jabari, then to Alex. She listened in silence, then leaned back, arms crossed, thinking hard.

"I'm out of my depth, Alex," she said finally. "Something must have gone wrong in the surgery. I suggest Emily go to Pronimos. The cybernetic surgeons there are the finest in the galaxy. If anyone can help her, it's them."

Alex nodded slowly, gaze shifting to Emily. "That makes sense. And it's time to return Kyros anyway."

"I know how important this mission is, Alex," Emily looked down, whispering, "I don't want to slow it down by returning to Pronimos and having you all wait on my surgery."

Alex leaned forward, voice firm. "You don't slow us, Emily. You are family and far more important than any other task."

"Understood, but…"

"Stop, Emily. Here's the way we handle this. Drop Shelby and me at the next planet on our list and we'll continue following the records. You, Jabari, and Kyros take Tranquility to Pronimos. Once your medical issue is handled, meet us again on the trail."

Emily gave Alex a long look. "That's a risk."

Alex met her eyes. "Your health is important and so is pausing our search. Time is the one thing I don't think we can waste. I know how important this is to you and Jabari, so go take care of it."

"Okay," Emily looked up at last, her face softening. "Then it's decided."

"What's the next planet, Emily?" Alex asked.

"The next one is Gamma Crux, but it no longer supports a population. Since we are splitting up, I suggest Oiketerion, an interesting planet where the population is entering its industrial age. Since you and Shelby will be out on your own for several weeks, I want to be certain you have sufficient resources."

"Of course, you always think of everything, Emily."

"I have analyzed our trip to Pronimos and back will likely be a minimum two weeks, and a maximum of six."

Alex arched a brow. "That sounds reasonable."

"As you know, it's called parallel processing." Emily gave a faint smile. "We will arrive tomorrow. For now, I suggest you and Shelby get some rest. I will work on final plans.'

The following morning, Alex found Emily in the galley. "What do we know about this planet?"

"They do not use a traditional money system there, Alex. Their economy is entirely barter. Goods for goods. Services for services."

Shelby joined them, holding a glass of water, and sat down.

Alex leaned in, curious. "So how do we fit into that?"

"While you were sleeping, I tunneled into one of the small towns and researched what might offer you stability," Emily said. "I secured the title to a ranch on the eastern plains. It comes with one hundred and twenty head of bosque, which are the local equivalent of cattle. They are prized for hides, meat, and their horns, which believe it or not, are used to make musical instruments."

"How did you accomplish that?" Alex furrowed his brow.

"A little bit of technology mixed with old fashioned paperwork. Other than that," Emily smiled, "well, just don't ask."

Shelby blinked, then broke into a grin. "Alex… we just became ranchers."

Alex chuckled. "Texans through and through. Guess we'll see if bosque taste better than Texas beef."

"Or if they buck harder than longhorns," Shelby teased.

Emily tilted her head, studying them. "I believe you are joking, but the herd is real. It will give you standing there, and plenty to barter with while we're gone."

Emily interfaced to the cameras, so Oiketerion filled the viewport. They could see green plains cut with rivers, settlements shining like pearls along coastlines.

Alex took the controls and brought Tranquility into a landing spot on the meadow near the ranch. Outside, the prairie stretched in rolling waves of gold and green, broken only by scraggly trees that looked like live oaks and a silver ribbon of water cutting through the grassland. The house stood a hundred yards off with stone walls, a wide wood porch, and several chimneys that reached like old sentinels above the roofline.

Shelby stepped down the ramp of tranquility and took in the view, eyes wide. "It's beautiful, Emily. Looks like a *real* home."

Alex smiled at the tone in her voice. "Not quite Texas, but close enough for you to claim it."

They stepped down the ramp together, the dry grass crunching under their boots. A warm breeze carried the scent of wildflowers, dust, and the faint musk of cattle. The ranch house had a prairie-style porch running its length, railings hand-hewn, with a hearth at the far end built of rough-cut stone. The wooden beams glowed golden in the sunlight, as if they'd grown here instead of being placed by human hands.

Shelby let out a low whistle. "That porch is beggin' for a couple rockers, an acoustic guitar, and a long Texas evening. I swear, Alex, if you'd never told me this was some remote planet, I'd say we'd landed halfway between Abilene and the Brazos River."

Alex chucked, taking it in. For a moment, his engineer's brain went quiet. "It's… more than I expected. Almost like they built it with us in mind."

Shelby laughed, her voice catching just slightly. "You mean with *you* in mind. Straight lines, clean walls, sturdy as a bunker. But look at it with the stonework, the porch, the open fields. This place was made for sittin' outside with a cold beer and listenin' to the cicadas."

Emily and Jabari studied the area, grinned, and shook their heads. To them, it was just another old beat-up house in the country.

"I guess you did good, Emily." Jabari commented with a smile. "Our family will be happy here while we are off traveling to Pronimos."

Alex hugged Emily and Jabari. "Take care of her," he told Jabari.

"I will," Jabari said firmly.

He then looked at Kyros, "Stay out of trouble, young man, and best of luck back in the university."

"Life's no fun when I stay out of trouble." He responded and hugged Alex. "Thanks for the opportunity, sir."

Shelby embraced Emily, whispering in her ear, "Get well. We'll see you soon, hopefully expecting."

Emily's eyes softened. "Yes, we will plan on that."

"Shoot, one more thing," Alex said, raising a finger before turning back toward *Tranquility*'s engine room. He retrieved the Archē crystal from its platter and slipped it carefully into a padded compartment on the backpack. Then he checked the two tunnel backpacks Emily had prepared once more for good measure, making sure everything was in place.

Shelby slung hers over her shoulder and gave him a half-smile. "Ranchers with a side of cosmic archaeological treasure hunting. A nice mix of Indiana Jones and Star Wars."

"I'm glad you know both of them movies," Alex laughed, the sound carrying a touch of the old Texas drawl. "Then let's get'er done."

Tranquility's engines whispered to life. The ramp closed, and with one final wave, the ship lifted off, carrying Emily, Jabari, and Kyros back toward Pronimos. Alex and Shelby remained behind, standing in the grasslands of Oiketerion, where bosque herds grazed in the distance and their own uncertain path was only just beginning.

○ ○ ○ ○ ∞ ○ ○ ○ ○

Tranquility slipped into the tunnel, its hull shimmering as the stars stretched into infinite ribbons. Emily stood at the console, calibrating the flow fields, her mind partly on the ship, partly on Jabari's steady hand resting on her shoulder. Kyros sat hunched over his workstation, eyes bleary, his computer glowing with half-written code.

"Kyros," Emily said gently, "you've been at that for hours. Take a break."

"Just one more cycle," he muttered. "I've almost got the emitter routines mapped."

Emily frowned. "Emitters? Which emitters?"

But Kyros didn't answer. His code loop ran silently in the background, pinging Tranquility's auxiliary systems, an experiment left open, testing various frequencies in the tachyon tunnel.

Emily should have checked it, but Jabari had asked if she'd join him for a bite to eat now that the ship was safe in the tunnel.

Not far enough away in the spiral arms, Daklin hunters stirred.

The Daklin had been searching for Tranquility for months, sifting through the static of tunnel-space, hoping for the faintest anomaly. And then, like blood in the water, Kyros's unshielded test signature rippled across the network. A beacon in the dark.

A squadron of Daklin warships reoriented in formation. Their command carrier pulsed with power, charging weapons tuned for tunnel strikes, something they had learned from the resistance.

Inside Tranquility, Emily's console suddenly screamed, alarms flaring red. Her eyes widened. "What…? That's not possible. We're being tracked inside the tunnel!"

Jabari grabbed her arm. "How?"

Before the sentence finished, the ship jolted violently. A piercing wave of energy ripped through the hull. Panels exploded in showers of sparks, the lights dimming to amber. Shields and attack detection had been turned off.

Emily's fingers flew across the console. "Shields offline. Tachyon field destabilizing." She looked up, eyes locking Jabari's. In that instant, the truth passed between them. No escape. No time. She tried to Plink Alex but realized there was no open tunnel to Oiketerion.

Alex was on his own.

Kyros's voice cracked. "I didn't mean…oh God, I did this."

The second-strike hit, and the ship tore apart in an incandescent bloom.

For a heartbeat, Emily reached across the smoke and chaos, her hand brushing Jabari's. She Plinked one last encrypted message up to her cloud storage on Pronimos, then the tunnel swallowed everything, and Tranquility was gone.

Out in the void, only the Daklin remained, their sensors confirming the kill. One of the officers hissed in satisfaction.

"The Earth ship is destroyed."

But the commander's voice was cold. "That pariah Durant is now gone. The remainder of the resistance will soon follow."

25

The Bosque Ranch

Morning broke across the Oiketerion plains with a soft gold light, the bosque herd moving like shadows in the mist. Alex leaned on the fence rail, watching their broad shoulders push through the grass. He exhaled slowly. "Well, Shelby, I guess we really *are* ranchers."

Shelby joined him, sipping from a tin cup. "Can't say I expected this when we left Pronimos. Let's enjoy it while we can."

Alex smiled faintly, but his eyes were already distant, scanning the horizon. "The Pronimos records described Oiketerion as one of the most unusual of the old worlds. Millions of years of civilization, but no machines, no ships, and very little technology-based engineering."

"Strange," Shelby tilted her head. "And yet, they're still here."

"They are," Alex said, almost to himself. "Physics without engineering. Arts and government without industry. It shouldn't work, but somehow it does."

Later that morning, they saddled up a pair of animals that were horse-like, but taller, with longer, slender necks. They rode to the nearest town, Drevarn. The journey took about an hour and proved a bit challenging for two people who hadn't ridden in quite some time.

The streets in Drevarn were alive with barter: merchants trading bolts of cloth for pottery, farmers exchanging hides for glasswork. There was no currency, as Emily had hinted, only agreements written in chalk or spoken in trust.

At the Drevarn Town Hall, Shelby handed the records to the clerk who noted that their ranch had been tied up in probate for several seasons. Emily, with her thorough logic, had somehow discovered the opportunity and transferred the title to Alex and Shelby by making Alex the beneficiary.

Shelby saw it as an opportunity for her and Alex, as the new owners, to meet the records clerk. They knew they needed recognition around town if they were going to trade, and even though they would only be here for a month or so, they decided to start off on the right foot.

The clerk smiled as he stamped the parchment. "Seems you two were meant to step in."

Shelby tucked the papers under her arm and grinned at Alex when they left the building. "Guess we just made ourselves legit."

In the afternoon, Alex and Shelby wandered over to Drevarn Collegium. The campus was a mosaic of stone courtyards and lecture halls; their walls etched with flowing murals of equations and philosophical maxims. The architecture wouldn't have looked out of place at an Ivy League college back on Earth. Students clustered in shaded alcoves, debating physics and sketching equations on old-fashioned chalkboards.

Alex didn't *need* to visit the science department, but his curiosity about the state of science on this new world was too strong to resist. That's where they met Fraklen, a man of middling years, sharp-eyed, with a permanent ink stain on his fingers. A professor of chemistry, Fraklen had just finished a lecture on bonding and electron shells on which Alex listened in. They struck up a conversation, one that quickly turned from polite interest to shared enthusiasm.

"You're Durant, the new Bosque Ranch heir?" Fraklen asked, adjusting the strap of his satchel.

Alex nodded. "That's me. I guess news travels fast around here." He wondered how he should introduce Shelby, then remembered the deed showed them as husband and wife. "This is my wife, Shelby, she's a medical doctor. Just so you know, my education is in physics, not ranching."

"Well, you two look young. Where did you say you're from?"

Alex realized he hadn't studied a local map and had no idea how to answer the question.

"We're from South Theslon," Shelby answered.

"Never been there," Fraklen nodded. "But I know that's a long trip."

"Yup. A couple of boat rides and a wagon from the coast to here." Shelby answered confidently, "but we are excited to be here in Drevarn."

Fraklen's eyes brightened. "That's... far." He turned to Alex, "But physics, yes. I could tell you were following along in the lecture. Not many do."

They walked together beneath the colonnade. Alex hesitated, then admitted, "Truth is, I'm more interested in the archaeology here than the ranch. Ancient ruins and historic records... they're the trail I'm following."

Fraklen's lips quirked into a smile. "Then we have something in common. Chemistry may be my profession, but archaeology is my passion. I've led expeditions to several of the ancient sites. The strata, the timeworn libraries, the artifacts... they are windows into a world even older than most people imagine."

Alex stopped, surprised and pleased. "Then maybe we should compare notes. You know the sites... Between the two of us, we might make sense of things others have missed."

Fraklen extended a hand, formal but warm. "Consider it a partnership, Mr. Durant. I will be done administering final exams in a couple days, and I need something interesting to do during the break."

Alex shook it firmly, a smile tugging at his lips. "Then let's see what secrets Oiketerion has been keeping."

Fraklen furrowed his brow, "Oiketerion? Is that what you people in Theslon are calling Oiket?"

Alex could feel his pulse race. Next time he came into town, he'd be better versed. "No sir, I just used that name because I saw it in one of the archaeology manuscripts. Call it a beginning to our adventure."

The afternoon sun had dipped low by the time Alex and Shelby parted ways with Fraklen outside the Collegium gates. The streets of Drevarn bustled with evening traffic, wagons rattling over cobblestones, vendors calling out the day's last trades, lamps being lit one by one along the square.

Shelby nudged Alex with her shoulder. "You handled yourself well back there. But next time, let's learn a bit more before someone asks where we're from."

Alex exhaled, laughing at himself. "Yeah. Nearly gave us away with that slip. Good save, Doctor Shelby."

"Doctor *and* wife," Shelby teased, flashing the parchment tucked in her satchel. "Never thought I'd see my name on a deed to a cattle ranch. Particularly one that says I'm Shelby Durant."

"And married to me…" he grinned. "I'm sure that's Emily's version of humor."

They wandered into the town square, drawn by the smell of roasting meat and the low hum of conversation spilling out from a timber-beamed tavern. A painted sign above the door read *The Golden Horn*.

"Think they'll serve bosque brisket?" Alex asked, his eyes alight with curiosity.

Shelby arched an eyebrow. "Only one way to find out."

Inside, the tavern was warm and lively. Wooden tables were packed with townsfolk sharing platters of food, mugs of frothy ale raised in easy laughter. A hearth at the far end burned low, sending ribbons of smoke into the rafters.

They found a table near the window. The server, a stout woman with an apron dusted in flour, brought them two mugs of dark ale, a platter of sliced bosque roast, and some fresh baked bread.

"Y'all are the new owners of the Bosque Ranch, right?" The server asked.

Shelby stood and shook the woman's hand, "I'm Shelby Durant and this is my husband, Alex."

"Good to meet you both. I'll send the owner over when he gets in. You have a credit here, but we're gonna need another bosque in the next day or so."

"Happy to help, but, since we're new here, just let us know the process." Shelby smiled.

"Will do, Shelby Durant, and welcome to our humble town."

When she left, Alex took a cautious bite, then blinked in surprise. "Shelby… this is *good*. Tender. Smoky. Almost like beef, but richer."

Shelby sampled a piece and closed her eyes with a smile. "You're right. Better than half the brisket joints in Texas."

"No! You're wrong there, Shelby. Nothing's better than Texas brisket." Alex raised his mug, foam clinging to the rim. "And the ale? Not bad. Malty, smooth, and a hint of chocolate. They've got something here."

Shelby tapped her mug against his. "To ranching, archaeology, and a few weeks away from the Daklin nightmare."

They both laughed, and for a moment the weight of their situation lifted. Alex leaned back in his chair, surveying the lively room. "You know… for a couple of Texans stranded on a world without engines or money, we're not doing too bad."

Shelby smirked. "Speak for yourself. Tomorrow you'll be mucking bosque stalls, professor."

Alex groaned theatrically, taking another long pull from his ale. "Guess some things never change."

○○○○ ∞ ○○○○

The next few days, they explored the ranch house, which was a beautiful combination of rock and split wood. The home had four bedrooms, and a tank for running water, with indoor plumbing. Candles and oil were used for lighting and fireplaces for heating. Mornings belonged to the ranch, managing the bosque herds grazing across the plains, the smell of fresh hay and damp earth, the crackle of the wood stove when Shelby or Alex cooked.

Alex found the work both humbling and strangely grounding. He patched fences, learned how to drive the herds from pasture to pasture, and even found himself arguing with Shelby about which cut of bosque meat tasted best over an open fire.

Shelby had invested in a full ranch wardrobe of rugged clothes for the workday and softer, more graceful outfits for the evening. Each morning, she pulled on sturdy jeans, scuffed leather boots, and a pair of gloves that soon carried the dust and sweat of the prairie. By nightfall, though, she always transformed. After a quick bath, she would trade the grit of the day for a clean western skirt that swayed lightly around her cute figure, and a pair of stylish cowboy boots, the kind that turned work-hardened Shelby into an elegant, graceful woman under the porch lights.

On the third day, exhausted from a hard day's work, Alex leaned against the porch rail, dust still clinging to his jeans. The prairie-style deck stretched wide, its rough-hewn rails catching the pale light of a rising moon. Beyond the rock walls of the ranch house, the dark pastures were serenaded with the sounds of crickets, cicadas, and the faint lowing of cattle. A hearth fire cracked at the end of the porch, sending out a glow that caught the edges of two old rockers and a bench worn smooth by use.

The door creaked open. Shelby stepped out, her hair still damp from her bath, the scent of soap and cedarwood drifting softly ahead of her. Her work clothes were gone, replaced by her captivating evening attire. She carried two beers, handed one to him, and took the chair across from him.

"You know, Alex," she said, settling in with a sigh, "I like this place. Reminds me of home in ways I didn't expect. Feels like the old west, even though that home is half a galaxy away."

Alex took a long sip. "Hard to believe this land's been here for millions of years waiting for us to stumble across it. Ranching cattle under another sun… it's strange. But it fits."

She laughed softly. "Fits better'n most places I've been. Out here, life feels simpler. We mend fences, work stock, chase down strays. Then the night falls, and it's just you and me, and the stars."

He nodded. "Yes… I suppose I need to begin ramping up the archaeology, but that can wait till tomorrow."

Shelby smiled, picked up the guitar propped against the wall, and strummed a few chords. Her voice drifted into a soft country tune, easy and warm. When she finished, she looked at him sideways. "You know how to dance?"

"Not much. I tried a two-step once, but I was terrible. Physics makes more sense than dancing ever did."

She stood, brushing her skirt, and reached out her hand. "C'mon then. It's time you learned."

He set his beer down, hesitated, then took her hand. They tried the two-step. As predicted, he stumbled, stepped on her boots, and muttered an apology.

She laughed, shaking her head. "Bless your heart," she joked in her most southern twang. "You dance like a Yankee."

Alex blinked, then grinned. "Wait, did your accent just… change?"

She exaggerated the drawl, her eyes twinkling. "Reckon it did, darlin'. Don't you worry none, I'll learn ya proper."

Alex chuckled. "Well, I do recall this version of Shelby from the bar on Pronimos. Kind of sweet and charming. …makes me happy."

"Let's try some simple math," she laughed, keeping the old twang in her voice as she guided him. "One, two, three, sugar. One, two, three. That's the waltz."

She smiled, realizing that with just that simple counting, he was actually dancing.

"You got this," she encouraged.

Something loosened in him. He stopped counting, let her lead the rhythm. The porch boards creaked under their steps, the fire crackled, and Shelby started humming a tune in that country drawl that was soft, sweet, and familiar.

"I know that song. It's an old one by Ernest Tubb." Alex grinned. "My favorite is the version by Shelley Laine."

"Yes, I like that one as well." She responded, keeping the step, then began singing again. "Waltz Across Texas, with you in my arms'" she sang, still half in character, and continued making up words, but keeping the melody. "Like a story-book ending I'm lost in your charms, I could waltz across Oiket with you…"

The moonlight painted her hair silver as they moved. Alex felt the weight of war and quest for lost archaeology melt away. All that remained was her hand in his, the sway of their steps, and her soft humming drifting out into the Oiket night.

○○○○ ∞ ○○○○

Over the next couple weeks, the friendship with Fraklen deepened. He often joined them at the ranch, sitting on the porch with a notebook while the bosque grazed in the distance. They debated chemistry versus physics, argued about whether societies collapsed by choice or by catastrophe, and shared mugs of the local ale late into the evening.

"Strange thing," Fraklen said once, gazing across the fields, "I teach chemistry, I study ruins, but I've never had a place like this. You are a lucky man to have inherited this kind of wealth and stability. The ranch gives you roots."

Alex nodded, watching the herd shift like a tide across the grass. "Maybe that's the point. Roots give us perspective. Even when we're digging for the past." A part of him wanted to tell Fraklen more about what was going on in the galaxy, and why he and Shelby were on the planet, but he resisted.

○○○○ ∞ ○○○○

Alex settled into the groove with days balanced between bosque ranching and archaeological discovery. The deeper they dug, the clearer it became: Oiket's civilizations had risen tens of millions of years ago, and somehow, in all that time, they had never turned to engines or machines. They left records of thought, not tools of progress. Alex couldn't shake the feeling that buried in those records was something more, yet to be uncovered.

The days were turning into weeks, and exploration was happening, but the seeds of concern were beginning to grow. Emily and Tranquility had not yet returned.

Like on most every evening, the bosque herd grazed quietly in the moonlight, their hulking shadows stretching long across the plains. Alex sat on the porch, elbows on his knees, staring into the distance where the grass met the sky. The soft creak of wood signaled Shelby settling into the chair beside him, mug in hand.

"You've been quiet all day," she said.

Alex rubbed his hand over his face. "Five weeks, Shelby. Five. I thought we'd hear something back by now. A message, a sign, anything."

"You knew it'd be at least two weeks," she reminded him. "Up to six if the surgeons needed time."

He shook his head. "It's not just that. I've come to realize that we're blind out here. No comms. No way to know if they even reached Pronimos. We're sitting in the dark with no technology and at least for me, it feels helpless."

Shelby leaned back, her gaze steady. "You're not wrong to be worried. Even the most complicated procedure, the kind that would take multiple teams, would be about three weeks in the worst-case scenario. I agree that Emily and Jabari should've been back on course by now."

Alex looked up at her sharply. "I don't know why, but I have a gut feeling … something's happened."

She sighed, swirling the dregs of her drink. "Maybe they were delayed for other reasons. Maybe the doctors asked Emily to run more diagnostics before they released her. Maybe Kyros got himself into trouble. But if you want my expert opinion, if this were just about surgery, they'd have been back by now."

Alex stood, and began pacing the porch, his boots thudding softly against the wood. "This planet, these people…they've been around for millions of years. They should've built machines, ships, something. We went from cave dwellers to space faring in thirty thousand, but they didn't. It's perplexing…" He gestured vaguely toward the hills. "The ruins tell a different story. There was technology once. Maybe more than once. It's gone now. Just… gone. What could have happened to them?"

Shelby frowned. "Are you changing topics Alex?"

"I'm trying to distract myself."

"I see," she smiled and put her arm around him.

"I'm saying civilizations collapse. Sometimes suddenly, sometimes over centuries. Maybe Emily's delay isn't medical. Maybe it's… something bigger."

"I'm not following you, Alex. Your stream of thought is jumping around too much for me to follow."

"Maybe the Daklin found Pronimos. We know they've been looking, and now they have tunneling." He could feel the possibility in his gut. The haven that had protected science, preserved liberty, and saved lives around the galaxy. "Pronimos has no military and would not be able to stop the horde."

The silence between them stretched, broken only by the lowing of the herd. Finally, Shelby set her mug down with a decisive clink. "Speculation won't change anything. Until we know, we keep working. The ranch keeps us standing, the ruins keep us moving forward. If Emily and Jabari are out there, they'll find their way back to us."

Alex leaned against the post, jaw tight. "And if they're not?"

Shelby's eyes softened. "It's not like you to be negative and speculate this way, Alex."

The wind stirred across the grasslands, carrying with it the faintest echo of something neither could name.

"You're right, Shelby. I need to focus on the task at hand."

26

Silence and Darkness

The weeks slid into months. Alex and Shelby worked the bosque herd and frequently spent afternoons in Drevarn with Fraklen poring over archaeological records. But the shadow never left. Each passing week without word from Emily or Tranquility deepened the silence in Alex's chest.

At first, he forced himself to shake it. *They'll be back any day. Pronimos is far. Surgery takes time.* But the math gnawed at him. Four weeks became six. By the end of the second month, he no longer believed the excuses he made for why Emily had not returned. She was literally a machine, and her failure to return or communicate could only mean one thing.

She was gone.

By the fourth month, the silence became unbearable. He had come to grips with the fact that Emily was not returning, but not with the circumstance where he had no way to reach anyone. No radio, no signal array, no Plink connection. The nearest star with a spacefaring planet, Asterion Prime, lay twenty-two light years distant. Even if he could send a message, it would be decades before anyone received it.

Alex Durant had never been one to sit idle, but the only technology he had was his computer and the tunneling backpacks.

He began with the smallest steps. He started growing silicon to make simple diodes and transistors which were primitive by galactic standards, but the foundation of everything. He scoured the Collegium's records for notes on magnetism and scavenged copper wire from local tradesmen. He learned of a city a few thousand kilometers away that was developing an electric train.

He tunneled there and was able to secure simple supplies. By the end of his eighth month, crude circuits blinked to life on his workbench.

Shelby found him one night bent over a coil of iron wrapped in wire. "What's this contraption?" she asked.

"Electromagnet," he murmured without looking up. "Next step's power. If I can spin it, I can build a generator."

Before the end of their first year, the ranch hummed faintly with new life. A windmill turned lazily above the plain, feeding power into a storage bank. LED lamps lit their kitchen and barn with steady white glow. Shelby joked that they were dragging Oiket a century forward with one LED at a time.

But Alex's mind never rested. The tunnel backpacks still held a significant charge, enough for years of careful use, but he knew they were finite. One evening, staring at the windmill, the idea struck him to build an interface. If he could convert wind power into the right current, he could trickle-charge the backpacks.

Thirteen months after their arrival, he stood next to his bench listening to the steady hum of a new transmitter. Its signal leapt into the night sky, weak but real, aimed squarely at Asterion Prime. Did anyone on Asterion still listen to RF signals? He did not know, but it was the best he could do, for now.

He leaned back from the console; exhaustion etched beneath his eyes like faint bruises. Outside, he could hear the hum of the windmill outside filling the silence until the old door creaked open. He swiveled his chair just as Shelby stepped in.

"Signal strength is good," he said, voice flat. "Direction's stable."

Shelby touched his shoulder, gentle and warm. "And it'll only take twenty-two years to get there," she teased, the lilt of her Texas drawl softening the jab.

Alex gave a tired smile. "Yeah. Twenty-two years. If anyone's even listening to old fashioned radio frequency on the other end."

He looked at her fully then, and for a heartbeat, the weight of the universe seemed to lift. Shelby stood framed in the lamplight, wearing a cream denim skirt that brushed her knees, a faded blue blouse knotted at the waist, and those tan cowgirl boots he loved. Her hair, still damp from her bath, spilled in loose waves over her shoulders, catching the glow like liquid copper. Just a few hours earlier she'd been the perfect picture of grit, sweaty, dirt-streaked, sleeves rolled, moving cattle beneath the twin moons. Now she was radiant, every trace of the day's dust transformed into grace.

That look which was soft, feminine, and unguarded, had a way of cutting through his despair like sunlight through storm clouds.

She sat beside him, and together they listened to the slow rhythm of the windmill turning outside, each creak translating air into power. The LED glow washed their faces blue-white as the night came alive with the sounds of crickets and the lowing of the bosque herd. Beyond the ranch, the plains stretched in endless silence, and above, the sky shimmered with a billion stars.

Alex was finally coming to realize, it was that silence he was trying to end.

While the windmill spun faithfully day and night, he spent his hours bent over coils and wire, piecing together transmitters from scrap. His hands, once skilled in precision instruments and equations, were now lined with calluses and burns.

Shelby liked to tease that he was trying to drag the whole planet into the twenty-first century by himself. But behind the humor was worry. She could see how thin he'd grown, how his mind never shut off. He ate little, slept even less, and sometimes sat staring at the transmitter long after the signal had vanished into the void.

"Emily would've told me if something happened," he muttered one night, tightening a coupling on the transmitter. "She would've found a way."

Shelby stood in the doorway, arms folded, her voice steady but sad. "You don't know that, Alex. All you've got is silence. You can't let it eat you alive."

But it did, quietly, piece by piece. In the still hours, when the bosque herd bedded down and the wind carried only the sound of crickets, she saw it taking him. His genius, once alive with possibility, now circled endlessly around a problem he couldn't fix in a lifetime.

Then, after nearly a month of this, something shifted. Alex began spending less time at the bench and more at the dig sites. At Fraklen's urging, he even started teaching a course at the College. For the first time in months, he laughed again..

He was finding purpose once more, inspiring a new generation on Oiket.

But as Alex's spirit lifted, Shelby's began to drift.

At first, it was small things. She'd find herself standing at the corral gate at sunset, watching the herd move in the long shadows, and realizing she couldn't remember the last real conversation they'd had that wasn't about archaeology, data or power output. The wind carried the scent of the tallgrass and wild sage, but even the beauty of it felt distant, like she was observing her own life through glass.

She told herself she should be happy. Alex was coming alive again, focused, teaching, and building. He was becoming the man she'd followed around the galaxy from fight to fight. But the more he returned to himself, the more she felt herself fading from his orbit, like a planet slowly losing the warmth of its sun.

He'd come home late from the College, his eyes bright with ideas, his mind already a million light-years away. She'd pour him a drink, kiss his cheek, and listen as he spoke of discoveries and students and plans for the next expedition. He never noticed when her eyes glistened, or when her smile faltered for a heartbeat too long.

She loved him, but there was a quiet ache in realizing that his true devotion was to the infinite, not to the life they'd built together here among the bosques and stars.

He had found his purpose again, and Shelby had lost hers.

Two ships, passing in the night. One was racing toward the stars, the other drifting slowly into silence.

◦◦◦◦ ∞ ◦◦◦◦

The southern hemisphere of Oiket was drier, its grasslands giving way to scrub plains and jagged ridges. Alex had tunneled in alone, the backpack's hum fading as he stepped out into the wind. He had developed an itch of curiosity that had been keeping him awake for weeks.

The site lay half-buried at the edge of a ravine with a tumbled wall of stone, its lines too precise to be natural, and too old to easily see human architecture. He spent the morning clearing rubble, his shirt soaked with sweat, until his hand struck metal.

At first, he thought it was just a beam. But as he brushed away centuries of dust, a seam appeared. It was a door, or perhaps a hatch.

He worked for hours, fashioning a lever from a broken slab. The latch groaned in protest but held through persistent scraping until at last, it gave way with a dry crack that echoed into the silence. Alex pulled the heavy door outward and peered into the darkness.

The chamber was small, no more than nine meters square. The air was stale, thick with the smell of rot and dust. A few objects rested on shelves along the wall. Some collapsed at his touch, crumbling into powder. Others were aged beyond recognition.

He spent several hours exploring inch by inch and was about to give up when his lantern caught the edge of something flat. It looked like slate with etched faint lines. He lifted it carefully, brushing the dust away. At the bottom, just barely legible, was a single word. Alex froze. It was Greek.

Λυσανδρος.

He pointed the camera of his handheld computer and translated: Lysandros. *What is Lysandros*, he thought to himself.

His hands shook as he turned the slate over. Etched on its face was a crude image that looked like a solar system. One of the orbits had four satellites carefully marked. The fourth bore a name, faded but unmistakable in the old Greek letters:

Ἄρης.

Translated: Ares.

Alex's breath caught. He stared at it in silence, his heart pounding. He slid the slate into his pack as though it might vanish if he lingered too long.

Somehow, Oiket was connected to Ares, or in the modern vernacular - Mars.

That evening, back at the ranch, he cleaned it under the glow of his wind-powered LED lamp. He used a soft brush and water, careful not to erase what little remained. He thought perhaps he should be consulting a professional archaeologist but decided against that. Slowly, the lines sharpened, and the letters stood clearer.

It was unmistakable: someone named Lysandros had been here, and he carried with him memory of Alex's home solar system.

Alex sat back, the slate resting in his lap. He could hear the sounds of the bosque outside and the windmill turning against the stars.

He glanced at the chair beside him, Shelby's usual spot, but he hadn't seen much of her lately. She had thrown herself into ranching, hiring a few laborers to help manage the growing herd, which had nearly doubled from 120 to 285. On top of that, she'd begun volunteering at the local hospital.

He looked at the stone, which was the most significant discovery he had made since being stranded on this planet. It meant something important, significant.

But the empty chair next to him suddenly held more significance.

Alex set the slate down carefully and pushed back from the table. His throat was dry, so he went to the fridge, grabbed a dark beer, and popped the top. The first swallow was smooth, silky, and refreshing.

It had been 14 months since he had fallen out of the sky and onto this ranch. In that span he had tried everything he knew to find ways to link back to Pronimos, Earth, and the fight.

During that same stretch of time, Alex became aware of the full cycle of seasons spinning past, marked by Shelby taking full control of the ranch: repairing fences, growing the herd, and improving the land in every way.

His head, heart, and creativity were all facing upward, focused on things he could not control, while Shelby maintained her balance, brought balance to him and focused on the things she could control.

The windmill outside spun in the night breeze, steady as the stars slowly marching across the sky overhead.

He was still staring at night sky when Shelby's boots crunched on the porch. She came in with her hat tipped low, dust on her shirt, and the smell of the barn clinging to her clothing.

"You're late," Alex said gently.

"Long day." She smiled, but it was not a real smile.

"Are you okay," he casually asked.

"Just busy." She shrugged out of her jacket and dropped into the chair across from him.

Her tone was light, but he could feel the distance in it. She was not holding a beer for him like she had done for virtually every night before. She was still in her work clothes.

When was the last time they had woken together, entwined, or the last time he had focused singularly on her? He couldn't remember. The pieces of reality crashed into him all at once.

"Shelby," he pressed, "that's not all. Talk to me."

For a moment she said nothing, staring past him. Finally, she drew a breath. "Alex, I've come to grips with something. We're not leaving this place anytime soon. Maybe not ever."

He opened his mouth, but she kept going.

"When we first got together, what, five years ago?" she stopped, thinking about the events, and the time that had passed. "We made that decision because we were both in need of simplicity and healing. You from Maria, me from Daniel. We needed each other to heal, and we did." She looked down at her hands, then back at him, steady. "But that healing is done, and maybe… maybe it's time to start thinking about moving on."

The words hit him harder than any Daklin plasma burst. He blinked, trying to process, his chest tight. "Move on?" Alex could barely get the words out. "Shelby, what the hell are you saying?"

She didn't flinch. "I'm saying we finally pronounce ourselves as healed. Mission accomplished, and perhaps… we stop pretending this," she motioned between the two of them "is forever."

Alex sat in stunned silence, the beer he had poured for himself, forgotten in his hand, the slate was now a meaningless weight in his lap. He leaned forward, setting the beer on the table with a dull thud. "Shelby, you're wrong. Something more significant is happening here. I can feel it."

She stared out to the pasture where her growing bosque were finding places to settle in for the night. "Is that right?"

"Yes," he answered tentatively.

"You know, you're not that convincing, Alex Durant," She tilted her head, studying him.

"I…" he sputtered.

"Tell me…what do you remember about the third night we got together at the Old West Bar on Pronimos?"

He frowned, sifting through memory. "I recall the neon lights, the oatmeal stout, the music," he paused, thinking. "I recall you, talking about what intimacy meant and didn't mean." He felt his face flush even now. "We had that talk about both of us needing to heal. About not hiding behind words. And it was the first night we… well, we slept together."

Her eyes stayed locked on his. "Anything else?"

He searched deeper, replaying the details. "That was the day you went to the longevity clinic, wasn't it? You looked amazing. Breathtaking."

"Thank you," She gave a small nod. "Yes. Why do you think I chose that day to do my de-aging?"

He hesitated, then tried to guess. "Because you wanted to look and feel young?"

"No." Her voice was quiet but edged.

Alex furrowed his brow. He had always thought she wanted to be 29 again, and feel the energy he had felt when he went to the de-ageing clinic on Andromeda. "Okay… what was it?"

"The last ten years of my marriage were devoid of sex and intimacy. I knew something was broken, but I wasn't ready to face it," she paused. "Daniel and I had zero intimacy in those ten years…" She paused, remembering something sweet and painful. "I don't know how it works in Andromeda clinics, but on Pronimos, the de-ageing treatments aren't just about reversing aging. They include a host of tests for disease, failing organs, and things like birth control."

Clarity was beginning and Alex froze. He remembered the doctor warning him about birth control.

"I had a pretty good sense that third night with you, well, that we were going to have sex," she continued, steady, and matter of fact. "It might have happened on the second night, but I stopped it. Do you remember that?"

Alex nodded, "Yes, I do."

"Fact is, I was concerned about the possibility of getting pregnant if I didn't have the treatments and I wasn't willing to take that risk. I firmly believed that you and I were brought together to help each other heal, not to make a baby on our first date."

"That makes sense, and together, we did heal."

"Yes Alex, we did. The problem is that, just like age reversal doesn't last forever, the birth control wears off after four or five years."

His mind jumped through the last months, the distance between them, her quiet refusals. He swallowed. "Shelby… are you saying you can get pregnant now?"

"Yes." Her eyes softened, but she didn't look away. "That's part of what I'm saying. You see, Alex, our relationship stopped being about healing a long time ago. These last 14 months on Oiket have been about convenience and finding a way back to Pronimos and the war… for you, but for me," She stopped and studies his eyes, "I have planted my feet and lived. Sure, I want to get back, but I've adopted this new place. Alex, this is now my home."

"I understand," Alex finished the thought. "If we continue intimacy now, it will mean something else. It could result in children, a family. You're telling me that's the choice in front of us," he leaned forward, his voice low but sure. "So, let's discuss *that* Shelby… not walking away from each other! Jabari and Emily made a great point of the fact that life must go on. It's what makes us real, especially in times of war."

She stared at him with concern flashing in her eyes. "Alex, in five years together, neither of us has ever even said that we *love* each other. Not once. I've heard you tell Emily you love her. I've heard you tell Megan, and you use it when you talk about Maria, and Paula. You've said it to every woman in your life, except me."

Her words hit him like a gut punch. He froze, the beer suddenly heavy in his hand. Something shifted, like the night breeze outside had changed direction. His mind spun. She was right. Why had he never said it? He'd felt it, certainly. But somehow, the words never came.

Was it because they had started as a mission to heal? Because he'd been so careful not to blur lines, not to lose focus? Or was it fear… fear that once spoken, the words would bind him to something deeper than healing and survival, ending any possibility of a reunion with Maria?

He looked at her. Really looked. The woman who had stood by him through battles, who had embraced living on this ranch out on a forgotten planet, who had steadied his soul when it was fractured. And he knew. He did love her. He had all along. At this point, he did not know who or what Maria represented, but she was absent, and Shelby was here. She had been here when he needed her most. She had been a rock.

But saying it now felt hollow. Instead, he rose slowly, crossed to her, and took her hands.

She searched his eyes. "It's okay, Alex…"

"No, I think it's time for a dance, Shelby."

She rose, slowly, uncertain.

The began a waltz. In silence, driven by years and memories.

Then Alex began to sing as they slowly waltzed on the porch. "Waltz across Oiket, with you in my arms…"

She started singing along, both making up words to the old Ernest Tubb song. "How many times have we done this same exact dance, Alex?"

"Eighty-seven," he made up a number.

They both started to laugh.

He silenced her with a kiss, gentle at first, then deeper, pouring into it what his words had never carried.

"Mmm," she murmured, feeling a warmth in her body, half-laughing. "That's not fair. You know we can't."

"Sometimes life's not fair," he said with a grin, "but tonight, I think we *should*."

He kissed her again, this time deeper. His hands slid along her shoulders, down her arms, then to her back, holding her close. They were still waltzing, in their own way, to a song that played on only in their heads.

Shelby sensed a new and different version of Alex, melting into his touch. Her hands slid around his neck, pulling him close. She felt his touch on her shoulders, then he caressed her arms, lingered at her waist until she wriggled and laughed, breathless. "As always, you're impossible."

"Persistent," he corrected, kissing her throat. "You've always said that about me."

"Yes, persistent is definitely what you are…"

He scooped her up and held her in his arms.

"Alex Durant, put me down before you drop me!"

"Not a chance of either," he said, carrying her into the bedroom. He laid her on the bed and admired the woman who had given him so much. "I am ready to stop pretending."

Her smile trembled, but her eyes shone. "You're serious, aren't you?"

"Completely." He brushed his lips over hers, slow and tender, then kissed her cheeks, her jaw, the corners of her mouth until she was laughing and tugging him closer.

"Just so you know, I'm ovulating…"

"Perfect timing, then." He brushed her hair from her face, eyes locked on hers. "It's time," he whispered. "Time that we shift from healing to what this has really been, maybe since the beginning."

Her eyes glistened, uncertainty completely gone, and she didn't resist. She drew him down, her heart hungry, anticipating a new version of their connection that was long overdue. Clothes fell away, and the distance of the past weeks disappeared to skin on skin.

When they came together, the world seemed to still, everything outside the two of them fading. He held her face between his hands, moving with her, every touch deliberate, every kiss a promise. She gasped his name, her body shivering beneath him.

Only then, when he was deep inside her, did he finally say the words that had been locked inside for too long. "I love you, Shelby Coates."

"Durant," she corrected raising an eyebrow with a crooked smile.

"Yes, Shelby Durant." With that, he reached the summit.

Shelby's eyes filled, tears slipping free. She clutched him harder, and for the first time in five years, she was absolutely certain, the healing was complete.

○○○○ ∞ ○○○○

The sun was already spilling through the shutters when Alex stirred. He blinked, turned, and found Shelby curled against him. For nearly five years, every day, he had woken beside her until a few weeks ago, when she had abruptly stopped sleeping in the bed with him. Now she was back, and her soft face was peacefully asleep. For a long moment, he just lay there, absorbing the quiet weight of her body against his.

When her eyes finally opened, she gave him a crooked smile. "Morning, cowboy."

"Morning, Mrs. Durant," he murmured, brushing a strand of hair from her cheek. "How'd you sleep?"

"Like I hadn't in months," she said, stretching. Then she rolled onto her back, staring at the ceiling. "So… Mrs. Durant, eh? Did I miss something last night?"

Alex tilted his head and smiled. "I'm just referencing the deed for this ranch, which calls us husband and wife."

"Well, you delivered something last night that will very likely have lasting impact." She smiled and pulled him close.

Alex chuckled. "Going straight for the hard stuff?"

"You're a big boy and I suspect you know how the birds and bees work," she countered, smirking. "It felt like you knew what you were doing… so don't act surprised."

He grinned. "I'm an engineer. I'm familiar with cause and effect. The birds and bees are for biologists and teenaged kids."

She swatted his chest. "I'm serious. Alex, we've probably just changed the next 20 years of our lives. Last night we planted seeds at the peak of my cycle…kids aren't theoretical anymore."

His smile softened. "Planted seeds, eh? I'm hoping you're right, but just in case, I suggest we try again this morning before the ovulating ends."

Shelby laughed, burying her face in the pillow. "I like that you're insatiable."

"Last night, it was persistent, but for this task, I prefer *thorough*," Alex said, removing the pillow away and pulling her close.

She shook her head, still grinning, but when he began to slowly kiss her breasts, she melted, letting out a soft moan that betrayed her affection. "Fine," she whispered, trying to recover and seem distant. "But only because I have learned it's always a mistake to leave your engineering experiments left half-finished."

Their laughter gave way to something deeper, more urgent but still entangled with tenderness. The sunlight climbed higher across the room as they moved closer, not rushed, but savoring. Shelby's teasing gave way to quiet murmurs; her fingers tangled in his hair.

The puzzle pieces fit together again, and caused her to gasp. "Well," she whispered between breaths, "if we didn't make a baby last night, we sure as heck will this morning."

Alex chuckled, brushing a kiss against her lips. "Redundancy. All engineers know that every good system needs backups."

When they finally stilled, tangled in the sheets, she rested her forehead against his. "Alex," she felt the warmth deep inside, "Why did it take us so long to get to this moment?"

"I have been here for years, Shelby, and I apologize for not letting you know sooner."

"You've been wanting a child for years?" She asked in a bit of shock.

"No, not that. I meant what I've felt for you. The confidence and the perfect connection. The baby question is an easy one…but I do love you and what we are together."

She pulled him tight, memorizing the moment.

They lay together in the easy warmth of morning, the tension of the past months replaced by something quieter, steadier. Shelby was the first to break the silence, her voice soft. "You know… this feels different. I think maybe we'll always be healing. But *this love*," she paused, searching his eyes, "it feels like home. And Alex, I don't think I've ever really been home before."

"It's funny you say that. We are on such a parallel path, and yet there are so many tasks tugging in different directions."

Her smile softened. "I've already been thinking about that. The herd's doubled. We've got steady hands helping. This place is becoming more than two refugees playing house."

"And now we put kids in the middle of all that." He answered with a warm tone.

She shrugged, but there was light in her eyes. "They will be *our* kids."

He leaned down, kissed her forehead and furrowed his brow. "Wait, how many kids are we talking about here?"

"I cannot do the math on that one, Alex, but I can tell you there is no real birth control on this planet, other than rhythm, and based on your insatiable appetite, well... it could be dozens." She laughed, but continued, "In seriousness, my biological age is now 35 and having personal knowledge on the state of healthcare on this planet, I don't want to be having babies after 40."

Alex thought about her comment. "I don't think we have a pathway to getting off this planet in the next five years, Shelby."

Silence settled for a beat, broken only by the creak of the windmill outside. Then Shelby propped herself up on an elbow. "But you, Alex... you're still half an archaeologist. Still chasing mysteries under every stone. Would you really be happy with cattle and kids?"

He laughed softly. "I never would have guessed I would end up with cattle and kids. Still, I remain optimistic about getting us off this planet." He paused, thoughtful. "But wherever I go for now on, I need it to be with you."

"Thank you, husband, that means a lot, hearing you finally say it."

"Oh, I almost forgot, speaking of archaeology..." His eyes widened suddenly, and he sat up. "I found a slate."

"What slate?" she asked, puzzled.

"Yesterday, I discovered a sealed chamber at a dig site." He swung his legs off the bed, grabbing for his pants. "Shelby, it wasn't just some artifact. It had a Greek name: Lysandros. And a map with *our* solar system. Mars is specifically marked as the fourth planet on that slate. Someone from our solar system's ancient history was here. On this planet."

She pulled him back in bed and rolled over on top, "Does that mean we get to have sex again?"

"I don't understand, Shelby."

"Uhhh, you're clearly excited about this slate, and it's showing up, well, you know," she winked and looked down under the covers.

They both broke out laughing.

"You are such a kid, Alex Durant. You get so excited about all the challenges and discoveries."

"Hold on there, Shelby. Am I supposed to be deciding whether to have sex again or tell you about the slate?"

"We can do the sex part later, as much as you desire." Her face grew serious. "You're telling me that you found something that isn't just a relic, but proof?"

"Proof," he said, voice hushed, "that humans, or at least someone who knew Mars, walked here fifty or sixty years before us."

The room felt suddenly smaller, as if the weight of history had pressed in on them. Shelby sat back, biting her lower lip. "So, kids, ranching, and now… uncovering history? You sure know how to complicate a morning."

Alex turned, meeting her gaze. "Yeah. But I think this time, in all cases, the complication matters."

27

Life on Oiket

The months on the Bosque Ranch had grown into years. Alex wouldn't have believed it possible when he first set foot on the planet, that life on Oiket could ever settle into a rhythm, but it had. The herds grazed thick across the meadows, windmills hummed softly in the steady trade winds, and the ranch had become something more than mere survival. It was home. Under Shelby's steady hand, it had grown into one of the largest bosque ranches on the continent.

Shelby thrived on ranch life. Her days were filled with managing ranch hands, tending stock, and periodically volunteering at the hospital in town. Her laugh came easier here, and Alex found himself listening for her light-hearted joy each night when the house grew quiet.

And then there was Austin. Their daughter was nearly three now, bright-eyed, endlessly curious. Her name was a deliberate nod to the Texas city Alex and Shelby had both loved. She toddled through the halls, giggling, pointing at everything, seeing the world for the first time.

To Alex, she was living proof that even in exile, life moved forward.

And then, of course, baby number two was just a couple months away.

But even with family, even with love, Alex's mind refused to rest. The ancient slate etched with Greek letters sat on his desk, its faded solar system taunting him with questions he could not answer. Who was Lysandros? How had he known of Mars and its moons? More than that, could all of this connect to the greater challenge of getting off this planet?

It was during one of Fraklen's visits that Austin came running to him with a squeal of "Unko Frak," her name for Fraklen. The old family friend arrived, as always, with trinkets from town. But as his eyes wandered across the room, his grin slowly faded.

On a side table, half-forgotten, rested the crystal Alex had once carried from Tranquility's engine bay.

Fraklen stepped closer, his expression darkening. "Alex. Do you know what this is?"

Alex stiffened. "Just a keepsake. Nothing important."

Fraklen snorted, his tone suddenly sharp. "No, sir. This is one of the most treasured pieces of Oiket work. A crystal lattice formed from noble gases. Only advanced human chemistry could create this."

Alex frowned. "Noble gases don't bond. They have full shells and are inert. You're a chemist and should know that, Fraklen."

"That is true for your primitive science," Fraklen cut in. He leaned closer but did not touch. "But the Oiket Polychemists have learned to strip electrons from closed valence shells using high-energy tunneling. Once destabilized, they forced orbitals into overlap and bonded them to active elements. Neon woven with silicon, argon chained to carbon, krypton meshed with transition metals. Bonds that *should* be impossible are created by humans and the proper annealing."

"High energy tunneling?" Alex's breath caught. How could a preindustrial civilization even know that term? "So, they break the orbitals, combine the right elements with valence electrons, and the lattice holds?"

"Exactly," Fraklen said. "The result is stronger than diamond, immune to entropy, and resonant across tachyon frequencies."

"Wait, did you just say tachyon frequencies?" Alex asked incredulously.

"I know, I know," Fraklen started. "Tachyons are theoretical, but I spent time with the Polychemists and that is what they believe, but they have crystal structures and materials outside the periodic table of possibility. This," he tapped the air above the crystal, "is the signature of a civilization that understands matter itself, and it is the finest example I have ever seen."

Alex stared at the Archē, realization dawning. *That would explain how it carried Tranquility through the tunnel. Why it didn't fracture under that energy load.* He thought to himself. "Did you use the term *primitive science* when talking about me?"

Fraklen's eyes narrowed. "I did. Sometimes physicists can be so stiff and unbending."

Alex rubbed a hand over his face, then stood, crossing the room. "You'd better sit down, my friend. There's more you need to know."

Fraklen lowered himself into a chair, his eyes never leaving Alex. "What'cha got mister physicist?" he challenged, confidently.

From outside came the sound of Shelby laughing as she lifted Austin high into the morning sun, the little girl shrieking with joy. Alex could see the silhouette of his gorgeous pregnant wife, playing with their precocious daughter.

Alex exhaled, then began. He walked to the lantern hanging from the wall, twisted it off its mount, and pulled the cover free. "These aren't made with Oiket glass or flame. Look closer."

Fraklen leaned in, his eyes widening as he saw the delicate glowing diodes. "It's not hot and this… this isn't wax or oil."

"It's a Light Emitting Diode, or LED," Alex said simply. "It's technology that was invented on a planet far from here. It is energy efficient, and long-lasting. It's pure photons that get their energy from things called batteries and from those windmills outside." He replaced the lantern and moved to the corner, lifting the vented housing of a compressor unit. A faint hum filled the room.

"Have you ever wondered why it's always more or less the same temperature in the house during the summer and winter months? This device chills air through compression and expansion cycles. Cool air in summer, warm in winter. I call it an air conditioner." He walked into the kitchen and opened a cabinet door, revealing milk, meat, and vegetables stacked neatly, preserved in a steady chill. "And a refrigerator. Keeps food fresh without the need of preserving winter ice. Oh, and I can make my own ice, on demand."

Fraklen blinked, equal parts wonder and suspicion. "I don't understand, is this technology from your home country of Theslon?"

Alex's voice lowered. "No. I'm not from *here*." He walked to the closet, unlocked a chest, and pulled out the tunneling pack. The straps were worn, the casing scarred, but the faint shimmer of its dormant core still pulsed inside. Alex set it on the table between them.

Fraklen leaned forward, breath caught. "What in the name of the Seven Valleys is this?"

"A tunneling backpack," Alex said quietly. "Built on tachyon tunnel principles. It's how Shelby and I arrived here. We're not Oiket-born. We travelled through a tachyon tunnel… from another world."

Alex then picked up the slate, "I do not know how, or why, but this slate depicts my solar system, which is over fifty thousand light years from here."

The room fell silent, save for the low hum of the compressor. Fraklen's gaze shifted between Alex, the device, and the crystal still resting on the side table. At last, he sat back slowly, rubbing his jaw, eyes narrowing in thought.

"I knew," he said softly. "Not the details, but I knew. The way you spoke, the tools you built, the ideas you couldn't hide. You were always just slightly out of step with the rest of us. Not wrong, but sometimes you said things that made no sense. What was it you called Oiket in the beginning?"

"Oiketerion, which is the name of this planet on our star maps." Alex met his gaze, steady. "Yes, we made a lot of mistakes in the learning process, but now you know the truth. Can I trust you to keep it?"

Fraklen studied him for a long moment. Then a slow smile crept across his face, not with mockery, but with respect. "You've given me the greatest gift a scientist could ever dream of, Alex. You've shown me living proof of another world, another history. I will keep your secret. Gladly. Because some truths are too dangerous for open ears."

He tapped the table near the crystal before continuing. "And because if the wrong people knew you carried all this, neither you, nor Shelby, nor that little girl laughing outside would ever be safe again." He smiled thinking of all the fun times and memories he had made with his niece, Austin.

Alex nodded once, relief mingling with the heaviness of the revelation. "Then we understand each other."

"Yes," Fraklen said, eyes gleaming. "And now that I know this story, together, we can understand the rest."

Alex rested his hand on the tunneling pack. "Fraklen, if what you say about these Polychemists is true, then I need to meet them. They may know more about this crystal than anyone alive."

Fraklen's brows rose. "It's a two-week journey, Alex. Across the eastern ridges, through river valleys that wash out half the year. Not easy travel."

Alex grinned faintly, tapping the backpack. "Or we could get there in about a second."

Fraklen blinked. "What exactly is it?"

"It is a tunneling backpack. I t creates a tachyon tunnel so I can travel from point to point. I have used it thousands of times," Alex said. "Safe as walking through a doorway. Watch."

Before Fraklen could object, Alex swung the straps over his shoulder and adjusted the controls and grabbed Fraklen's arm. The air shimmered faintly, a rippling distortion like heat rising off stone.

"Just relax."

The ranch blurred into darkness followed by a brief millisecond rush, like falling through a dream, and then light returned. They stood on a bluff overlooking the ocean, waves crashing white against jagged black cliffs. The salty wind tore at their clothes, the horizon stretching endless and blue.

Fraklen staggered back, eyes wide. "By the rivers… have we crossed half a continent?"

"Not half," Alex said, smiling. "All the way to the coast. Go touch the water."

 Fraklen put his finger in the water and tasted it. He took a deep breath and smelled the ocean.

"One more," Alex grabbed his arm.

The shimmer swallowed them again. This time they stood among snowcapped peaks, the air sharp, thin, and cold. The mountains stretched in every direction; valleys carved with glaciers that glowed faintly under the northern sun.

Fraklen turned in a slow circle, his breath steaming. "This is impossible. It should take months of travel, and yet… you move as if the world were nothing but rooms in a house."

Alex's hand found the controls once more. "And just like that…" The shimmer came, and suddenly they were back in the ranch house, the compressor still humming, Shelby and Austin's laughter carrying in from the porch.

Fraklen braced himself against the table, then let out a low laugh, half awe and half disbelief. "Alex, you just rewrote the laws of distance. The Polychemists need to see this. They *must*."

"I don't really think we can show them the backpack tech, Fraklen." Alex set the pack down carefully. "In any case, let's go tomorrow. We can bring the crystal with us and see what we can learn."

Fraklen nodded slowly, still staring at the device. "Tomorrow, then. I never thought I'd live to see technology like this. You've given me a glimpse of the impossible."

Alex glanced toward the window, where Shelby pushed Austin on a swing, the child's laughter spilling into the morning. "Then let's make sure we use the impossible for something that matters."

○○○○ ∞ ○○○○

The Polychemists were cautious at first. Their speech was clipped, their demonstrations measured. They treated Alex as though he were a curious outsider who might misunderstand or misuse what he heard.

And perhaps he was.

But Alex persisted. Patient, steady, with questions that revealed both humility and insight. Fraklen vouched for him, sitting beside him through long evenings where nothing more was shared than tea and guarded pleasantries.

Through all of that, Alex never revealed his crystal. They only spoke of science, chemistry, and history. Trust would not happen on the first visit, so days stretched into months. Months became years. Slowly, their connection, and trust, grew.

Over the course of five years, Alex made regular visits with the Polychemists. In that time, he came to learn that their science was not new, not even ancient by human standards. It was an inheritance that had been handed down for millions of years. The Polychemists spoke of formulas and lattice equations the way a farmer might speak of planting season. They spoke of particle accelerators, though none of them had the faintest idea how to build one.

Even their description included the fact that knowledge was passed down through hands and tongues for as many generations as stars in the night sky. Tens of millions of years, they said, though no one could be certain. They did not guard history or science. They guarded a long-forgotten craft from which, only relics remained.

"We do not know where it began," one of the elders admitted one evening, her wrinkled fingers tracing symbols in the dust. "Only that it has always been. We are keepers, not creators. Our task is to preserve, not to question. You clearly think of it as science, but to us, it is craft and art."

This stance frustrated and fascinated Alex in equal measures. The science behind the Archē Crystals was elegant and precise, but the origins were lost in the fog of time. No records of the technology survived, only stories, like techno jargon in a science fiction novel.

They spoke of creating new crystals but did not possess the accelerators to make them. They did not have the technological knowledge of how to build the accelerators. It was just a term in their art.

So, while the Polychemists revealed their formulas, Alex and Fraklen sought answers elsewhere. Together they roamed the ruins of Oiket, digging through strata of fallen empires. They found collapsed cities swallowed by forests, eroded temples carved with symbols too old to decipher, and fragments of tools that hinted at civilizations with knowledge rivaling or surpassing that of Pronimos.

The ancient Martian, Lysandros, had accomplished his objective of removing the great achievements from the Daklin, but not from the forces of nature. Four times, it seemed, Oiket had risen. The first fall arrived in the form of pestilence from a virus unfamiliar to Martian biochemistry that decimated over 90% of the population in a matter of days. The survivors experienced lawless pandemonium and thousands of years of dark ages where much of the great science and art was lost. The other three came over the millennia at the hands of natural disasters that Lysandros' original technology would likely have survived.

Each collapse left memories in stone and silence which were finally pieced together by Alex and Fraklen. Unfortunately, almost every element of great Martian accomplishments in the arts and sciences had been erased, with one exception: the production of Archē Crystals in the hands of the Polychemists.

The Polychemists were fond of describing in great detail how to create molecular bonds with inert substances from Group 18 on the Periodic Table, but they lacked the engineering technology to do so. Alex knew this knowledge, if brought back to Pronimos, could advance materials dramatically.

Over the years Alex spent a lot of time studying the art held by the Polychemists. Through it all, life at the ranch carried on. Shelby was no longer just the woman who had helped Alex heal, she was his partner in every sense. Their love had grown with the years, deepening as naturally as the roots of the trees outside their home.

Their family had grown too. Austin was eight now, sharp-eyed and endlessly curious, already pressing Alex with questions that reminded him of himself. Tyler, five, was sturdier, more reserved, a boy who loved the rhythm of ranch life. And little Abilene, only three, had Shelby's smile and a stubbornness all her own.

Alex often found himself caught between worlds: the warm chaos of family life, the endless puzzle of archaeology, and the tantalizing mysteries of Polychemistry. But in those moments when Shelby laughed across the table, or when Austin quizzed him with another question about the stars, he felt something he had not known since leaving Earth.

Hope.

○○○○ ∞ ○○○○

One evening, energized by time spent with his family, and 18 years after his arrival on Oiket, Alex made the decision to reveal his own Archē to the Polychemists.

He set the Archē down on their long oak table. Even dormant, its facets caught the lamplight and bent it in ways no glass or gem could mimic. The crystal seemed to glow from within, lines of color chasing each other across its flawless lattice.

The Polychemists drew close, their usual reserve slipping into audible wonder. One whispered, "Not a flaw. Not a fractured line. It is… perfect. This truly is ἀρχή."

Alex nodded. "Where I come from, this was used to channel power. Enough energy to tunnel shortcuts between stars. It never cracked, never burned out."

They exchanged glances. One leaned in, his magnifier trembling in his hand. "Channeling… power? With a crystalline dielectric this pure, you could step beyond our crude copper dynamos. This could resonate at frequencies no coil could endure."

Another, her fingers hovering just above the surface, added, "Do you see the way the planes align? If you pressed an induction field across this, you would create oscillations stable enough to drive current for a city. No loss. No heat. It would never wear out. This crystal was perfectly formed and perfectly annealed."

Alex tilted his head. "You think it could power a city?"

"More," she said firmly. "With proper alignment, it could replace every boiler used to power our electric train. Imagine steam turned directly into electric charge, funneled through crystalline resonance rather than iron rotors. No explosions, no soot. A machine that hums forever."

Another elder cleared his throat. "Not only that. With this lattice density, you could store charge as though it were a compressed spring. Capacitive reactance the size of a fist that could hold more than an acre of Leyden jars. A spark that never fades."

Alex thought about Tranquility's reactor, about how the Archē had accelerated its pathway through the hyper tunnel from Andromeda. He felt a chill. He knew it would not be appropriate to tell the Polychemists, but the realization came together that the crystal was capable of that and more. Alex recalled that when it was fitted into his ship, it channeled power that no metal, no crystal, or no alloy could have survived.

The oldest Polychemist whispered, "Then it is not only for power. With modulation, this could alter resonance of matter itself. A crystal that sings to the bones of the world."

They all stood back, as though suddenly reverent.

Alex studied them, hearing their late-century vocabulary with dynamos, boilers, and pistons, but beneath it, he sensed the echo of knowledge deeper than they knew. They spoke of capacitance and field coils, yet the words were fragments of a legacy stretching back tens of millions of years.

○○○○ ∞ ○○○○

The lanterns of town glowed warm against the twilight, their soft yellow light casting long shadows across the cobbled streets. The Durant family walked together, Shelby's arm looped through Alex's as Austin, Tyler, and Abilene walked just ahead. The little ranch town had grown in the time since Alex and Shelby had arrived. While most of the shops still used oil lamps on the outside, Alex had brought electricity and LED lighting to his adopted town. A few larger businesses had replaced their ice boxes with real refrigeration. Wind turbines were generating power alongside a new oil burning generator.

Tonight, the Durant family had come to town to celebrate 20 years on the Bosque Ranch, just outside the town of Drervarn of course, Fraklen was the only person on Oiket who knew *just* how far they had come in the last 20 years.

Austin, who was now 17, had begun being pursued by half the boys in town.

Alex never thought he'd say it, but life had been good here. Not simple, not easy, but good. He had a wife who still made his heart skip and took his breath away every time he looked at her. He had three children who filled the house with noise and hope, and a community that treated them as their own.

They ducked into a tavern-restaurant that smelled of roasted meat and fresh bread. The owner, a stout woman with silver hair pinned back in a bun, greeted Shelby by name. "Table's ready for you, dear. Congratulations to the whole family."

The five Durants, along with Uncle Frak, settled in at a long wooden table. Alex looked at them, smiling. Austin blushed when a young man from town slipped her a shy grin from another table. Tyler, fifteen, had shot up like a weed, already broad-shouldered, a ranch hand in the making. Even the older boys knew they needed to treat Austin with respect, or they'd hear from Tyler. Abilene, thirteen, still had her mother's stubborn spark, her eyes dancing with curiosity.

Shelby raised her glass. "To twenty years. To family. And most importantly, to a life worth living."

They all clinked mugs, the sound sharp and bright in the cozy room.

"So, Austin," Fraklen said, leaning back, "your mom tells me you've begun thinking about your studies."

Austin blushed, but her smile was proud. "I want to study medicine, like Mom. Maybe not just in town, but in the cities, maybe even with the hospital in Rivelon. They're experimenting with new surgical methods and antibiotics." She looked at her mom who had shown her how to make antibiotics before anyone on Oiket knew their value. "There's a lot I can learn, uncle Frak, but mostly, I want to help."

Shelby squeezed her daughter's hand. "You'll do it, sweetheart. You've got the patience and the brains."

Tyler rolled his eyes, smirking. "As long as she doesn't run off with the first doctor who wants to marry her."

"Shut up," Austin shot back, laughing.

Abilene piped in, grinning wickedly. "She's just excited because she's got a boyfriend who says he wants to be her nurse."

"Stop it, Abby!" Austin hissed, cheeks going scarlet. Shelby laughed, and even Alex couldn't hide his grin.

Alex raised his mug again. "To boyfriends, antibiotics, and whatever the future holds."

The table erupted in laughter, the sound mingling with music drifting from the tavern corner. For a moment, Alex let himself sink into it. He was surrounded by the warmth, the ease, the ordinary joy of it all.

Yet even as he laughed with his family, a part of him was still tugged towards the larger problems in the galaxy. It was always there, and he considered himself fortunate to have Shelby as an understanding partner of over 20 years in this fight.

He and Shelby knew that one day soon, the door would open up for them to leave Oiket and stop the Daklin so that people all over the galaxy could continue to enjoy the life he and Shelby had found here.

Later that night, after the kids were asleep and the Oiket cicadas had quieted in the grass, Shelby and Alex sat hand in hand on the expansive porch, listening to the windmill creak slowly and steadily under the stars. It was old and needed new bearings.

Shelby leaned back, enjoying the feel of the chair beneath her. "20 years," she said softly. "We've built a life here like nothing I have experienced in 224 years, not since 1800s Texas. We have three children, a ranch, and a town that knows us by name. If I didn't know better, I'd think we were just… normal folks."

Alex smiled faintly. "I never, ever would have guessed this when we sat in The Old West Bar all those years ago."

Her gaze stayed on the horizon, where the last of the light had bled away. "But you and I both know this isn't the end of the story. Sooner or later, we'll have to return. Back to Pronimos, back to the fight. That's who we are."

He didn't argue. There was no point. "And when we do," he said quietly, "we'll have to have the age reversal. 50 years old here, back to 29 there. Time hasn't beaten us yet."

Shelby turned, her smile catching the lantern glow. "It won't beat us, Alex. In the scope of the galactic war, time is on our side."

They sat in silence for a while, listening to the night. Then Shelby's expression grew thoughtful. "You've told Austin. About Pronimos. About Earth. About the tunnels. But not Tyler or Abby."

Alex shifted, uneasy. "Austin was ready. She's always been the most precocious of the three, and she has constant questions. Better to tell her than have her figure it out on her own. The other two, well, they're still kids."

"Tyler's nearly a man," Shelby said firmly. "And Abby is sharp enough to sense when something's being kept from her. Secrets don't last in families, Alex. They weigh people down. Sooner or later, you'll need to tell them, too."

Alex rubbed his hands together, staring out into the dark fields. "I just… don't want to take their childhood away before I have to. Let them think the universe is simple for a little longer. The scope of evil in the Dalkin Empire is too much. Most of the time it's too much for even me to think about."

Shelby reached for his hand, her fingers warm against his. "That's the parent in you talking. But you're forgetting something; they're *our* children. Stubborn. Curious. Tougher than we give them credit for. If they're old enough to ride fences and drive cattle, they're old enough to hear the truth."

He nodded slowly, her words sinking in. "Maybe you're right. Maybe it's time."

"Not tonight," she said, squeezing his hand. "Tonight is for us."

Alex leaned back, letting his shoulders relax. He glanced at her, the woman who had carried him through grief, given him new life, and had stood with him through years of exile. "Us," he echoed softly.

The porch fell into silence again, but it wasn't empty. It was full with the weight of years behind them, the laughter of children that constantly echoed in the walls of their ranch house, and the knowledge that the future, however uncertain, was still theirs to shape.

28

Frozen in Time

The wind rattled the shutters on the north wall of the ranch house, The wind generators were at max production, which was always a good thing. Alex leaned back in his chair, boots propped on the railing, while Fraklen thumbed through one of his weather-worn notebooks.

"We've been over every one of them," Alex said. "The southern dig at Dathris, the equatorial cairns, even those cliff vaults you swore were untouched. We've visited all the official sites and found almost nothing. Just fragments and dust. Ultimately, I think that Oiket is interesting from an historical perspective, but it does not have the answers I came here hoping to find."

"I am sorry Alex." Fraklen nodded, his eyes distant. "Every path seems to have a dead end. It's like the story was half erased before we arrived."

"Well, it's hard to imagine tens of millions of years. Not much can survive that. Think about this ranch house. As well built as it is, if we walked away, it would be dust in two hundred years. Weather and nature are a powerful force."

"I know," Fraklen tapped his pen against the page. "But there might be one more."

Alex sat forward, eyebrows raised. "You've been holding out on me?"

"Not holding out. Just… uncertain." Fraklen's voice dropped lower. "When I was at the Academy, I read a reference in an obscure archive. A possible site in the far northern polar region. No official coordinates. Just a mention that something exists beneath the ice." He looked up. "If it's there, no one has touched it. Temperatures and terrain that have made it too dangerous to get to."

"Well, we can get anywhere on the planet," Alex muttered, clanking at the tunneling backpacks. "If it's real, we can find it."

Fraklen folded the notebook. "If it's real. But tell me, Alex Durant, wouldn't you prefer to spend another 20 years wondering?" He grinned with sarcasm.

Alex's grin was sharp. "You already know the answer. We'll need provisions, heavy cold-weather gear, heat packs, and insulated shelters. We can minimize our exposure time by tunneling back and forth whenever we need to warm up."

Fraklen gave a rare smile. "Another adventure."

The portal shimmered, depositing them onto a windswept expanse where sunlight never touched at this time of year. Above stretched a gray vault of sky, looming over ice crusted with jagged ridges that groaned under shifting pressure. The biting cold pierced through Alex's outer shell, even with the heated layers humming softly against his skin.

Fraklen pulled his hood tight, his voice muffled. "North polar latitude, sixty-three degrees west. Nothing but ice."

"Not nothing," Alex replied, setting down his pack. From it he pulled out a crude rig of coils and sensors fashioned to a homemade magnetometer cobbled together from Oiket alloys and Earth engineering. He adjusted the dials, watching the needle twitch erratically.

Fraklen squinted. "You think a magnetometer will help us find this facility?"

"We are looking for metal in an ice field," Alex said simply. "If there's a doorway cut into these mountains, it'll leave a signature."

For an hour they trudged along frozen escarpments, checking, tunneling and checking with the instrument whining faintly in the gusts. Then, on their eighth jump, as they rounded a ridge, the needle jumped and held steady.

Alex exhaled in a plume of vapor. "There. Field distortion. Something ferrous under the ice." He stepped back and surveyed the scene. The mountain, the ridge line and the clear area. If he was building a facility, hidden and difficult, this would meet the criteria.

They hacked through the frozen layers until the dull ring of metal echoed back at them. Alex scraped away frost until he could see the first part of a massive door, carved seamlessly into the face of the mountain, its surface coated in uncountable years of ice.

Fraklen pressed a gloved hand against it, reverent. "Holy crap, perhaps it wasn't myth after all."

Alex traced the seams with his fingers, the cold biting deep even through his gloves. "I'm crossing my fingers that we've just discovered a facility that's been sealed for megaanum, and we just found the front door."

Fraklen's gloved hand lingered on the seam. "It's sealed tighter than the vaults back south. We'll never force it open bare-handed."

Alex stepped back, squinting against the icy wind. "I have a torch back at the ranch, and it's a snap to get there."

"Agreed," Fraklen said. "This door has waited centuries. It can wait another day."

The shimmer of the tunneling backpack brought them back onto the wooden porch of the ranch. Alex stomped snow from his boots. "Feels wrong to be warm again after that."

Fraklen laughed. "That tunnel backpack is amazing. I never would have dreamed how easy it is to travel."

"I know. Let's call it a day and get back to it in the morning. Once we start, I don't intend to stop until that door gives." Alex said, already heading to the storage shed to inspect his propane torch.

The next day the mountain greeted them with a cold that gnawed into their bones. They set to work. Hours blurred into days as sheets of ice chipped away with the propane torch sputtering in the wind, hammers and chisels ringing against the stubborn face of the door. Every evening, they staggered back to the ranch, bodies aching, gloves stiff with frost.

On the ninth day, Alex leaned on his hammer, breath fogging thick. "One more centimeter and the seam will give."

Fraklen braced with his boots. "Then push."

With a final shriek of metal on metal, the door groaned inward. A draft of ancient, preserved air spilled out, smelling faintly metallic, untouched since before Oiket's recorded time. They stood shoulder to shoulder in the opening, lantern light spilling into the black.

What they saw inside was not a tomb, but a time capsule. Above the door was an engraving: Φυλάκιον. Alex pulled out his handheld computer, pointed the camera: "Phylakion," he said, translating the inscription. "It's the Ares language, or what we call Martian Greek, and it translates to *guard post*."

"You mean, like the Mars in *your* solar system?" Fraklen turned slowly taking in all of the technological wonders that were stored in this vault under the mountain. "The one on the slate you found years ago?"

"Yes," Alex nodded, trying to contain his excitement. "I think perhaps we have hit the jackpot, Fraklen."

They wandered through the large entrance chamber, discovering several doors and rows of crates stacked neatly along the walls stamped with the red insignia of the Martian pioneers. A shelf of tools stood nearby: spanners, vises, even a pair of old EVA gloves, waiting as if their owners had only just stepped out.

Fraklen whispered, "Is it possible this is one of the first settlements, untouched?"

"I'm not sure…It doesn't really feel like a settlement." Alex opened one of the doors and spotted a console, brushing frost from its surface. His light swept across a hulking cylinder in the corner. The fins and shielding were unmistakable. "And that…that is a fusion reactor."

Fraklen knelt beside him. "Fusion?"

"Yes. We use fusion to generate massive amounts of electricity. My guess is that this reactor is capable of producing a hundred thousand times the output of my wind turbines." Alex ran a gloved hand along the casing with reverence. "If I can get this operational, we might bring this entire facility back online."

The weeks that followed became a rhythm. Each morning, they tunneled in from the ranch, their packs heavy with tools and components. Each day Alex tore deeper into the reactor's guts, tracing circuits with his crude meter, re-insulating cracked conduits, grafting Oiket made components to Martian alloys.

Fraklen stayed in the main room and catalogued the artifacts: journals that had been sealed in polymer, maps etched on metal plates, data rods stored in vacuum containers. Every discovery hinted at a civilization bridging Mars and Oiket, the forgotten story now spread before them.

On the twenty-first day, Alex tightened the final coupling. Sweat ran down his back despite the cold. "All right. Let's see if they built this the way I think they did."

Fraklen stood ready with a fire suppressor, just in case. "Could it blow up?"

"It won't, and if it did, that fire extinguisher you're holding won't help." Alex grinned with absolute confidence as he flipped the master switch.

For a moment, silence. Then the reactor hummed with a steady low resonance that vibrated through the floor. Ancient lights flickered along the walls, bathing the chamber in simulated daylight.

Fraklen's eyes widened. "You've woken the dead."

"Definitely not the dead," Alex let out a long breath, his hands trembling with both relief and awe. "We've just brought the voice of your ancestors back online. Prepare yourself, my old friend. I think you are about to see some of the miracles of modern engineering."

"Or ancient engineering, as the case may be…" Fraklen countered.

With full power and lighting, they were now able to explore. Doors and chambers that had been locked were now accessible. Alex chose a computer terminal and began researching. The deeper Alex read, the clearer the design of the place became. This was no accident of geography. Phylakion had been buried in the northern polar wasteland for a reason.

"They built it here with purpose," Alex murmured, his breath fogging in the chilled air. "The cold wasn't an obstacle; it was the shield and a method of preservation. For millions of years, this facility was entombed in ice, waiting and defying time. Lysandros and his Martians had thought about it in the same way as the founders of Pronimos. Preserving their work, their hope, their future. It was nature that decimated the Ares colonists, and nature that preserved their works in this frozen fortress."

Fraklen said nothing, just rested his hand against the glowing console, trying to take in the wonders.

Alex's chest ached as he shut the terminal down. "It worked. Against all odds, Lysandros preserved the important aspects of their accomplishments in this time capsule, and we found it."

That evening, the golden shimmer of the tunnel carried him home. The sharp, metallic hum of the facility was replaced by the sound of cicadas in the brush and the warm crackle of the outdoor hearth on the back porch with a full fire lighting the evening.

But as Alex stepped onto the porch, he heard something else, something that made him stop in his tracks.

Shelby sat in the rocker, guitar balanced on her thigh, her voice soft against the night air. Tyler leaned on the railing, coaxing a mellow, haunting line from a saxophone crafted from the twisted horn of a bosque. Austin and Abilene sat on the steps, their harmonies weaving through the chords, filling the Texas-like twilight of Oiket with something achingly familiar.

Alex leaned against the post, silent, the stars cold above him, his heart full.

Austin was in her third year of college now, driven and confident, but still laughing like the girl who once followed him around the ranch with endless questions. Tyler, lanky and restless in his first year at the local collegium, blew another riff on the horn, his music already as solid as his stride; he was a good musician with a great creative mind. And Abby, their youngest, her voice rising like Shelby's own, was bright, unyielding, and pure. Her singing wasn't perfect, but her energy and confidence were about as close as a 16-year-old could get to being flawless. She was the superb mold of her mom.

Tears stung Alex's eyes. He thought of Phylakion, frozen archives, lost voices, the desperate hope of Lysandros's people, the encroaching Daklin Empire, and then of this porch, his porch, which had become the focus of the Durant family, filled with warmth, music, meals, and science.

Seeing the surge of emotion, Fraklen put his arm around his friend. "Enoy the moment, brother Alex. The vast universe is full of war and shadows, but here, now, you can enjoy something that is worth fighting for."

"You are correct," Alex looked at his insightful friend. "Thank you."

A few hours later, the night settled soft and warm across the ranch. The kids' laughter had faded into memory. Austin off with her boyfriend, Tyler was already back on campus with his books and coffee, and Abilene curled up in her room. Only Shelby remained on the porch, her guitar set aside, her gaze on the wide band of stars overhead.

Alex was sitting in the chair beside her. For a while he said nothing, just listening to the creak of the wood, the rustle of the trees, and the quiet cadence of her breathing. Finally, he turned toward her. "You know," he said softly, "after all these years, you're still the most breathtakingly beautiful and perfect part of my life. What we've built here, you and me, with the kids… it's everything I never thought I'd have."

Shelby turned and a smile touched her lips, but her voice carried an undertone he couldn't miss. "You say that, and I believe you, Alex. But I need to be honest with you. I'm 227 years old, and for the first time in my life, I am beginning to *feel* old. Biologically, I'm now in my fifties, and that's the oldest I've ever been. My hair is just a shade duller; my hands are not as quick with my ranching tasks. And yet… this life with you has been the best I've ever had. I would take the effects of aging if it meant we could be together on Oiket."

"Well said," he drew a deep breath, the words heavy in his chest. "I need to tell you about Phylakion."

"Yes, Phylakion," Her head tilted, curious. "The new archaeological site you and Fraklen have been visiting every day for the last month."

"More than a site," Alex said. His voice lowered, and urgent. "Today, down one of the corridors, locked in a warehouse, I found a starship. Not a relic, Shelby, a tunneling ship. And in its vaults were 20 Archē crystals, exactly like ours. The site has records and videos with full instructions on how to construct hyper tunnels. Not just small portals like we built with Tranquility, but the kind that connect the stars in a galaxy."

Shelby was shaking her head. "I don't know the numbers like you, Alex. Give me a sense of what this means."

"My first version of Tranquility could travel a few light years per day. Our best ships now, are capable of about 400 light years per hour," Alex explained, "which means we can travel just under ten thousand light years per day. The galaxy is two hundred thousand light years across, so it would take us 22 days to travel from one end of the Milky Way to the other." He paused for a second so she could process the numbers. "Using the crystals and hyper tunneling, we can make that trip in ten hours."

"And the Daklin?" She asked.

"Our best guess is that they can do about 150 light years in an hour, which means it would take them 55 to 60 days to travel that same distance. Unfortunately, our speed is not really an advantage when they have billions of cruisers that are based all over the galaxy."

"Okay, so what are you thinking, Alex?" Shelby requested, considering the numbers on speed and distance he had just given her.

"I am thinking we could potentially establish several bases in the galaxy, so we can be anywhere in three hours." Alex clarified.

Shelby's breath caught, her hand tightening around his. "Alex… do you realize what you're saying?"

He nodded. "This isn't just a discovery. It's the foundation of everything the Martians tried to preserve. If it's true, we now hold the keys to link the stars on our own terms. To build what the Daklin have always kept from us."

She turned away, staring into the night. "What you are saying changes everything. For us, for Oiket… for Earth. Maybe for the whole galaxy."

Alex reached across and touched her hand. "Then why does that sound like you're trying to prepare me for something?"

She looked out at the dark horizon, her thumb brushing his knuckles. "Because you found Phylakion. You found a ship buried under the ice, and 20 Archē crystals, and records that show how to build hyper tunnels. Alex… that's not just a discovery. That's a doorway. You've given us a way off Oiket, a way back into the fight, maybe even a way *home*."

He studied her profile in the dim light. "And that scares you?"

"Of course it does." She swallowed hard. "We've been here for over two decades. We've raised children, lived like ordinary people. No wars, no empires killing our friends and destroying entire civilizations. Just love, family, and quiet."

"But…" Alex started.

"I have a new definition of home." Shelby cut him off. "Not the one we left on Pronimos or Earth. I do miss some of the conveniences, but I think I would be willing to give that up. Do you understand?"

"I'm not sure, Shelby."

"Part of me wants to stay here forever."

Alex's grip tightened on the arms of the chair. "Is there a part of you that thinks we can't?"

Shelby leaned forward, elbows on her knees, her voice steady but raw. "Alex, look around. Austin's thriving in college, Tyler's just finding his footing, Abilene still needs us at home. This porch, this ranch… it's not just shelter, it's *our home*. For the first time in two hundred years, I feel like I belong somewhere. Why would I risk tearing that apart?"

Alex drew a long breath; eyes fixed on the stars. "As much as I want to stay here, I know we can't, or at least, I can't. In an inexplicable way, the weight of the galaxy is on my shoulders. It always has been, and now, knowing Phylakion holds a tunneling ship, enough crystals to power a fleet, *and* records on how to build more crystals and hyper tunnels? Shelby, that kind of knowledge can't just sit buried under ice while the Daklin exterminate entire planets. If we turn our backs, the next war won't give us a second chance."

She shook her head, her hair catching in the porch light. "And if we go, what happens to the life we built here? To the kids? To us?"

Alex's voice cracked, almost a whisper. "I don't know. I wish I did. Every part of me wants to stay here, wake up with you every morning, hear the kids laughing in the yard, grow old on Oiket. But every time I close my eyes, I see the reactor humming, the crystals glowing, Lysandros's records staring back at me. It's a call I can't ignore."

Shelby's gaze hardened. "I see all of that in you, Alex. *You* are the problem solver, and perhaps as Polonius has said, the one who is destined to save the galaxy, but me? I see Austin's energetic smile and curiosity, Tyler's love of science and music. Abilene's whole future. I can't just abandon that for ghosts and war."

Alex turned to her sharply. "They'll never be safe with the Daklin capable of tunneling anywhere. Oiket is no longer remote and safe. The only reason Oiket has been untouched is because no one knows it matters. If they ever discover it, this porch, this peace will either become a subject of Daklin rule or be decimated."

Shelby's eyes filled with tears. "So, what are you saying? That the only way to keep them safe is to leave them? To drag me and our family back into an impossible fight with trillion to one odds, a war that nearly broke you once already?"

He reached for her hand again, his grip firm. "I'm saying the only way to keep them safe is to finish what started long before us. Phylakion isn't just a relic. It's a message from Lysandros pleading that we *don't stop.* If we ignore Lysandros' plea, it is tantamount to betraying our kids, and the future of all humanity."

A long silence stretched between them, broken only by the final crackle of wood in the outdoor hearth. At last, Shelby whispered, "For me, it's about whether our children will understand and forgive us. But I can't make that decision right now."

Alex felt the question, and the pain hit deep in his gut. He had once been close to his son, Steven, but had missed much of the joy of watching him grow, of being there to guide and inspire him. By now, Steven would be in his thirties.

But the three children here on Oiket had been part of his life every single day since they were born.

Alex knew, in spite of the pain, he only had one choice, and that was to leave.

○○○○ ∞ ○○○○

For the next few weeks, every morning, Alex tunneled directly into Phylakion. He managed to get the heater running well enough to push the temperature above freezing, allowing him to work comfortably on the slumbering starship.

Lysandros and his team had clearly accounted for every variable when they built the outpost. It had been over sixty million years, an impossible span of time, yet nearly all the technology still functioned on the first attempt or could be repaired.

During one of his breaks, Alex stumbled across a perplexing file. In it, Lysandros described a colony that sounded almost exactly like Pronimos, down to its structure and ideals. But that couldn't be possible. Phylakion and Lysandros's writings predated the founding of Pronimos by millions of years. Lysandros had referred to the colony's founders as *the Sophists*.

Alex remembered his initial search for Pronimos had been because of a rumor of a planet populated by the sophists. It seemed mythology and legends permeated the galaxy. He ran intensive searches, digging through every archive he could access, but found nothing else about them. The mystery of the Sophists would have to wait.

For now, he returned to the important task of making the starship flightworthy.

Day by day, he made progress on the starship. Circuit by circuit, panel by panel, he tested, studied, and rebuilt what Lysandros, and his people had left behind. He poured himself into the ship as though it were a living thing that needed his heartbeat to rise again.

Five weeks later, it did. The tunneling drive hummed low and steady, with the Archē crystal aligned in its socket, glowing with a light that seemed to pulse in time with his own blood.

He walked through the ship and tried to guess what Lysandros, and his team were thinking when they left it here. It was not a fighting vessel, lacking shields or weapons, but more like transport. Alex estimated it could carry maybe 50 people with cargo and provisions for a year. Why was this one ship here?

Alex could only guess, but the engineer in his spirit hated guessing.

Everything seemed to be functional, so he did a test hop, first to a remote location on the planet, then up into orbit. When he was done for the day, he didn't tunnel home right away. He sat in the pilot's chair, running his hand along the console, soaking in the significance of what it meant.

Elsewhere, on the ranch, Shelby was asking the same question.

That night, Alex and Shelby chose one of their favorite places in town, a small adobe-walled cantina lit with LED lighting, thanks to Alex. The owner knew them well enough to bring two dark beers without asking. Shelby carried her guitar, as she often did, and played sitting on a stool with a makeshift stage, her voice threading through the hum of conversations.

For a time, Alex let himself pretend this was all there was. The sound of her singing, the warmth of the room, the cold beer, and the glow of her smile in the soft lighting. For a time, he let himself forget the ship in the mountain hangar under the ice.

But when the last notes faded, and she sat back down at his table, he couldn't hold it back.

"She's ready," he said quietly.

Shelby set the guitar down; eyes fixed on him. "The ship?"

He nodded. "The tunneling drive is stable. I ran a couple tests and am confident I can take her to Pronimos. I have to. They need to know what we've found, what's been preserved. It's too important to leave buried."

Her gaze faltered, falling to her hands. She turned the beer glass slowly in her fingers, the lamplight catching in her eyes. Her fingers were trembling. "I can't go with you, Alex."

The words landed harder than he expected. He forced himself to breathe. "Shelby…"

"I know you have to go, and it breaks my heart, but I can't leave the kids," she said, voice breaking. "Austin's just finding her path. Tyler's struggling to grow into his. Abby still needs her mother every day. If I go, I will tear apart the one thing we've created that survives after we are gone. I've lived for two centuries searching for meaning, and I found it here, with them. With you. I won't walk away from that."

His chest ached as though a blade had found its way in. He reached across the table, caught her hand, held it tight. "You're the reason I want to stay. You and the kids. You're the best thing I've ever had, Shelby."

"I feel the same, Alex," she whispered. "But I know the galaxy won't wait for us. And I can't follow you into it this time."

The silence that followed was thick, broken only by the faint sounds of other patrons talking and restaurant servers performing their duties.

Alex's eyes burned. For over 22 years, Oiket had given him a family, a home, and a peace he never believed possible. Now the Daklin conflict, and the Phylakion discovery, was tearing him in two.

"Take me home, Alex. I want to sit on our porch with you and enjoy the Bosque Ranch."

When they got home, he looked at Shelby, the woman who loved him, who raised his children, and he knew with bitter clarity that the next stage of his life would change everything and take him away from the four people he loved most.

They sat for a few minutes, sipping on a beer in the familiar environment.

Alex stood, took her hand, and she knew what was next.

In her perfect skirt, her cute cowboy boots began to slide to a Waltz.

I have waltzed across Oiket, with you...

29

Return to Pronimos

In the three days since Shelby's decision to stay, Alex had buried himself in work, testing the ship at Phylakion. He did not have the benefit of his AI computer interface that had always been available on Tranquility. Tunneling into local orbit was a very different task than tunneling to Pronimos.

Once he had a handle on the calculations with the ship, he began testing the array of crystals. It all seemed to function identically, producing a hyper tunnel that allowed him to travel over 200,000 light years in a day. While that was only 40% of what he had hoped, his belief was that with proper calculations, that number could be improved. The advanced AI on Pronimos would make that happen.

Shelby had come with him the first two days, standing silently in the cockpit, watching him fuss with systems she couldn't begin to name. But on the third day she stayed behind.

"The herd won't wait," she'd said with a sad smile. "Neither will all the other responsibilities of operating the ranch."

So, Alex finished the task list alone. When the final diagnostic hummed green on the fourth day, he tunneled the starship south to the ranch. The vessel materialized just beyond the barn, startling the livestock, its red hull dulled by uncountable millennia in the Phylakion hangar bay. Alex had selected the location specifically because it was hidden from view of the ranch hands.

He disembarked, his chest tight. He still had to pack, still had to say his goodbyes.

But the moment he stepped onto the porch, his world shifted.

Shelby stood there, eyes red from crying but fierce in their resolve. Tyler and Abilene flanked her, bags already slung over their shoulders.

"Shelby…" Alex's throat closed.

She shook her head, cutting him off. "I couldn't let you go alone. Not this time. Not when the path leads back to Pronimos."

Tyler stepped forward, awkward but determined. "Dad, I'm coming. College can wait. You'll need hands, and I can help."

Abilene's voice wavered, but her chin was high. "Me too." Then she straightened up and became the image of her mom, a woman who had fearlessly walked into battles of the civil war to care for wounded. "If this is our family's fight, then I'm part of it."

For a moment, Alex couldn't speak. The weight that had been crushing him, leaving Shelby behind, leaving his children, lifted so suddenly it left him unsteady. His vision blurred as he pulled Shelby into his arms, holding her tight as though he could fuse them together.

"You're sure?" he whispered against her hair. "This isn't a journey we can turn back from."

She drew back, tears shining on her cheeks. "I'm sure. The ranch will endure. Austin will stay, finish her education. She's strong. Stronger than we ever were at her age. She'll keep this place alive until we return. I have spoken to Fraklen and he has agreed to live here and run the ranch until our return."

The door creaked, and Austin stepped out, her backpack still over one shoulder. Her eyes were wet but steady. "Don't look at me like I'm a child," she said, trying to smile. "I'll be fine. Somebody has to finish what we started here. And somebody has to keep the beer cold for when you all return."

Alex pulled her into his arms, holding her as long as she would let him. "I'm proud of you," he said.

"I know," she whispered. "Now go do what you always do. Save the galaxy and fix things no one else can."

When they broke apart, Shelby took Alex's hand. "I have already packed for you," she said winking.

The kids fell in beside them. Together they walked toward the ship waiting under the evening sky, its crystals already glowing faintly, hungry for the stars.

Alex looked back at the ranch house, at the porch, the home, the life they had carved from dust and silence. He had a flash of Emily telling them about the ranch 22 years ago. It was only supposed to be a place they stayed for a month or two.

Then he turned and walked to the starship ramp, heart aching and full at once. "Pronimos awaits," he said.

The ship hummed with power, the Archē crystal glowing as Alex punched in the course.

"How long to Pronimos?" Tyler asked.

"Not Pronimos. Not yet," he said. His fingers danced over the console. "We'll tunnel to a resistance safe world first. Safer to reach out on Plink before we fly straight into the Pronimos system."

Shelby leaned forward. "How long a jump?"

"Twenty-three thousand light years," Alex answered. "At this drive's speed, two hours and forty-five minutes."

Tyler let out a low breath. "That's all? Wow! That's like thirteen thousand light years per hour." He had grown up on a planet that still used horses as the primary means of travel.

The crystals flared, and the ship lunged into the tunnel. Reality smeared into shifting light, a kaleidoscope of geometry bending around them.

"This is very different from traveling in Tranquility," Shelby observed.

"Agreed. Why don't we all go to the galley? For now, the ship can fly itself."

Two hours and forty-minutes later, the ship notified them it would exit the tunnel in four minutes.

When they emerged, silence swallowed the cabin.

Below them floated a dead planet. Its crust fractured, oceans dark and devoid of life.

Abilene pressed against the viewport. "Oh my God… who could do this?"

Alex's voice was flat. "The Daklin." The name came out of his lips with disgust.

Shelby's hand went to her mouth. "How long ago?"

Alex studied the still-burning lines across the surface. "Probably years ago."

Tyler's jaw tightened. "How many people lived there?"

Alex closed his eyes. "Too many."

The cabin fell quiet, the weight of loss pressing in. Finally, Alex checked Plink, which for him, had been silent for 22 years.

The plink channel buzzed to life. "Zander?"

For a moment, only static. Then a voice, ragged, disbelieving: "Dad? … No. No, it can't be. You're supposed to be dead."

"As you know, I'm pretty hard to kill," Alex's throat tightened. "I don't have time to explain. Don't talk, not here. Just know I'm alive, and I'll be back shortly."

"Dad…" Zander's voice cracked, heavy with emotion.

"Later," Alex cut in, firm. "It's safer if we say nothing more, just… I'll be there soon."

He killed the link, the silence deafening in its wake.

Shelby reached across, her hand warm over his. "They thought you were gone. And now… you're coming back into their lives."

Alex's eyes stayed fixed on the ruined planet. "The Daklin have been busy. It's time for us to move fast. No more waiting." He punched in the program for the trip to Pronimos, checked the calculations. "Five hours to Pronimos."

oooo ∞ oooo

Once they came out of the tunnel in Pronimos orbit, Alex Plinked Zander so he could meet them at Spaceport.

The Pronimos Spaceport provided coordinates for a docking assignment and Alex navigated in. They watched on the monitors as it came into view spread like a jeweled crown with rings of docking platforms and bustling terminals alive with traffic.

Alex's hands tightened on the controls as they touched down. "We're here," he said quietly. His chest ached with the weight of everything waiting on the other side of the hatch.

The airlock cycled open. They stepped out and took in the spectacular towers of Pronimos, Shelby holding Alex's hand, Tyler and Abilene trailing behind.

Zander greeted them first, tall and broad-shouldered, his expression froze for a moment as though he wasn't sure the sight was real. Lyra was at his side, her eyes bright with tears. And just behind them was Steven. Taller than Alex thought he would be, his boyhood gone, his frame filled out with the confidence of a full-grown man who had matured too quickly by war.

"Dad…" Steven's voice caught as he stepped forward eyes filled with tears. "It's really you."

Alex's breath left him in a rush. "Steven. God, you've grown." He pulled him into a fierce embrace, holding on as if there was a way to make up for lost years.

Tyler and Abilene exchanged wide-eyed glances, then smiled as they were pulled into the circle.

Zander blinked, sizing them up. "Dad, Shelby, you had kids?"

"Yes," Shelby responded with pride.

"So, these are my brother and sister?"

Tyler stuck out a hand, half-nervous, half-proud. "I'm Tyler."

"Abilene, but I go by Abby," she added quickly. "And it's really good to meet you. Dad has been telling us about you for our entire life."

Steven grinned through damp eyes, hugging both of them. "Looks like I gained a brother *and* a sister in one day. I'll take that."

They stood together in a moment that was both messy and beautiful, stitched together with disbelief, tears, and laughter.

Then Zander leaned back, finally taking in Alex and Shelby fully. His brow furrowed. "Dad, Shelby…" He shook his head. "You both look like hell. Like, seriously, you look like shit."

Shelby laughed through tears running down her cheeks. "Nice to see you too, Zander."

But Zander's expression hardened. "I'm not joking. The resistance needs you both in fighting form. Your first stop is the de-aging clinic. No arguments. If you're going to stand with us, you have to be young and at full strength."

Alex glanced at Shelby, a wry smile tugging at the corner of his mouth despite the sting of truth. "Guess my son's giving the orders now."

Shelby squeezed his hand, her voice soft. "And maybe for once, we should listen."

"We can do that tomorrow, Zander. First, we catch up."

Steven wiped his eyes, still staring at the ship that loomed behind Alex's group on the landing pad. "Dad… where did that come from? I don't recognize it."

Alex's expression sobered, his voice low. "It's very, very old. We found it buried under the polar ice of Oiket, uhhh, Oiketerion. A settlement that was built by one of the original Martians named Lysandros. Inside, it's a starship like no other. It uses Archē crystals to hyper tunnel up to five hundred thousand light years per day."

"Holy shit! Are you sure?" Zander exclaimed, but Lyra pinched him and looked at Tyler and Abilene. "I'm sorry. Didn't mean to swear, but that speed is unimaginable."

"It's okay Zander," Shelby reassured him. "These kids grew up on a ranch. They've heard worse."

"The ship has historical records I haven't even begun to touch, plus instructions on building Archē crystals for travel in hyper tunnels, like the one we used to return from Andromeda."

Zander's eyes widened, his hand tightening on Lyra's shoulder. "You're serious?"

Alex nodded. "Deadly serious. And if the Daklin realize what we've uncovered, they'll reduce Oiket to ash. We have to keep this quiet." He drew in a breath, his tone shifting, heavier. "We need to catch up, Zander. What happened with Emily and Jabari?"

The brightness drained from Zander's face. In an instant, he looked years older.

"Dad… 22 years ago, the Daklin broadcast across every channel. They bragged that Tranquility was destroyed. That Alex Durant was dead."

He paused, his jaw tight.

"They wanted the resistance to collapse under the weight of losing you. And for a while… it almost worked."

Shelby's fingers gripped Alex's arm. "They destroyed Tranquility?"

Zander nodded grimly. "We never knew exactly how. Just that it was gone, and the Daklin made sure everyone believed it was final. At first, we didn't believe it, but then the years of silence finally convinced us."

Steven's voice cracked. "How did you escape?"

"We weren't on Tranquility." Alex explained. "Emily and Jabari were returning to Pronimos so she could get a specialized surgery to have children. The Daklin must have tracked them. We were stuck on a planet that had pre-industrial age technology and was 22 light years from the nearest tunnel."

"So, if you hadn't found this ship," Steven looked back at the Martian ship, "You would have died of old age on that planet, and we would never have known?"

"Looks like you're already dying of old age, Dad," Zander persisted on the point.

"We're just fine, son," Alex deflected the comment. "We lived…"

"I'm sorry to be the one to deliver the news about Emily, Dad," Zander said, apologetically. "It's been over twenty years for us."

"I know, and I had long since come to the same conclusion, Zander." Alex let it set in.

"As I was saying, the Daklin built their narrative around your death," Zander said, eyes fixed on Alex. "But Megan never gave in. She's alive and still fighting. Quietly. Patiently. She's the only reason the resistance still exists."

"Megan's a badass," Shelby clarified.

Alex's chest tightened. "Megan… she survived."

"She's a tough fighter, for sure," Zander exhaled. "She's been the backbone of it all. But Dad, you need to understand, Earth wasn't spared either. They came for it, and Adamez led the defense. Somehow, against all odds, Earth held. But…" He looked away, grief catching his words. "None of the other planets in the resistance did. Every single world in that was aligned with us is… gone. Burned. Just like the planet you passed on your way here."

Alex's voice was raspy. "Every other world in the resistance… destroyed," he repeated, not quite believing the reality.

Zander's gaze came back to him, steel hard. "The resistance is down to ashes, Dad. Adamez's forces still are fighting for Earth, and a handful of cells are hanging by threads, scattered around the galaxy. But that's all that's left."

He stepped closer, lowering his voice. "Dad, hopefully you're not *just* back. You're the fulcrum, but if the Daklin learn that you're alive, they'll come for you harder than ever. And if you fail… there won't be anything left to save."

"We need to get you, and the best Pronimos engineers, working on this Martian ship." Alex put his arm around Zander as they walked. "It was not designed for war, but some of the tech is far advanced of even Pronimos."

○○○○ ∞ ○○○○

The Old West Bar hadn't changed. Same dark wood paneling and same row of taps with craft stouts and ales that somehow never ran out. Alex and Shelby slid into a corner booth, the smell of smoked mesquite and hops hanging in the air.

The cybernetic bartender recognized Alex immediately, even after all the years. "Two oatmeal stouts?"

Alex gave a small nod. "Perfect."

The glasses landed heavy on the table. He lifted his glass and waited until Shelby raised hers.

"To Emily," he said quietly.

Shelby's eyes softened. "And Jabari."

The clink was soft but carried weight. They both drank, letting the silence sit for a moment.

"So," Shelby finally broke it, "what's next for my cowboy engineer?"

Alex exhaled. "Integrating Martian tech into the Stinger ships. Hyper tunneling, new alloys, their drive symmetry… it's elegant in ways we barely understand. If we can mesh that with Pronimos tech, it will give us a start."

Shelby arched an eyebrow. "And after that?"

"The crystals. Making materials from inert elements on the periodic table. I don't know yet how that will impact us beyond making ships faster, but I'm looking forward to handing it over to the scientists here." He stared into the foam at the rim of his stout. "I also want to rebuild Tranquility. Not just the name, Shelby. The ship itself. She was more than metal to me… she was home."

"That's a big task, and I get it, but I'm not sure anything will replace the Bosque Ranch on Oiket."

"I know," Alex nodded, appreciating the woman who sat across from him. "It started in this bar, sweet Shelby."

She got up and sidled in beside him, the two of them sat silently for a few minutes.

He leaned closer and kissed her on the cheek, then took a sip of his oatmeal stout. "Emily used to update the Tranquility files to

Pronimos on a regular basis. Specs, logs, memory matrices. If those files are still out there, then our ship and part of her is, too."

Shelby tilted her head, studying him. "You're thinking about bringing her back?"

"At least as an AI," Alex admitted. "Maybe even in that sassy Jamaican body. For now, if I can revive the core of who she was, we won't just have a ship. We'll have Emily and all her amazing attributes with us again, in a way."

Shelby's smile was slow, touched with sadness. "Alex, you never *could* leave ghosts behind."

"Some ghosts are worth following," he said.

Alex set his glass down, the stout half-finished. The task list, assets, and end goal had taken over. "I'm sorry Shelby, I can't wait. I need to start tonight."

Shelby gave him a firm nod. "I know my Alex, and this is one of the great things I admire about you. You do whatever you have to so we can get her back."

Hours later, in the engineering workshop where he had spent so many hours, Alex was bent over three holo-screens stacked in a triangle. The Pronimos cloud interface shimmered, demanding authentication in archaic encryption protocols that hadn't been touched in decades.

"C'mon, Em… you always left me breadcrumbs."

Shelby leaned against the wall, arms folded, watching as his fingers darted across keys. "Do you think the data survived?"

"Absolutely." His voice carried that old stubborn certainty. "She backed up every major systems update, navigation logs, diagnostics, even her memory journals. If the packets are intact, we'll have her."

The last key sequence lit the screen green. The Pronimos crest flickered, then a cascade of file streams poured across the displays.

Emily's archives. Tens of thousands of them. Tens of exabytes of data.

Alex's chest tightened. "There you are."

He routed the files through a sandboxed core and began assembling the AI kernel. Lines of code folded into place, fractal-like, as though the ghost of Emily knew how to rebuild herself. A soft hum filled the workshop as processors spooled to full load.

Then the AI began to form.

"Alex?" The voice was faint, electronic, like a whisper from underwater.

Shelby straightened. "Oh my God… It's Emily!"

Alex swallowed hard. "Yes Emily, it's Alex. Can you hear me?"

"Yes. Fragmented… but here." The voice gained steadiness, a familiar tone emerging. "How long… offline?"

Alex laughed, raw and relieved. "Too long, kiddo. Too damned long."

Shelby wiped a tear and whispered, "Welcome home, Emily."

"Alex," Emily started, "It will take several days for me to reformat into this system. I will update my logs on events since, well, *whatever* happened."

"That's okay Emily, we have lots to do."

Early the next morning, Alex stood with a cup of coffee in hand. The realization that he was back on Pronimos made the process of integrating Emily into a new cybernetic body a more manageable task. Still, he couldn't help but recall how the Pronimos engineers had marveled at the upgrades Megan had implemented. He needed to contact her.

He opened a Plink channel to an old frequency he hadn't used in decades. The link crackled, then steadied.

"Holy shit! Alex?" The voice was unmistakably Megan's.

He grinned. "Been a while."

A pause, then a laugh, warm and disbelieving. "You bastard. They said you were dead 20 years ago. I knew you weren't dead. There was no way in hell they could get Alex Durant."

"Yeah, well, death didn't stick."

Her laugh softened into something tender. "It's good to hear you, Alex. Damn good."

"I need you," he said, dropping the pleasantries. "The Daklin did destroy Tranquility, and we lost Jabari, Emily, and a young student named Kyros."

"Okay," Megan waited.

"Emily did regular backups, and I've gotten her partially back online from the Pronimos cloud. But if we're going to restore her fully, we need the best systems mind I know."

Another pause, longer this time. Then her voice came, steady, resolute. "Then I'm coming back to Pronimos. I've been waiting for a reason. This is it."

Alex exhaled. "I'll send you a gate sequence. Pack light."

"Light? Alex, I'm bringing hell with me." Megan's voice hardened. "Oh, and tell The Old West to put a keg of vanilla porter on ice for me."

Alex smiled. God help anyone who stood in the way of this woman. "Okay. After we wake Emily all the way up, we're going to make sure the Daklin never sleep easy again."

30

Reviving the Resistance

The Pronimos spaceport gleamed like polished stone under the twin suns. Alex stood with Shelby, Abilene, and Tyler at his side, tension coiled in his chest. The docking portal shimmered, then opened with a rush of light.

Out stepped Megan Hoglund, her hair a little longer, curls bouncing as she laughed and crushed Alex into a hug.

"Damn, Durant. You look like hell."

"That's the first thing you say after twenty years?" Alex grinned.

Megan kept her arms on his shoulders, studying him. "Seriously. You look like you're pushing sixty in Earth years. Get your stubborn ass into the de-aging clinic. Resistance doesn't need an old man; it needs the Alex I knew."

Shelby chuckled. "I've been telling him the same thing."

Megan hugged Shelby, "you look great for an old woman, Shelby."

Behind Megan, the tall figure of Sun Tsu emerged from Singularity 2. His dark eyes scanned the spaceport with tactical precision before softening at the sight of Alex. "It is good to see you again, my friend. The fire still burns in you, though your frame betrays the years. Megan is right. You need to correct this weakness."

Alex gave a resigned nod. "All right, all right. I'll book the clinic, but first, I want you to meet my family."

Shelby introduced Tyler and Abilene.

"We've been in the fight for two decades, getting our asses kicked around the galaxy, and you've been playing house with this sweet Texas girl?" Megan grinned broadly.

"Making the best of being stuck on a remote planet, Megan." Alex defended.

"It's okay Alex, I'm just screwin' with ya." She hugged him again. "Having you back is the best thing that's happened in decades. Anyway, I appreciate Shelby as the reason you're likely still breathing."

Abilene and Tyler stepped forward shyly. Megan hugged both of them. "Your dad's a pain in the ass, but he's also a badass, and the best damned engineer and most creative thinker in the galaxy. You should be proud of him."

Tyler grinned proudly. "We know."

That night, in the engineering hangar of the Pronimos Spaceport, the reunion turned to work. Holo-screens glowed with schematics, and Emily's voice, steady now, echoed from the central core.

"Alex, Megan, systems integration of my AI into a cybernetic body is feasible. The Pronimos bio-labs have scaffolds and the neuro-matrix from my last body. I'd like to prioritize and create a dedicated assembly window and timeline."

Megan leaned forward, excitement lighting her eyes. "Then let's get you a body, Em. Walking, breathing, fighting beside us. You're way better in a body than trapped in circuits."

The next holo-display filled with star maps, Tranquility and Singularity outlined in ghostly light.

"It's time for us to rebuild them," Alex said, conviction in his voice. "But not as they were. We fold in Martian alloys, Andromeda engines, and an upgraded neural net. Stinger compatibility across both hulls." Alex tapped a sequence, bringing up new design overlays. "The engineers here have gone wild with Archē crystals. They've prototyped one that doesn't just focus power, it bends it. The simulations show it could form a shield strong enough to deflect a Daklin planet-killer burst."

The room went quiet.

Sun Tsu spoke first. "A perfect shield. That changes everything."

"Well, we are decades from having enough power to stop a DPK with shields, but the good news is that it's possible." Emily clarified.

"Does anyone have any familiarity with the old Kardashev scale?" Alex asked.

"I'm not familiar with it," Megan was shaking her head.

"It is basically a theory about a civilization's ability to create and control anergy and power. Fire was the beginning, followed by mechanical, fossil fuels, electricity generation by harnessing chemical and electromagnetic power sources. Above that was nuclear fission, then fusion. Beyond fusion was the Dyson level which is equivalent of controlling the entire energy output of a star."

"We aren't there, yet..." Megan said, half asking, half stating as a comment.

"We aren't but I wonder if the Daklin are ahead of us in energy production. How do they generate enough energy to destroy planets?"

Everyone in the room looked at each other, but no one had an answer.

"Pronimos has been living on fusion power for millions of years. It's cheap and reliable." One of the Pronimos engineers offered.

"It's an area, we need to improve," Alex concluded. "I think the Daklin are ahead of us, but there's no reason we can't start working on achieving Type II, Dyson level."

"Another task, but a valuable one." Emily added.

"Sorry to drag us off, but I think we need to consider everything here," Alex added. "Anyway, back to the current tasks." He nodded at Zander.

Zander, seated near the end of the table, stood. "We need to build production, but one assembly plant is not enough. We saw what happened on EtaKatz when all our hope rested in one place."

Megan jabbed a finger at the map. "Exactly. We need to replicate and build manufacturing on half a dozen worlds across the galaxy. They should be highly classified locations that are hidden, fortified, and capable of being self-sufficient. If the Daklin take one, the others still stand."

Alex leaned back, letting the idea settle. "Distributed resistance. Factories the Daklin can't strangle. Tranquility, Singularity, Stingers all fed from a network of production sites. Is this enough so we can win?"

The room got quiet as they remembered the numbers. Billions of cruisers and millions of DPK.

"Maybe we can be ready in 100 years," Sun Tsu announced somberly.

oooo ∞ oooo

Two weeks later, life on Pronimos began to settle into rhythm. Tyler and Abilene had started classes in one of the academy towers, their days filled with new friends, languages, and technology that stretched their imaginations. Both of them wished that sister Austin had joined them on this adventure.

For Alex and Shelby, the day had come for their appointment at the de-aging clinic. Because of their advanced ages, it was preceded by hours of scans, cellular resets, and molecular infusions.

When it was done, they stepped out into the evening light.

Shelby caught her reflection in the glass doors and laughed. "Well, hell. Look at me. I haven't seen this face since we arrived on Oiket."

Alex stared, momentarily speechless. "Shelby… you're stunning, beautiful."

She gave him a playful nudge. "You're not so bad yourself, cowboy. You look like the man who dragged me into all this madness."

He reached for her hand, squeezing it tightly. "I know exactly where we should go to celebrate."

After a short walk they stepped into the familiar oak smell at the Old West Bar, the bartender didn't even ask, just poured two oatmeal stouts and slid them across.

Alex lifted his glass. "To being young again."

Shelby clinked his. "And making it count this time."

"Oh, we made it count pretty well, if you ask me," Alex smiled broadly.

They both drank deep, laughing like they hadn't in years. Shelby leaned across the table, eyes shining. "The beer tastes better."

Alex took a sip and enjoyed the flavors, "You're right, but the hormones right now…"

"Hormones raging, are they cowboy?" she winked with a sensuous grin.

"Uhhh, yes. How about you?"

"I could hold them off for a few more seconds, if I had to." She chuckled, feeling her pulse rate spike. 'But it appears you ain't gonna let me try."

"Let's get out of here, gorgeous wife." He stood and took her hand. "The hormones are calling and, well…"

Back in their high-rise, the door barely closed before Alex pulled her into his arms. The kiss was urgent, hungry, like they were discovering each other for the first time.

They tumbled onto the bed, laughter breaking through the passion. Alex brushed her hair back, breathless. "Shelby… are you fertile?"

She shook her head gently, smiling. "No. I switched that one off."

"Well, shoot," he teased, kissed her again, slower this time. "I'll take you any way I can. Always."

Their clothes fell away, and for the first time in decades, their bodies moved with youthful strength and abandon. The room filled with heat, laughter, and whispered memories. They made love until exhaustion claimed them, falling asleep tangled together, their hearts synchronized in the same rhythm.

For Alex, it felt like more than passion, it was a declaration. They weren't just young again. They were alive, together, and ready to face whatever came next.

oooo ∞ oooo

Five months later, the Spaceport hangar on Pronimos shimmered with construction drones, their lights weaving like fireflies against the night. Alex watched two sleek silhouettes ready to rise above the city towers and on to the edges of the galaxy.

Tranquility II and *Singularity III.*

Both ships gleamed with the sharp edges of new alloys and the soft pulse of living systems. Each carried two Archē crystals at its heart, one tuned for hyper tunneling, the other dedicated to shielding and weapons. The design was bold and experimental, but the Pronimos engineers believed it would give the resistance what they needed most: speed and survival in the worst of fights.

Shelby stepped out beside him, wrapping a shawl around her shoulders. "She looks different."

Alex nodded. "They both do. Less like ships, more like… living fortresses. The advanced materials and second Archē crystal changes everything."

Behind them, the planning chamber buzzed with voices. Megan leaned over a holo-map, her fingers dancing across the display as she fine-tuned the distribution of the resistance's future.

"Twelve worlds," she said firmly, pointing as each system lit up in pale blue. "Every one of them is isolated from the main Daklin tunnel network. Hidden, hard to reach, and rich enough in resources to sustain production. If the Daklin find one, we will defend it like hellcats so the other eleven stand."

Emily's voice came from the central console, now carried by her fully tested cybernetic body. "Probability of simultaneous destruction is less than one in 10,000. This configuration gives us resilience the solo base at EtaKatz never had."

Zander leaned back in his chair, arms crossed. "That's the point. No more single points of failure."

Alex glanced at Steven, who stood with confidence that reminded him of his own youth. "We'll coordinate the assembly facilities. He knows the tech; I know the logistics. Together, we can make it happen."

Steven's eyes met his father's. "You created the dream. We'll build the infrastructure."

Alex felt the weight of the moment; pride and fear balanced in equal measure. "Don't underestimate the Daklin. They'll find ways to reach even off-network planets if they think it matters enough."

Megan leaned back from the holo-map. "Earth has stopped the Daklin, what, three times now? I don't completely understand why the Daklin haven't hit with the same kind of blitz they used with the Persiori…"

"I suspect it is because they don't understand Earth's limited capabilities." Alex speculated. "Maybe they see it somewhere between threat and unimportant."

"Every other planet was in the Empire. Earth wasn't." Steven was standing and looking from one person to the next. "Maybe their lack of information or intelligence on the planet is creating their pause?"

"Likely correct," Sun Tsu stepped forward, his voice measured but resolute. "The resistance is no longer a cornered force, but instead, a defeated one. The Daklin probably feel like they have won. In a sense, they are right because the resistance lacks the dozen supporting civilizations. With these ships, these shields, and these factories, we can become the storm. The Daklin will adapt, but so will we. And this time, we make certain to not underestimate their asymmetric response."

Silence settled for a heartbeat as all eyes turned back to the two new ships glittering above the skyline.

○ ○ ○ ○ ∞ ○ ○ ○ ○

The Pronimos data core pulsed like the living heart of the city, threads of light weaving through crystalline matrices. Alex paused at the threshold, always struck by the room's beauty. At the center stood Sasha, graceful as ever, her hands moving across a holographic lattice.

"Alex Durant," she said without looking up, "it is good to see you." Then her expression turned to somber, "I heard long ago that we lost Mark. He was a good man and became a true friend."

"Yes," Alex recalled the infatuation Mark had for Sasha, which had caused him to stay on Pronimos on their first visit decades earlier. "For me, he was a lifelong friend. I guess we never get over those losses."

"No, we don't, Alex," Sasha motioned for Alex to sit. "Word is you want to test the limits of my computer data capabilities."

Alex smiled. "If possible, I'd like a copy of the entire Martian ship database downloaded to Tranquility II. Their alloys, their drive harmonics, even their myths. If there's a clue in there to stopping the Daklin, I want it aboard my ship."

Sasha lifted her gaze, dark eyes sharp. "It's possible, but not trivial. That Martian starship has technologies we are still beginning to understand."

"I know," Alex remembered his own analysis of the ship.

"The new version of Tranquility was designed with impressive capabilities Alex, but it does not have that level of storage. You'll need a full systems upgrade, new neural grids, and expanded resonance memory. Without it, the data would overwhelm her."

Alex crossed his arms. "Then we upgrade. I won't accept less."

Her lips curved in a faint smile. "You sound like Mark. Always pushing for more than the system was designed to carry." She gestured for him to follow, leading him deeper into the glowing chamber.

"But Alex, there is a mystery. My teams have been studying a discrepancy in the Martian archives. Lysandros spoke of a colony… its description mirrors Pronimos exactly. But the entry is dated several million years before Pronimos was ever founded."

"I saw that same piece of data, Sasha," Alex stopped short. "Pronimos was built after the Daklin began their rise."

"I think you know, it was not Lysandros or Oiket that founded Pronimos," Sasha said softly. "So, either Lysandros carried only the plans, and they lay dormant for eons… or someone bent time itself. Either way, the vision existed long before we raised these towers."

"So Pronimos might have been born first as an idea? Or…" Alex frowned, then glanced at the pulsing core. "Is it possible there is another Pronimos?"

"Oh no. *That* is not possible. We would definitely know if there was another place in the galaxy like Pronimos." Sasha's expression softened, a flicker of memory in her eyes. "I think you know of my late husband, Aristotle?"

"I know who he is of course, but I never had the pleasure to meet him." Alex thought about the fact that he was standing next to the wife of one of the greatest thinkers of all time. "My wife, Shelby, studied under him."

"Shelby is quite extraordinary Alex…"

"More than extraordinary, Sasha. She stabilizes me and everyone around her."

"I am glad you see that, Anyway, my husband spoke often of Archē," Sasha continued, her voice carrying reverence. "The beginning, the first principle that underlies all. He believed it was not just philosophy but something that might one day be real, a force or artifact that could shape existence." Her eyes went to the faint glow of the crystals powering the matrices. "And now, Alex, I see you working with Archē itself. To find my husband's teachings made manifest… it is surprising, and I must admit, unsettling."

Alex leaned closer, voice steady. "Then maybe he wasn't just teaching. Maybe he was preparing you for this moment."

Sasha held his gaze for a long, silent breath, then returned her eyes to the data streams. "Perhaps. Either way, we will give Tranquility II what she needs. The Martian archive will live aboard her. And we will see what truths emerge."

○○○○ ∞ ○○○○

Six months after Alex's return to Pronimos, Megan called the team together.

"I'm leaving tomorrow," she announced, her voice steady. "My team is ready to establish the resistance's first manufacturing forward base. From there, we can print our assembly line in about four

449

months. It is remote enough so we should run unimpeded without the Daklin finding us."

Alex clasped her hand firmly. "Be careful, Megan. You're carrying the future on your shoulders."

She smirked with that familiar spark in her eyes. "I always do. Besides, you've got your own assignment, returning to Earth."

"Yes, well I am sure the return to Earth will be interesting, but I need to understand how much Adamez has developed technology. I would not have guessed they could survive the Daklin assault when every other resistance system had fallen."

"Bring me a couple kegs of Breckenridge Vanilla Porter, please."

"I will do that, Megan." He hugged her one last time and watched her disappear into the new Singularity. Alex watched the ship depart and made the realization that every time he said goodbye, it could be the last.

A month later, the hangar gleamed with a fully updated Tranquility II. Emily ran a hand across the upgraded plating, pride flickering in her voice.

"Expanded shielding, modular weapon pods, and a new grav-core. She's ready, Alex. Stronger than her predecessor, and capable of 13 Quettabytes of storage."

"I'm not really sure what a Quettabyte is Emily?" Shelby asked.

"May I answer?" Tyler glanced at Emily and stepped in with a proud smile. "A Quettabyte is ten to the thirtieth bytes, which is something like a quadrillion terabytes. The first-time dad left Earth in Tranquility, he had four hundred terabytes of storage."

Shelby took a deep breath and exhaled slowly. She knew this could go on with a piece of paper and lots of zeros, but instead smiled proudly at her son, "Wow, that's a HUGE number!"

"It's astronomical, Mom!"

Emily was watching them, and when they finished, she looked at Alex, "We will be ready for departure to Earth tomorrow."

Before Alex could respond, Tyler and Abilene exchanged a nervous glance. Tyler finally spoke.

"Dad, Mom… we want to stay here. Pronimos has the best schools in the galaxy. Our studies, our new friends, well, they're here."

Abilene nodded quickly. "If we're really going to be useful to the resistance someday, we need this foundation. Pleeeeaaasssee let us stay."

Shelby squeezed Alex's hand before he could argue. "They're right. They'll be safer here, and better prepared when the time comes."

Alex studied Shelby and his children for a long moment, then nodded slowly. "All right, but remember, I expect to be back for you as soon as possible, and I expect us to communicate daily on Plink."

31

Earth & Oiket

The next afternoon, Tranquility II popped into tunnel-space, carrying Alex, Shelby, Emily, Zander, and Lyra back to Earth. They landed in Dallas under cover of night and sent word to Adamez.

The next afternoon, they met Art Adamez at a table on the patio of Alex's favorite restaurant, Mexican Sugar. The sun lit the stone patio, and the smell of sizzling fajitas drifted past as servers carried trays of margaritas rimmed with salt and spice.

Adamez lifted his glass. "Welcome back to Earth. Best Mexican food in the galaxy, and I'll die on that hill."

Shelby laughed, tilting her hat back. "Best margaritas too. But tell me, Art, how does a place this good still serve beer that tastes like water?"

Alex grinned. "That's the first upgrade we'll bring to Earth. Advanced shields, fusion weapons, and proper beer at Mexican Sugar."

Adamez chuckled, leaning in with a conspiratorial smile. "Then let's eat, drink, and start planning how to keep this planet alive."

"Indeed." Alex took a chip, dipped it in the salsa, and enjoyed the flavors. "This is worth the trip alone!"

"So, what's the plan?" Adamez asked.

"We build out the network to detect every Daklin incursion to the edge of the Oort Cloud." Alex observed, eyes on his friend.

Emily didn't look up from her guacamole, "Using the standard outer boundary at roughly one hundred thousand astronomical units: that's about 9.30 trillion miles. In light-time, approximately 13,862 light-hours, which is roughly 578 light-days, or 1.58 light-years."

Zander nodded. "With hyper tunneling, we can deliver a bomb to any invading DPK on the outside edge of the Oort Cloud in about a quarter of a second."

Adamez folded his arms. "And if they pop a tunnel inside that fringe, we catch the ripple and hyper-tunnel a nuke right into their belly?"

"Fifty thousand warheads," Alex said quietly. "Let's hope deterrence still works on those monsters."

"Or that they don't send more than fifty thousand DPKs." Adamez added.

∘∘∘∘ ∞ ∘∘∘∘

Two months later, with most of Earth's retrofits complete, Zander's face went pale over a secure feed. "News from the Perseus relays. Two non-resistance worlds, both lightspeed-capable, but no tachyon tunnels, are gone. DPK destroyed them without announcement, and no struggle."

"What the hell are they doing?" Alex winced, perplexed.

Adamez's jaw clenched. "I suspect they're clearing the board. Anything not under the Daklin banner is now officially the enemy."

Emily's voice lost its usual warmth. "Now that they can open their own tunnels, nowhere is off-limits. Any system. Any arm. Anywhere."

Alex stared at the star map as it expanded showing Milky Way sectors webbed with faint lines, the new sensors shimmering outward past the Kuiper Belt, beyond the Hills Cloud, all the way to that thin, cold ring where Emily had finally put a number to the dark.

"If the Daklin are wiping out every system not connected to the tunnels," he said quietly, "it's only a matter of time before they turn their eyes toward Pronimos."

Zander leaned against the bulkhead, arms folded. "Pronimos is advanced, Alex. Their knowledge is deep…"

"They do not have a military," Alex cut in, voice sharp. "They've never had to fight. No fleets, no weapons infrastructure. If a single Daklin Planet Killer arrives in orbit, Pronimos is dust."

Emily rested her hands on the table, her dark eyes steady. "Alex, there are millions of systems in the galaxy. Even if the Daklin are systematic, probability says it will take centuries before they reach Pronimos."

"Centuries on a roll of the dice. Pronimos could be tomorrow, but either way the actual date means nothing when your children live there," Alex shot back. "Austin is still on Oiket. Pronimos has Steven, Tyler, Abby… half the people we love. Pronimos might see it coming and evacuate, but Oiket? They'd never even see it coming. They've got nothing."

Silence settled in. The only sound was the soft hum of life-support systems.

Finally, Zander exhaled. "So, what's your plan?"

Alex looked up, his jaw set. "We wrap up here with Adamez. Earth's defenses are as good as they'll get for now. Hell, they were the best in the galaxy before we arrived and gave the hyper tunneling."

"Agreed. What we have seen here is a model worthy of replication," Zander affirmed.

"Let's jump to Oiket, collect Austin, and head for Pronimos. If the Daklin are going to turn their attention there someday, we'd better start building a defense like Earth has as soon as possible."

Emily tilted her head. "You would make Pronimos into something it was never meant to be? A sanctuary turned fortress?"

"Better a fortress than a grave," Alex said. His voice dropped, almost a whisper. "I won't let Pronimos share the fate of those other worlds."

Zander straightened, a grim nod. "Then let's get moving."

The Tranquility team decided to meet one last time at Mexican Sugar with their friend Art. At the end of dinner, they all started hugging their Earth friend, each farewell spoken with quiet resolve.

Adamez's eyes lingered on Alex. "You've done more here in a few weeks than most do in lifetimes. When the Daklin arrive, Earth will be ready to deliver hell like they've never experienced."

"No doubt," Alex hugged his friend. "My home planet is lucky to have you, Art."

"We're ready. Now go take care of your own."

Alex nodded. "We'll be back when we can. Don't let your guard down."

Adamez allowed himself a rare smile. "I *never* do."

oooo ∞ oooo

The trip from Earth to Oiket was sixty-two thousand light years and took five hours. Alex had to double check the math. He had not yet grown accustomed to the fact he could span the width of the Milky Way in less than a day. He remembered that old *Star Trek* show where Discovery had gotten stuck in the Delta Quadrant and was going to take a lifetime to get home. His ship could make that trek before lunch.

When they arrived on Oiket, early morning sunlight was spilling across the Bosque Ranch. The ship settled into the meadow beside the stone-lined porch hidden from view of any ranch hands that might be out in the fields working.

Shelby stood at the top of the ramp, breathing in the warm air, then turned with a half-smile. "Alex… let's stay a few days. Just us. I need it."

He studied her, the strain etched in both their faces. "I feel like every minute counts right now, but I have some work I need to do at the Phylakion site. I want to bring Emily up there and see if she can find anything Fraklen and I missed."

"Can you spend the evenings here with me?"

"Yes, Shelby," he agreed. "I'll take every evening I can get with you."

Later that day, Shelby traveled to the university to find her daughter. She spotted Austin sitting on a stone bench under the shade of a wide-leafed tree at the university quad. Students streamed past, laughing and carrying slates, but Austin was lost in her thoughts.

"Austin," Shelby called gently.

Her daughter looked up, eyes widening. "Mom!" She jumped up and hugged her, holding the hug as if it had been decades. "You look…" she broke off, studying her face. "You look as young as me."

"It is so good to see you, Austin," Shelby hugged her again and smiled faintly. "Pronimos med tech has its perks with de-aging clinics. I wasn't trying to shock you."

"It's more than a shock," Austin said, standing. "It's… unfair. You don't even look like my mom anymore. You look like some grad student visiting campus."

"I'll take that as a compliment." Shelby reached for her hand, "I came to talk to you about leaving. Dad and I want you with us."

Austin shook her head immediately. "No. I can't go. My life is here, my work. My friends. And…" she hesitated, then pushed forward, "Blark. He's more than just some guy, Mom. We're serious."

Shelby's voice softened. "Serious how?"

"Serious as in, well, leaving the university, my studies and him would be tearing me away from the things I most love."

By then Alex had walked up, hearing the last words. His jaw tightened. "Austin, we don't have time for this. The galaxy is burning, and I'm not about to leave you behind. Pack your things. You're coming."

"No!" Austin's voice rose, sharp enough to turn a few heads. "You don't get to order me around anymore. I'm not 12. I'm an adult. I belong here and I choose to stay."

The tension cracked like static.

"Do you have any idea what's out there?" Alex demanded. "Do you know how many people I've already lost to this war? The Daklin are now destroying worlds that are not part of the conflict. I won't lose you too."

Austin's face flushed. "Maybe you should have thought about that before you disappeared into that tunnel in the first place."

"We didn't desert you, Austin!" Shelby cut in, but her daughter was already walking away, shoulders stiff, refusing to look back.

Alex made a move to follow, but Shelby caught his arm. "Let her go."

He shook with frustration. "I can't. I won't. I've buried too many family members and close friends. Most of the damned resistance is dead, and now you're telling me to just leave my own daughter on a planet with no defenses?"

"Oiket is as safe as anywhere in this galaxy," Shelby said firmly. "And safer than most. She's a grown woman, Alex. We can't drag her away like a child. She has a right to be with the man she loves."

Alex exhaled hard, chest heaving. "Safe? Nothing is safe anymore."

Shelby pressed her hand to his cheek. "If we push, we'll lose her for good. Trust her. Trust me."

The fight drained slowly from him. He closed his eyes, then nodded once, reluctant. "Grudgingly, Shelby. Grudgingly. She's my daughter. I love her and don't know what I'd do if anything happens to her."

Shelby's voice was steady. "Let's tell her we are okay with her staying and find time to meet Blark before we leave. We can go back and fight knowing she has her life, her love, and her choice."

"I can't even Plink her on this planet," Alex started, then said nothing more, but his eyes filled with tears and stayed fixed on the path where Austin had disappeared. Finally, he turned to Shelby, who hugged him.

"It will be okay, Alex."

"I know you will handle it, and I'll follow your lead." Alex kissed her lightly. "In the meantime, I am going to take Emily and Zander up to Phylakion."

Shelby's brow arched. "You and your ruins."

"Every answer we have starts with data," Alex said simply.

"You mean distractions. I know you, Alex Durant."

○ ○ ○ ○ ∞ ○ ○ ○ ○

Because he did not have the exact coordinates for the starship hangar bay inside Phylakion, Alex landed outside. Snow whipped across the barren ice field, driven by a constant wind that never seemed to stop. The entrance to Phylakion was once again covered in ice. Alex used a tunneling backpack to enter the main room, walked to the hangar, and transmitted coordinates to Emily.

Once Tranquility was in the starship hangar, Emily stepped into the vaulted chamber. "This place feels… different. Quiet in a way even the tunnels don't match."

"It's a fortress, not a city," Alex replied, stepping onto the steel gantry. "Phylakion was built to survive long after any disaster that might happen to the people who settled here."

"I know what it is. This place reminds me of the research facility we found on Mars sixty-six million years ago."

Alex looked at Emily. She was right, and that facility flooded back in his memory. The architecture, the smells, everything was similar. "I had that same feeling."

Emily had walked over to a terminal, her eyes unfocused as her neural link began scanning the system at a rate thousands of times faster than Alex could. "I found a hidden directory."

Alex frowned. "Hidden?"

"Encrypted," Emily corrected. "Layered so deep the surface metadata loops on itself. It's clever. Someone didn't want this opened."

"Can you crack it?"

She tried. Lines of code spilled through her interface, recursive locks knotting into knots. After several minutes she pulled back, eyes narrowing. "No. Not here. The cipher uses a seed tied to things I have never seen before. The password structure reminds me of the code we used to enter the hyper tunnel from Andromeda. Brute force is not prudent because I risk tripping a purge routine if I probe too hard."

Alex laid a hand on the console, feeling the cold vibration. "Can we copy it?"

Emily nodded reluctantly. "Yes. I already have a full image. I can wrap it in a sandbox aboard Tranquility. But to break it we'll need Pronimos specialists. Sasha's team. She has cryptographers who love working on this kind of lattice noise."

"You said it reminds you of Andromeda?" Alex clarified.

"Yes."

"Hmm," Alex nodded thoughtfully. "Let's wrap it up and move it to Tranquility."

The data stream poured into their secure channel, a silent river of symbols glowing across Emily's retinas. She layered checksums, locked them behind parity firewalls, and finally sealed the image into Tranquility's vault.

"Transfer complete," she reported. "No decryption attempted. Integrity is one hundred percent. Once we get back to a place where I can communicate with Sasha's team, I will work with them to see what hidden secrets we can uncover."

Alex glanced back at the walls of Phylakion in the frozen light. "Whatever this is, it was important enough to encrypt and bury in the most secure vault on Oiket. I feel like there might be some real answers here."

Emily's expression softened. "And you'll get them. But not here. Not now."

"I hate to wait…" Alex thought about the situation.

"I could tunnel to the nearest Plink location, but I'm sure you don't want a repeat of twenty-two years ago."

"You got that right, Emily, but now that you mention it, We could be there in minutes, transfer the file, and return to Oiket."

"Let's do it!" Emily agreed.

Fifteen seconds later they had tunneled 22 light years. They spent less than one minute in 3-space to transfer the file, then back to Oiket. The entire trip took less than a minute and a half.

When they touched down at the Bosque Ranch, Alex was dizzy. "That was one of the most amazing trips ever."

"It was like Tranquility delivery service Alex."

As promised, Alex spent his evenings with Shelby on the back porch of the Bosque Ranch. She played her guitar; they talked and reminisced about the decades they spent here. Both of them felt like this could be their last time enjoying the quiet of Oiket and their ranch home.

On their last night, they had dinner with Austin and Blark at their favorite restaurant. Blark was so much like Alex that the two talked nonstop.

"You have my blessing, sweetheart. Blark is amazing, but we are gonna miss you." Alex said as he hugged his daughter goodbye.

After a long evening, Shelby and Alex returned to the porch of their ranch house. They both agreed that Austin was doing the right thing.

The following morning, they had a cup of coffee and watched the sunrise.

"Ready?" Shelby asked.

"As I'll ever be."

The tunnel flared open, a river of light swallowing them as the ship leapt between stars. Mid-transit, alarms barked.

Once in the tunnel, Emily checked and the response from Sasha's group had been delivered. They had created backups and tried several times, all to no avail. The encryption was beyond the capabilities of Pronimos.

As they came out of the tunnel, they were greeted by a fleet of Daklin cruisers.

Static cleared into Sasha's face, pale, strained, her voice cracking. "Alex, Zander, Megan, anyone! The Daklin are here! They've come to Pronimos!"

For a heartbeat, silence froze the deck. Then Shelby whispered the words they were all thinking. "It's too soon…"

Alex's jaw hardened. "We're here Sasha."

32

The Battle of Pronimos

"Alex…" Emily's voice cracked. "Look."

The main display filled with their worst nightmare. A hundred Daklin cruisers tangled the system, their black hulls flashing with sensor beams as they probed Pronimos below. Orbital fire drifted like lightning storms.

"God," Shelby whispered. "It's already started. I need to get my kids."

Alex's jaw clenched. "The Cruisers are mapping every inch before they send the planet killers. We've only got minutes."

On the surface, 12 sleek second-generation Stingers crouched like predators, their hulls reflecting the fires of the sky. They were waiting, unpiloted, except for the AI scaffolding Sun Tsu had coded for each.

"Zander," Alex barked.

"I'm on it." Zander's voice was tight. He slammed a tunnel-pack against his chest, vanished in a flare of light, and a heartbeat later his voice came through the comms again, ragged with adrenaline.

Thirty seconds later, Zander reported in. "I've got one. Controls are live and coming up to greet our Daklin guests."

Emily overlaid telemetry. "AI flight modules engaged. All Stingers online, but Alex, none of them know how to fly like Megan. Not even close."

"I know," Alex muttered. His stomach twisted at her name. *God, Megan, we need you now.*

The first wave of Daklin cruisers broke atmosphere, sending thousands of black spears diving toward the planet.

"Deploy all 12!" Alex shouted.

The Stingers roared skyward, brilliant arcs of plasma trailing them, but the formation shattered almost immediately. Two pilots, Zander and one young woman who had trained briefly under Megan, peeled into clean intercept vectors. The rest lurched and spun, AIs fighting to compensate, wings jagged as frightened birds.

"Hold formation!" Alex yelled into the channel.

"Negative control!" one pilot screamed. "I can't..." Static swallowed his voice. A flash on the horizon marked his death.

Another Stinger clipped a Daklin cruiser but over-rotated, spiraling back into the atmosphere evaporating in a stream of overheated plasma.

"Chaos," Emily whispered. Her eyes tracked dozens of red icons converging. "They're not going to hold, Alex."

"Then make it a diversion!" Alex snapped. "Tell the AIs to distract them. We need to get as many people off the planet as possible!"

An AI's calm synthetic voice cut through the noise. "Directive updated. Maximum chaos mode. Expect losses in excess of ninety percent."

Shelby looked at him sharply. "Alex, I need to get our kids."

For an instant, Alex knew he could lose his entire family, but he also knew Shelby had to go. "Take a tunneling pack and come back to me sweet wife."

She grabbed a pack, kissed him and disappeared.

Alex was already strapped in. "Emily, battle configuration. Full systems online. We're taking the fight to them."

"Confirmed," Emily said, her voice sharpening into the calm, combat tone she had adopted in her AI core days.

Tranquility II's hull glowed as its engines spooled to combat output. Alex's hands moved like a pianist across the controls. "Time-hop drive armed. Run program for intervals in microbursts."

"Intervals set. Target priority: cruiser class."

He flashed through the memory of the training session he had done in Andromeda, but executed a more advanced version of the program they had used at the end of the battle in the Perseus Arm. He was grossly outnumbered and knew he would likely die today, but the Daklin would pay in holy hell first. He pulled the trigger, and Tranquility II vanished.

It reappeared behind the first Daklin cruiser, less than a hundred meters from its stern. An X-ray burst punched through the aft core, the ship detonating in a white blossom of fire.

"Kill confirmed," Emily reported flatly. The AI will adapt to that one, so let's switch to multi hit super close strikes.

"Hit one more and transfer program to Zander and…" Alex didn't know if he even knew the name of Megan's protégé flying the other Stinger. "heck, whatever her name is and clear the others off the field."

They vanished again. Reappeared. Fired. Another cruiser tore apart.

Then strategy shifted with three Stingers executing close in strikes destroying cruisers at a rate of three per second - each.

The deck of Tranquility II rattled with the tempo of impossible war. To the Daklin fleet, it was madness: three Stinger blinking in and out of existence, reappearing just long enough to gut another cruiser before vanishing again.

"Thirty-eight down," Emily counted. "44…51."

Alex's face was a mask of concentration, sweat running down his temple. "Keep me lined. Shorten hops. Faster. The crystal is handling the thermal issues we had in Perseus."

"Confirmed. New intervals…"

Another four bursts. Another cruiser gone. Then three in a row, x-ray after x-ray, faster than the Daklin could track. Alex was using time hops to take out ships almost four per second.

"Eighty-six confirmed kills," Emily said. "Elapsed time: eleven seconds."

Alex exhaled, his voice hoarse. "More," Alex said covered in sweat, but nowhere near finishing. "No stopping until they're all gone."

The comm crackled with Zander's voice, ragged but fierce. "Dad, this strategy is working! These bastards can bleed!"

Another voice broke in, higher, breathless but steady, the young woman who had trained under Megan. "They can be killed!"

For a heartbeat, just one heartbeat, it looked like the impossible was turning. Cruisers fell burning toward Pronimos as their swarm faltered.

Then the darkness came.

Three titanic signatures bled into the system, blotting out the stars.

Emily's voice dropped to a whisper. "DPKs. Three of them."

"Zander, the two of you finish the cruisers, I'm gonna figure out how to handle the DPKs."

The displays lit with the cold outlines of Daklin Planet Killers, their hulls stretching kilometers long, weapons arrays glowing with the power to scythe entire continents.

Shelby's voice came over the Plink, "I can't find them," Her voice trembled. "Alex… oh God."

"Shelby?" Alex closed his eyes, "don't get distracted." He muttered to himself.

The fleeting hope of stopping the cruisers drained away, replaced by the terrible silence that came before annihilation.

"Emily, what is that?" Alex demanded.

Her eyes glowed with cascading data. "Daklin Planet Killers are aligning. They came out of the tunnel with weapons arrays charging. Core output climbing past eighty percent. Now ninety-five. They are firing, Alex. We are out of time."

Alex's stomach turned to ice. "Shelby!" he barked into the comms. "Shelby, answer me! Get out of there…Now!"

Only static.

"Emily, can you find her?"

"I'm trying," Emily said, multi-tasking, voice clipped, calculating. "No signal return. But the tunnel packs are tethered to Tranquility. If she jumps, she'll materialize on our deck as long as we are within a light year distance from Pronimos."

"Damn it, Shelby, come on…" Alex slammed a fist against the console.

Alarms shrieked as the DPKs locked onto their target. From the dark giants came a slow, terrible flare, twin spears of energy gathering at their cores, bleeding into converging lances aimed at the planet a million miles below.

"Alex." Emily's voice was low, almost human. "We cannot stop this attack. I am initiating short-hop escape."

"Do it," he bellowed, still desperately trying to contact Shelby.

The ship lurched sideways into a slice of nothingness, the stars smearing as the DPK beams unleashed.

For an instant, all of the chaos disappeared as Tranquility entered the calm of the tachyon tunnel.

As they emerged two million miles from the planet, they could see the impact of the DPK energy pulse as it engulfed Pronimos.

Then, all three DPKs exploded.

Megan's voce came over Plink, "Sorry Alex. I destroyed the DPKs, but it doesn't look like I got here on time."

All of the Cruisers and DPK had been destroyed, but it was too late.

A slow-motion horror show was unreeling on the screens, Pronimos, with its green valleys, silver seas, shining towers, flared like paper in a furnace. The beams from the now destroyed DPKs wrapped around the planet's surface, tore the atmosphere away in boiling storms, shattered the crust into oceans of magma. The cataclysmic death spread until no eye on Tranquility could look at it.

Alex covered his face, but still saw it, seared into his mind: his adopted home, the sanctuary of humanity, obliterated in a handful of heartbeats.

When the glare faded, only silence remained. Pronimos was gone, its orbit filled by a blackened husk, the last bits of life, choking on, would soon be a barren sphere adrift in the void.

Alex's voice cracked, barely more than breath. "God help us…"

Emily's eyes dimmed, her voice quiet but final. "Pronimos has been completely destroyed. No life signs. Nothing remains."

Then a soft hum, and Shelby collapsed onto the deck in a tunnel-flare of light, coughing, stunned, but alive. "Too many… too many gone."

Alex dropped beside her, pulling her into his arms, his whole body shaking. "You made it. Thank God, you made it."

But behind his closed eyes, he still saw Pronimos burning. A sanctuary for the best of humanity, an entire world obliterated in less than a minute.

END of Part 3

Thanks for reading

***Please take one minute to
write a review on Amazon***

Watch for the next exciting book in the Tachyon
Tunnel series…

Coming Spring 2026!

<u>Other books by Michael Gorton</u>

1. **USSA**, political thriller written in 1994
2. **Lex Talionis**, political thriller and sequel to USSA, written in 1998
3. **Born Again American**, inspirational, written in 2011
4. **Forefathers & Founding Fathers**, written in 2016 is a historical fiction from the beginning of colonial America taking place in the early 1600s. This book became a #1 best seller and won several literary awards. Brown Books republished the book in 2017
5. **Broken Handoff**, business book, written with co-authors Seth Gordon and Darien George. The book became the #1 M&A book of 2019
6. **Digital Medical Home**, written in 2022 with co-author Jay Sanders, MD. The book won awards and became a #1 best seller. It tells the history of the telemedicine industry.
7. **Tachyon Tunnel 1**, written in 2023 is a science fiction that won awards and became #1 bestseller.
8. **Calamistunity**, written in 2023 is a business book that teaches how to turn calamity and mistakes into opportunity.
9. **Tachyon Tunnel 2, The Daklin Empire**. SciFi, 2025 sequel. #1 bestseller, 7-literary Awards
10. **Telemedicine Wars**, historical fiction written in 2025 with co-authors Jay Sanders, MD and Harvey Castro, MD.
11. **Tachyon Tunnel 3**

Appendix A: The Science of the Tachyon Tunnel series
A plausible framework for faster-than-light travel

If time flies, then let's study the aerodynamics
and build the wings to soar on it.
-Alex Durant, Tranquility Ship Logs

1. The Problem with Light-Speed

For over a century, Einstein's theory of relativity has held one unbreakable rule: no object with mass can accelerate beyond the speed of light. As mass approaches light speed, the energy requirement to continue acceleration rises toward infinity. That law applies in 3-space, but it says nothing about what lies beyond those three dimensions.

The Tachyon Tunnel Theory assumes that light-speed is only a barrier in 3-space. In the deeper fabric of spacetime different rules apply.

2. Tachyons: Beyond the Barrier

Tachyons are theoretical particles that always move faster than light. Because they never slow below light speed, they don't interact normally with the particles of our universe. Instead, they move through imaginary time, where cause and effect are not bound by our sequence of events.

In this sense, tachyons might not be "particles" in the ordinary sense, but information carriers or energy ripples that traverse spacetime in a dimension we cannot directly perceive. Their interactions could form microscopic bridges between distant points or quantum tunneling on a cosmic scale.

3. Quantum Entanglement: A Familiar Clue

Quantum entanglement, where two particles remain connected no matter how far apart they are, gives us a hint. When one particle changes, the other reacts instantly, without any detectable transmission of energy. This "spooky action at a distance," as Einstein called it, appears to violate relativity, but only if we assume the particles are limited to 3-space.

If instead, both particles are connected through a hidden higher dimension or subspace of spacetime, then no law is broken. Information doesn't move faster than light; it simply takes a shortcut through an unseen dimension.

4. Tachyon Tunneling: Entanglement Scaled Up

The Tachyon Tunnel combines the two ideas of tachyons and entanglement into a single physical model. When a ship enters a tachyon field, its particles are temporarily entangled with their future position in spacetime.

By creating a controlled field of tachyon energy, the Tranquility's engines distort the local geometry of spacetime and link two coordinates the origin and the destination into one continuous surface in higher-dimensional space. The ship doesn't accelerate; it slides through a tunnel of entangled spacetime.

From the outside, it appears to vanish from one place and reappear elsewhere instantaneously, or nearly so. Inside, travelers experience smooth motion and normal passage of time because locally, they never exceed light speed.

5. Relativity Intact

This model doesn't violate relativity because, within the tunnel, the ship's velocity relative to local spacetime never surpasses the light barrier. The "faster-than-light" effect exists only when measured externally, across the endpoints of the tunnel. Relativity forbids breaking the barrier in 3-space, but it doesn't forbid using the geometry of spacetime to bypass it.

The process is similar to quantum tunneling, where particles "disappear" from one side of an energy barrier and "reappear" on the other without ever crossing it in a classical sense. The difference is scale: quantum tunneling happens across nanometers; tachyon tunneling happens across light-years.

6. Implications

Tachyon tunneling redefines our understanding of distance, time, and causality. The Daklin Empire understood how to use the tunnels without understanding how they were built.

In theory, the galaxy could be threaded with countless dormant tunnels, relics of an older civilization that once mastered the quantum architecture of the universe.

7. Conclusion

Tachyon tunneling doesn't break the laws of physics but instead suggest a new one yet undiscovered. It uses the same deeper geometry that makes quantum entanglement possible, applying it at macroscopic scale. The Tranquility's drives don't force matter beyond light-speed. They simply fold spacetime into alignment and ride the entangled bridge through.

From our limited human perspective, it looks like faster-than-light travel. From the universe's perspective, it's simply the shortest possible path between two points in spacetime.

<u>Mars & Greece</u>

Humanity has always had a fascination with Mars. While that fascination goes back to the dawn of mankind, since the beginning of the space age we have sent 68 missions to the planet!

Well into adulthood, I held the dream of being on the first human expedition to the red planet. Thanks to SpaceX, a human mission will likely occur before 2032. I believe that when we finally send people there, we will find traces of an ancient civilization. Some of that belief is reflected in this book. The fiction in this series assumes the Galaxy was colonized millions of years ago, and part of the residue of that colonization shows up in Greek mythology, and Greek names scattered throughout the series. For clarity, I am not suggesting the ancient Greeks explored the Galaxy, but that they got some of their language and culture from those much earlier explorers.

<u>Plasma</u>

I did my graduate work in physics, building a computer model of the magnetosphere and how it is shaped by the solar wind. Back then, plasma was just the 4th state of matter. Plasma is what shapes the magnetosphere, it is lightning, and it is the Aurora Borealis. Robert Temple's 2021 book *A New Science of Heaven* introduced a new perspective. Temple explores the concept of plasma physics as a potential key to understanding consciousness, intelligence, and even the nature of the universe. He suggests that complex plasma structures, such as those found in space and possibly in Earth's atmosphere, could have self-organizing properties that resemble cognition or sentience. The concept of consciousness in plasma brings a much larger idea to the forefront. Organic life is fragile and short lived. Plasma is much more tenacious and therefore could exist as a living entity for billions of years.

<u>Characters</u>

All of the characters in this book are creations of this author's imagination. While it is true that some situations and personalities or credentials are loosely based on people I know, most characters are a variation of my personal perspective.